Praise for Peter Murphy's
Born & Bred:

"The author did a splendid job in portraying many diverse relationships, city life, church life, family life, corruption and crime, which makes it an engaging read."
– Hotchpotch

"As the first book in a series, Murphy has created a lasting story with great potential in future installments."
– Savvy Verse and Wit

"*Born & Bred* is part historical fiction, part political thriller and part social commentary. With a bit of magical realism thrown into the mix it makes for a commanding read and a compulsive page-turner."
– Brendan Landers

And for his first novel, *Lagan Love*:

"The best books are not forgotten because you can never stop thinking beyond the story. This is true of *Lagan Love*. Murphy is a natural storyteller. I look forward to reading more."
– Examiner.com

"*Lagan Love* is more than your ordinary novel and Mr. Murphy is a skilled writer with the ability to tell a story that teaches a life lesson everyone can benefit from."
– Simply Stacie

Wandering In Exile

Wandering In Exile

Peter Murphy

THE
STORY PLANT

The Story Plant
Studio Digital CT, LLC
P.O. Box 4331
Stamford, CT 06907

Print ISBN-13: 978-1-61188-182-0
E-book ISBN: 978-1-61188-183-7

Visit our website at www.TheStoryPlant.com

First Story Plant Printing: January 2015

Printed in the United States of America

0 9 8 7 6 5 4 3 2 1

The boundaries which divide Life and Death are at best shadowy and vague. Who shall say where the one ends, and where the other begins?
– Edgar Allan Poe

For Jim G.

Chapter 1 -1977

THE IMMIGRATION OFFICIAL WAS POLITE as he checked Danny's passport and stamped his papers. He had a strong accent and told Danny he was originally from Sherbrooke, in Quebec. He seemed a little disappointed that Danny couldn't speak French but smiled when he told him that his girlfriend did.

"She can speak all sorts of languages," Danny enthused in case his lack of bilingualism might be held against him. "She's going to come over, too, after she's finished university."

"*C'est bon*, Monsieur Boyle, *et bienvenue au Canada.*"

"Merci," Danny acknowledged in his best French accent that would have made Br. Arnold proud. He wished he could have remembered more but it didn't matter now. He was officially "landed" and walked out to where Martin was waiting for him.

"No problems?"

"He says you have to speak French to me or they'll throw us both out."

"He can feck-off. This is Ontario. We only have to speak English here."

"And I thought I was comin' to some multicultural paradise."

"Save it for when you go for citizenship and you'd better do up your jacket before we go outside. Didn't you bring a coat?"

"I got my anorak in my suitcase."

"It'll be nice and warm there."

When they stepped through the sliding doors, Danny gasped. The inside of his nose grew stiff and when he inhaled it felt like needles. "Sweet Jesus."

"This is nothing. Wait until the winter comes."

"You're kidding, right? How feckin' cold do you think it is?"

Martin hailed a cab with his gloved hand. "Minus ten . . . or fifteen."

It took a few minutes before a large salt-stained Pontiac pulled to the curb. Martin slung their baggage into the trunk while Danny huddled in the back seat, blowing on his bare hands. "Jesus Christ, I'm totally fuckin' frozen."

The driver checked him in his rearview mirror. "Are you Irish?"

"Yeah," Martin answered as he finally sat in, blocking the wind and closing the door.

"From the north or the south?"

"From Dublin."

"Is that in the north or the south?"

"It's in the east, actually," Danny piped in but the driver didn't seem to get the point as he edged the huge car into traffic and accelerated away.

"Where to?" The car wobbled as he turned to look over his shoulder.

"Balliol Street, just south of Yonge and Eglinton."

"Young and eligible?" The driver turned again but Martin just nodded.

They careened along wide streets and into a curving ramp that led to the 401 before the driver spoke again. "My aunt is married to an Irish guy and, boy, does he love to drink!"

"Yeah," Martin answered like he had heard that far too often.

"Yeah, man." The driver carried on regardless with just one hand on the wheel, weaving through traffic and tailgating anyone who wasn't moving fast enough. "You gotta see this guy. He does a forty-pounder and a two-four every night."

"Well, we do practice."

"And shit, does this guy like to fight." He cut across two lanes and back again to overtake someone who blocked his way. "Just last week, we were having a few beers in a bar on the Danforth—the Newfie place. Know it?" He turned again and the car veered far too close to the wheels of a huge truck. Martin nodded but Danny didn't and just stared out the window, across lanes and lanes of enormous cars, some the size of boats. And everywhere he looked he saw rust spots on the passing cars and on the metal rails that kept traffic separated.

"Well a bunch of Newfies were watching the Leafs, so my uncle starts cheering for the Habs. The Newfies didn't like that and before long two of them went for him."

Beyond the furthest lanes, Toronto rose in towers between darkened snow-lined streets, compressed layers and layers of people's lives, lit up for Christmas.

"And before we could do anything, he'd decked the pair of them. And then, do you know what he did? I swear to God, he picked the two of them up and bought them a tray of draught. Can you believe it?

"And then he says: 'You always buy them a drink afterwards so they'll know there was no malice in it.' Can you believe it? They sure make you guys tough over there." The car wobbled again in its lane as he checked over his shoulder for their reactions. "Isn't that the coolest thing you ever heard?"

"Yeah," Martin agreed languidly and looked past the driver, willing him to watch the road ahead. "Only we come from a rich part of Dublin where we hire people to do our fighting for us."

"There is a rich part?" Danny muttered, joining in.

"You guys are shitting me. Right?"

"Course we are. If there was a rich part of Dublin, do you think we'd be over here in the colonies freezin' our balls off?"

Danny meant it as a joke but it didn't go over well with the cabbie.

"Listen," he said, about to turn around again when Martin sat forward pulling Danny with him, into the driver's peripheral view. "I like you guys so I'm gonna let you off with a warning: Don't ever, ever," he slapped his hand on the dash for emphasis, "ever complain about the winter in this country. That's the only rule. That and never miss the hockey game, eh?"

He swung the wheel as he finished and swerved across three lanes and into an exit ramp, fast enough for the tires to squeal, until Yonge Street stretched out before them. He gunned the car again, all the way down into Hoggs Hollow, and then back up the hill. Then on again toward the lake, blowing through yellow lights like they were only there for decoration.

*

After Martin retrieved their bags and tipped the driver, Danny stood for a moment looking up. The apartment building was square and reached up toward the orangey-blue clouds. "Thank Christ!"

"What are you thanking him for? I was the one who smuggled your ass over here before you got yourself killed."

"No, I meant for gettin' me through that taxi ride. Are they all like that?"

"That was one of the better ones." Martin also looked up at the night as a few flurries drifted down and settled on their heads. He wished that when they finally got home and put their cases down for good David would be waiting for him.

"So which floor do you live on?"

"The fourteenth but don't worry, we'll take the elevator."

"Good, because I'm not carryin' my bags up there. So, how long is your roommate away for?"

"His name is David and he's not my roommate; he'll be back in a few weeks."

"Does he go home every Christmas? Must be nice. How come you didn't go with him?"

"Because I had to go back to the bogs of Ireland to get you."

They crossed the shining floor of the bright, posh-looking foyer with pictured walls and columns of what looked like light-brown marble. "You're doing all right for yourself." Danny whistled softly as he looked around. "This is very nice."

"It's all right," Martin shrugged. He had always liked fancy stuff and he always looked after himself. They squeezed between the doors of the elevator and struggled to turn around. "Push fourteen."

Danny tried but couldn't reach.

"Put that bag down and you can get it with your left."

Danny tried again but stumbled, lighting up floors eight through sixteen. "At least there's no thirteen." He looked at the glowing buttons again. "You live on thirteen?"

"I know."

"Aren't you nervous?"

"I'm getting there."

While Danny settled into his room and began to unpack, Martin ordered a pizza. David had decorated for Christmas before he left, with lots of little white lights and a little pink love note on the fridge to welcome him back. Martin was home again with their huge color TV and the great stereo with speakers in all four corners. Their living room was like a big 'L' with a smaller room as a kitchen, full of jars of spices and bottles of sauces that David had brought from home, that he couldn't live without. There were a few bottles of rum, too, and the door of the fridge was lined with beer. But there were only two bedrooms. Danny would be sleeping right next door.

When he came out, Martin was sitting on the couch with his legs on the coffee table, something he wouldn't have done if David was there. "Look. I don't want to freak you out or anything, but I need to know that you're going to be okay with David and me."

"I told you, it's no sweat off my nose. And besides, I'll get my own place as soon as I can."

"I don't want you to feel like you're under any pressure. David is cool with it. It was his idea you come out here."

And it was Martin's idea that David should not be around when Danny got here. David rarely went home. It was part of the deal. He stayed out of his parents' lives and they paid his way—school, apartment and a generous allowance. David always claimed he got the better of the deal, something he brought up every time he got drunk and homesick.

"C'mon, Martin. You know I'd only be crampin' your style. Besides, after I get a job, I'll need to have my own place. I wouldn't want anyone thinkin' that I was like you."

"You should be so lucky, but be careful what you tell your mother. I don't want anyone from home knowing."

"My Ma and Da know."

"They do not. They only think they know and I don't want anyone else knowing."

"They're goin' to find out some time."

"I know. I'm just hoping that it's after I die."

"Fair enough then. I'll mention it in your eulogy."

"You're not going to outlive me, you daft bollocks. You'll probably get yourself killed long before I croak."

*

"How can you even be thinking of celebrating with our only son off in some heartless place in the middle of winter?"

Danny's mother was in no mood for Christmas and pestered his father every time he even mentioned it. She was finding it hard to adjust to life on their own again even though she agreed when everybody said he'd be better off over there. It had been a terrible few months with Danny getting mixed up in the Scully murder, and then his own kidnapping, and being taken up the mountains to be shot like a dog. He had been saved, of course, and brought back to her, only to have to leave the country and she wasn't ready to go on like nothing had happened.

"Ah, Jaze, Jass. He only went to Toronto, and he has Martin there to look after him."

"But Martin is not his mother."

"Maybe not," Jerry agreed. "But he's the next best thing."

Jacinta had decided to let it go at that; Jerry was trying to be so nice to her. He'd even invited her whole family over for Christmas dinner so she wouldn't feel alone. Only it never occurred to him to ask her first and she'd had to run out at the last minute to buy a bigger turkey and more of everything. But it didn't go as badly as she feared. Her mother did most of the cooking while Jacinta and her sisters sat around the kitchen table drinking sherry. Jerry and her father sat in the living room with Donal, smoking and drinking whiskey. All in all it was grand, but afterwards, when everybody got on with their lives, she was alone again to feel her loss. It was like a hole inside of her that was getting bigger. Her pills didn't help except to make the edges less jagged but it was still there. And everywhere she went, to the shops or to get her hair done, it followed. Except when she sat in the church. Nora was gone but Jacinta was okay with that. She knew Nora's job was done. She had been there for Danny and her and Jerry too. Now she could do no more and had gone off with Bart. Jacinta couldn't explain how she knew. It was just a feeling that came over her whenever she knelt in the shadows before the Virgin Mary. Jacinta could face her now, woman-to-woman, now that they had both lost their sons. Just like Mrs. Flanagan who always sat a few rows over and a bit to the back, where she could cry in the shadows. Jacinta always wanted to say something but could never think of the right thing to say. She even prayed for guidance on it but, like every other time, Mary just smiled back. She reminded Jacinta of the Mona Lisa.

On the way out, Fr. Reilly was waiting. He wasn't wearing a hat and his coat was open to the winds.

"Father, what are you doing out in the cold dressed like that?"

He looked a little surprised and, for a moment, Jacinta thought he might piddle himself.

"Ah Mrs. Boyle. I was wondering if we could have a little chat? We can go over to the house and have a nice hot cup of tea."

"Grand so," Jacinta agreed, but he hesitated.

"Would you mind if we just waited for Mrs. Flanagan. She should be out shortly."

*

Fr. Reilly had been hoping to run into the two of them. It was time to get back to some parish work. The bishop had sent him home for Christmas and had a few ex-missionaries fill in. It was well meant but, if anything, it just confused things more. His mother was dead, God rest her soul, and his father lingered like a wraith without her. He still lived in the old place even though he had sold up the last of the land. He had his pension, too, and had more than enough put aside. Patrick wanted him to move into a home where he could be looked after.

**

"I can look after myself well enough." His father had looked craggy—the way he got when he was digging his heels in.

"I'm not saying that, Daddy. I just think it would be better to have someone mind you. What would you think if we asked someone from social services to drop by and check up on you again?" He had driven the last one away but the bishop had smoothed that over by now.

"Patrick," his father sighed and sat down beside the fire and pulled his chair forward. He stopped looking craggy and looked the way he did the night before Patrick went away. "You've always carried the cares of the world on your back. Don't put me up there too. I can be getting along fine for a bit yet."

"But you'd tell me when you can't anymore?"

His father didn't answer and just stared at the fire. He looked older than so many Patrick had been with at their ends. His skin was wrinkled and crinkled around his neck. "Like an old tom-turkey," his mother used to say before she died. It was a blood clot in the brain and she died out in the fields. His father insisted that it was the way he wanted to go too. "The fields have had the blood, sweat and tears of this family for years. They may as well have what's left of me, too, for fertilizer."

"Daddy?" Patrick felt strange calling him that but he was so tired of hearing 'Father' everywhere he went.

"I will so. If it's the only way I can get a bit of peace and quiet." He snuck his pipe out from under his hat. He had put it there so Patrick couldn't hide it like he did whenever he came over. "But you'll have to tell me what you're going to do. His Grace has been telling me that you're thinking about Rome. Are you thinking about it and wondering if I will be all right?"

"No, Daddy. I'd never think like that."

"Good enough," his father said and smiled as his face faded into his cloud of smoke. "Because if things were like that I'd die tonight. I've had my life, Patrick. It's time you started enjoying a bit of yours."

***

"Grand now." Fr. Reilly leaned to pour the tea as Mrs. Boyle and Mrs. Flanagan settled at opposite corners of the coffee table. It might be a bit too soon, but he couldn't watch them suffer any longer, particularly Mrs. Flanagan. She had come to him after her son's funeral and begged him to tell her what really happened. She said the version the Guards had given was very formal and stilted. She had made no sense of it and wanted him to find out what he could. He had gone to his uncle for advice and was told to bring the two of them together and let the holy mother of God do her work.

"Do you both take sugar and milk?"

His guests nodded without making eye contact with each other.

"Grand so." He served their tea and followed up with a plate of finger sandwiches that Mrs. Dunne had made in advance. "Well then," he explained as he sat in his armchair and tried to balance his cup on the armrest, "you might be wondering why I brought the pair of you together like this."

"Well," he continued when they didn't answer, "I was hoping that we could have a little chat about all that has happened with Danny and Anthony." His guests stiffened so he offered more sandwiches. "It has been a terrible tragedy that has touched you both."

The two women nodded and briefly made eye contact but Fr. Reilly pretended he didn't notice and smiled to himself; he had them. "And when a mother's heart is broken, who could offer more comfort than a mother with a broken heart?"

They looked at him like he was mad so he had to continue. "I thought I could give you both the chance to share some of the things you are feeling—things that might be helpful."

Neither woman spoke so Fr. Reilly was silent too. The whole room was silent except for the passing sounds from outside and the ticking of the clock on the mantle, ticking off each moment of silence.

"I'm very sorry for your troubles," Jacinta finally blurted toward Mrs. Flanagan and quickly raised her tea cup.

Mrs. Flanagan didn't respond so Fr. Reilly rose and offered more tea and sandwiches. "Now, Mrs. Flanagan, do you have anything you would like to say to Mrs. Boyle?"

Mrs. Flanagan shuddered a little and struggled to compose herself. When she did look up her face was whiter and her eyes were darker. "That's kind of you to say, Mrs. Boyle, but it's like the heart was torn out of me. At least you still get to see your Danny; I'll never see my Anthony on this earth again."

"But," Fr. Reilly gushed before Mrs. Boyle had a chance to speak, "it still means more coming from a woman whose only son is far away."

Both women looked like he had punched their hearts. He'd never get the hang of talking to them. Perhaps he'd be better off in Rome, in a dusty part of a library where no one else's problems would come poking, like cows through a gap. "I have always believed that a sorrow shared is a sorrow halved."

"You don't have children. Do you?" Mrs. Flanagan snapped at him as she began to shake. "You don't have any idea of a mother's suffering."

He didn't, but at least Mrs. Boyle was nodding in approval and moved a little bit closer to Mrs. Flanagan and sat like an old chicken roosting. "It must be terrible for you," Mrs. Boyle comforted as Mrs. Flanagan shuddered and sobbed some more.

"The worst part," she managed to get through her tears, "is that no one remembers the real Anthony."

"Well now, Mrs. Flanagan," Fr. Reilly tried to encourage but was cut off.

"Well now nothing. I've heard them with my very own ears. 'Good riddance' they say and my poor little boy lying dead in the cold ground. And the worst part is that I can't even get a reason why he had to die."

Before Fr. Reilly could try to take charge, Mrs. Boyle moved closer and put her arm around the other mother and rocked gently back and forth.

"My Anthony," Mrs. Flanagan said, her cadence in time with the rocking, "would never do a bit of harm to anyone. Isn't that right?"

Fr. Reilly looked at his feet as he tried to think of the right thing to say, but Mrs. Boyle jumped in to save the day. "Of course he wouldn't—not really."

"Then why did he end up shot and left on the side of the mountains? The Guards tell me nothing but lies."

"Well Mrs. Flanagan," Fr. Reilly said as he tried to regain control, "it was a delicate matter. And at times like these we have to remember that God has a plan, even if it is not apparent to us. Remember that he does work in . . . "

"He died saving my Danny," Mrs. Boyle announced when it was obvious that the priest was going to make a mess of it all. "He gave his life so my son could live. Just like Jesus," she added in Fr. Reilly's direction, but he just sat there in stunned silence.

*

Danny rode the elevator down to the lobby where the heater blasted every time the door was opened. He walked across the carpeted floor and was shocked when he reached for the metal handle. There were a lot of things to still get used to. It was fuckin' freezing all the time and everyone was talking about the wind chill—that that was what really got to you. But everyone still went out in it.

He and Martin had holed up from Christmas to New Year's and only went out when they had to. But Martin went back to work and Danny started getting cabin fever. Martin told him he had to start going out on his own. He'd have to get used to it when he was working and all. Martin had friends looking out for anything Danny could do while he was getting his band together.

He tugged at the zipper of his anorak, which was nowhere near as warm as it had been in Ireland. It didn't really block the wind; it just deflected it down to his thighs and made his arse freeze. He kept one hand in his pocket as he cupped his cigarette with the other.

The wind made smoking miserable as it squeezed down between the high-rises and scraped the length of Davisville Avenue. Martin had told him how to get to the subway and gave him a few tickets too. He would go southbound and get off at Bloor. It was just a few blocks east of there—whatever a block was.

He was a bit disappointed when he got to the subway platform; it wasn't really underground like it was in London. The platform was open to the winds and he shivered until the train arrived.

It was warm and clean inside and he settled by the window and watched the graveyard slide by until the train tunneled beneath the street. "St. Clair station," the distorted, scratchy voice announced and Danny checked the map again. Summerhill,

Rosedale and then Bloor; it was only going to take a few minutes. Martin had even suggested where he could go for lunch.

Dooley's wasn't what he had expected. It was large and clean and bright with deliberate little Irishisms everywhere. It was the type of place he would have to bring his parents to, after he got settled and all. The young woman who came to take his order didn't look very Irish. In fact she looked Vietnamese or Filipino, but she was friendly. She smiled and asked what type of beer he wanted. Her skin was clear, a yellowish brown, and her eyes were dark like pools. Her lips were almost too big for her face and her hair was straying from under the white hat of her maid outfit.

"What type do you have?"

He ordered Carlsberg. It was what Martin had filled his fridge with, along with some anemic light beers that were for David. Danny tried one but couldn't finish it and, without thinking, said he thought it was faggoty.

"Over here we're called gays," Martin had warned him. He also asked Danny to stay out for the day. David was coming home and they wanted the place to themselves for a few hours. Danny didn't mind; it would give him a chance to explore his new city.

After lunch, he wandered toward Parliament Street in the bright cold sunshine. He wanted to see Corktown and the old church down on Queen Street. Martin had marked it on the map for him even though he hadn't been down to see it.

Martin's tour led him through Cabbagetown where the Irish had migrated to from Corktown, once the Irish ghetto that waited for those who survived the "Fever Sheds." He had read all about it and wanted to see the places for himself—where the children of "Black 47" had fought their way up. Martin had suggested he not talk like that in front of other people; it was all in the past now and besides, Canadians got very sensitive when immigrants criticized them. "And they have every right to, too. People come over here from the backend of nowhere and, no sooner than they get set up, they start telling everybody they're doing it wrong, that everything was better back in the old country. Don't be one of those guys, Danny. Please?"

Still, he had to go where those who had gone before him had been and he'd pay his respects. A lot of Irish had come to Toronto and had to claw their way up. Just the Catholics, mind you. The Protestants got to run the place right off the boat, but Martin said it was better to forget about all that too. "It wasn't like being Catholic was such a great thing." Danny knew what he meant.

Still, the houses along Winchester didn't look like the kind of houses that Irish people would own. The Irish had moved into them when their more Anglo residents had moved up the ladder. That, Martin had told him, was how it worked. Each time a new group of immigrants arrived, they started near the bottom. "That pushes everybody up a bit. Well, almost everybody."

Most of them were rooming houses now, with rows and rows of buzzers implanted into their Victorian facades—a public notice of their continuing decline. Danny had noticed a big change in his uncle too. Now that Martin was openly gay, he wanted people to start accepting each other and not judge. And not just gays; he was on about the way Danny talked about black people, too, but that was understandable.

Danny agreed and tried but, sometimes, it was just reflex. Everyone at home talked about black people like they were afraid of them. Most of them had never met one but they inherited the attitudes of those who said they had. But Martin was right; Danny didn't want to be a part of anything he was back there. He was being given a new beginning—just like everybody who came over.

Martin was still Irish, but in a different kind of way. He always acted like he never missed it but sometimes, after they had been drinking, he'd let it slip out. He also made it plain that he had no time for religion anymore. He missed Ireland— not being Irish. It was understandable. The Church was against people having sex unless they were trying to have children and there was no way two guys were ever going to be able to convince anyone that that's what they were up to.

He shivered in the blast of wind and the noise of a highway right in the middle of everything that met him at the edge of Riverdale Park. It was right beside the overgrown river, white in its winter stillness except for a few bits and pieces of garbage that flew off the highway. Most of Toronto was clean. He couldn't believe it—almost sterile—but Martin bristled a little at that and said he needed to see the rest of it before deciding. Sometimes, Danny was beginning to wonder if he ever really knew his uncle. Most of what they had shared had been all about him. That's why he wanted to try so much, for Martin's sake.

The cold cut his tour short but he did get to walk along a part of Queen Street. It wasn't what he expected, especially around Sherbourne, where a steady flow of shabby-looking men filed in and out of the tavern on the corner. It was called the Canada House but it didn't look like the type of place he'd go to.

He did stop in at McVeigh's New Windsor Tavern. Martin had marked it on the map, too. It was dark and smoky and warm, and he felt at home in a moment. It was a quiet afternoon but Martin had told him it was the place to go when you were in the mood for being Irish.

Danny was. He missed Dublin and he missed Deirdre, even though they weren't really back together. He felt totally alone and wanted to be somewhere warm and familiar for a while. He wasn't second-guessing coming over—he had no choice really—but it was hard to get used to. Everything was all very different now that he was actually here.

"What can I get you?" the waitress asked.

"I don't suppose I could get a pint?"

"Not the type you're thinking about. Most of the guys who come in drink 'EX.' It's a bit like Carlsberg but they seem to prefer it."

"Can I get a pint of that?"

"Most of the guys drink it by the bottle."

"Okay then, that's what I'll have. Thanks."

There were a few others tucked into the shadows and alone with their thoughts, glowing every once in a while when they pulled on their cigarettes. But one was different. He was very dark-skinned but he had a white beard, a neatly trimmed hedge along the side of his face. He wore a beret and a checkered shirt, like the ones lumberjacks wore only his was blue and black. He was very tall even though he was sitting down and, when he crossed his legs, Danny could see that he was just wearing sandals and no socks. He reminded Danny of a Yeti or something from the bar in Star Wars.

The beer brought little comfort. It had a hard taste to it, but, if it was what the locals drank, he'd get used to it. It wasn't bad, it was just different and the bottle was weird, a short stubby little thing with a big label on it. He thought about having another but decided against it. Sitting alone in a pub always made him feel like his father. He would have headed back toward the apartment if it weren't so early. Martin and David would have just gotten home.

So Danny Boyle walked along Yonge Street as the city rushed home from work. But the cold got to him again and he stopped at the Duke of Gloucester. It was packed. They served beer in pints and you could stand along the bar—just like a real pub. He even got talking with a few people, a Brit and two Scots who had been over for a few years and acted like they owned the place. They spoke about Toronto and Canada in terms of them and us, them being all the non-Brits. And, after a few beers, implied that Danny was one of 'us.' His Irish might have bristled at that but he was happy to feel included. They assured him he'd be okay as long as he stuck to his own kind. "Canada, mate, is British," the Brit explained. "And all these foreigners need to remember that."

"You're right there," one of the Scots agreed, burping beerily.

"It's really more Scottish when you think about it," the other insisted, smiling as he said it.

"Yeah," the Brit agreed with both of them. "But the main thing, Paddy, is that we all stick together over here."

"My name is Danny, not Paddy."

"Danny, Paddy, Jock or Tommy. We're all the same over here and we have to stick together."

*

He left them after eleven and found his way home by twelve, sloshing around inside of himself all the way. David had gone to bed but Martin had waited up for him—to make sure he got in okay.

"Thanks," Danny slurred as he staggered through the doorway. He barely managed to relieve himself before going to bed, collapsing onto it as he struggled to take off his jeans. The room spun for a few moments before he passed out.

So? Are you getting all settled in?

Danny answered without waking up. "It's okay."

It's well for some. I'm stuck here waiting for some bollocks to decide what to do with me. It's worse than before.

"Before what?"

Before you had me whacked, ya bollocks. Ya didn't think I was going to let you get away with that.

Danny finally recognized the voice. "Ah, for fucks sake. Not you?"

Yes Danny fuckin' Boyle, ya back-stabbing little rat's twat.

"Anto. How the fuck did you find me?"

I followed you.

"You can do that?"

I can do anything I want. I'm a fuckin' ghost, ya dopey little fuck.

The room grew colder and colder as Anto Flanagan flickered in the shadows.

He was wearing a dark suit and his dark-glasses, darker against the whiteness of his skin. Except around the hole in his forehead. It was still red and crusted. But there was something else that was different. He didn't seem as menacing as he had been in life. He almost seemed like he was lost and unsure. "And what the fuck do you want with me?"

We have unfinished business, Boyle. You and I are going to be bound to each other for a while yet.

"Great, and I thought I was getting away from all of that." Danny rolled over, pretending he was not afraid.

Not by a long shot, Boyle. Not by a long shot.

Chapter 2 -1978

A FTER A FEW WEEKS, Danny got a temporary job with the government. Martin knew a guy who knew a guy who could offer Danny a few weeks here and there without him having to commit to a steady job. It was only to keep him going until he got a few gigs.

He hadn't actually gotten around to asking at any of the bars yet; he was working up to it. The Gloucester didn't have live music but he ended up there most nights. He usually stayed until closing time and Martin didn't stay up for him anymore.

So Danny came in as quietly as he could and struggled out of his new parka and his heavy lined boots. He had taken Martin's advice and bought winter underwear too. He made his way to his room and peeled off the rest of his clothes and threw them on the floor.

He lay on his back and began to fondle himself. It was how he got to sleep every night, masturbating to his mental image of the barmaid at the Duke. Slimmer than in real life, but still with huge breasts and bigger, poutier lips. And at night in his room she wanted him, tearing her shirt open and flicking back her hair before leaning forward and taking him in her mouth.

He always felt guilty afterwards and it wasn't just all the stuff that he had been brought up with. He felt guilty about Deirdre but he couldn't imagine thinking about her when he was doing it.

The barmaid knew.

He told her all about Deirdre. He told her that he phoned Deirdre every week to ask her to come over. The barmaid told him that was cute and patted his head but she still came to him, when he was alone at night, with only one thing on her mind—to bring him pleasure. She almost had him there when he heard noises from the other room. Martin and David's bed squeaked amid the sounds of muffled love.

The barmaid vanished as he realized what was going on. He sat up quickly and his jeans slid off the bed, his heavy buckle making a sound that silenced all others but for whispers and stifled laughing.

He lay for a while and wondered what to do next. It was all very well joking around so that Martin wouldn't think that he was against it, or anything, but it really freaked him out. He couldn't help but imagine what they were doing. He'd never be able to look Martin in the face again. He'd have to pretend that he hadn't heard a thing—that he had kicked his jeans to the floor while he slept, deeply, where nothing could bother him. He covered his head with the pillow and tried to remember Deirdre that day in the Dandelion when she gave him another chance.

She had worn a summer dress that made her seem so tall and cool. Not aloof, but she stood out from the crowd that had gathered. And when he finished his song and looked over she gave him the same smile she used to give him, back in Bushy Park, before everything got fucked up.

He wanted to keep thinking about her but he couldn't and finally dozed off again and slept fitfully until he heard sounds outside.

*

Martin was sitting on the couch, looking a little flustered but trying to remain calm. He wore a thick, heavy robe, though the room was warm. He wore slippers, too, and his hair was all flattened against his head, like he had slept on the couch.

"David's just getting up. We were going to go over to that new place for brunch, if you're interested."

Danny wasn't; he just wanted to be alone for a while. "I'm just going to go to McDonald's and then I might go downtown and have a look at the apartment you were telling me about." He put on his parka and his boots without making eye contact and rose to leave.

Martin looked up at him like there was no other choice. After he had gone, David came out and sat with Martin.

"You don't think he heard us?"

"Martin, he knows."

"I know he knows, but I still don't want to be doing it while he is here. We'll have to be more careful until he moves out."

"I can't wait." David put his arm around his shoulders and kissed his cheek. "Not that I mind having him here."

Martin turned and kissed his lips. "Thanks. It won't be long now."

*

The super was gay, too, and was friendly—but not like 'friendly.'

It was more like he was letting Danny know that he knew Martin and friends looked out for each other. And the apartment was great. He'd have his own bedroom with his own kitchen on one side and his own shower on the other. The kitchen was more like a closet but there was a little booth where he could have his breakfast. The front room was huge and looked out over Jarvis and Isabella.

"Where it all happens," the super nodded at him. "And you can start moving your stuff in anytime."

"Stuff? I don't have any stuff yet. I'm just over."

The super's eyes softened. "Listen. We have a room full of furniture that tenants leave behind. You're welcome to look through it. Some of it is not bad. I found some chairs, a kitchen set and a radio from the 60s. It might give the place a more . . . you're not really into decorating, are you?"

Danny was getting a little uncomfortable. He wasn't sure if there was more going on. He was never sure around gays; not that he was an expert or anything like that, but he was learning a lot.

He'd been putting a lot of strain on Martin and he didn't mean to. It was just the way his face would change before he could stop it. Or sometimes, he'd say something that he shouldn't. He couldn't help it. It was the way he was brought up and even though he was trying to change all that, it was all still a bit new to him.

"Listen, Danny. The apartment is yours if you want it. And, if you ever need my help, you know where to find me."

He had gone and done it now. The guy had picked it up from him. Homophobia must have a smell that only gay guys could get, like the way men sense desperation in women. The guy was doing him a favor, getting him a place so fast, and keeping the rent the way it was.

"No, I do want it."

He had plenty of money for the first and last month's rent. His parents had given him nearly two thousand before he left. It must have been the last of Granny's fortune and they wanted him to have it. Even the old family solicitor, Davies—the one who got the cops to leave Danny alone—agreed, but he was so old that he might have been nodding at anything.

Still, everybody was happy with the way things had turned out and he'd been able to emigrate with some money in his pocket. He'd be able to buy his own TV and a nice stereo. And he'd get a couple of lamps around the place, like the way Martin had done up his place. Martin said that David did it all, that he was very artistic and creative.

He'd get a bed too. A big one for when Deirdre came over. He'd get some nice drawers, too, for her to be able to put her things in.

*

"Hey, Jerry, what's the difference between inhuman and degrading treatment and torture?"

Pat Magee was sitting at the bar, over the dregs of a pint. He'd been a fixture since Jerry was at university. He and the lads always stood Magee a few pints—to show support for the cause. "I don't know, Pat."

"The European Court of Human Rights!"

"I know! Can you believe it? The Brits must've paid them all off."

"They didn't have to. These fuckers are all the same when it comes down to it. They all look out for each other and to hell with the people. Amn't I right?"

"When you're right, you're right." Jerry patted the old man on the back and nodded to the barman for two pints.

Magee puffed up in his attention and softly murmured into song, low enough so the barman wouldn't object:

> No saviour from on high delivers, no faith have
> we in prince or peer.
> Our own right hand the chains must shiver,
> chains of hatred, greed and fear.
> E'er the thieves will out with their booty, and to
> all give a happier lot.
> Each at his forge must do their duty, and we'll
> strike the iron while it's hot.
> So comrades, come rally, and the last fight let us
> face.
> The Internationale, unites the human race.
> So comrades, come rally, and the last fight let us
> face.
> The Internationale, unites the human race.

"Fair play to you, you still have it in you," Jerry acknowledged.

He'd just have one and get out before Magee had him there all night. He wasn't the worst of them but if he got hold of you, you'd have to listen to his whole life story, again.

"Good man, Jerry," Magee acknowledged as the pints were placed before them. "It's good to see that not everyone has turned their back on the Brotherhood."

*

He'd been nursing his drink for an hour and now drained it and pulled the fresh pint toward him. He only spent the wet afternoons in the pub and he couldn't even afford that on his pension. A free pint was straight from providence and let him avoid his damp, empty room for a while yet.

On a fine day he'd sit in the Green; there was no place else for the likes of him to go. He liked it there among the flowers and the men that died for freedom. And when it was time to go, he always took his leave of them, statue by statue. There'd never be a statue to him or any of the others. Their war was not something the people wanted to remember—when they lined up behind their priests and let the fascists overrun the world.

"Did I ever tell that I was out in Spain with Frank Ryan?"

*

He asked the same question every time they met. Jerry glanced at his watch before answering. "You must've been awful young."

"I was just a gossoon of nineteen. Can you believe that? Can you picture any of these young fecks today going off to fight for the rights of the working man?"

"You said a mouthful there, Pat."

The old man looked delighted with himself and raised his fresh pint. "Here's to the lads: Charlie Donnelly and Eamon McGrotty, Bill Henry and Liam Tumilson, Bill Beattie and Frank. We were all at Jarama, you know? That's where the lads were all killed and Frank got wounded."

"And yourself?" Jerry asked for the umpteenth time.

"Do you see that?" The old man raised his trouser leg ,exposing a long white scar from his knee to his ankle. "That's what I got up near Suicide Hill. They had to carry me out of there and that's what saved my life."

"Well, here's to you and all of them." Jerry raised his pint and took a long swig. It was his first today. He didn't go at it so much anymore. He wasn't able for it. Besides, he and Jacinta liked to sit out, when the weather was fine, and enjoy a few glasses of wine in the glassed-in room where his mother used to grow her tomatoes. They'd all died, but Jacinta had planted flowers and things.

She seemed to have gotten over Danny's leaving fairly well. She still said she missed him all the time but she was putting on the brave face. He knew she was trying so he took every chance to just sit and talk with her. The worst was over and now it was time for the two of them to sit back and enjoy a bit of life. There was no point in worrying about all of the terrible things that went on in the world. They couldn't do anything about them, anyway, but they could share a little peace and quiet between them. They deserved that after all they had been through.

Magee was getting lost in his memories so Jerry left him alone. He didn't really care about all of that anymore. It had never gotten him anywhere. He was doing all right for himself now. His pay wasn't great but the benefits made up for it— stuffed envelopes from grateful contractors and the likes.

At first he had qualms, but if he didn't take them somebody else would.

His manager wasn't a great one for work, preferring to leave it to his assistants. As long as Jerry looked after his cronies, he had a free hand in how the more minor public contracts were doled out. It was all small stuff so nobody ever came nosing around. There were far bigger deals going down, further up.

"We used to stand up for each other back then," Magee commented to no one in particular. "Didn't matter what race or creed either. If you were a working man, that was good

enough. And we were fighting to protect a democratically elected government too. And just for the principle of the thing. We
don't do stuff like that anymore—not unless they have oil or
something."

Jerry nodded in agreement. Every time he stuffed an envelope into his pocket he agreed. The working man had to get a
bit of his own back every chance he got. All the big shots were
doing it and pocketing a lot more than the hundred or two
that Jerry got. And God knows he needed it; there was always
something.

"Have you any news?" Magee nudged him to let him know
he was almost finished.

"Did you hear about Johnny Giles?" Jerry asked as he
ordered one more round and then he'd be gone.

"Who?"

"The manager of the football team. He just quit."

"We used to play football in Spain too. We used to play
against the English and the Scots. We played against the Span-
ish too. They were a bunch of cheating bastards, but we still
fought for them, you know?"

*

Danny phoned his mother's house most Saturday mornings
and Deirdre got to talk with him there. They didn't risk him
calling her parent's house—not yet. Her mother knew about
the calls but said nothing to her father.

Danny always said he was fine but Deirdre could tell he
sounded lonesome and homesick. Though he might have been
drinking, he did phone late at night, his time. He told her how
much he missed her and he couldn't wait until she came over
for the summer.

She still hadn't agreed to it, not for the whole summer
anyway. She might go over for a few weeks, just to see what it
was like. Her mother wouldn't mind a few weeks. Her father
wouldn't be too happy about it but Deirdre was sure that her
mother was probably chiseling away at him. She would remind

him of how proud he was of her and how well she was doing at university. Her mother would tell him that she was quite grown up, almost enough to make her own choices in life and to find her own happiness.

Her studies were going well but the shadow of the future was looming. The world was changing again and having a fine arts degree was of little value.

Ireland was changing, too, looking more and more to the Continent. Everyone told her that, after she had gotten her degree, she should get away somewhere else and find a good job. They were, she was told, crying out for people who could speak French. She could move to Brussels and get plenty of work translating. She heard the money was good but she couldn't see herself being very happy doing that. She wasn't really sure what she'd be happy doing and she hoped that a few years in Canada would help her see things differently. She wasn't even sure if she loved Danny, but she missed him. She could go over and spend a few weeks with him and find out, one way or the other. It wasn't like she was going to spend the rest of her life with him.

Her mother had always told her to try things because that's how she would find out what she liked, but she probably meant vegetables and things like that and not going to live with a boyfriend. She was very liberal about a lot of things but she was having enough difficulty getting her father to accept that Grainne had a child with a painter. And they still hadn't gotten around to getting 'Church' married.

Grainne had explained it all patiently—that they loved each other and wanted to have children but they just didn't believe in marriage.

"Not believe in marriage?" her father had fussed and bubbled. "How can you not believe in marriage? You can dread it and fear it, but you can't not believe in it. That's like saying that you don't believe in death."

Her mother had eyed him coldly until he sat down and accepted the whole thing but Deirdre could tell that it never sat well with either of them. And her going off to spend a few weeks with Danny in Canada would be no different.

*

Jacinta had been very formal so Deirdre couldn't say no. She wanted to say she was busy but she didn't want to lie. She'd just stay and have tea and they would probably talk about how much they were missing Danny.

Jacinta made a fuss and insisted on serving tea in china cups, a part of Granny's collection that she had been able to retrieve from the pawn. She also insisted that they sit in the conservatory that Jerry had rebuilt for her. "He didn't actually do the work," she explained. "A friend of Donal's did the brickwork and new glazing and Jerry painted it and put in a bit of outdoor carpeting." But it looked grand and was warm in the spring sunshine.

"You're not still thinking of going over, are you?" Jacinta asked after she had poured their tea and settled back into her wicker chair.

Deirdre was hesitant. "I was thinking about it."

"Are you sure? Danny might read something into it and you don't want to be leading him on, do you?"

*

"You'd be better off forgetting about her and getting on with your own life," his mother told him the next time he phoned.

"I can't, Ma. She means the world to me."

"Well I hate to be the one to break the bad news, Danny, but she's going out with someone else."

"She can't be. She just wrote to me and said she was still thinking about visiting."

She hadn't. Her letters were vague, talking only about how much studying she had to do and how she was worried that she might not do as well as she hoped in her finals. But he couldn't admit that to himself. And certainly not to his mother, who almost sounded happy with her news.

"Well I'm only telling you what I know."

"But she can't, Ma."

"Oh, Danny. You don't know women. They do whatever their hearts tell them. Not that you can blame her. You're over there and she's over here with the whole world between you."

He didn't blame her; he blamed himself. He had no right to expect her to give up anything for him. He wasn't worth it. He had proven that so many times before. When she came to see him, that day in the Dandelion, she was probably just doing what was right. It meant everything to him and helped him get through it all, but now that he was safe in Canada, he had no right to ask anymore of her.

It was like the guardian angels his granny used to tell him about; good people didn't stay in his life. He spent a lot of the day thinking about all that his granny used to tell him. He didn't feel so bad about most of it anymore but he wished she had talked to him about what happened to his mother—rather than finding out the way he did. He was still a little pissed at his father over that, but who was he to hold a grudge?

He had, he decided as he leaned on the bar of the Duke of Gloucester, survived the worst of it.

He liked to spend Saturday afternoons there. He liked the neighborhood and each evening, as he walked from Yonge, across Isabella, everyone he met asked if he'd like some company.

He was embarrassed the first few times but he knew them all by now; young girls running from frying pans to fires and young men, showing their real selves only at night, offering every sexual possibility for nothing more than money.

Some nights Danny was so lonely he was tempted. But he couldn't—they were even sadder and lonelier than he was. And he always had the Windsor. He spent his Saturday nights there and one of these nights he'd chat someone up and take her home with him. He hadn't before because of Deirdre, but she wasn't going to be a part of his life anymore.

*

It was one of those nights—a blur of bearded bands belting out *The Wild Rover* and *Whiskey in the Jar*. Crowds of young women, second and third generation mostly, danced and gyrated with abandon as young men, recent immigrants mostly, hovered by the bar until their courage grew.

She slipped through the crowd and popped up like a daffodil in the space between Danny and the bar and waved her empty glass at the barman, like it was his fault.

"I'll get that," Danny drawled as he lit a cigarette, "and gimme one too."

He was trying to look her up-and-down, casually, but his own smoke was drifting into his face, causing it to twitch and causing his eyes to water.

"FOB?" she asked as she turned toward him and struggled to contain her smile. He was trying to read her face so she batted her eyelids and dazzled him a little more.

"Is that some kind of French thing for WOP?" He was wearing polyester pants that were low on his hips and were tight around the crotch, leaving little to the imagination.

"Just over?" She smiled at him like she was a little concerned—like he might be a bit slow.

"Me? No. I've been here for a few years now. Just got back from a business trip to Europe, ya know."

"What type of business are you in?"

She was probably giving him a little more rope but he had to go for it. "International business, ya know?"

"Where were you?"

"Do you know Ireland?"

"I read about it once—something about a war or something." She tilted her head and let her blonde hair tumble down her shoulder to where her sweater swelled.

"Yeah! We've had a few of them. I was in the North, ya know, where we're still trying to get the Brits out, ya know?" He checked from side-to-side before he leaned closer to her face. "That's what I was on business about, ya know?"

Her skin was almost perfect and her lips were big and warm. Her eyes were a deep sea green, deepening as he got closer.

"Really, are you one of the Freedom Fighters? What do call yourselves, I.R.B. or something?"

"Ah now, I've said enough ya know." He leaned back against the bar and tried to jam his thumb into his waistband but his pants were far too tight. He was getting erect, too, and turned to one side and drained half of his beer as he rearranged himself.

"What's your name?"

"Billie. What's yours?"

"Danny. Danny Boyle."

"Isn't that a song?"

"Not with the 'le.' So what do you do with yourself then, Billie?"

"Guess."

"I bet you're an art student, or a model or something like that."

"Close, Danny boy." She took the cigarette he offered and let her hair trail along the back of his hand as she leaned forward toward the match. "I'm doing my Masters in Celtic Studies. Right now I'm doing a paper on Irish caricatures and clichés."

She watched him as his smile wrinkled at the edges. His bulging withered, too, and for a moment he felt like a total fool. But he had to shake it off and looked her straight in the eye. "I really just came over a few months ago. I'm sorry about all that. I was just trying to make an impression, ya know?"

"Okay, I suppose I can let that one pass but do me a favor, Danny boy? Don't be such an asshole."

He was unsure and hunched over his drink so she couldn't see the side of his eyes where little tears were gathering. He should never have tried to be smooth. He should have just been himself. She was probably one of those libbers that always felt she had to put men in their place.

"Danny? I was just teasing you."

"Well then, I'll forgive you. Just this once."

She leaned closer and smiled. "So what do you think of the band?"

"They're all right. I'm a musician myself, ya know?"

"Really? Maybe I'll come and hear you play sometime."

"So am I going to get a second chance then?"

"Just until someone better comes along." She nudged him with her elbow and pressed closer as the crowd at the bar grew tighter and tighter. The bearded bands became more boisterous, enlivened now as the close of night approached. When they could stand solemnly, with the total reverence of the crowd, and proclaim to the entire city of Toronto, and the cobweb morality the old Orangemen had imposed, that: "Ireland long a province be a Nation once again."

> A Nation once again
> A Nation once again
> And Ireland long a province be a Nation once
> again.

After the cheering died and the lights were raised, intruding on soft intimacies and pools of boozy passion, the crowd thinned out, leaving only those still in negotiation. Mostly young lads trying to pull birds as well as a few pockets of older men, still trying to solve the problems of the world.

When Billie and Danny stepped outside, Richmond Street was empty. Cold winds had scoured it clean and white-stained by salt, but he wasn't ready to say goodnight. "You could come to my place. It's just up on Jarvis Street and we could stop at Harvey's and I can buy you a burger."

"Why? Don't you have any food in your place?"

"I have bacon, Canadian bacon, but it's in the freezer."

"Keeping it for a big occasion?"

"At least until I buy some knives and forks."

"As tempting as that sounds, Danny boy, I'm going to go home."

"Well, I'll come with you then."

"No you can't. I live with my parents and my father has a shotgun. A really big one."

They laughed all the way to the subway and he didn't stop there. He went with her, all the way out to Victoria Park and then on the streetcar where he placed his arm around the seat rest behind them.

"You still can't stay, Danny."

"I know that. I just want to see you safely home—that's all."

"That's very gentlemanly of you."

"Good, because I would love to go out with you again."

"Are you sure you have room in your business schedule?"

"I was going to ask you the same thing."

"Well, as a matter of fact I do have one night open next week. Next Saturday, same time, same place?"

She insisted that he stay on the streetcar. "My house is just around the corner and I don't want the neighbors to see you walk me home. They'd tell on me and I might get grounded."

"Are you serious?"

"Of course not! Listen! I don't know you so I don't want you knowing where I live. You might try to sneak back and climb in my bedroom window."

"And what makes you think I might do something like that, unless you'd like me to?"

"Good night, Danny boy. See you next Saturday."

*

As the autumn settled in, Patrick Reilly jumped at the chance to see her again but convinced himself that it was for the cause. "We can't just let them destroy it." Miriam's voice had sounded strained. He had called to see how she was; she'd been away for the summer. "We're all going down. You have to join us." They

were all going down to Wood Quay to try to save the recently uncovered Viking ruins from being covered up by progress.
"You will come won't you, Patrick? I know it's your evening off
so you can have no excuse."

He had never done anything like this in his life. He was
more inclined to shake his head and say it was a shame—or a
holy shame if the situation was bad enough to warrant it. But
Miriam had a very contagious fire inside of her. She took issue
with the things she thought were wrong and always spoke out
against them. He wanted to ask her if she wasn't afraid of getting into trouble again. But that was just stupid of him. What
more could they do to her now? Excommunication?

Besides, it was just Dublin Corporation. The Church didn't
concern itself too much with them. It would be different if they
were going to build the cathedral there and not an office block.
No! There was no reason why he shouldn't go down and lend
his support to a good cause. This was the bones of the city they
were going to pave over. He kept telling himself that but he still
felt a little guilty, like he was sneaking off to do something he
shouldn't be doing.

"I'm off now," he had called up to Fr. Dolan. "I won't be too
late."

He didn't like his new parish priest, God forgive him.
There was something shifty about him. But he had to give the
man a chance. It was a big change for both of them.

He wasn't the only priest that went. There were even a few
monsignors with their flashings of red, strutting among the
crowd like robins among starlings. He hadn't worn his collar
and he regretted it. It wasn't your everyday class of protest.
There were people from archeological societies from all over,
standing shoulder to shoulder with union members and assorted activists and young lads just hanging out and, of course, the
university crowds.

Miriam waved him over. They had torches and were
just getting ready to light them as the sky darkened above

Christchurch, standing out on the crest of the hill like Mary Shelley's castle.

He didn't dare carry a torch but walked along beside Miriam as she marched with hers held out in front of her. The glow sparkled in her eyes and her cheeks blushed and flickered. Her hair shone, red and yellow and black. He almost wanted to reach out and run his fingers through it.

Everyone around them was outraged.

They were there to try to save Wood Quay, the heart and soul of Dublin, from the talons of those that had been elected to serve them.

"It could be so much more," they encouraged each other with visions of urban spaces where people could gather, not for profit but for the sheer pleasure of it. "It could be the center of a living, breathing city. It would let the people reach out and touch the past that made them."

But Patrick could see the doubt in their eyes. They would march and make speeches, but in the end, everybody knew—those in power did as they pleased and had the gall to say it was for the public good.

Miriam chatted with everyone around them, growing more and more indignant with every step she took, heels hard on the old cobblestone. She opened her coat as she grew warm and he tried to look somewhere else. He wasn't afraid of her; he was afraid of himself.

He shouldn't have come. It was only leading himself into temptation but he couldn't help it. She made him feel like no one else ever had. She made him feel like he shouldn't have to go through life alone anymore, despite everything he had been taught.

He stopped himself as they walked up Winetavern Street. He had no right to think of her like that. She had enough to do in rebuilding her life without the likes of him mooning over her like some lovesick schoolboy. But still, there were times when even just the thought of her made his days seem a lot less empty. Who could a priest take his loneliness to? But he could never allow himself to think about anything else. It was bad enough that she had fallen from grace but to take him with her? That could never be forgiven. But they were doing nothing wrong. They were taking part in a public protest, in public. What harm was there in that?

She looked over at him and he smiled back to let her know he was happy to be out walking with her at night, in torchlight, even if it was for a lost cause.

Chapter 3 -1979

THE YEAR OF THE THREE POPES had been very hard on the bishop. Rumors were rife of intrigue in sacred places, echoes of the times when popes murdered each other like kings. It was all they needed now with the Church being attacked from all sides.

Not that he wasn't up for one more fight; what bothered him the most was something far more fundamental. How could they sell the idea of being anointed—rather than appointed—when the Holy Spirit couldn't pick a winner to save His life? The ruddy-faced man had raised the same question the last time they met at Moss Twomey's funeral. The bishop had thought long and hard about going. The Boys were out of favor but he had known Moss since they were young and starting down the paths they were given.

He went, but wore his hat and scarf in the hope that prying eyes would pass over him. And, as they filed out to their cars, he and John Joe had the chance for a quick chat. They still enjoyed each other's company but they were both buckling under the weight the years were piling on them. They had lost their places of prominence in Irish life. Decisions that had been made behind closed doors could now be openly challenged in foreign, less friendly courts. Some of the darkest secrets from before were beginning to surface and, although both their hands were clean, they would still be called out for betraying the people's trust.

The bishop more than the other. John Joe could still claim lineage to the 'Men of 16,' and those that had kept the flame burning. All the bishop would have to cling on to was the love of God—to evoke forgiveness for all the sins of Rome.

And on top of that he had Fr. Dolan to deal with, an ambitious sort who disdained anonymity, claiming instead that the people should know what their Church did on their behalf. The bishop didn't approve of all of that even though he had to agree that Fr. Dolan had really perked things up since he took over. Dan Brennan had let the parish go so Fr. Dolan brought in a lot of new-fangled ideas with him. He harangued the married couples into Marriage Encounter and had galvanized the whole parish around the killing of Anthony Flanagan. He even had Jerry Boyle and that Fallon blowhard out talking to parents about the danger of drugs. And he'd set up a new youth club where he could get to know the local lads and lassies and give them somewhere to go—other than getting into trouble. But the bishop could see that the new broom would end up sweeping Patrick Reilly out too.

He could have given him the parish but he didn't. Not because of the nepotism of it all, but rather because he couldn't put that cross on his nephew's shoulders. Patrick was at one of those crossroads that people have to face at some point in their lives. He'd been a priest long enough to know what it was really like and not the way his mammy had told him. By now, he'd have learned what it meant to be really alone and apart.

Patrick was going to have to decide and his uncle didn't want him deciding until he had a chance to sit back and contemplate his life from the Holy See. That was where the bishop had made his decision in the years leading up to the war, when the Church and the rest of the world had sat back while the black crows spread their cloaks. They were beholden to Franco and all that flocked to his side, even the Austrian, but later when the smoke cleared, they had backed the wrong horse and the Communists were still spreading their godless creed.

He came back to Dublin and became a monsignor after that. There was more than enough going on in Ireland to keep him busy and not be second-guessing himself. And in time they made him a bishop, to guide his priests with only God's silence to rely on.

His nephew had phoned to say that Fr. Dolan was making it difficult for him to connect with the young people, instead sending him to tend to the sick and the aged. The bishop advised patience and reminded Patrick that he could still go to Rome. All he had to do was to say the word and the bishop would make it happen. But Patrick still hadn't made up his mind and the bishop didn't want to have to order him.

He knew he wouldn't have to. Fr. Dolan would drive his nephew out with all the new and wonderful ideas he brought back with him from America. He could fascinate for hours with his stories of Boston. The way he made it sound it was a wonder that he should ever have chosen to come back to Ireland, but the bishop had to take priests wherever he could find them. There was talk that the new pope might drop in and he wanted every parish running like clockwork.

So he called Patrick in for a friendly chat—to feel the velvet around his iron fist.

*

Patrick was shown in on the hour, looking as sheepish as ever. Mrs. Mawhinney announced him and frowned. She had told the bishop to go easy on him and the frown was to remind him. The bishop wasn't offended; she'd been around long enough to have her say.

"Patrick, are you well?"

"I am, thank God, and yourself?"

"Still living when all around me are dying." He reached for his desk drawer and poured two nips. He offered one to his nephew and stared at him for a moment. "Well? Have you given anymore thought to Rome?"

"I have, but I can't leave now. Isn't the pope supposed to be coming over later in the year?"

"Ah, that's still just talk you know. Our people and his people are still trying to figure it out. I don't think anything has been decided yet."

He sipped from his glass so his nephew wouldn't know he was lying. He just didn't want his nephew run over when Fr. Dolan swept up in a Cadillac and drove off with the pope before poor Patrick would get near him.

"You need to speak up soon or the position might be gone."

"Well if Your Grace doesn't think . . ."

"It's not that at all, Patrick. Fr. Dolan just wants to make the parish more like he's used to and he might be right. Over in America they have to compete with all those evangelists on the television. Fr. Dolan has a bit of the impresario in him and the likes of you would be better off teaching than playing second fiddle to the likes of him."

Patrick sipped his whiskey and almost made a face. His uncle always enjoyed watching him. He still looked so much like the young man who came to see him years ago—just before he finished secondary school. When he had come to tell him he had decided on the priesthood.

"And you don't think I have anything to offer the people?"

"It's not that, Patrick. I just think that a young man like you, with your love for studying, could serve the Lord and the Church better doing what makes you the happiest." He let it sink in but they both knew he wasn't really giving the young priest any options.

"Very well, Your Grace. I'll go. When should I travel?"

"You can go over any time you like. You'll enjoy being in Rome. It gets a bit hot but you'll be used to that in no time."

They finished their drinks and Patrick rose to leave.

"You'll not regret it," the bishop repeated a few times as he ushered his nephew out.

When he sat back down, he poured another nip. He had no choice. Fr. Dolan was making a fuss about Patrick and the ex-nun. Fr. Dolan knew all about her from Chicago and made sure the bishop knew too. "An undesirable sort," he had called her and the bishop had no defense. Patrick was better off out of there, for everyone's sake.

*

Miriam got to Bewley's early and found a table near the back. She wanted a little seclusion in which to re-read her letter. She hadn't heard from Fr. Melchor in a while, though she wasn't surprised. The last time she met him in Rome, she could tell he was up to something.

He had been banished there rather than face possible conviction at home. Neither the State Department, nor the Society of Jesus, had any appetite for a public trial and he had taken the option his superiors offered and agreed to the position in Rome.

But she knew he would never let that be the end of it. He had been angling for a teaching position in Central America and wrote, *I only want to 'strive especially for the propagation and defense of the faith and progress of souls in Christian life and doctrine,' while spreading liberation theology among the downtrodden!*

Miriam feared what he might get up to there, but he wrote about it like it was nothing.

What else can they do with me? I have done my penance and my superiors are happy to believe that I am reformed in their image. They have, however, insisted that I do not go back to the States. It seems that in trying to be Christ-like, I have offended the sensibilities of those who claim to be a Christian nation.

Miriam smiled at that. John Melchor could always cloak his casuistry within his cassock. But she worried, too. He had always shown disregard where others might be afraid for themselves and what their dissent might cost. Not Fr. Melchor though. He always said that a true Christian would suffer death rather than go along with the murder and repression of any who disagree. He said the Church had done enough of that. And his country.

My beloved United States has gone from being the policeman to the world to being the hired thug of despots. But the world will, as it must. The shah has gone to Egypt and some ayatollah is taking over. I doubt he will be our puppet for very long. Everyone is blaming the president. They say he isn't strong enough on the world. He can't be that bad, though, he commuted Patty Hearst's sentence. Maybe he will put in good word for me—if it comes to that.

His mood changed again as he went on to write about the death of Pedro Joaquín Chamorro Cardenal. *He was blasted from this world by cruel men with shotguns. The people of Nicaragua knew who was responsible and over 30,000 rioted against Somoza. I must find a way of doing what I can in this.*

Miriam knew exactly what he meant and worried for him, but she had to smile again as she continued to read. *Don't worry about me. Tell me all your news. How are the Mother-loving Catholics of Ireland accepting you?*

*

"Sorry I'm late; the buses seem to hide when it rains."

Miriam folded her letter away and smiled. "Not at all Deirdre, I was just catching up with an old friend."

She caught a passing waitress's attention and watched her friend while she ordered. She didn't look too happy. Danny had been pestering her to go over but Deirdre wouldn't go without her parents' approval.

"Have you asked them yet?"

"Not yet. I just haven't found the right time."

"Is there ever a good time to ask your parents if you can go live in sin for a few weeks?"

"I know. It's not like I'm still a child. And besides, he's been away for over a year."

"That might be what they are afraid of."

"Danny's not like that. And neither am I for that matter."

Miriam started to laugh. "Not that I would know anything about that type of thing."

She had tried. She tried to do all the things that women did to suggest interest without being overt about it, but men never responded to her. She knew why—men just weren't into hitching up with ex-nuns. Deirdre had told her that she probably intimidated them but Miriam knew better. She had once been married to Jesus; no man alive would try to follow that.

"So who was the love letter from?" Deirdre smiled.

"Father Melchor. He is about to get himself into trouble again."

"And you are worried about him?"

Miriam smiled. "To know John Melchor is to worry about him. He has no concern for his own safety and always answers when social injustice calls. He said that the war made him like that. He was a bombardier in the Air Force and took part in the fire-raids over Tokyo. He said it changed his life. He had nightmares for years."

"It must have been awful for him."

"It was. After he got out of the Air Force he spent a few years in Mexico trying to forget, but he couldn't so he became a Jesuit. Since then, he has been using the protection of the collar to speak out.

"He galvanized us all to do whatever we could to protest against Vietnam. That was when I got into trouble too. We got caught pouring pig's blood on draft records. We weren't formally charged, as the Diocese got involved and promised to look after the matter internally. I was banished to Ireland and John was given a desk job in a basement somewhere in Rome."

"Do you ever regret it?"

"Never. I would have regretted not doing it no matter what it cost me. I'm just not one of those people who can sit silently by while . . . but you know all that. Tell me, what are you going to do about Danny?"

It was Deirdre's turn to look troubled. "I think I will wait until I graduate and then I might think about going over for a few weeks. They wouldn't mind that?"

"And do you think Danny Boyle will wait for you?"

"I'm not asking him to. I told him I couldn't this year."

"Are you testing him?"

"No! Not at all. I'm just letting fate take its course."

They fell silent for a while until Deirdre looked at her watch and gulped down the rest of her coffee. "I'm sorry. I have to run and catch my lecture."

She rose and gathered her things but Miriam stayed where she was.

When Deirdre was gone, Miriam ordered one more coffee and thought about all that she had given up, both as a nun and as an anti-war protester. It didn't make sense to her anymore. Evil was openly rewarded while people like Fr. Melchor and her paid dearly. She wished she didn't know that. She wished she were still like Deirdre, still able to believe in something.

*

Billie knew Danny was still hung up on the girl he left behind and hadn't wanted to push him. She hadn't wanted to change the way things were between them. He was off limits but she liked hanging around with him. He was safe. The only time they ever messed around was on St. Patrick's Day. She'd had a little too much to drink and they both decided that she could stay at his place and that nothing would happen.

**

"Are you saying," she had asked as she twirled in the falling snow, "that you don't find me even the least bit attractive?" The snow was heavy and wet and would be gone by morning, but tonight she was happy—drunken happy, but happy.

He stood waiting for the lights to change, clutching the bags from Harvey's. They'd be cold but it wouldn't matter. Tonight, she was going to make out with Danny Boyle.

She didn't want to have sex with him. Getting laid on St. Patrick's Day was far too clichéd, but fooling around with someone who wouldn't try anything was just what she needed.

It would appease the wanton within, the Harpie that emerged when she drank too much. She had been very popular during her first few years away at university. Only, she got a bit of a reputation. Boys were still studs and girls were still sluts, just like it had been in high school. There hadn't been anybody since, except Danny Boyle and he had a girl back home.

"Come and sit beside me," she beckoned from the couch as Danny returned from the kitchen with a bottle of Mateus Rosé.

"No, you're fine there."

"Come on, I won't bite."

"Only if you promise then."

She pulled her knees up to her chin as he sat and poured. "Danny, play me a song."

"I'm too drunk. Besides, we spent the whole night listening to songs."

"Not those kind of songs. Sing me one of your songs. I've heard you singing bits and pieces of them and I want to hear a whole song. Sing me a song about you."

She really had to pester him until he picked up his guitar and twanged and tuned for a while.

"Close enough," he laughed in his shy way and began to strum as she lowered the lamp behind her. He changed as his strumming became a rhythm. His hands grew steadier and his eyes began to clear, the boozy blur began to part and he sang. Unsurely at first, but steadying, and he sang about being alone. About being so terribly alone, about love and all good things coming and going but always leaving him alone. But not in a whiney way, Danny sang like a man who had been all the way down and had come back to tell about it. She couldn't help it. She almost began to cry for him, for her, and for them. She uncoiled beside him, reaching one arm around his back as she rested her head against his shoulders, listening to him singing in time with his heartbeat.

He sang another. A sweet gentle song of hope but it was almost like a lullaby. She couldn't help it and let her hand slide between him and the guitar.

He pulled away and stood, placing the guitar gently against the couch.

"Oh, Christ, Danny, I'm sorry."

She started to sob so he led her toward the bathroom, to clean her face but he had to steady her, one hand holding her arm, his fingers softly brushing past her breast.

She leaned a little more and bumped his hip. It made him stagger toward his bedroom so she did it again. They were both laughing by the time they fell across his bed.

"We can't, Billie. It's not right."

"I don't want to have sex with you. I just want you to hold me." She nestled across his chest, her face next to his. "I just want to kiss and stuff. Nothing that we ever have to feel guilty about." She reached up with her lips but he pulled back and pushed her away.

"Fuck's sake. We can't, Billie. Don't ask me to do stuff like this. I can't do something like that to Deirdre."

He turned and left and slept on the couch. She snuck out when the subway opened and they avoided each other for a while.

**

She stayed away from the Windsor for two months before she could face him again.

"How ya?" he smiled from the bar, the night she finally walked in.

"Listen, Danny," she brushed her hair behind her left ear so she could look up into his face. "I'm really sorry about what . . ."

"Don't worry about that. What harm was done?"

"I couldn't face my best friend for months." she smiled back.

"Come here to me." He hugged her roughly and ordered her a beer and they were back to normal by the time the bar closed.

"I'll only see you to subway."

"Aren't you worried about me alone on the train?"

"I'd be more worried if I had to go with you."

"Listen, Danny Boyle. You're not that cute."

"You didn't think so on Paddy's Night."

"What can a colleen say? Sometimes I overdo the Irish thing. Sue me."

"Go on then, while you still have a handle on your libido."

She dropped her token and brushed through the turnstile but she did turn and blow him the sexiest kiss she could manage. He caught it, too, and held it to his heart.

⁂

They were fine after that and she started dropping by his place on Sunday afternoons, just as a friend again, and listened to him play. They spent hours drinking coffee and smoking up a little. He'd sit on the couch and she'd sit on the floor, across from him. Sometimes, she'd even clap when he finished but it only seemed to distract him, so she stopped.

His songs were good and getting better. He re-worked every one and she listened to each improvement. She told him he was good enough to play in coffee shops and places like that. She even offered to introduce him to people who knew people, but Danny wasn't sure and wanted to start somewhere more familiar.

He finally arranged a gig at the Irish Center and pleaded with her to come for moral support.

She did and it was a total disaster. The crowd was like her parents, older, having come over in the fifties and sixties. They weren't there to hear what was new from Ireland. They wanted to hear the songs from their day and Danny didn't know any of them. But they were a good-natured crowd and just talked and laughed through every song he sang.

While Danny was recalling the last night of some poor unfortunate that got mixed up in the drug scene—he made him sound like another martyr for old Ireland—they asked after each other and their children. Some openly boasting and some putting-on-the-poor-mouth, even as they paid for their drinks from wads of freshly minted dollars. They worked hard for them and they knew how to enjoy themselves.

As Danny switched and tried to sing songs they might know, they just grew louder until Danny couldn't be heard at all. He kept going, though, with sweat streaming down his face and darkening his armpits through his lime-green t-shirt.

Because no one else would look at him, he stared at her, sitting alone at a table in the front row, putting her in the spotlight where she could suffer along with him.

In time a small man with a big accordion joined him on stage and the whole crowd got up to dance. They danced jigs and reels, foxtrots and waltzes without ever changing gait. They were all the same to them and the small man played on and on.

"What key?" she could hear Danny's loud whisper as he tried to join in.

"B-Flat!"

Even Billie could tell it wasn't, but Danny fumbled with his capo until he found the key. That was when she started to have real feelings for him—when she glimpsed him as he really was—a voice crying in the wilderness.

"Would you consider coming home with me?" he had asked on the cab ride back, his voice sadder than she had ever heard.

"Do you really think I should?"

"I do."

"Why?"

"Because Deirdre's never going to be coming over. It's over between her and me."

*

Jerry had a great afternoon, sitting in the pub picking horses. He had a three-cross-double come in but he only had a few pounds on it. Still, it paid over two hundred and he was in the mood for a night on the town. He'd take Jacinta for a meal and a few bottles of wine but the lights were all out when he got home and the house seemed empty.

"I'm home," he called into the darkness as he reached along the wall for the light switch.

The breakfast dishes were still on the table and the house was cold. Jacinta usually had a fire going by now. "I'm home," he repeated as he wandered into the living room.

She was sitting on the couch in the dark with a half-empty sherry bottle on the coffee table.

"Ah, Jaze, Jass, what are you doing sitting in the dark? I thought you might have died on me."

"I may as well be dead, Jerry. I've done a terrible thing."

Jerry sat down opposite her and lit a cigarette. He should have known better—God never gave with the one hand but he didn't take away with the other. "What's the matter with you now?" He didn't mean to sound impatient but he couldn't help it, even after all these years.

"I got a call from Danny that's after upsetting me."

"What's he done now?"

"It's not his fault, Jerry. It's mine."

"Why, what's happened?"

"He told me that he has met someone—a Canadian someone."

"And why's that a bad thing. He's a good lookin' lad. He was bound to meet up with someone."

"But don't you see? He'll never come back now."

"But how's that your fault?"

She looked up at him with tears rolling down her cheeks as she pulled a cigarette from his pack. Her own pack was empty and the ashtray was full. "I was the one," she said, pausing slightly, "who told him that the young Fallon girl wasn't interested in him, and now he has gone and got someone who is probably giving him sex and he'll never want to come back."

Jerry might have laughed. "Ah now, Jass, I think you're getting a bit carried away." He was about to say something else when he noticed her pills on the cushion beside her. She normally kept them in the bathroom cabinet. "What are those doing there?"

"I must have brought them down and forgot about them."

Jerry reached for them and opened the lid. He always kept an eye on her medicine just in case she forgot herself and took too many. "You weren't thinking of doing anything stupid, were you?"

"Ah, no, Jerry, don't be thinking that. I'm not mad anymore."

He said nothing for a while and they smoked in silence, both knowing the other knew what they knew.

"I'm so sorry, Jerry. I'm so sorry I turned out like this. Your mother was right about me."

"She was," he lied. He had to; he had to say something that would turn her away from the darkness. "She said that you were good to her to the bitter end."

"Did she really?"

"She did. And you know Nora. If you ever think about doing something like this she'll come back and haunt sense into you."

"She did before but it wore off."

"If you don't promise that you'll never think of doing it again, I'll hold a séance."

"I promise you, Jerry." She waited until his eyes began to soften and reached for his arm. "I don't suppose that you would make me a cup of tea now?"

*

"What are you going to do?"

Jerry had confided in Gina, and she in Donal, but they all agreed it would go no further. Jerry had told Jacinta to have them over on Sunday and, as was pre-planned, he and Donal had to go out to get more cigarettes while the women shared a pot of tea. Normally, Jacinta would have caught on but she seemed to want to spend some time with her sister and Donal and Jerry were happy to make themselves scarce.

"Jeeze, Donal, I don't fuckin' know. This is the last thing I needed right now. Should I have called the hospital?"

"No! You did the right thing. You don't want your poor wife to die of shame. But don't worry, you probably saved her life." He placed his arm on Jerry's. "You're not afraid that it might happen again?"

Jerry paused to light a cigarette. "I don't think so, only Jacinta is not like Gina and the others you know? She's a bit delicate and sometimes she does things because life gets to her."

"Has she ever tried to do this before?"

He thought about it but he couldn't tell him. That whole night was still a bit of a blur.

**

He'd been out having a few drinks and when he came home she went right for him. She was complaining about how hard it was for her with the baby and all. It never occurred to her that it was hard for him, too, getting used to it all. He probably should have tried to be a bit nicer but he was getting awful tired of her.

"I'll take the baby," she had screamed at him. "We'll go down to the river and I'll throw the two of us in and then you'll be happy. You and your mother will be rid of us and you can all go back to being the big shots and everyone will be happy. Is that what you want?"

He should have said something else but he didn't. "I don't give a fiddler's fuck what you do; just let me go to bed, will ya?"

He didn't really mean it but he didn't think that she really meant what she said either. He couldn't believe it when she grabbed the child and ran out the door in her nightie. He ran after her of course, but she was screaming and carrying on until the Guards arrived and took the three of them to the station.

Fr. Brennan arrived with his mother a few hours later. They had talked it all through and were going to step in and do what had to be done. Jerry and Jacinta had no say in it and were packed off, him to England and her to the hospital and Danny went to live with his granny.

***

"You know, Jerry." Donal nudged him when the silence had dragged. "You could be rich and get real doctors to look at Jacinta."

"With what? I can barely afford aspirins on my wages."

"And that, me-auld-flower, is what I want to talk to you about. You and I could be rich as kings soon and be able to treat our wives like queens."

"Will I have to wear a fuckin' crown?"

"You'll be able to wear your arse for a hat if you like. When you're rich you get to do what-ever-the-fuck you like."

"And how are we going to get rich then?"

"You still handle contractors, don't ya?"

"Ya. Why?"

"Well, you see, I know of a few rundown houses over on Lesson Street."

"I'm not going to be a fuckin' landlord's agent. Not for all the gold . . ."

"Shut up, will ya? I'm not talking about renting them. The auld-fella who owns them is dying and his family won't want them. We could fix them all up and sell them. It's called flipping. Everyone over in London is doing it."

Jerry nodded as he absorbed it all. "But come here to me. Where are you going to find the money to be fixing houses? Gina says you can't even change the jack's-roll."

"That's where you come in. I got the houses and you got the men and the material."

*

After that, Jacinta was back to her usual self and tried to convince him that she had just gotten mixed up.

"I was just having a few drinks and I forgot if I had taken my pills. I must have taken them before because as soon as I took some more I didn't remember anything. I'm so sorry for scaring you all like that but there's nothing for anybody to be getting worried about."

Jerry was more than happy to accept her explanation; he had too many other things to be thinking about.

And Jacinta never had to mention that Deirdre had come by to see her, too, to ask why Danny wanted nothing more to do with her. Jacinta had lied to her but Deirdre's tears were like acid and burned all the way into her soul.

Chapter 4 -1980

A RE YOU WELL, MRS. BOYLE?"
        "Fair to middling, Mrs. Flanagan, but I suppose I shouldn't complain."

The two of them stood on the steps of the church as the winds swirled plastic bags up into the trees. They had seen each other often but they hadn't really had a chat since that day in the priest's house. Jacinta was ready to leave but Mrs. Flanagan had something to say. She just didn't seem to know how to begin.

"Is there anything I can do for you?" Jacinta asked nervously.

"I would like to have a little chat, if you can spare the time."

"Of course, but not here in the wind. Let's go over the road and have a cup of tea," Jacinta offered and nodded toward the Yellow House, "or something stronger if you prefer," she added as the two women linked arms and forced their way through passing cars.

"I've been thinking about what you said about my Anthony," Mrs. Flanagan finally announced after she had sipped her sherry and placed it carefully on the paper doily.

It took Jacinta a moment to remember what she had said. "Sure of course you would. You'd think on nothing else."

"Well," Mrs. Flanagan paused like she was measuring what she was about to say. "It's no secret that my Anthony was no saint, but he wasn't the worst of them either."

"Not a bit of it," Jacinta lied and wondered where Mrs. Flanagan was taking her.

"I know he got mixed up in things that would have been better left alone, but he wasn't the only one."

"No, he wasn't."

"Well, I have been praying to God because I know he hasn't got to heaven."

"Sure how can you be sure? Maybe he said a good act of contrition before . . ."

"Ah now that's very nice of you to say, Mrs. Boyle, but I think he'll be a while yet before he gets there."

"You don't think that he's in Hell?" Jacinta asked as earnestly as she could. If there was any justice, and if God paid any attention to all the neighbor's curses, Anto would have a front seat close to the fire.

"No. I have a feeling that he is going to have to stay in purgatory for a while."

"Lord save us," Jacinta answered because she could think of nothing else to say.

She didn't believe in any of that anymore. All the grey days in the hospital had chased all that nonsense from her mind but she knew better than to say that aloud.

"What I was wondering," Mrs. Flanagan said as she finally got to the heart of the matter, "was if you would have a word with your Danny about this?"

"And what can Danny do?"

"Well, if Danny was to remember him in his prayers, then the bit of good that Anthony did wouldn't be forgotten."

Jacinta almost laughed but controlled herself.

"You can rest assured, Mrs. Flanagan; he gets down on his knees every night and thanks God for sending Anthony to save him that night. He was just telling me that he wants to send flowers for the grave only he's not sure how to send them from Canada."

And before Mrs. Flanagan could unravel her story, Jacinta continued. "Let's just have one more and we can chat a bit more."

*

Danny was down on his knees all right, as he clung to the sides of the toilet bowl and hurled his insides out.

"Are you okay?" Billie called from the bedroom.

They'd been making love with wild, boozy, abandon when Danny got dizzy. At first, she seemed to think he was trying something new and bounced along on top of him. But soon he began to groan and sweat and rushed off before he threw up on the pair of them.

Every time he mixed hash and beer, it got the better of him.

"I'm fine," he managed when he finally stopped retching and rose to splash cold water on his face. "I'll be out in a minute."

He looked up at his reflection. His face was white and his eyes were red and bleary, but at least the bathroom had stopped spinning. He was so relieved at that he didn't notice Anto standing in the corner of the mirror.

Fine me arse. You look fucked to me.

Danny shook his befuddled head. He had often heard the echoes of Anto's voice in his nightmares while he flayed around in a distorted reliving of the night they shot Scully and the night they buried the dog. And the night Anto and the driver got theirs, but he had never actually seen him. He splashed more water on his face and looked again.

I'm still here and you're still fucked.

Danny wanted to argue but he thought better of it. It was one thing to be seeing and hearing things, but it was another to answer them. He knew he couldn't be having the DTs—he hadn't been drinking that much, but he had been hitting the hash pretty hard.

Maybe he was having flashbacks. He heard about people having them and they were always bad.

Or maybe it was like all the stuff his granny used to go on about—the wages of sin and all that. Since that night in the mountains, every time he got stoned, it all came bubbling back up. He remembered his terror and the smell when he shit himself in the booth of the car.

And he remembered the shots—two, and then two more.

He hadn't actually seen them die but when he replayed it in his mind, he saw every detail. Both of them falling and twitching until the second shots made them calm and disturbed a far-off dog in the quiet of the night.

He was still riddled with guilt like, somehow, it was all his fault, and no matter how much he dismissed it as his Catholic upbringing, he could never wipe that smear off.

At various times, when he was young and foolish and deep in trouble, he tried making a personal deal with Jesus—that he'd pray to him as God and they would forget about all the Church stuff. But, when the heat was off, he forgot about all his pleading and got on with his life. They all did. It was how everybody dealt with all the shit in their lives.

Denial, he'd often argue with himself when he was drunk or high, was the opiate of the masses. That and the false hope of forgiveness. Otherwise, when we'd really look at life, we'd all go off and commit hari-kari, or something.

He splashed more cold water on his face and wiped it with a towel, but when he looked up, Anto was still there. Anto-fuckin-Flanagan had come back from the bowels of hell like his own personal devil.

He had to be hallucinating and tried pinching himself but it didn't make Anto disappear; it only made him smile.

I'm real, Boyle, so you better get used to having me around.

"Danny? Is everything okay?" Billie was standing on the other side of the door. He could hear her breathing heavily. She liked to go a little crazy whenever they made love.

"I'm fine, love. I'll be out in minute."

*Love? Ya didn't tell me you were in love, Boyle. And what happened
to the Fallon one you were seeing before?*

"Danny let me in, please?"

"Just a minute. I just got a bit sick but I'll be fine in a
minute."

*Y'er the last of the great romantics, Boyle. That girl just made mad,
passionate love to you and what do you do? You almost vomit on her.*

"Danny. Open the door. I'm getting worried."

Danny checked himself in the mirror again. He was still
white but he wasn't so clammy anymore. He rinsed with
mouthwash and put on some more deodorant and reached for
the door.

*Jazus, Boyle. Ya smell great. You smell like a bunch of roses that
someone got sick on.*

"Fuck you."

"Danny. Did you say something?"

He didn't answer but fumbled with the handle and slowly
opened the door as Anto disappeared.

"Are you all right?" Billie's voice was edged with concern
and she reached out and took his hand in hers.

"I'm fine now."

"You're white as a ghost and you're shivering."

She led him back to bed and covered him with her warm
body and pulled the covers around them. She laid her head
across his chest and touched his skin with her fingers. "Your
heart is racing."

"I'm fine, so don't be worrying. It must have been something I ate."

"Danny?" she rolled away and sat up, holding the bedcov-
ers against her. "You'd tell me if there was something wrong?"

She looked so concerned he was mad at himself for
not being able to hack it. He felt like a lightweight. She had
matched him drink for drink. And she toked up too. She must
think he was a real bummer.

"I told you. I'm fine. I just felt a bit sick but I'm fine now."

He tried reaching for her but she moved back. "Not now, Danny. Go to sleep."

"I just want to know that you are here beside me, that's all."

She moved closer, but after he fell asleep, she moved back to the edge of the bed.

*

Still, she knew she was beginning to fall in love with him. It started the night he was on stage at the Irish Centre, when she had been dragged along for moral support. He looked so lost and alone she wanted to reach out and put her arms around him. She never told him that. He liked to act all tough—like nothing really got to him—but she was beginning to notice things.

It wasn't just his shyness. There were things he just never spoke of. He didn't mention Deirdre anymore. It was like she had been erased. And he never told her why he left Ireland even though he had often talked about growing up there and finding out that all he once believed had been lies. He didn't complain about it, though. He made it all seem so matter of fact, like he was grown-up enough to know that everyone fucks up. Even his granny.

Billie wanted to know more and always encouraged him to talk about himself.

**

"But I don't want to bore you with all my shite," he'd argue.

"You're just like my father. All you Irish are the same. You're all bound up so tight. Nothing can ever penetrate. Even Freud said you were all impervious to psychoanalysis."

"You say that like it's a bad thing."

"Isn't it?"

"We don't need a doctor to tell us we're fucked in the head; we've got clergy who'll do it for free."

"But you say you don't believe in them."

"I also don't believe there is such a thing as well-balanced or well-adjusted. It's all shite. Do you really think we're supposed to be tuned like radios every time what passes for reality changes?"

"So you think we should all run around mad?"

"We do anyway. That's why the Irish drink so much. We're the only ones who know how mad we really are. That's why we make such good poets and all."

"God's gift to humanity?"

He laughed at that and tried to hide behind self-effacement but she was beginning to know him better than that—big and bruised, shy and awkward.

"Well I wouldn't go that far. I'm just saying that we know what's really going on—just like the blacks. That's given me an idea for a song, the 'Growing up in Dublin blues.' And in my first album notes, I'll mention that it came to me while I was talking to you. You'll be famous, too."

She couldn't help herself and smiled. He was full of it, but she wouldn't want him any other way. Where her father had become dark and brooding, shying away in the basement and drinking himself to sleep while he listened to his old jazz records, Danny still had life and hope in him.

She kissed him slowly and passionately to let him know that she wanted to believe in him. Why not? He had as good a chance as any of them.

"What's that for?"

"So you will remember me when you're famous," she laughed and turned away from him.

***

"Jerry? Do you have any regrets?"

He knew better than to answer without thinking. Jacinta didn't want honesty—no woman ever really did. They only wanted to hear what they wanted to hear—assurances. He had no problem with that. Who wanted to know what their partner really felt? Who wanted to find out that they had wasted their lives on the wrong person?

"What do you mean?" He reached out for the wine and refilled their glasses. The garden was in late summer bloom around them and, when the rain held off, it was warm and lazy.

"You know, did you ever regret getting involved with me?"

"Not at all. What would make you ask such a thing?"

"Well it hasn't all been rosy."

"It's not supposed to be, Jass."

"I know that, but I was wondering how you were feeling about things."

"To tell you the truth, I have never been happier—or as close to it as the likes of me can get."

He lied of course but what else could he do. It was like his mother had said: He'd made his bed and now he was lying in it. Not that it really mattered anymore; he was as happy as the next man.

When he was younger, he thought it would be very different. Back then he thought he would get through university and go on to do something great in the world. He thought he might be the one to find the cure for something or the missing piece to a puzzle that had mystified them all for eons.

But as it turned out, he wasn't really the learning type. "I'm happy, Jass, and that puts me ahead of most of them."

"Are you really?"

"I am, and the big reason is that I'm smart enough now to know what's really important."

Jacinta lit up. She probably thought that he was referring to her and he did nothing to correct her. What he did mean was that he had come to realize that the plight of mankind was never going to be his concern. His purpose was to tidy up his own little corner of the world and look out for himself and those that depended on him.

Things were going well for him too. His boss was a total idiot and was useless without him. Jerry knew better than to let on he knew but he was the one they all came to when something needed to be sorted out. Even the higher-ups knew and came to him directly.

"That's so nice to hear. Sometimes I wonder what things would have been like for you if we hadn't . . ."

"But then we'd never have had Danny."

Jacinta blew him a kiss and sipped her wine, her eyes shining above the rim of the glass. "Do you think he's getting on okay?"

"Why wouldn't he? Doesn't he have my brains and your good looks? What harm could happen to him? Unless he wears himself out on all those Canadian girls."

"Oh, don't say that. I don't like to think of him off alone. God knows what type of trouble he could be getting himself into."

"He'll do just fine. And besides, it'll do him good to see a bit of the world for a while. Then he can come back and go to university. You know if I had done that, then I would have been ready for life and not always be trying catch up after everything that happened."

"Jerry? You don't feel like you wasted your life with me?"

He paused and thought about it. Sometimes he did, particularly when he was younger and lost his patience with her and all that being married meant. That's what he smoldered over in so many bars in London during his banishment. That and guilt, and that only made things worse and drove him deeper and deeper into that downward spiral. And in the morning as he downed a cure, remorse would settle on his shoulders. He was a piss-poor father and a total fucking failure as a husband, and he had his mother's voice worming through his head and heart.

"No, I don't Jess. I think what I wasted was the time it took me to get to where we are today."

"You know, Jerry, I think that's the most romantic thing you have ever said to me." She looked happier than he had seen her since . . . the day he asked her out.

"I still got it then?" He shouldn't have said that. She deserved a bit more honesty from him. That was one of the things he wasted a lot of time trying to deal with. He shouldn't have been afraid to show his true feelings. He was no better or worse than any of them. Even his parents. Even Jacinta. "I'm sorry for spoiling the mood and all. What I really wanted to say was I'm not good at that yet—you know—sharing my feelings and all."

"You know one of the things it took me a long time to get?"

"What's that?"

"That we share our feelings in a lot of different ways."

"I know what you mean."

"I wasn't talking about you, Jerry. I was talking about myself. You know, sometimes when I look back, I can't understand why I spent so much time in hiding."

"Ah now, Jass. Don't be getting all serious on me now."

"Let me just say this and then I'll drop it. Okay?"

"Okay then. Let's hear it." He didn't want to be rude but sometimes, when she had a few glasses too many, she could go very dark on him, almost pulling him back down there with her.

"I want to tell you that I'm sorry that I wasted so much of our time too." She raised her glass for a toast. "To you and me, Jerry, for making it this far."

"To you and me," he agreed as the warm summer sky looked more and more burnished. All of their hard edges were getting dulled and now they could get close without pricking each other. She was right to look at it that way. They had made it this far and things were only going to get better.

"Jerry? What'll we do now that Danny is out on his own?"

"We'll try to mind our own business for one thing. We'll let him fall flat on his face a few times."

"But we'll always be there to pick him up again?"

"Of course we will. We weren't the worst parents, you know? I know we made a few mistakes, here and there . . ."

"Here and there?"

"C'mon, Jass? What the hell did we know and now look at us. Sitting out in the back garden drinking wine and discussing our son. Who, by the way, is heading out to find his place in the world with a good Leaving Cert in his back pocket. There was many before him with less. Some of them didn't even know how to read or write and they did okay for themselves."

"But he must get awful cold there, in the winter."

"He'll be fine. He'll figure it out—after wasting some time, of course. But he'll be all right. And besides, it's not what it was. We can jump on an airplane and be over to see him anytime you want."

"Could we really?"

"Sure. We can go wherever you like." He sipped his drink and measured the moment. "Did you talk to him about the business yet?"

"I wasn't the one who was supposed to ask him."

They had argued about it for weeks until they could both see that it was a chance they would be mad to miss out on. Donal was looking for a few shrewd partners. And Gina vouched for it. All they had to do was to borrow some money against the house.

*

Danny and Billie stopped at Harvey's, just like they did every other Saturday night, coming home from the Windsor or wherever he was playing. He had started to do regular gigs with Frank and Jimmy. They played mostly the old shite, but they were good at it and the crowds were starting to like them.

And Danny was getting better all the time. He even sang a few of his own songs, early in the night before the crowd got going. After that it was *The Wild Rover*, *Whiskey in the Jar*, *The Black Velvet Band* and *The Unicorn*. It made her smile when Danny looked over at her and pretended to cringe.

She went to all of his gigs before heading back to his place where they'd eat, drink, talk and make love. She'd even started leaving a few things there. He was pretty cool about that, even when he found her pads in the bathroom.

She could tell he liked having her around, and not just for sex. He liked waking up beside her and always got up to get her a coffee, walking all the way to Church Street to get it. And he brought back pastries.

She loved spending Sundays with him, too, wandering through the neighborhood, more and more renovated each week, passing the 'Gardens' on their way to the Eaton Centre. She had once answered his if-you-could-only-have-the-same-meal-question with crepes. She could eat them all the time so Danny brought her to the Magic Pan every Sunday before she took the subway home.

"Did you ever want to try something else?"

"Like what? I like Harvey's."

"But it's every Saturday night. Why don't we order a pizza next week instead?"

"Why is it that women can never be satisfied? You're always trying to change things."

"Like what?"

"Like me."

"You weren't that much of a catch."

"Oh. Am I not good enough for you now?"

"You are now, after I changed you."

**

When they finally had sex for the first time, he had fumbled so much—and squeezed too hard—she just had to roll him on his side so she could talk to him.

"What's the matter? Am I doin' it wrong?"

"You're in such a hurry. Slow down and let me enjoy it."

He looked so hurt she regretted it immediately. It was obviously his first time.

"I'm sorry," she mewled and trailed her fingers along the side of his chest and across his stomach. "I just want it to be special between you and me."

"Trust me," he gasped as her fingers trilled along his soft stomach and onto something hard, "it's getting more special all the time."

"Really?" She smiled and reached forward to kiss him while her hand stroked him. She slowly changed her rhythm until he rolled on top of her and poked at her until she guided him inside. He plunged into her and took her breath away. She wanted him to start slowly but he was getting carried away.

"Danny, oh Danny, slow down," but he didn't seem to hear and ground into her faster and faster. The bed groaned and thumped against the wall but it didn't slow. And then she didn't want him to, urging him deeper and faster but he came too fast.

But he got better.

***

"What is it that you want to change about me now?"

"Well, when we get home I want us have sex that is not all about climaxing."

"What?"

"Trust me, you'll like it." She moved ahead and walked backwards in front of him.

"I like the sound of that." He stepped beside her and wrapped his arm around her, pulling her around until she was back by his side. "What did you have in mind?"

"Well. What do say we get naked first?"

She paused to look up into his eyes, to see if she could trust him to understand. "Then we'll both put on blindfolds and explore each other all over."

"How will we know if we're not peeking?"

"Danny."

"What?"

"Don't ruin the mood."

"Okay, so we get naked and blindfolded. Why couldn't we just turn the lights out?"

"What I want is for both of us to totally trust each other—at the same time. I want tonight to be a journey of trust."

"Will we get to eat first, before the journey?"

She flipped his arm away and stood on the sidewalk and glared at him. "Forget it." She crossed her arms and ignored his pleas. "I'm going to get a cab and go home."

She waited a few moments until a passing car slowed and the driver asked if she was available.

"Very well," she compromised. "I'll call a cab from your place."

"Billie! C'mon. You know I was only messing."

"Don't," she snapped and pulled away when he tried to take her shoulder.

"Okay. We'll just walk along together and not say anything. Will that make you happy?"

"What would make me happy is if you'd grow up."

"Just don't give him any, honey," a passing hooker encouraged her before turning to glare at Danny. "Make him beg."

"Thanks," Danny called after her. "Thanks for making things worse."

"You're welcome, Danny," the hooker said as she waved and climbed into the curbed car.

"How the hell does she know your name?"

"Sugar? I've known Sugar since I first moved down here. Sometimes she asks for a smoke or something."

"Something?"

"It's not what you're thinking." He looked like he really wanted her to believe him and led her toward his apartment. "I never . . . ya know . . . hired her or anything like that. I know I come across all cool and suave but," he held the front door open for her. "I'm dead shy inside. That's why I was all joking before. I just don't feel right talking about what we are going to do."

"What we were going to do."

He unlocked the second door and followed her up the stairs. "Fair enough, I deserved that."

They ate in silence for a while but the food helped them relax.

"Why is she called Sugar?" Billie decided to break the ice. He was right. He was shy. That was one of the things she first liked about him. And the way he smiled—it always melted the frost from her heart.

"Who?"

"The . . . prostitute."

He held up a joint until she nodded and lit it. He took a few deep drags and handed it to her. "They prefer to be called hookers. That way nobody will confuse them with politicians." He had tried to say it without exhaling and ended up coughing and spluttering.

"So why Sugar?" Billie asked as she inhaled.

"Cos she lets guys snort coke off her body."

"How do you know that?" she handed him back the joint.

"She told me," he hissed but he had to cough it out again.

"You can talk to her about sex, but not me?"

"We were just talking one night. She was on break and I was coming home from the Duke."

She believed him. He was so easy to see through. "Maybe we should try that some time?"

She rose and headed for the bedroom where she picked out two of his ties.

"Does this mean I'm getting another chance?"

She didn't answer but tied his tie around his eyes and unbuttoned his shirt.

She was nervous too. Despite her reputation, she really only had three lovers before. Two of them in university and both of them were always in such a hurry. She came with them—their determined pounding forced it out of her. It was easy; she was drunk enough but it was never really satisfying and she felt a little ashamed afterwards. Particularly when the boys talked to other boys and within weeks she was known as 'easy' and invited to every party.

When she found out why, she stopped seeing anybody but, in her last year, she let herself be seduced by one of her visiting professors. He was fourteen years older than her and promised to teach her so much more. She didn't mind; sex was complicated and she enjoyed that he took control of everything.

They always had good wine after dinner, listening to Leonard Cohen while he talked about all the brilliance in the world—all the things that others overlooked. In time he'd produce a joint and they would get closer. He never made the first move but responded when she did, touching her and tempting her to open, like a flower.

He talked about it, too, afterwards, as they shared the rest of the joint. He told her all kinds of wonderful things—stolen from poets and dreamers. She knew that, but she didn't mind. She knew the end of term was coming.

But with Danny, it was different. She would have to guide him and, in doing so, she realized that she cared for him and she loved that feeling.

*

"What would you think?" Billie asked from the bed. The two ties were twisted in the corner and the sheets and blankets were draped across the side of the bed. She was wrapped in his robe—a white one from some hotel in the Caribbean; his uncle brought it back for him. "Of me staying over more often?"

He was about to answer when his phone rang.

Chapter 5 -1981

Patrick Reilly was packed and ready to leave. He wasn't taking too much as he had his books sent over by ship. He had packed each one lovingly in an old trunk he had dragged everywhere with him. It made it feel more like an adventure.

His uncle was good to his word and had arranged a position for him, teaching, just like he said. He phoned to wish Patrick well too. "All roads . . . you know?"

Patrick couldn't be sure but he thought he heard a quiver in the bishop's voice. It might have been doubt or remorse, but it was quickly covered up. "I envy you—a young fella going off to Rome. You have the best part of your life in front of you."

Or perhaps it was envy?

Notwithstanding, he thanked him for all he had done and meant it. He didn't blame his uncle. His life was probably just unfolding according to a bigger plan and all that fell to him was to accept it with enthusiasm. The pope had come and gone and filled the whole country with pious renewal, but Patrick Reilly was not going to be a part of it.

"I could send the car to take you out to the airport?"

"No thanks, Uncle, I have arranged for a lift, but let me thank you again and I hope you'll come out and see me before too long."

"I will, indeed, Patrick. Now take care of yourself until then. And don't forget to drop into the café I told you about— the one in the Piazza Della Rotunda. Tell them I said 'ciao.' And, if you ever get to the Campo De' Fiori, say hello to Bruno too."

"Who?"

"You'll know when you get there. Take care now, Patrick. God speed."

*

After the bishop hung up he poured himself a ball of malt. It was a tough business but he had done the right thing. Parish work wasn't for the likes of Patrick. It was more suited to the likes of Fr. Dolan, a more mercantile-minded individual. Patrick was a good man who would rekindle his relationship with the Lord in the center of it all.

The bishop had no doubts about that. The rest of the world could be going mad, but Rome was eternal. He should never have left it and the gang he knew there. But they were getting fewer. Poor old Giovanni Montini had given up the ghost and gone to his heavenly reward. And Óscar Galdámez was shot dead while he was saying mass down in El Salvador. The world was spinning out of control again. And there was more than enough to worry about at home. An IRA hunger striker was elected to the House of Commons, while in Dublin they all mourned the young people burned to death in the 'Stardust.'

"What is the world coming to?" he asked the crucifix on the wall and smiled as silence settled all around him.

"Keep your mysteries, then, but would you be good enough to keep an eye on young Patrick. You know fine well what can happen to a young priest in Rome."

*

Miriam insisted on seeing him off to the airport and had cajoled her friend into driving them. She also called to say they were on their way and would be there in no time. So Fr. Patrick Reilly carried his case outside and waited in the concrete space that once was Dinny O'Leary's garden, now the parking space for a shiny new car. There was nothing left for him here anymore. He'd be better off starting out again, somewhere new.

Fr. Dolan was out but had called, too, to wish him good luck—like what had happened had nothing to do with him. "Good luck to you, too, Father," Patrick replied with just a small tinge in his voice. *And good luck to the poor people of the parish,* he added after he hung up. Tongues would be wagging for a while. "The bishop's own nephew—packed off to Rome. You'd have to wonder what was going on."

People were like that and there was no point in dwelling on it. Rome would be good for him; he'd get the chance to separate his lives there and find some time for himself, again. He hadn't been able to do that since the seminary. It was all going to be so exciting.

He hoped he could get through saying goodbye to Miriam in front of her friend. He would have preferred if it was just her, but it was probably for the better. The last thing he needed was somebody seeing them alone at the airport. His uncle would find out and phone the pope and he'd probably end up being burnt at the stake, just like Joe had always predicted.

Joe was delighted he was going. He had been urging him to do it for years, insisting that Patrick should get out and see a bit of the world. He'd come over for a visit as soon as Patrick got settled. He was due a trip to 'Head Office;' it was the least they owed him.

It would be great to see him again and they could walk and talk like they once did. He'd have to learn as much as he could about the place so he could make an impression and not look like some lost paddy. He'd have to bring Joe out for dinner in one of the piazzas and he'd have to know all the best places.

That's the first thing he would do when he got there—he'd explore every little street. If Miriam ever came over he could bring her to them, too, with her friend of course.

They pulled up in a shiny car and bundled him and his cases into the back and chatted so much that he hardly noticed that he was leaving behind all he had ever known.

*

"So this is it?" Miriam smiled when he finally got to the gate. She was unsure and didn't know what to do with her hands. She wanted to hug him but she wasn't sure how he'd feel about that. He looked so lost and far too young to be heading out on a journey like this.

Still, he was older than she was when she went away. Only she was always older than she was. "Are you forgetting anything?"

"I don't know." He looked more confused and afraid.

"You have your ticket and your passport? And your wallet? You can get by without all the rest of the stuff."

"You don't think that my luggage will get lost. I wrote the address as clearly as I could."

"Don't worry, Patrick. I'm sure you could borrow something from the pope if you get stuck."

That seemed to calm him so she pecked his cheek and shook his hand and then walked away, leaving him at the gate and never looking back.

*

"Did he get off okay?" Karl politely inquired as they drove away, but Miriam didn't answer and turned to look out the side window so he wouldn't see her tears.

"He'll be fine. I'm sure John Melchor will look after him." Karl took a moment to touch the back of her hand before Miriam withdrew it.

"John has gone to El Salvador. He's not there anymore."

They drove in silence for a while, thinking about Jean Donovan, Maura Clarke and Ita Ford, beaten, raped, and murdered for trying to spread the word of God. Beaten, raped, and murdered by America's friends. The world might have looked the other way but they both knew that John Melchor wouldn't. They both knew why he had to go there.

"And what are you going to do?"

Miriam wasn't sure. She felt left behind but she couldn't go to Rome now. John was gone and it wouldn't be fair to Patrick. He needed the time and space to find himself again. And he didn't need her around. She was a little flattered that he had such an obvious crush on her but she couldn't. It just wouldn't have been right.

"I'm not sure," she finally answered. "I should be finished with my degree by the summer. I just have no idea what to do with the rest of my life."

"I don't suppose you'd consider spending some of it with me?"

*

They cruised along the 401 in David's Trans Am, long and sleek with a golden Firebird across the hood. David drove while Martin checked and re-checked his tickets and his papers. Danny sat in the back, pressed against the sides and the sloping back window.

"You've checked your stuff ten times already. Relax, man. You're only going for two weeks."

"It's long enough," Martin answered and checked himself in the mirror in the visor. "And I look like shit."

"What's the matter now, Toastie?"

"Look at me. I look like something that has been left in the fridge too long."

"You look fine, doesn't he Danny?"

"What?" Danny was sitting between the two bass speakers and couldn't hear a thing. David always drove with his music blaring, causing the car to reverberate.

"I said," David repeated as he lowered the volume, "that Martin looks great. He is worried about that."

"Why? He's only going to Dublin. Everybody looks like shite there."

"Oh, come on. I bet you wish you were going with him."

"Are you kidding, I wouldn't be caught dead in the kip."

David laughed. "Still got all those bad men wanting a piece of you?"

"Fuck them. I'm not afraid of them. It's the cops I worry about."

"Such a bad ass," David laughed as they veered off on the 409, past industrial yards of dirty trucks and assorted rusting cranes as Martin fussed again.

"What's the matter now?"

"I don't know. I just don't feel well. I feel like I might be coming down with something."

"You'll feel better when you get on the plane and have a few drinks. Right, Danny?"

"What?"

Martin was going home for a few weeks. He didn't consider it a holiday; it was more of an obligation. He hadn't been over in a few years and his parents were getting old; otherwise, he would have put it off. He wasn't feeling well and hadn't been for a few weeks.

"You'll keep an eye on Danny while I'm away?" Martin asked as he checked his pockets again. He had checked his luggage and was lingering by the gate. He wanted to go inside and find somewhere to sit until he felt better but he didn't want to be rude.

"Don't worry, we'll be fine." David took him in his arms and hugged him while Danny shuffled and waited.

"Bye, Danny, and behave yourself."

"I'll be fine. You're the one who is going back."

"Yeah," Martin forced a smiled and walked away.

*

"So, Danny," David asked as they drove from the airport, "what's new?"

"Ah, sure you know yourself."

"I don't. That's why I was asking. You still seeing Billie?"

"Ah, no."

"What happened? I thought you guys were good together."

"So did I, but you know women."

"You fucked it up, didn't you?"

"A little. I got a call from Deirdre and she said she wanted to come over this summer so I told Billie and she got all mad at me."

"How did you break it to her?"

"Over breakfast. I thought I'd come clean and tell her."

"And what did you tell her."

"I just said that Deirdre was thinking of coming over. I also told her that I loved her and that Deirdre was just a friend from before, but she got all mad and stormed out. I mean, I used to love Deirdre but I love Billie now."

"Did you tell Deirdre about Billie?"

"No. I wanted to, but she was all excited and stuff. I figured that she could just come over and, after she'd gone back, Billie and I could just go on."

"And Billie didn't go for that? Oh, sweetie. It doesn't work like that!" David was laughing so much he nearly lost control of the car.

"Why am I talking to you about this? What would you know?"

"Oh Danny boy, you crack me up."

"What? I was just trying to be honest with her."

"Danny, that's not the type of honesty that people want when they are in love. Billie doesn't want to know you are being fair to another woman. What's she supposed to do—sit around while you make up your mind? She isn't going to want that."

"Then why is she always telling me to talk about my feelings?"

"Because she wants you to tell her that you feel the way she wants you to feel."

"Is everybody like that?"

"Not everybody, Danny, just those who are really honest with themselves."

"Life was a lot easier when I didn't worry about being honest."

"Yeah, it was great. Look at the mess you got yourself into."

Danny fell silent and watched the passing cars for a while.

"Danny, do you think Martin is okay?"

"I don't know—should I be honest?"

"Why, what's he said?"

"Nothing."

"You bastard. I just get the feeling that things aren't right with him."

"What do you expect? He's going back to Dublin. He's probably just de-gaying himself."

"Do you miss it?"

"Fuck no!"

But Danny was lying. Deep down his heart was bleeding. He couldn't go home. The ruddy-faced man had let Jerry know that Danny shouldn't be showing his face around Dublin. Not for a while yet. Not until all the fuss died down.

*

Martin wished he hadn't come. It was raining and no matter what he did, he couldn't feel warm.

"I thought you'd be used to the cold," his sisters jeered as he shivered and sniffled around the house.

"Are you not well?" his mother asked. "Would you like a nice hot cup of tea?"

"Not right now, thanks, Mam."

His mother was showing her age, totally grayed and bent-over as she shuffled. He didn't want her doing for him but she was insistent. He would always be her little boy. His father said she was failing, but that she wouldn't hear a word of it. He wondered if Martin could have a word with her and talk a bit of sense into her. But his mother said the same thing about his father so Martin gave up and went over to see Jacinta.

*

"She's out with Mrs. Flanagan," Jerry explained, "but we could go down and meet them. They're just down in The Yellow House."

Martin nodded wearily and waited while Jerry got his coat. "So is that Anto Flanagan's mother?"

"The one and only. They became friends in the church and have been meeting there a few times a week."

"What's that about?"

"Jacinta says Mrs. Flanagan was going mad with grief."

"Over Anto?"

"The very same. Jacinta says that having Danny away helps her understand. I wasn't too crazy about it at first but I think it's good for Jacinta. She says Fr. Reilly brought them together because he thought Jacinta would be the best to counsel the poor woman in her grief.

"I've been doing my bit, too. Me and Dermot Fallon. We go around talking to parents about what they should do when they think their kids are taking drugs."

"You and Dermot Fallon?"

"He's not the worst, only we don't really agree on things. He's all for having the parents grass on their kids."

"And you agree with that?"

"No. And I told him, too, only he says to me: 'we don't all have IRA hit squads to call on.' I don't pay him too much mind though. He's just doing it because he's going to run for the council. I think he wants to become the Lord Mayor or something."

"The more things change . . . eh?"

"What?"

"Never mind."

Jerry looked at him like he was trying to see if he was okay. "Do you know what I wanted to ask you? I was wondering if you could do me a favor. I need you to ask Danny to sign the house over to his mother and me."

"Why?" Martin didn't mean to sound so leery.

"Well, it's just that I'm going into business with Donal and I need to raise some cash. I even have the papers all drawn up. You just need to take them over and have Danny sign them. We need to do it quickly too. Donal has found a place that we just have to snap up before some other fuckers get their hands on it."

"Are you sure you can trust Donal?"

"Why wouldn't I? Isn't he married to your own sister? C'mon," he held the bar door open. "We can have a drink and discuss it."

"Holy mother of God," Jacinta laughed as she saw them enter. "The Canadian has come home to us."

She rose and hugged him tight, warm and quivering and sobbing. "Ah Martin, it's so good to see you. Do you know," she asked as she released him, "Mrs. Flanagan?"

Martin greeted her as he sat.

"Hello, Martin. Welcome home."

"Thanks, Mrs. Flanagan and I'm very sorry for your troubles."

"That's nice of you to say."

"Well," Jerry shuffled from foot to foot, "what's everybody having."

"I'll be heading off home," Mrs. Flanagan decided as she finished her drink, "so you can have a proper home coming. It's nice to meet you, Martin, and please ask Danny to remember my Anthony in his prayers."

"You'll have to excuse her," Jacinta said after Mrs. Flanagan had left. "She's still grieving. Did Jerry get a chance to ask you?"

"He did. He just told me on the way over."

"You'll get Danny to do it?"

"Are you both sure about this?"

"We are," Jerry insisted when he returned with their drinks. "We have talked it through."

Martin waited until Jacinta nodded in agreement. "I'll ask him but I'm not sure."

"Not sure about what? It's a sure thing. Donal has found a house on the other side of Terenure on Ashdale Road. We can get it at a good price and fix it up. All the yuppies are dying to live there."

Martin was tired; he had jet lag on top of the flu and was in little mood to argue. "How much is Donal putting in?"

Neither of them answered so Martin asked again.

"Well," Jerry hesitated, "he is the one who finds the houses. He has all the connections, ya know?"

Martin sipped his beer. He was in no mood to discuss it further and shivered a little in the damp.

*

Deirdre had come back from her vacation in Canada with a sparkle in her eye. But she was careful to keep it hidden from her father. Her mother had convinced him that it was all above board; that Deirdre and Danny had been carefully chaperoned by his uncle—all of the time. She politely inquired if Deirdre had enjoyed her visit but avoided making eye contact.

She had. Danny's time in Canada had changed him. It almost seemed like he had grown up. He dressed much better, too, and took more care with his appearance. It was like being with someone new and someone familiar at the same time. He had a day job with the government and was getting steady gigs with the band. Deirdre had gone to hear them a few times and enjoyed the show, and stopping for Harvey's on the way home where he slept alone on the couch.

He brought her to the museum, and the art gallery, and of course, the CN Tower. He was proud of his new life and he made it very obvious that he wanted her to become a part of it. He even said it: "You should think about moving over, after you get your degree of course."

"I might," was all that she could bring herself to say, at least until she thought about it some more. They could be good together, in a brand new city with hot lazy days and warm evenings when he would touch her bare arms as he guided her from place to place. After the first week it was obvious; in Toronto she could become the type of person she wanted to become.

They went to Niagara Falls on her last weekend and spent the night in the King Edward, in Niagara-by-the-Lake. He took her to a charming little restaurant and behaved like a gentleman all night. It was all very, very romantic, strolling back to the hotel on a warm night, scented with flowers hung in baskets along the way.

She kissed him again as they got to their room, large, Victorian, but with one enormous bed.

"We don't have to, you know? If you don't want to, I could sleep on the floor."

She did want to. She was ready. She wasn't giving herself to him; she was stepping out of everything she had been and joining him in the new world. She was ready to fall in love with him again, only she didn't say any of that. She just smiled and went to the bathroom to change into the long dark satin slip she had brought—just in case.

It felt so right, she encouraged her reflection, as she touched up her lips and teased out her hair. And she wanted it to be special. Danny seemed to want that too. He had lowered the lights and opened a bottle of wine. He smiled at her without a trace of his leer—the one he used to wear to hide his real feelings. When she emerged from the bathroom, she walked slowly toward him, silhouetted in the light she had left on. She had seen it in a film and decided, then and there, that's how she wanted to look.

He rose and took her in his arms, gently kissing her as his fingers thrilled along her skin. He tasted like wine, warm and soft to her lips, sending little tremors through her. His hands were cool, gliding along her skin, up her arms and across her shoulders, freeing them from her straps as they passed. He touched her throat and ran his fingers through her hair, brushing it back from her ears. His lips fluttered along her cheek and she began to shiver.

They shivered together underneath the sheets even though the night was warm. His eyes were soft and deep and his lips were bigger than she had ever seen them before. And they were soft. They stroked and petted each other, twisting and writhing. Getting closer and closer until he was inside of her, filling her and straining her but in time, delighting her until it all became too much, for both of them, and they crumpled together. He rolled on his back and eased her head on to his chest where she could hear his heart pound.

*

"His past will always be there, hanging over you," Miriam had said before she went.

Deirdre respected most things that Miriam said to her but on this issue she was wrong. Deirdre understood why. Miriam was struggling with her own feelings. Her relationship with Karl was in a bind. He was ready to have sex with her but she was still a nun when it came to that. Deirdre wished she could talk with her about it. She had so much to say on it now.

"And what about love, Miriam?" Deirdre asked as they settled in for coffee and a chat. "People fall in love and become better people..."

"Love?" Miriam answered like she was thinking aloud. "I am beginning to realize how very little I know about love after all. It is ironic, isn't it?"

Deirdre wished she could take her in her arms and whisper to her that it would be all right. That if she could just open herself, like she had done with Danny, everything would be fine. It took a lot of trust to believe that you were giving yourself to the right person. But she couldn't so she just reached over and touched the back of Miriam's hand.

Miriam was in the same position as her—only she couldn't see it. Karl had a past too.

He seemed very normal and talked about himself in a very assured way but Miriam had told her that there was more to it than that. She admitted that she once peeped at his diary. It was full of strange drawings of the things he had brought back from Vietnam. Things that he never spoke about. There were pages and pages of dark shadowy things that were alien but familiar to her. "I know I shouldn't have looked but what am I supposed to do now?"

The question had hung in the air, unanswered since before Deirdre went away.

"Then you just have to trust in your feelings," was all that Deirdre could offer.

*

Patrick Reilly woke with the bells as Rome started to bustle in the early morning. It was when all that was ancient woke from its memories and smiled down on the never-ending comings and goings.

At first it had all seemed frenetic but he had become attuned to the Romans and the way they lived in the shadows of faded glory. He found hope in the way that life could continue after the pomp of pride was gone.

He could learn from that and give up any notion of being the force that would set the world to right. He was but a common priest in the city of cardinals and he was happy to shed the burdens he once carried. He would find himself and his new purpose in the place where it had all happened.

He had so much more time on his hands with no parish duties to attend to. He did his teaching and had hours alone in the libraries. At first he had felt guilty and wrote to his uncle, who assured him that it would do him the world of good. *'It'll give you a chance to savor the place. Get out and enjoy it. You've earned every bit of it.'* But Patrick couldn't help but feel that he had been carefully and diplomatically placed on the sidelines.

He had found lodgings in Trastevere, just off the Piazza Santa Maria, the ancient place where Christians gathered before taking the city from the pagans. It was a monastic type of place and that suited him fine. His books had arrived and were placed around his room within reach. He had added the reproductions of Giuseppe Vasi's ten books of etchings showing the monuments of Rome. He handled them with the greatest care and made notes for the tours he began to take, visiting each one of Augustus's fourteen Rioni. He spent a few days in each to absorb all they had to offer. He visited the churches and the ruins but all the time he kept an eye out for the better places to eat, for when Joe came over, and Miriam.

He had managed to put it all in perspective.

He hadn't really been doing anything wrong with her. She was his friend and all that stood between him and loneliness. He understood how it might have looked to others, especially his uncle, but there was no shadow of sin in his intentions.

He gave her up for all their sakes. She had enough to get over and he knew that a priest couldn't afford to indulge in the luxuries that other people enjoyed. He had chosen the life, the lonely walk in Christ's footsteps. He had chosen it freely and would see it out to the end. But he did think about her. Every time he stopped to marvel at something, he wished he had someone there to share it with and he usually wished it was Miriam.

He kept up with the happenings from home, too, reading the Irish papers as the hunger strikers died, one by one, the ancient symbolism of their sacrifice lost in the righteous rhetoric of the wrong. He felt a little guilty about that as he sipped his café lattes in the Piazza, as others downed espressos and rushed off into the day.

He still shivered a bit at the taste of coffee but, as he had so often heard, 'When in Rome . . .' He never thought the words would one day apply to him.

He wrote to Miriam often, on the back of a postcard, and was careful to sound casual, like a friend. He told her how wonderful it was and that he hoped all was well with her.

*

"Did ya get it sorted?"

"I did, ya."

Danny had signed the papers and sent them back. Jerry had taken out a mortgage and would have the money in a few days. He talked it over with Jacinta again and she had assured him she was fine with it. She and Gina were already planning how they were going to live when they were rich.

"So, do you have the money?"

"I do, but it'll just take a few more days."

"A few more days, Jerry? I'm not sure we can wait a few more days."

"I told you," Jerry repeated carefully so as not to give any offense. "I'll have it for you in a few days."

Donal shook his head slowly. "That's not good enough, Jerry."

"It's the best I can do."

"Well, maybe your best won't be enough. Ya know I got people lining up to get in on this deal?

"Maybe," he said as he eyed Jerry over the rim of his glass, suspended before his face for effect, "you're not cut out for this kind of thing. I'm doing you a favor, ya know, because we're brothers-in-law but I'm beginning to wonder. I don't need a partner who's not sure."

"But we're not really partners if you're not putting any money in. I'm more of an investor."

"That's right, Jerry. You're investing in my savvy. I know all about buying and selling property. All you're doing is throwing in the seed money and there are lots of places where I can get that."

"Ya, but how many investors can supply the men and material too?"

Donal looked at him for a moment and smiled. "Right enough, Jerry. Maybe we're both getting a bit edgy. Bring the money when you get it and we'll say no more about it."

Chapter 6 -1982

As I was going over the far famed Kerry
Mountains,
I met with Captain Farrell and his money he was
counting.

Frank sang and the whole bar clapped along. He played
guitar, too, laying down big fat chords while Jimmy slapped
and tickled along on the bass. Danny went around the melody,
plucking the banjo and trilling where the beats allowed.

I first drew out my pistols and then produced
my rapier
Sayin': Stand and deliver, for I am a bold
deceiver!
Mush-a-ring da-ba-do da-ba-da. Whack for the
daddy-o,
Whack for the daddy-o. There's whiskey in the jar.

Jimmy and Danny joined in on the chorus, filling the
whole bar like a choir.

I counted out his money and it made a pretty
penny,
I put it in my pocket and I took it home to Jenny.
She sighed and she swore that she never would
deceive me,
But the Devil take the women for they never can

be easy.
Mush-a-ring da-ba-do da-ba-da. Whack for the daddy-o,
Whack for the daddy-o. There's whiskey in the jar.

They had played this song a thousand times and even though it was threadbare, they played it with perfected polish, even making mistakes look impromptu.

> I went unto my chamber all for to take a slumber,
> I dreamt of gold and jewels and for sure it was no wonder,
> But Jenny drew me charges and she filled them up with water,
> And sent for Captain Farrell to be ready for the slaughter.
> Mush-a-ring da-ba-do da-ba-da. Whack for the daddy-o,
> Whack for the daddy-o. There's whiskey in the jar.

The crowd joined in on the chorus, singing along and beating their tables like bongos.

"They love this shite," Frank loudly whispered over his shoulder, his voice carrying across the room but nobody cared. The crowds loved Frank, with his Luke Kelly hair and his accent that never faded.

> T'was early in the morning just before I rose to travel,
> Up comes a band of footmen, and likewise Captain Farrell,
> I first produced me pistol, for she'd stolen away me rapier,
> But I couldn't shoot the water so a prisoner I was taken.
> Mush-a-ring da-ba-do da-ba-da. Whack for the daddy-o,
> Whack for the daddy-o. There's whiskey in the jar.

"Banjo solo," Jimmy shouted, catching Danny off guard, but he had been practicing, listening to hours of Barney McKenna. He didn't really like the banjo but the crowds loved it and its penetrating twang. He played off the melody, doubling and trebling as he could, and bringing it around again for Frank to take. But Frank was lighting a cigarette and missed. "Bass solo," he announced and grinned at Jimmy.

"Ya bollocks," Jimmy laughed and changed rhythm, doing the next verse as Thin Lizzy had done, with Danny taking the guitar licks on the banjo.

> Now there's some take delight in the carriages
> a rolling
> And others take delight in the hurling and the
> bowling.
> But I take delight in the juice of the barley
> And courting pretty fair maids in the morning
> bright and early.
> Mush-a-ring da-ba-do da-ba-da. Whack for the
> daddy-o,
> Whack for the daddy-o. There's whiskey in the jar.

Jimmy and Danny stopped and started, playing a musical game of hide-and-seek before handing it back to Frank who sang on without missing a beat.

> If anyone can aid me, 'tis my brother in the army,
> If I can find his station in Cork or in Killarney.
> And if he'll go with me, we'll go roaming in
> Kilkenny,
> And I'm sure he'll treat me better than me own
> sweet, sporting Jenny.
> Mush-a-ring da-ba-do da-ba-da. Whack for the
> daddy-o,
> Whack for the daddy-o. There's whiskey in the jar.

"Now we're going to take a break for a few minutes," Frank announced when the crowd settled down again, "so we can get a few beers into us."

"And maybe some of that funny tobacco," Jimmy added leaning across to share the same mic.

"Don't be talking like that in front of the people," Frank reacted in fake shock. "Y'er not in one of your rock bands now. Irish musicians get drunk—not like the rest of them. It's lucky for you that they banned corporal punishment in the schools."

"Where?"

"In Ireland, ya dope."

The crowd loved the banter but Danny needed to relieve himself. "Fuck the pair of you'se; I'm goin' for a piss."

"Well there you go, folks. The bass player is goin' to get stoned, the wanker on the banjo is goin' for a piss and we'll all be back so don't go anywhere."

*

When Danny came out of the washroom, Billie was standing by the bar and acted like she was surprised to see him. He was unsure for a moment but walked over and stood beside her and ordered a beer.

"Enjoying the show?"

"I just walked in. I didn't know you guys were here tonight."

"Do you come here often?"

"Oh, Danny, that's so corny, even for you."

"No, I meant it's all the way out past High Park and you live in the east end."

"I moved. I'm not living with my parents anymore."

"That's nice. And are you finished with school?" He wasn't sure what else to say.

He wasn't even sure if he should be talking to her. Since Deirdre had moved over he often wondered about that. Frank and Jimmy were still pulling birds but not him; he and Deirdre were living together—almost married—and he had to behave himself.

"Yeah, I got a job at the museum."

"That's great."

"And you, how have you been?"

"Are sure ya know yourself. Not much ever changes in my life."

"I heard your girlfriend moved over."

"She did, ya."

"And that's not news?"

"I just didn't think it was the type of news you'd want to hear."

"You do think highly of yourself."

Danny might have blushed but there was something in the corner of Billie's eye, something that contradicted her tone.

"C'mon ya bollocks," Frank nudged him as he headed back to the stage.

"I gotta go . . . but it was nice seeing you again."

"Yes, Danny boy. It was."

*

"We're goin' to start with a slow song," Frank said as he quieted the crowd down again. "For all the poor Newfies that died on the Ocean Ranger. It's a song called *The Springhill Mining Disaster*."

"Springhill is in Nova Scotia," a drunk heckled from the back.

"It doesn't matter. They all died trying to earn a living, ya feckin' eejit. Now shut up and listen to the song."

Jimmy began on the bass, sonorously, as Danny picked through the chords on the guitar and Frank added the whistle, high and ethereal, fluttering like the candles in the darkness of the caved-in mines. They played the song beautifully, even calming the drunken heckler and causing a few eyes to well up with tears. Even Billie was moved.

"And now," Frank roused them again when it was over, "we're goin' to play a song for the bollocks at the back because he had the decency to shut up."

Danny went back on banjo as Frank put on his guitar and found the chords, leading them into *Farewell to Nova Scotia*. They played it with wild abandon until everyone was up and clapping again.

"It's like they're his puppets," Jimmy muttered to Danny as Frank went on charming the asses off everyone all night.

*

"So how was the gig?" Deirdre had let him sleep late and had gone for the Saturday papers and coffee. She seemed to have settled in very quickly and liked the neighborhood because it was so central. She had managed to find a job in St. Mike's, on the other side of Bay Street, and often walked to and from work. She had come over at the end of the winter and had no idea how bad it could get.

"It was all right. Frank and Jimmy said to say hello."

"That's nice." She smiled at him and picked up the paper and sorted it in the piles that she would read first and a pile she would leave on the coffee table to read during the week. She had made friends at the university and they liked to talk about books and stuff like that. She even went to the art gallery with a few of them. She had invited Danny but he couldn't— the band was rehearsing that night.

They would sit in Frank's basement with a two-four and have a few hits. Then they would try to learn new stuff but, too often, they just got far too wasted. "We should do something by Moving Hearts," Jimmy often enthused but they never got around to it. They were doing a bit of Planxty but it took Frank forever to learn the whistle parts. "It's because it takes skill and precision," Frank would explain. "It's not like slapping on the bass and hoping that some fuckin' sound comes out. And what the fuck are you laughin' at?" he'd ask Danny. "Your banjo sounds like a hyena fartin'."

*

"Listen," Deirdre leaned toward him and put her hands on the table. "How would you feel about me going back to school over here?"

Because he felt guilty about talking to Billie, Danny agreed without thinking, even though it meant he wouldn't be able to quit his day job and go on tour with the band. They didn't really have definite plans but it was something they were going to do, one of these days, when they got their shit together.

"Are you sure? It would mean living on one income for a while."

"Two." Danny corrected her.

"Yes." She stroked the back of his hand without looking into his eyes and went back to sorting the paper as Danny tried to read the headlines upside down.

"What's happening with the Falklands? Has the Ice-Queen had her pound of flesh yet?"

Danny wanted to be topical with her. Lately she spent a lot of time talking about the conversations she had with the people around the university and he wanted to show her that she could have those talks with him. "I heard the Brits lost the Sheffield and twenty people were killed. And the Argies lost one, too, and lost over three hundred!"

*

She didn't mean to, but sometimes she got a little impatient with him. It wasn't his fault. She didn't like being away from Dublin. Toronto was nice but it was so different. Danny had shown her all the Irish places but they were always filled with the type of people she found hard to talk to. Miriam always told her that she was a bit of an intellectual snob.

And he was different too. He was becoming more Irish. Not the natural type of Irish, like he was at home. He was becoming more . . . stage Irish.

Her friends at the university liked him when they came to see the band play, but Canadians were like that. They seemed to enjoy everything that was different from them and embraced it all, even the ethnic villages tucked into their downtown neighborhoods, and made a point of experiencing them. They often had lunch on Spadina, eating Chinese food that she didn't recognize but was determined to try.

"It's not a football game, Danny. Those are real lives that are being lost."

"I know what ya mean. In football, England never wins."

She gave him a look but he ignored her and lit a cigarette.

She would have to find a new apartment—one with a balcony. She really couldn't stand the smell of smoke. It wasn't all his fault; it was just that living together was a lot harder than she imagined. Harder, too, because she could never go home again. At least not until her mother had time to work on her father, but that might take an age. But she would get through it.

Her friends told her it was normal and that all she had to do was to change things until she was happy with them. "But what if Danny doesn't like the changes?" she had asked. "Then you change him for someone else."

She had laughed along, but later, when she was sitting on the couch with him, she felt a little guilty.

"Here," she said as she handed him the front section. "Someone tried to stab the pope."

"Where?"

"In Fatima."

"Then there's no problem. He can get cured without having to move."

She smiled briefly and found something to read about a new disease called AIDS.

"Have you seen Martin recently?" she asked when she was finished.

"I saw him a few weeks ago."

"We should go and have brunch with them tomorrow. They always know the nicest places."

"Sure," Danny answered and went back behind the sports section.

"Good. I'll call them."

"Them?"

"Why? Don't you like David?"

She rose before he could answer and lifted the phone. She liked spending time with Martin and David. She told her friends about them. It was so 'Toronto' of her—having gay friends.

"Just don't make it too early. We get paid tonight and we always go for something to eat afterwards."

*

"You are very much like your uncle. He used to sit here for hours too."

Giovanni had come out from behind the counter to sit with Patrick. It had become a part of his ritualwalks around the city—stopping at Giovanni's for coffee and watching the crowds come and go across the cobblestones of the Piazza Della Rotunda. He liked the Pantheon, with its roof open to the heavens.

"What was he like, back then?"

"He was like you—young. And his head and his heart were full of all the good he was going to do in the world."

"Did you think he was foolish?"

"Of course, of course. Only the fool can lead us away from the—how do you say—the edge of the cliff. I was a young fool too."

Patrick studied the old man's face, broad and affable and prone to smiling. Giovanni liked to make people laugh. Even during the morning rush, as Romans jostled for their coffee, Giovanni would tend to them with a broad smile.

"So what changed you?"

Giovanni liked to shrug, too, and did before answering. "I am still a fool at heart. I still believe that, like all of this," he waved his arm across the piazza, "the whole world will live long enough to know that the only thing that really matters is how we treat each other. Nothing else is important. We are remembered for how we treat the people."

It was Giovanni's turn to study Patrick's face, something he did openly. "And you. Why are you so burdened with all that is wrong with the world?"

"It comes with the collar," Patrick reached for his neck but he hadn't worn his collar for weeks. There was no point here where priests were as common as beggars.

"I don't think that is so." Giovanni reached forward and touched the pocket of Patrick's shirt, right above his heart. "You carry great weight here."

Patrick sat back in his chair and raised his cup between them. Giovanni was a wise old man who could look into the soul of anyone he met. He might have blushed but Giovanni just laughed. "Do you think you are the first priest who has carried the burden of secret love in his heart?

"And now, Giovanni must have his rest."

The old man rose and briefly placed his hand on the young man's shoulder. "But remember one thing: everywhere you go in Rome, someone has walked before you."

Patrick watched him leave, collecting cups and glasses as he went. Giovanni was a part of the city. His family had run the café for generations, serving priests and plunderers alike.

Patrick turned again to watch tourists filing in and out of the old temple, built to honor all of the gods of man's creation. He liked that; it gave him hope that one day the human race might see all that they shared and worry less about the things that divided them.

Giovanni's words stayed with him all the way home, along the Via Arenula, across the Ponte Garibaldi and in among the trees of Trastevere.

*

"Deirdre, Danny, are you well?"

Martin and David rose from their chairs as Danny and Deirdre approached. David kissed both of her cheeks but Martin declined. "I still haven't shaken off the bug I picked up in Ireland," he explained and waited for her to sit.

"I love your hair," David remarked as he sat opposite her. "It's like Lady Di meets Madonna."

"That's exactly what I was going for." Deirdre laughed and raised her menu. She loved David's attention but she was a little embarrassed too."

"I mean it girl. You look so chic."

"And don't you like my hair?" Danny intruded.

Deirdre could never understand that. Danny was jealous of David and the way he was with her. "It's bad enough," he'd complain to her after every time they got together, "he's with my uncle. Does he want to be with you too?" Deirdre might have chided him but she understood. Martin meant everything to him.

"That depends," David played along, filling the awkward moments when Martin coughed from the depths of his lungs. Martin was pale and had lost weight—almost like he was beginning to waste away. "What look are you going for?"

"The I-don't-give-a-shit look."

"Oh, honey. You've nailed that."

Deirdre knew that Danny was getting pissed. He always came out second-best in his banters with David, so she changed the subject. "You're very quiet, Martin."

"He's sulking," David interceded. "He won't take my advice and get a second opinion."

"I don't need a second opinion. The doctor said it's viral and that the antibiotics will take care of it."

"Well, I think you should see someone else. It's your health."

"Maybe I will," Martin answered, looking tired and grey.

"So," David moved them all along like a guide. "How are the young love-birds? I hear that you are thinking of moving. I know of a wonderful, newly renovated place down on Winchester Street."

"Does it have a balcony? I'm going to make Danny smoke out there."

David put on his most shocked face. "Danny. Are you still smoking? Don't you know how bad it is for you? You know," he continued, talking to Deirdre before Danny could answer, "you should cut him off until he quits."

Deirdre couldn't help it and giggled. She wasn't comfortable talking about sex, but with David, it all seemed so natural. "Maybe I will."

"So," David pronounced the subject decided and raised his menu. "What's everybody going to eat? They do a wonderful quiche. You must try it."

"I will then, if you insist."

"I do. And for you?" He turned to Danny.

"Bacon and eggs."

"How original. And Martin?"

"I don't really feel like eating. I'll just have a cappuccino."

"You must eat something," Deirdre and David both said, practically in unison.

"Try the Eggs Benedict."

Martin nodded like he didn't have the energy to argue.

"And can I get a Bloody Mary?" Danny asked after the waiter had taken their order. "Anybody else?"

"Danny. It's a bit early."

"Not really. It's evening in Ireland."

David looked askance at Danny for a moment before turning to commiserate with Deirdre with his eyes. He had made it obvious, so many times, that he thought she was far too good for him. She liked that and remembered it every time Danny complained about the little changes she was making to his wardrobe, and his hair, and his shoes. He complained that she was killing off the old him, bit by bit, and David was a willing accomplice.

*

Deirdre and David chatted throughout, giving Martin and Danny a chance to catch up on the news from home.

"Did he do it?"

"Yeah, your mother told me they have almost finished the work and should be able to put the house for sale in a few weeks."

"Do you think they'll do okay?"

"I'm sure they will. Whatever we might think about Donal, he does seem to have a nose for money."

"Yeah, other people's."

Martin didn't respond. He didn't trust Donal; there was something about him. But he said nothing for Gina's sake. She was enjoying the ride and he knew her well enough to know that she was more than capable of hitting the brakes. If the time ever came.

Even remembering his trip made him shiver a little. Everything back there was cold and damp and mean-spirited. Normally, he could handle it, but this trip had really brought him down.

"Danny? How the hell did we ever survive in such a cold damp bog of a place?"

"Don't be such an emigrant; it wasn't all that bad. Except for the cold. And the damp. And the smell of bog on everybody. And the rain."

"Still miss it, then?"

"Like fuck! I don't know how they put up with it. Even Ma was telling me that they're all goin' on holidays when the money comes. They're goin' to the Costa Del Sol."

*

"You know you were flirting with him."

"With who, David?"

"Of course, David. The two of you were like giggling girlfriends."

Deirdre turned and faced him seriously. "What bothers you more, Danny, that he's black or that he's gay?"

"Both, if you must know. And I don't see why you have to be all . . . with him."

"All what Danny? Say it."

He hated when she did that. She was so much better at explaining her feelings than he was. He was better off changing the subject. "I suppose we're goin' to have to look at the place he was tellin' you about."

"Don't you want to? We need a bigger place. We have nowhere to put anybody if they come to visit."

"But I'm happy where we are."

He knew it was a lost cause. They would go and look at the place and, if it was right, move. His whole life was becoming a self-improvement project, constantly guided by the new ideas Deirdre brought back from the university or from David. He was getting tired of it but everyone told him he was just being an asshole. "You're so fuckin' well off, ya bollocks," Frank often reminded him. "And just be thankful that she has whatever is wrong with her. Otherwise she wouldn't want to have anything to do with you." Even Jimmy agreed, "You're one lucky bastard."

Danny still resented all the changes but maybe she was right. She had started school and was taking courses in Celtic Studies. She had become so immersed in it all—sometimes not even coming home to make dinner for them.

"Trust me, Danny. It will be a lot better and, after I graduate, we can have family over to visit. By the way," she deflected before he could comment, "they are planning a Celtic evening at school and I mentioned your band."

"Us? Playing in front of all that crowd? It's a bit big house, don't ya think?"

"Oh, Danny, you must try to broaden your outlook."

*

"I don't know, but what I do know is that I cannot stay here. The past is too oppressive here—the tit-for-tat and the ongoing suffering of the women and children. Why can't men just fight each other and not drag the rest of us into it?" Miriam was close to tears. She had been watching the news and the pictures of dead horses in Regent Park had really torn her up.

"They are often no more than disillusioned boys told they are fighting for freedom." Karl held her hand as the evening sunshine began to fade.

She had been on edge for months, as the British took back the Falklands, and the Israelis pounded the Lebanese before letting loose the Phalangists to slaughter thousands in the refugee camps. Miriam had wanted to go and stand between the women and children and the righteousness of murderers and assassins.

Karl wouldn't let her. He knew what happened when the world looked the other way. Miriam was bright with hope and optimism, refusing to believe that there were men in the world who would shoot her down without a thought, but he knew better. He had been in Vietnam when his troops had done things that would haunt him forever.

"We could still go to Rome?" He reached across and took her small hand in his. Touching her skin to remind her that she was not alone. "We can find something to study and pass our days somewhere warm."

She knew he was trying to ease her mind but she tried to smile. "Yes, we could apply for the position as God's Banker."

"Oh I don't think things are that desperate." Karl touched her cheek. He loved her deeply for the peace she brought to his soul, even while she railed against all that was wrong with the world. He loved her for that. When he first came home from the war he had gotten lost inside of himself. He had no one to talk to about the terrible things he had seen. Young men shredded by mortars and bombs hidden in the fresh, green jungle. Young men, whose eyes once shone with innocence, began to look like old men. Growing more and more haggard as their tours dragged on.

No one at home could understand, least of all his parents. They tried, but he couldn't burden them with it. They had changed too. They had once supported the war but, as it dragged on, rejected it and not just for their son's sake. Karl's war always made the six-o-clock news and even though the images were grainy, the horror of it all came home to roost. When they got to see it as it really was, war was never righteous—it was always total human failure. A failure that was always being perfected.

He did two tours. Not because he was a hero, or a fool. He was a good junior officer who had learned the ways of the jungle. The night before he was to ship back, he stood before the men who had followed him. Young, downy-faced boys who would never survive without him.

He phoned his father before he signed up again, and explained why he had to do it. His father assured him he understood but Karl could hear his mother crying in the background.

When he finally came home she held him and wouldn't let him go. Even when he went for a walk around the old neighborhood, she followed him with her eyes and stood by the window until he returned.

He had tried to fit back in, but America wanted to forget and he couldn't let them. Nor could he agree with the hippies who called him a baby-burner. None of them knew or understood either. His father did. He had fought in the Pacific and Karl followed his lead and never spoke about it again.

Going to Dublin was his father's idea. When he came home from his war he studied there while he tried to write his book. He never did, but he always remembered Dublin with a smile on his face. "All their wars were happy and all their songs are sad," he laughed when Karl's mother was out of earshot. "Go there and find yourself again." He found Miriam instead, resplendent in her shame.

"We could always go back to the States and fight for the Equal Rights Amendment?"

"I doubt they would let me in."

"They wouldn't have any choice if you were my wife."

"Oh, be serious."

He knelt before her, in the middle of Stephen's Green, and asked for her hand.

*

"Of course I told him to get up before people started looking at us," Miriam wrote to Joe. "I was shocked and delighted at the same time. He is a good man—you'd like him—but I am unsure. And it's not just what my 'ex' might think. I am too old to be falling love—amn't I?"

Joe would know what to say to her. He always did.

She wasn't going to have a Church wedding. It wouldn't feel right. Besides, Karl wasn't Catholic and she didn't want to deal with any of that. They weren't going to have children—she was far too old for that type of thing.

She thought about writing to Patrick, too, but she couldn't bring herself around to it even though it was for the better—for her and Karl and for Patrick too. She would tell him when enough time had passed and he had gotten over his crush on her. Poor Patrick. She hoped that Rome was being good to him.

Chapter 7 -1983

FRANK LOADED THE VAN while Jimmy and Danny lugged everything down from the third floor. Deirdre had packed the boxes and marked them. They were easy to move but Frank wanted the couch and the bed first.

"What's it matter?" Danny asked when Frank chided him.

"Because you have to put the big stuff in first. Now fuck-off and get the couch. And the mattress and box spring."

"Alright, alright, don't get all fucking snarky."

"I'm doing you a favor, ya bollocks. Do you think I like wasting a whole day on you? I could be out working and earning a few bucks."

"I thought you said there was no work around." Jimmy had been asking Frank for work—if any was going. Frank was a carpenter and Jimmy could carry wood and tools.

"Fuck-off the pair of you and do as you're told. It's my van and we'll load it my way—the proper way."

They ceded and fetched the bed. The mattress was awkward but at least it could be bent around the corners of the stairwell. The box spring required a rudimentary knowledge of geometry that was beyond Jimmy and Danny. They got stuck on the last turn until the super came out to help. But after a couple of hours or so, they got it all done and piled in to drive the few blocks over to Parliament and Winchester, in the heart of Cabbagetown, now almost half-renovated.

"You're moving up in the world, Danny, I heard this is going to be the place to be."

"He is like fuck. He's just riding along on Deirdre's skirts."

"Leave him alone, Frank."

They pulled up at the back of the renovated house that shared its parking space with the Beer Store, the government-run outlet where they slung the boxes of beer along the rollers like they were begrudged.

"You'll be alright for beer anyway."

The liquor store was just the other side of Winchester. There, all the bottles were kept hidden and customers had to write down their selection from the descriptions on the boards. Then hand them to a man who seemed unwilling to offer any assistance. 'Toronto the Good' suffered intemperance and the resulting tax contributions—but could not seem encouraging, for one reason or another.

Moving in was a lot easier. They just had to drag everything up to the second floor deck and shove it through the back door. The apartment was open with a large room with a working fireplace, a smaller room where they could eat and an even smaller but well equipped kitchen behind a bar-like counter. The bedrooms were small, too, and the washroom was little more than a closet but it was all tastefully finished.

"This place is alright," Jimmy agreed as Deirdre showed him around.

"It is, isn't it?"

"It used to be a roach-ridden flop house."

"Thanks for sharing that, Frank."

But Deirdre just laughed and directed the incoming boxes, depending on their markings.

When they were done, Danny brought them across the street for a few beers while Deirdre began to unpack.

The Winchester Hotel was typical of the older taverns in Toronto. "Watch yourself in here," Frank said, nodding in a knowing way as he held the door and let Jimmy and Danny go before him.

"Why?"

"'Cos it's Pogey Day."

Frank smiled as the tray of draught arrived and each one of them was given two small glasses—the legally allowed allotment. But the waiter hovered by their elbows as they drained their glasses and quickly replaced them.

Built as a hotel, the Winchester once offered cheap rooms to travelling salesmen and others of the working class in transit. Never a place of beauty, it used to have a clean orderliness about it but salesmen now preferred the sameness offered by the low-end hotel chains and the Winchester's rooms were rented on a monthly basis—welfare cheques exchanged for the surety of a bed and a place to wash and shave. It was the last fixed abode of those that life had passed by—East-Coasters and others who hadn't risen on the tides of emigration. Old men now made older by years of grind, ending their days in musty little rooms, walking the streets until the end of the month when their cheques finally arrived.

After rent and board there was hardly enough left to be stretched until the next so they splashed it around like confetti in the men-only bar; another relic of when the city fathers frowned on such behavior—at least in public.

And when it was gone they would stand up and, acting on the prodding of some inner demon, flushed with alcohol, erupt against all the injustices cruel fate had visited upon them. Some sang lewd ditties and some called out all who tried to silence them. Some spoke of government plots, while the most succinct simply pulled their pants down and wagged at the world with their pale pinched arses.

They were ejected by the burliest waiters but it was better that way—leaving with a flourish before facing another long month asking for change and searching for butts along the street.

"So, Boyle, is this going to be your new local?"

"You never know. I kinda like it."

"Are you fucking mad?" Jimmy gaped around in disbelief.

"We'll all end up here sooner or later." Frank laughed and lit a cigarette.

"Speak for yourself. This won't be me."

"Look around you. How many of them do you think said the same thing?"

"You're so fucking morose."

They drank their beer as the waiter stood over them, seeming to disapprove that they were drinking so slowly.

"We should do a gig here."

"Only if they have chicken wire."

"I forgot to tell you," Danny interrupted them. "Deirdre got us a gig at the university."

"Great. Can we do some Moving Hearts?"

"We can't play stuff like that. We should do something intellectual."

"Like what?"

"I've been working on some stuff of my own."

"I don't know," Danny interrupted them, "Deirdre told them we were Celtic."

"What's that even mean?"

"It means we have to sing the 'Black Velvet Band' in Scottish accents."

"Hey, I know someone who plays the bagpipes."

"Why don't we just kick you in the bollocks while you're singing? It'll sound the same."

*

"He doesn't want Danny to know. At least not yet—not until we know for sure."

David was worried. His broad smile was gone and his eyes were haunted. Deirdre reached out and touched his hand but David pulled it away. She knew what hung over him. There had been talk of a 'gay cancer' for almost two years, of a plague passing among them. "God's retribution," the righteous scorned, and seemed to take delight in the tragedy.

"I won't say anything, for now, but we will have to tell him."

Danny hadn't seen much of his uncle recently. He'd been busy, working all day, and the band was gigging four or five nights a week. The other nights, he'd sit on the couch watching the hockey game and drinking beer. Sometimes Deirdre got a bit frustrated with him but she didn't complain. He was bringing home enough money for her to study in comfort. Some Saturdays he even insisted on taking her shopping and waited patiently while she tried everything on. Sometimes, she wished he wasn't so busy so they could do more together, but for now she let it pass.

She saw Martin and David regularly and had often chided Martin for not taking better care of himself. Since he had come back from Ireland he seemed to be wasting away. It all made perfect sense now. Perfect in the most horrible way.

"And what about you? How are you doing?"

David almost seemed embarrassed. "I'm fine, girl."

"David. You are the world's worst liar."

He looked cornered for a moment before he began to cry and Deirdre couldn't help herself and took him in her arms, ignoring those sitting around them. They often met in The Senator. David worked nearby and Deirdre loved its nostalgia. Too much of Toronto was rushing into change.

"I'm scared, Deer-dree." He always had difficulty with her name. "I'm scared for myself and for Martin. I'm also afraid that I might have given it to him."

"But that's ridiculous."

"I really wish it was but I was Martin's only."

"But you're showing no signs of anything wrong."

"Maybe I'm a carrier. Not everybody gets infected."

"But you have been with Martin for so long. How . . ." She stopped as he hung his head in shame.

"It was just once. Just a stupid little fling one night when Martin and I had a big fight. Only, after we got back together I lied and now . . . how can I tell him now?"

*

"Have you heard of one Humpty Dumpty?" Frank sang and silenced the room full of men in tartan skirts, groomed beards, and sporrans dangling between their thighs, while their wives stood primly in lace-edged linens beneath their tartan sashes.

"How he fell with a roll and a rumble?"

Even the caterers paused their dashing between the tables and the younger professors nodded and smiled to each other.

"Curled up like Lord Olofa Crumple."

Frank was on a roll and closed his eyes while clutching his whistle in his hand. They would do an instrumental verse if he hesitated on the words. It was all very well rehearsed. "At the butt of the Magazine Wall."

"The Magazine Wall, hump, helmet and all." Danny and Jimmy joined in on the chorus.

"They're doing James Joyce," the crowd acknowledged and edged a little closer. Earlie,r when the band first arrived, they had looked disappointed and somewhat alarmed that Danny and the lads looked more like a rock band or drug dealers.

> He was one time our King of the Castle,
> Now he's kicked about like a rotten old parsnip.
> And from Green Street he'll be sent by order of
> His Worship
> To the penal jail of Mountjoy,
> To the jail of Mountjoy! Jail him and joy.

Deirdre's friends flocked around her and whispered. "They are great, Dee," but Deirdre had to force herself to smile. She would have to tell Danny about Martin—when they got home.

"He was fa fa father of all schemes for to bother us," Frank stammered as Ronnie Drew had done.

> Slow coaches and immaculate contraceptives for
> the populace,
> Mare's milk for the sick, seven dry Sundays a week,
> Open air love and religion's reform,

"And religious reform, hideous in form." Danny and Jimmy were beginning to make it sound like a Gregorian chant.

> Arrah, why, says you, couldn't he manage it?
> I'll go bail, me fine dairyman darling,
> Like the bumping bull of the Cassidys
> All your butter is in your horns.
> His butter is in his horns. Butter his horns!

> Sweet bad luck on the waves washed to our
> island
> The hooker of that hammerfast Viking
> And Gall's curse on the day when Eblana bay
> Saw his black and tan man-o'-war, saw his man-
> o'-war, on the harbour bar.

By now the professors were joining on the chorus, puffing up like baritones while their wives checked to see how much they had drunk. They weren't a bad lot. Most of them were only Celtic by ancestry but they would not be denied the opportunity to sing along with the real thing.

"He was joulting by Wellinton's monument," Frank sang on with one hand cupped to his ear, his accent becoming more pronounced until it almost sounded guttural.

> Our rotorious hipppopopotamuns
> When some bugger let down the back strap of
> his omnibus
> And he caught his death of fusiliers, with his
> rent in his rears. Give him six years.

Jimmy added a stifled strum on the bass for effect, sounding almost like a snare drum.

> Then we'll have a free trade Gaels' band and
> mass meeting,
> For to sod the brave son of Scandiknavery,
> And we'll bury him down in Oxmanstown,
> Along with the devil and Danes, with the deaf
> and dumb Danes, and all their remains.

By now, the professors were mouthing the phrases to each other in total communion with the playful words of one of the greatest writers, the one they all offered courses on, explaining and deciphering all that Joyce had put there to keep them busy for years.

"Will ya look at them," Frank whispered aside. "You'd think they were at a fucking rock concert." And turning back to the mic, he hushed them before continuing.

> And not all the king's men nor his horses,
> Will resurrect his corpus.
> For there's no true spell in Connacht or hell,

He paused as Jimmy's snare drumming rose to a crescendo and came to a sudden shocking halt.

> That's able to raise a Cain.

*

Deirdre knew he would take it badly and debated waiting until the morning.

Danny was high as a kite all the way home, on adoration and some strong smelling dope. The band went on from high to high, even surviving the moments when Frank stopped in the middle of *The Irish Rover* to tell the audience how great they were. "You'se are the best crowd we've ever played to. Even the bars we normally play don't get this wild. And you," he had turned from the mic and whispered across to Jimmy, his whispering leaking out into the room. "Said that they'd be a

pretentious bunch of stuck-up bastards. All liver-spotted—
and their hatchety old wives."

After a moment of hesitation, the crowd roared back to
life, laughing and shaking their heads. Even some of the wives
laughed too, at least the ones who had been drinking.

"Did you see the looks on their faces? They fucking loved
us, man! They fucking loved us."

"They did, Danny."

"Is that all?"

"You guys were brilliant."

"Brilliant?" He stepped across in front of her, his face right
before hers. His eyes searching deep inside her. "We were far
more than that. It's like those old farts got to see the real thing
for the first time. We were more than brilliant."

He turned his head slightly to one side, casting a shadow
across his face, making one side look so dark. And it made him
look like he was sneering, the way he once did.

"Can't you admit? All the times you complained about me
going over to Frank's. Admit it, you thought we were just getting wasted. Didn't you?"

"Danny. Stop a minute. I got to tell you something. Something serious."

"What! Just tell me that you were wrong." He reached out
and lifted her in his arms, up against him, hugging her with
sheer delight.

"Danny!"

"Go on. Admit it, you were impressed. Eh? Admit it!"

"Danny, please listen to me."

"Not until you tell me how great we were." He began to
squeeze her a little.

"Danny, please. It's about Martin."

"Martin?" He blinked at her and lowered her gently until
she was looking up into his face. "You mean my uncle and best
friend who wasn't even there tonight?"

"He's in the hospital. It's serious."

He got caught between his feelings for a moment and looked lost.

"He's very, very sick, Danny."

"Is it . . . you know?"

"We don't know. They are running all kinds of tests and won't know for a few more days."

"When did he go in?"

"Last week."

"Last week! Why didn't you tell me?"

"Because I didn't want you thinking about it before the gig."

It took a moment for it to sink in but it did. He blinked some more, like he was holding in his tears.

"I love you, Danny boy. Martin loves you. Even David loves you and we all agreed to wait." She kissed him more sweetly than she had ever done before, letting her lips brush across his. "And yes, I admit that I thought you guys were getting wasted. And I admit that you guys were great."

She linked her arm in his and steered him toward home.

"Thanks," he muttered after she had left him alone with his thoughts for a while. "Thanks for telling me. And thanks for waiting to tell me."

She rested her head against him as they walked, buffing up against him from one side while his guitar buffed against his legs on the other. "Danny. When I was watching you tonight, I felt so great. All my friends were jealous because I'm the one who gets to go home with you."

But he wasn't in the mood. As soon as he got home and got a beer from the fridge, he sat on the couch staring off somewhere she couldn't see. He'd stare and swig from his beer and no matter what she asked him, she couldn't distract him.

He'd acknowledge her but never knew what she was talking about. He apologized for getting so dark but he couldn't help it; he was thinking about Martin. He said it so often she finally realized that she was intruding, trying to force herself onto him when he needed time alone.

"Good night." She decided to go to bed and leaned forward to kiss him but he hardly lingered and rose to get another beer.

"You're not going to stay up too late?"

"Me? No. I just need to sort the evening out. It's been a bit of a wild ride."

"Yes, Danny. It has." She kissed his cheek gently and turned toward their bedroom, hoping he would follow.

She stayed awake as long as she could, but Danny didn't get up, except to go to the fridge a few times. She had left the door open.

*

She woke again when he was in the washroom and it sounded like he was talking to somebody.

"Of course I'm drunk. It's the only fuckin' way I know of getting through life.

"It's the only way I can handle all the shite the spite of God showers down on me.

"What's the point, anyway? What's the point of destroyin' everyone I come into contact with? What kind of a fuckin' malicious God would kill all these people just to teach me somethin'?

"And it wouldn't be so bad if He just killed them. No, the great and merciful God has to kill them slowly, suckin' life out of them before me so I can sit and watch them wither. What kind of a sick pervert can do stuff like that?

"I used to try to believe in Him, you know, and that he was good and kind. I even used to go to Confession and tell Him I was so fuckin' sorry for all the little things they told me were wrong with me. And what did I get for that? Absolution? No, I just got even more shite thrown at me.

"I used to go to mass, too, and pray. And not for myself. I prayed for my mother when He let my granny lock her up in the fuckin' nuthouse.

"And I prayed for my granny when sickness stole life from her, one day at a time. When we got to bury her, there was nothin' left but skin stretched over bones.

"And now Martin. What did he ever do to anyone? He was always the good guy.

"Well fuck God and this being good shite. What's it goin' to get you in the end? God is nothin' more than a malicious fucker that preys on the weak—and the kind—while rewardin' all those fuckers that use His name to do all kinds of evil.

"I'm done with God and all His twisted schemes. He doesn't work in mysterious ways. It's so fuckin' obvious—God goes around pickin' off anybody that is not just like Him, vicious and malignant.

"And we shouldn't be surprised. He killed His own son too.

"He gave him over to some fuckin' righteous mob to nail the poor fucker up on a cross. Fuck God, that's what I say. Fuck God and all the shite that clings to Him. Fuck them all. Fuck the bishops and the priests and the bloody pope in Rome.

"And another thing. Where was God when they were burnin' people at the stake—when the Inquisition was huntin' down and killin' people? Where was God then?

"I'll fuckin' tell ya where He was. He was sittin' on His fucking throne laughin' at us all.

"That's all we are, ya know, court fuckin' jesters. This whole fuckin' circus of life is nothin' more than God's coliseum. We're like the poor fuckin' gladiators fightin' over which one of us has the true God while all the time He sits up there waitin' to give us the 'thumbs-down.'

"He doesn't love us; we're just playthings to Him. He makes us to keep Himself amused.

"And when He tires of us—He kills us."

*

The weather was fine as May drew to a close. Jacinta was sitting in the garden, in the last of the sunshine, sipping a glass of wine.

"You're like a Duchess, sitting out here. The Duchess of Dublin." Jerry sidled up behind her and leaned over with the flowers he had picked up on the way home.

"What's that for?"

"It's because I love you."

"I know that, but why flowers—today?"

"Because I love you more today than I did yesterday."

"Did you stop for a few on the way home?"

"I had to. They had to get the flowers special for you and I would have had to wait anyway. I only had two pints."

She sniffed his breath as he leaned in to kiss her. "Well, thanks so much. And I love you, too."

"More than you did yesterday?"

"No. Just the same, but don't be disappointed. I've loved you the most for years now. Anyway. What's the occasion?"

"Can a man not buy his wife flowers without it being an occasion?"

"Of course they can, but they don't, so out with it."

"Okay then. Donal phoned and said we have a buyer lined up. They are willing to meet the asking price and just want to have it inspected first."

"Will it pass?"

"Of course it will, but we might have to cut the inspector in too."

"Is that right?"

"It's the way everybody is doing it and don't worry. The work was done by good qualified tradesmen. They'll find nothing wrong."

"And how much will we get out of it."

"Donal thinks we should take ten grand each and put the rest back in for the next one."

"And what are we going to do with it?"

"It's a surprise."

"You know I don't like surprises, Jerry."

"Okay then, but promise you won't tell Gina until Donal has a chance to talk with her."

"I promise."

"We're going to go to the Costa del Sol."

He expected her to be more delighted. "What's the matter? I thought you'd be over the moon."

"I am, Jerry, only I got a call from Danny today with a bit of bad news."

"What's he done now?"

"He's done nothing. It's Martin. He's been taken into hospital."

"Ah Jeeze, I'm sorry to hear that. Nothing too serious, I hope?"

"Well, Danny wasn't too sure. He said it was some kind of virus or other and that he might be there for a while."

"Well, he's in the right place. I'm sure they'll have him right in no time."

"I hope so. Danny seemed to think it might it might be one of those new viruses or something he brought back with him from Jamaica? What was he doing down there all these times? Do you think he has a girl down there?"

"Probably," Jerry agreed while avoiding her eyes.

"I wonder why he had to go all the way down there to find a girl. Aren't there any nice Irish girls in Toronto? You don't think she's one of them, do you?"

"And sure what harm if she is? It's a different world now, Jass, and you and I don't need to be worrying about any of it. Why don't you give Gina a call and we can all go out for a meal to celebrate."

"I will, so. Do you think I should tell her about Martin?"

"I wouldn't if I were you. Not yet anyway. There's no point in worrying anybody when he'll probably be fine in a few days."

She seemed happy with that and went off to call her sister while Jerry sat smoking and staring off into the distance.

*

"It's like he's the one who is . . ."

"It's okay, Deirdre." Martin assured her but his voice was dull and tired. He was propped against his pillows in a honeycomb of wires and tubes. "I'm dying. You can say the word. It's not so frightening anymore."

She gazed at him with total adoration. As the end approached, he grew braver and braver, while Danny's world was melting away. He had quit the band, even though they called every day to try to persuade him to come back. They had cancelled all their gigs too. They weren't prepared to go on without him. But even with Deirdre's secret involvement, they couldn't budge him.

He just went to work every morning, stopping in the liquor store, as well as the beer store, every evening. After dinner, when he would barely say a word, he'd sit on the couch, watching hockey and pounding down beer and whiskey too. She tried talking to him, even told him to snap out of it.

Danny would just smile at her and shake his head. "I can't, Deirdre. This is my life. This is what I've had to deal with since. . . Just leave me alone to deal with it. I'm not hurting anybody. I'm just sitting here, easing the pain. I'll be all right soon. Just leave me alone for a while yet."

As the fall gave way to winter and everybody else was getting ready for Christmas, Danny withered. More and more each day until he started missing work too. They were able to cover that up for a while. Danny's supervisor was a friend of Martin's, only nobody at work knew.

Danny had been to see Martin on his own too. Standing, looking at his own reflection in the dark windows, except for the lights from the street below. "It might be better if he didn't," David had told Deirdre the last time they had lunch together. But Martin wouldn't hear of it and insisted Danny come, whenever he could.

"You know, Deirdre," Martin rasped from his bed, "I don't worry about myself anymore. I've found peace, but I worry for Danny. I was the only family he ever really had."

Deirdre and David exchanged glances but said nothing.

"He needs to feel that he belongs to something—something that will last."

*

His words followed her all the way home. She loved Danny Boyle. More so now that he was so lost and helpless. He was losing the only friend who had always been there for him, even when she wasn't.

She had been thinking a lot about it lately anyway.

Only she usually thought against it, even though it kept coming back. Her friends said it was 'the clock.' Every woman had to deal with it. She argued that she was too young—that she was just past her mid-twenties.

"Happens," her friends laughed, "when you least expect it."

She had never felt the time was right before, but now it was all clear to her. She might not be ready to become a mother but Danny had to become a father. It was the only way he'd find his way back from the edge. That's what Martin must have meant.

Chapter 8 -1984

AFTER THE DOCTOR HAD CONFIRMED IT, Deirdre felt even more divided, part Madonna and part whore. She had been giving her body, night after night, to save Danny from the depths he wallowed in, making love to him when he came home, reeking of beer and hardly able to manage. And after, when he was soundly sleeping, she would lay awake and stare at the ceiling.

What was she thinking? Everything in Danny's life would always be shrouded with heartbreak. It was like he was cursed and damned from the beginning. And voices from the shadows were quick to remind her that she had played her part, sending him spinning off the path before he even began. Sometimes she wondered if she was only with him to appease her guilt.

Miriam had once asked her about that but Deirdre knew; Miriam wasn't impartial. Despite her best efforts, she often allowed their friendship to shade her judgment. She always said that she only wanted what was best for Deirdre, but sometimes it felt like she was living vicariously.

They still kept in touch, writing letters every other week, but Deirdre hadn't mentioned any of this. It was a matter of the heart, something that Miriam often said she knew little about. And she certainly couldn't do it now. She couldn't mention Martin, wasting away while becoming more and more spirit-like every time she went to see him. He was adamant that no one at home should know. No one! The little energy he had left was directed through her, toward Danny, to guide him back on track once again.

Besides, she knew that Miriam wouldn't understand. Deirdre was in love with Danny and people who were in love didn't turn their backs when things were going badly.

It almost made sense when she looked at it that way. She just wasn't sure that she loved him enough to spend the rest of her life with him. A life with a child and all the things children brought with them. She wasn't sure that he loved her enough either.

She had called him at work and asked him to be home in time for supper, that she had something important to tell him. He showed up an hour late, but he brought her flowers and a bottle of wine.

"No. Thank you," she declined when he offered her a glass.

"Is there something wrong?"

He hadn't noticed. She hadn't had a drink since his birthday, just after Christmas. "I'm fine, Danny, and I have some big news."

"I hope its good news. I could use some of that." He poured himself a glass and sat down opposite her. He looked so tired. The band had gotten back together before Christmas and they were working three nights a week again, on top of his day job. And those nights when he was home, he'd sit up drinking and staring into space if she let him. Frank said he was like that at the gigs, too, playing away like he was robotic, just going through the motions.

"I hope so, too."

"Well?"

"Well." She took a deep breath and dived right in. "Danny. You're going to be a father."

He lit up immediately. So many times she had tried to imagine how it would go but she never once imagined he would be so happy. He stood up and took her in his arms, squeezing her and twirling her around until he realized.

"Oh my God. I'm so sorry. I shouldn't be doing that." He put her down again, ever so gently. "I didn't hurt it, did I?" He touched her cheek so tenderly that she couldn't help it and began to cry.

"I haven't done anything wrong, have I? 'Cos I want to be the best father of all time. I'll never let anything happen to the baby—and you. Ya know that?"

"No, you didn't hurt us, Danny. And I agree, I think we're going to make the world's best father out of you."

"I hope you'll know how because I don't know anything about it."

"Well," Deirdre looked for the right thing to say, "you'll know all the things not to do."

"Yeah, I'm an expert in that."

"You are happy about it, aren't you?"

He almost had tears in his eyes. "I'm so happy I could . . . shit balloons."

She pushed him away from her but they were both laughing.

"Can I tell everybody?"

"Let's wait a bit; I just got the news today."

"But I can tell Martin, right?"

"Yes, you can tell Martin, but nobody else for a while."

He hugged her, much more carefully this time, and rested his head on hers. "What would you think if I told him that we were going to call the baby Martin?"

"I think that would be beautiful, but what if it's not a boy?"

"No problem. We'll call her Martina." He swayed them around like a slow dance until she pushed him away.

"Go on and see Martin. I'm sure he'll be delighted for you."

Danny agreed and got ready to go. "You'll be all right—here on your own?"

"Go on."

He kissed her again and was gone.

She sat on the couch and pulled her legs up under her. She was happy he was happy. So happy that she could almost forget that she had also made alternative plans. She wasn't really considering abortion; she just wanted to know she had options. She had even made an appointment but she didn't keep it. She couldn't do it, to the baby, to Danny, or to herself.

*

The doctor finished his examination and stood over the bishop.

The bishop hated that; a doctor had no business looking down on a bishop. He tried to sit up but he couldn't. He was far too sick for that.

"It's pneumonia, all right."

Mrs. Power had been telling him that for a few days before she and Mrs. Mawhinney tricked him into bed and called the doctor to come. The bishop would have gotten around to seeing him on his own. They had no right . . . but they did.

He had been a damn fool and a proud fool. He refused to admit, even to himself, that he didn't have the strength to carry on. He'd been so busy down at the diocese. There had been a most un-immaculate birth in the grotto up in Granard and the papers were full of accusations. Then Brendan Behan's mother had died and he really wanted to get down to the funeral. Kathleen was the last of her stock.

"And it might be better if we get you into hospital for a few days." The doctor looked at him over his glasses and waited.

"Tell me, Doctor. Would I really do any better there? If it makes no difference, I'd rather stay in my own bed."

"You'll need antibiotics, and you'll need round-the-clock treatment for a few days."

"I can be given those here. Bishops are a bit like Sea Captains, Doctor. We prefer to die in our own beds."

"Your Grace, without wanting to cause alarm, I must stress that your condition is serious."

"Of course it is. Do you think I'd be lying in my bed if it wasn't?"

"Well then, you'll know why I think you should go in."

"I'll take my chances here and that will be the end of it."

"Your Grace, as your doctor I would think that my opinion would hold more sway here."

"Not in my palace."

The bishop had raised his voice so loud that Mrs. Power and Mrs. Mawhinney, who were listening through the door, came rushing in.

"And what do you two want?" But his voice was lower as he sank back into his pillows. "I suppose you are here to agree with him."

"Well," Mrs. Mawhinney ventured while Mrs. Power urged her on. "I've had nursing training—during the war—but I can still remember the basics."

"I think that would be for the best," Mrs. Power joined in. "After all, where would he get better care than here?"

The doctor opened his bag like he was weighing his options. "Very well." He drew out a small bottle of pills. "See that he takes these and I'll come back tomorrow and see where we go from there. And make sure he gets lots of liquids into him. We'll see what the morning brings and make sure he takes two of those, every four hours."

"We will indeed," Mrs. Power assured him and saw him to the door.

"I'll not take them," the bishop protested meekly.

"Your Grace," Mrs. Mawhinney said, tidying the bed around him, "with all due respect, you'll do as you're told until you are well enough again. Then, when the doctor says it's okay, you can go back to ordering us all around." She sat in the chair beside his bed and reached for his forehead.

"What do you think you are doing?"

"Checking your fever, Your Grace."

"And?"

"And nothing." Mrs. Mawhinney handed him the two pills and a glass of water. "Take these and try to get some sleep."

He gave in and took them and settled down beneath the covers. "You don't think you're going to stay here?"

"I will for a while, Your Grace. Now go to sleep and give the medicine a chance to work."

"But you can't. What if I was to die in my sleep and they found you in here with me?"

"Did I ever tell you how my husband died?" Mrs. Mawhinney tucked his blankets in around him. "He was returning from escorting the bombers over Germany. He came across a lone bomber being attacked by German fighters and, even though he was low on ammunition, he tried to do what he could. He saved the bomber but it cost him his life."

"And I suppose there's a morale in that?"

"You'd know best, Your Grace."

He protested some more but his protests grew weaker and weaker until they were nothing more than a muffled rattle. He was asleep by the time Mrs. Power came back and the two women sat in the semi-dark, praying for the only man in their lives.

*

"Father Reilly? It's Janet Mawhinney. I'm just calling to let you know that your uncle has come down with pneumonia."

"It's bad, but the doctor has been in to see him."

"No. He refuses to go but, for now, we'll be able to look after him here. You know how stubborn he can be."

"Well, you'd know best yourself, Father, but I don't think there's any need for you to rush over. I'm sure he'll be fine in a few days."

"Good enough, Father. We'll wait and see."

"I will indeed, Father, and take care and I'll tell him that you will be calling."

"Don't worry about Mrs. Power and me; we're more than a match for him."

"Good bye to you, too, Father."

*

"Here is your son, Danny Boyle." Deirdre handed him the little swaddled bundle she had been carrying around for months. Pink and wrinkled, with his little hands around his ears as if the noise of the world was too much, the baby seemed to peep up at his father.

"Oh look, Dee. He's smiling at me. He knows his Daddy already."

Danny huddled over him, like he did with his mandolin, and gently rocked where he sat. He looked at peace with the world for the first time since . . . Deirdre couldn't remember a time when he looked like that.

Pregnancy was not as difficult as she had heard but there were times, particularly in the last few months, when her bump was too much. Sometimes she even wished someone would reach inside and pull the child out. But his birthing was quick. Danny had borrowed David's car and driven her to the hospital as soon as her water broke—just another in a long line of body functions that were no longer private. He had settled her in and gone for a smoke and by the time he came back, the baby was well on his way, pushing through her and out into the world.

"He's beautiful," Danny said as he looked up at her. "Just like his mother."

She knew he was just saying it. She hadn't been beautiful for months, with her swollen body and her fat face, and her hair—it had suffered the most, always stringy around her face, no matter how often she washed it. And none of her clothes fit and those that did were shapeless and ugly. But it was nice of him to say. He had been so nice to her about everything. He had stopped sitting up drinking and had involved himself in all the preparations. They had gone to prenatal classes together and he had decorated the baby's room. He even promised that he would get up at night, when the baby called, and bring him to their bed.

Sometimes, in bittersweet moments, he said it was like the coming of the new Martin was easing the passing of the old. He had been to see him every night and seemed reconciled. He rarely spoke about it anymore, preferring instead to talk about how great everything would be once the baby had come.

"You know," he said and smiled over at her, "I think he looks a bit like your father."

"Oh God, don't say that."

Her father was fuming about it all. Her sister and her mother had tried their best but he couldn't be soothed.

"He's got his hair." Danny laughed and gently touched the little tuft on the baby's head. "But he has your smile."

Lying there, sweaty and disheveled, Deirdre was happy. The future would test them but for now, they were happy. She had learned to push all of her own dissenting voices to the back of her mind. Voices that clamored about all that she would have to give up. How was she ever going to be able to do anything for herself again? The baby would take all that she had and more.

But today she was happy. The baby had brought Danny back to her and between them, they would repay that kindness. Deirdre Fallon and Danny Boyle had brought a child into the world. A world that would never be the same again—at least for the two of them. "Are you happy, Danny?"

He clutched the baby close to his chest and leaned forward to kiss her sweaty brow. "I've never been happier in my whole life."

For a moment he looked wistful but seemed to dismiss it. "And I promise you that I will be the best father and husband that ever was. And I promise that I will never let anything change the way I feel right now."

"I love you, Danny boy."

"I love you, too, Deirdre Fallon." Danny leaned forward while the baby squirmed between them.

*

"I can't wait for you to see him. Both of you. I know everybody thinks their baby is the cutest, but you've got to see him."

Martin tried to smile but it was more like a gash on his sunken face. "I can't wait."

"I wanted to bring him in but Deirdre didn't think it would be a good idea."

"Well we're both very touched that you named him Martin. Aren't we, David?"

David flashed his big smile. He hadn't used it much recently and it seemed to take more effort.

"Are you going to get him baptized?"

Since Martin got sick he seemed to have changed his attitudes on the things that people used to get them through life. He didn't endorse any of it; he just wasn't dismissive anymore.

"Deirdre thinks we should get him christened, but we don't want him to be Catholic."

"There's a United minister that comes to see me. You could ask him."

"Have you gone Prod?"

Martin didn't even flinch. Not even a quiver. "Danny, from where I lay, none of that matters anymore."

"Yeah, but."

"Danny. The minister and I talk about life and death. We don't discuss who's right and wrong. None of that really matters. He listens to me and I listen to him and together, we help me find the peace that I need."

Danny lowered his head. He couldn't argue with that.

Since Martin had been hospitalized, he had become calmer, almost like he understood the bigger picture. Deirdre said that it was part of the process. That after feeling angry and afraid, people like Martin searched for peace.

She had been careful not to call him an AIDS patient. That still had so much stigma attached.

"There is just one thing," Martin continued like he was really talking to himself, "that I want to know before I leave." David kept his thoughts to himself and sat quietly, holding his dying lover's hand. Danny wanted to as well, but he was afraid until Martin solved the problem by taking Danny's hand in his. "I want to know that you will be all right, Danny. I want to know that you will go on from here and be a proper father to your son. I know things weren't great for you growing up but everything is different now."

Danny shrugged and tried to deflect him.

"Danny, I need to know that you will never allow all the shit we grew up with to ever affect your son."

"Don't worry," Danny choked back his tears. "Deirdre would kill me if anything like that ever happened."

"Danny. I need you to promise me that little Martin will never have to go through what you did."

"C'mon, Martin. Don't be getting so heavy."

"Promise me."

"Okay, okay. I, Danny-the-fuck-up-Boyle, promise that I will never let any crap happen to my son. Are you happy now?"

"And Danny, when I'm gone, I don't want you acting the bollocks."

"What do you mean?"

"I mean I don't want you drinking and brooding anymore."

"I won't."

"I'm leaving but little Martin has just arrived. I want you to love him and to be the good in his life."

"Like you were in mine?" Danny smiled but his tears began to fall.

Martin lay back and closed his eyes but, even though his face was sunken and his bones were sticking through his skin, he seemed happier than he had been for a while. When he seemed to have fallen asleep, Danny rose to go. He put his hand on David's shoulder but couldn't think of anything to say.

David didn't speak either, but he did put his hand on Danny's for a moment.

"Danny," Martin called out as he got to the door, "I'll always be there for you—if you need me."

Danny nodded and turned to go, crying all the way to the door and down the street and all the way home.

*

The bishop didn't survive the spring and died, as he preferred, in his own bed while Mrs. Power and Mrs. Mawhinney kept vigil, saying rosaries by candlelight. His pneumonia spread to both lungs and his last few days were spent in fitful, feverish, semi-sleep. So late one night, Pat McConnell passed from the world he had helped shepherd and his passing was marked in every parish with calls to pray for the soul of the faithful departed and a good servant of the Lord.

Patrick Reilly had come back from Rome just before the end. Mrs. Mawhinney had kept him informed with daily phone calls. "Come now," she had told him and Patrick was there within a day.

His uncle clung to his last few breaths so he could share them with his nephew. "I have had Mrs. Mawhinney put together a box of my papers," he had gasped, each word costing him. "I want you to have them and, when the time is right, read them."

"Hush now, Uncle, and don't be talking like that. You'll be back on your feet . . ."

"Patrick! I'm near done. Don't waste time pretending otherwise."

His voice was failing and Patrick had to lean over him to hear.

"I will die a contented servant of God and His Church. I want you to know that. I'm at peace with all that I did there. It's with you that I have business now."

"You have always been a good bishop and uncle. There is no need for making peace between us. We have always had it."

"Ah, Patrick. You were always a most loving and trusting sort and I have not been completely honest with you."

The effort to speak was causing him to gasp and Patrick Reilly looked at the two women to see what he should do. But they sat with stone faces, like the angels in the churches, watching life come and go.

"Now, Uncle. Don't be upsetting yourself on my account."

"I am not upset, Patrick. In the box you will find all that you need to understand why I did the things I did. I did what I thought was right and I will meet my maker with that and let Him be the judge."

He fell silent for a while and the priest and the two women sat and waited.

"I've been a most fortunate man," the bishop spoke again, a frail rasping sound. "And I leave life in the company of those I love dearly. I have provided for you all as I think best and ask just one thing of you all." The priest and the two women leaned forward. "Remember," the bishop gasped and struggled for the last time, "remember me kindly."

**

He left instructions for his funeral too. Patrick was to say the mass and lead his uncle to his last resting place in the world. It was an honor that Patrick felt unworthy of but he did his best. Mrs. Power and Mrs. Mawhinney told him he did his uncle proud.

Mrs. Mawhinney even drove him to the airport when it was time for him to return and handed over the old wooden box containing the bishop's papers. "He made sure I had this ready for you, but insisted that you're not to open it until you are good and ready."

"Do you know what he meant by that?"

"I don't," Mrs. Mawhinney laughed, "but then again I was only privy to what His Grace wished to share with me."

Patrick looked at her and, for the first time, could see how much she truly loved the old man.

"What will you do with yourself now?"

"Well, your uncle left money to Mrs. Power and me. Enough to keep us for the rest of our days."

"It's no more than you deserve."

She seemed touched by that and smiled at the young priest. "And will you be okay, Father?"

*

"Sing us a song about Ballyporeen," someone called up to get Frank going. Ronald Reagan had recently gone there to look for his roots and Irish votes.

"Fuck Ballyporeen," Frank dismissed it with a smile, "and all belonging to it. We're going to dedicate this song to Luke Kelly who died earlier this year."

"Who the fuck was Luke Kelly?"

"He was the greatest singer ever to come out of Ireland, ya gobshite. Now shut up while we try to do a really great man some credit."

Jimmy set the beat and Danny strummed along, gently leading in until Frank sang clear and true:

> I must away now, I can no longer tarry
> This morning's tempest I have to cross
> I must be guided without a stumble
> Into the arms I love the most
>
> And when he came to his true love's dwelling
> He knelt down gently upon a stone
> And through her window he's whispered lowly
> Is my true love within at home?
>
> Wake up, wake up love, it is thine own true lover
> Wake up, wake up love, and let me in
> For I am tired love and oh, so weary
> And more than near drenched to the skin
>
> She's raised her off her down soft pillow
> She's raised her up and she's let him in
> And they were locked in each other's arms
> Until that long night was past and gone
>
> And when that long night was past and over
> And when the small clouds began to grow
> He's taken her hand and they've kissed and parted
> Then he saddled and mounted and away did go
>
> I must away now, I can no longer tarry
> This morning's tempest I have to cross
> I must be guided without a stumble
> Into the arms I love the most.

*

And even as the crowd clapped, Deirdre picked up the phone. It was David to tell her that Martin's suffering was finally over. He didn't think that she should call the bar. She should let Danny finish the gig. It's what Martin would have wanted.

*

As she told him, Danny could feel his heart break and all that he had strived to become, fracture. He sat and put his head in his hands, trying to hold on to all that was good in life, but with Martin gone, there was a huge hole inside of him. He tried to be happy that his uncle's suffering was over but he could never forgive the way fate had taken him.

Deirdre took the baby and left him alone—there was nothing else she could do.

By the morning he was done crying, and got himself ready to phone his parents. He wished someone else could have done it but there was no one else. Deirdre sat watching him, clutching little Martin tight.

Jerry answered and Danny was glad for that. His father took the news without too many questions but it was different with his mother. "What kind of hospitals do they have over there? Why didn't you bring him back here where we could have looked after him properly?"

Nothing Danny could say satisfied her and he couldn't tell her the whole truth—at least not over the phone.

"And why wouldn't he want to be buried in Ireland?"

"I don't know, Ma. I'm only telling you what he wanted. He made a will."

"But he can't have been sound in the head when he wrote that. Why else would he be thinking this?"

"He seemed fine when he wrote it."

He had been quite clear about it. He wanted to be cremated and wanted David to take his ashes to the spot they called theirs, a small cabana by a sheltered cove where they often holidayed without David's parents knowing. But Danny kept all of that inside him.

"And I suppose that this means that you're not coming over again this year?"

"Ah, Ma. You know the baby is too young to be going on an airplane but don't worry, we'll all come over next year."

"But you need to be here with me now, to help me through my grief."

There was nothing he could say that would soothe her and in time his father took the phone. He agreed with Danny; they would all see the baby next year when it would be better for everybody.

*

That Christmas Eve, little Martin's first, Danny stood alone on the deck, smoking and looking down on the sad state of the world that he and Deirdre had brought a child into. When he was inside with Deirdre and the baby he had to keep up the act, but he was getting tired.

Since Martin died, he'd get home from a gig and come in as quietly as he could. Deirdre and the baby would be sound asleep. But as soon as he got into bed, just as he was dozing off, the baby would cry out. He tried to keep his promise, rising and fetching the bawling bundle and bringing him to his mother's breast, but some nights he was so tired that Deirdre had to nudge him. And then, an hour before he had to wake, the baby would call again. Some nights, he even dreamed it and woke to find the apartment silent, except for Deirdre's breathing. She seemed to be able to fall asleep at will. She said she had to; otherwise she would never get any rest.

He never told her that it was all becoming too much for him, but being outside was calm and quiet.

What the fuck were you thinking of—bringing a child into a world like this?

"Ah, not you. I thought you only came by when I was wasted?"

What? And leave you to make a totally fucking mess of things. Danny, this life is tearing itself apart. There's fighting and rioting everywhere. And what about all those people that got poisoned over in Bhopal? And the fucking IRA tried to kill Thatcher. This life is no place for a child. What the fuck were you thinking?

"Why don't you just fuck off and pass over or whatever it is you're meant to do."

If you want me to leave just say so. I'm only trying to help you.

"Well that's very kind of you but I don't need your kind of help so please fuck-off and leave me alone."

Danny shook his head and rested his arms on the rail and lit another, softly singing 'Do they know it's Christmas?' as the snow fluttered down and made the lanes and back alleys magical.

Chapter 9 -1985

THE WINDSOR HOUSE HADN'T CHANGED TOO MUCH, except the crowd was younger and the beer was better; McVeigh had brought in Guinness a few years back and served a good pint too. Danny and the lads hadn't played there since Frank and Jimmy had a falling out.

"I hate when Jimmy Carton is here," Frank muttered into his pint. "How the fuck are you supposed to compete with that?"

Both bands split their sets between two floors, doing two sets in each and Danny and the lads were finishing upstairs.

"He'll have done his 'finale set' and they'll be fucking wired. How the fuck are we supposed to top that?"

Jimmy couldn't contain himself. "You could try singing in tune?"

"And you could learn to keep a beat. You're always off."

"It's called syncopation."

"Well stop it. You keep throwing me off. It's hard enough to remember the words with having to wonder when you're going to come in."

"It builds anticipation. It's expressive?"

"What?"

Danny just sat back. It was the same thing every night and he was getting tired of it.

"I like to come in with some panache," Jimmy continued regardless.

"Panache my arse. You sound more like a bull in a china shop."

Danny hardly paid any attention; he had other things on his mind. Deirdre was always putting on makeup, every time she went out. She explained that after looking like a beached whale for so long she just wanted to look pretty again. Only she hesitated before saying pretty.

"It complements your cracked voice. You really have to learn to sing properly one of these days." Jimmy almost made it sound like he was concerned.

Danny hadn't rushed to reassure her and she noticed that. And she turned it around on him. "I'm sorry if I don't look good all the time, but I do have a child and I'm studying."

He should have said something, but he didn't and that just made it worse.

"Fuck you; everybody says that I sound like Luke Kelly."

"Now or when he was alive?"

They hadn't done it since before the baby. In the last few weeks of her pregnancy, she used to get so horny and even get on top of him. But since then—nothing. He knew it was going to be like that so he didn't make a big deal of it and now she was probably thinking that he didn't fancy her anymore. Anto kept telling him that she was probably having it off with one of her study group.

"And what would you know about singing? You sound like Elvis getting a blow job."

"I wouldn't know what that sounds like, but I do know good singing. Just go down and listen to Carton and you'll know what I mean."

"Fuck you too."

Danny hadn't mentioned Anto to anybody. He didn't have to—he knew what was going on. His granny was right; the devil was reaching up for him. It was like Anto was his own Mephistopheles, like in *Dr. Faustus*. He hadn't actually read it. Deirdre did and explained it all to him. They were watching something on the television when she mentioned it. She was always doing that. She always wanted them to talk, only she wanted to talk about smart stuff and Danny didn't know how, so he pretended like he couldn't be bothered.

Anto said that was why she was probably doing it with somebody else. *She probably needs to be with someone who stops grunting when they are not in bed.*

Danny had bristled at that but he knew Deirdre wasn't like that. Sure, they had things to work through just like every other couple. And he had a lot of changes to make but he was going to make it with Deirdre. That's what was really pissing Anto off—that and getting shot in the head. They were just going through a rough patch, just like every other couple.

"And you, ya bollocks," Frank turned on him. "What are you sneering at? You should learn to tune that banjo; it sounds like you're banging a bull's balls together."

Danny looked at him but he had no idea what he was going on about.

"Where's your fucking head, Boyle? You've been all fuckin' broody again lately."

"Are you having problems at home?" Jimmy asked, almost sounding sympathetic.

"No, no. It's nothin' like that. I'm fine. I'm just tired. You know how it is with a baby in the house. It's fuckin' hell."

"Well, I'm glad to hear it's only that," Frank smiled and turned to Jimmy. "Pay up!"

"That's no way to act when a friend is sharing his troubles. It's obvious that the baby is keeping them from . . . you know."

Danny decided to go back to ignoring them and took another swig.

"What's fuckin' eating you?" Frank asked when they got no reaction.

"It's nothin' really, only . . ."

"We're fucked now. Here comes McVeigh."

"Would you ever," Jimmy McVeigh asked with his head slightly tilted, "get back on stage. I'm not paying you to stand around drinking. And try to keep the crowd from leaving."

Frank looked like he was about to say something but probably thought better of it and walked back on stage.

"We're back," he announced and looked around at the crowd, "but before we begin I have an announcement."

Danny and Jimmy followed and slung on their guitars as they waited for the other shoe to fall.

"Jimmy McVeigh needs you all the get shit-faced drunk before you leave."

The crowd roared back in approval but Jimmy McVeigh walked away shaking his head.

"And now, the 'F-an'-DJs' would like to do a song that is currently very high on the charts in Ottawa."

"What's he doing?" Danny mouthed at Jimmy, who just shrugged and waited for Frank to sing:

"When Irish eyes are smiling." He raised his arms like a conductor and led Jimmy and Danny into a very exaggerated waltz.

> Sure, 'tis like the morn in Spring.
> In the lilt of Irish laughter
> You can hear Mulroney sing.
> When Irish hearts are happy,
> All the world seems bright and gay.
> And when Ronnie Reagan's smiling,
> He's gonna blow all the Commies away.

*

Billie walked in just as they began their second last song. She was wearing a black spandex skirt and the type of underwear that Madonna wore with nothing over it. Only Billie wore a jacket, like the ones that bullfighters wore.

When she took it off she nearly impaled the guy she was with—a dorky looking git with parachute pants and a black tee shirt with no sleeves. And arms like a junkie. She leaned forward enough for Danny to see her at her best and blew him a kiss. Her lips were dark and wet looking and her eyes looked so bright in all the dark makeup she had on. She even wiggled a little while her boyfriend was at the bar.

She did it again when they started their last song, and Danny had to turn to hide his bulging behind his guitar.

"What the fuck is he doing now?" Frank asked between verses of *The Irish Rover*—their party piece. They played it with almost enough energy to drown out Jimmy Carton from the floor below. He was singing *The West Awake* and the whole building seemed to be shaking.

"It looks like the Duck Walk—only he makes it look like he's humping the guitar."

*

Danny woke around eleven. Deirdre let him sleep in after gigs and even went out with little Martin to get the papers. She kept him quiet, too, when they got back. She'd keep him on her lap while she read the paper aloud but soft enough so as not to wake Danny.

He lay on his back and thought of Billie. She was just fucking with him—showing up like that—and carrying on like that. She left before he got a chance to talk with her but he knew what she was up to. Stuff like that was always happening to Frank and Jimmy, only they weren't married.

He wanted to roll over but he had to get up; he had promised Deirdre that he'd call his mother. He hadn't called her since Christmas. He made all kinds of excuses—that's she'd still be going on about his uncle and why he wasn't buried in Ireland but the truth was, he just didn't want to have to deal with her right now.

He felt guilty about that and every time he held little Martin and stared into his eyes, he had to look away. Little Martin trusted him and so did Deirdre. The problem was that he couldn't ever really trust himself. He never let on, though, and went on like everything was great. Deirdre seemed to sense that and said she thought he might be bottling things up inside him, but he just laughed. "I'm fine," he insisted. "In fact I'm better than fine. I'm the luckiest man in the world."

That always seemed to work and she'd stop bugging him. It was, however, one of the things he was beginning to dislike about her—she was always trying to get him to change. When Billie used to do it, she made it all seem like an adventure, but with Deirdre it was different. It was like she was a school teacher. She had even started to tell him that he should go back to school too. He could do it part-time. And where the fuck would he get the time? He was already killing himself, working night and day. But he had known it was going to be like that and didn't feel right complaining. It was his job to go to work and provide for them. But with Deirdre finishing her degree and little Martin going to daycare, he felt he was the only person not learning anything.

Maybe that was it. Maybe she was getting embarrassed by him—in front of all her university friends.

*

"Well! It's about time you called. I've been worried sick that you'd caught whatever it was that took my poor Martin."

Danny made a face while Deirdre balanced little Martin on her hip and went into the bedroom so Danny could have some privacy. With the baby, the apartment was beginning to feel so small.

"Well I'm calling now. Besides, you could have called me."

"Listen to yourself. We're not made of money over here, you know."

"Well they don't give it out free here either."

His mother seemed to sense his mood and changed tack. "Well, you're phoning now. I know you'd never turn your back on your own mother. And how's Deirdre—and the baby?"

"They're both fine. Martin is starting to walk only he falls over a lot, but he should be able to get around by the time we come over."

"It'll be great to see you again son; it really gives me something to look forward to."

For a moment Danny felt she was trying to turn things on him again. Deirdre said that she did that. She felt that Danny had to stand up to her more—for both their sakes. He wasn't doing his mother any good either.

"So? Any news on your end?"

"They made a big fuss over that Bob Geldof down in the Mansion House. That could have been you, ya know, if you hadn't gone running off to Canada."

She was doing that again. Twisting everything around on him and forgetting what really happened.

"How's Da's business coming along?"

"Mister big-shot? Don't be asking me; he never tells me anything."

"Is it raining there?" She always got like this when it rained.

"It's always raining around here, Danny, only I'm sure it will be fine for when you come over."

"With my luck?"

"Danny? Can I ask you something?"

"What?"

"Did you do it?"

"Do what?"

"Did you burn up what was left of Martin?"

"Ah, Ma. Don't be bringing all that up again. He was cremated—just like he said in his will."

"I know that, but what happened what was left of him?"

David had taken his ashes to spread on the sands around the cabana. Danny had promised David that he would go and visit it, as soon as he got the chance. They held a celebration for him, too, on Valentine's Day. Deirdre was busy with the baby so Danny went on his own. He didn't mind being around gays anymore.

"He had his girlfriend spread them on the beach where they met."

"Is she white at least?"

"She is, Ma. You would've liked her." He lied but there was no point telling the truth—there never was.

"We'll never know, now, will we?"

"Well," Danny searched for something to lighten the mood. She was dragging him back to the days when he and his granny used to visit the hospital. "We know you're going to love little Martin."

"I will, but I'll never be able to hear his name without thinking of my brother."

"That's the way Martin would have wanted it. It was his idea to name the baby after him," he lied again.

"That was the way he was his whole life—always thinking of others."

*

"So? How is your mother?" Deirdre emerged from the room as he hung up.

He wished she hadn't asked. He wanted a bit of time to himself to come back from the places his mother had taken him to. It was always like that when he phoned. She always made him feel like he'd run away and deserted everything. "Morose, but she's happiest that way."

"Danny, you really shouldn't let her get to you anymore. I know she can't help it, but she can be very negative." She balanced the baby on her hip as she kissed him. "Now," she handed little Martin over, "please look after this lump for a few hours while I catch up with my study partners."

"Ah, Deirdre. I'm working again tonight. I was hoping to take a nap."

"You can take a nap when he does. Maybe you can take him for a walk first? That always tires him out."

She kissed the pair of them and gathered her papers and things. "I won't be long."

"Deirdre," Danny asked as she got to the door, "do you ever get ashamed of me?"

"Oh, Danny, not now. I'm already late. You always get like this after you talk with your mother."

"Yeah, but do you?"

She assured him she didn't and rushed off leaving Danny holding his son, who was watching him closely.

"What are you looking at?"

Little Martin made some sound and poked at Danny's face with his tiny fingers.

"I suppose you'll grow up to be ashamed of me too?" But he made it sound like a joke and little Martin laughed along with him.

*

There were three of them in the study group: Deirdre; Jean, who Deirdre suspected was lesbian; and Edward.

His real name was Eduardo but he wanted to hide his ethnicity. Sometimes he seemed to forget himself and called her 'Dee,' like they were so much closer. When she pulled him up on it, he'd get flustered and said that he had difficulty saying her name properly.

"Deer-dra," she'd correct him.

"Dee-dree," he'd say, no matter how often she pronounced it for him.

He was alone when she got there. Jean had called him to tell him she couldn't come. She'd tried to reach Deirdre but her phone was busy.

"So what are we supposed to do now?"

"You could stay . . . and have a coffee with me."

"Eduardo, you know I am married with a child?"

"I do. That's why I thought you might want to take a little rest from all that for a while. It's only coffee and I promise—I will behave like a gentleman."

"Do they have those where you come from?" she laughed and flopped into the chair beside him. She hadn't taken time for herself in so long.

"According to my father, we invented that too."

"Oh, dear. Did I hit a nerve?"

"We Portuguese are so proud that we do not get upset by little things like that."

"So what do you get upset about?"

"Amor. In Lisbon we say that you can leave your house unlocked, but you cannot leave your love alone."

*

"And did you know?" Patrick was almost rude. The whole thing was too incredible to believe.

Giovanni shrugged and looked trapped. "I knew, but nobody else did. Except . . ."

"And you didn't think to tell me?"

"What was I going to do? Welcome you into my café and tell you that your uncle was once in love with my sister?"

It was even more incredible when someone else said it. Patrick had to sit.

"Yes, that's it. Sit down and we will drink some coffee, okay?"

"Yes, yes, whatever." Patrick was waiting until his whole world stopped spinning around the rotunda.

Giovanni beckoned to someone behind the bar and a tray emerged with coffees and small glasses of Irish whiskey. "We will drink a toast to a good man."

He waited until Patrick raised his.

"Your uncle was a young man back then. And sometimes, even the purest of young men can fall in love. It was very hard on my sister too. She didn't want it to happen either. They were young and she was working here. He used to come in and she would bring him his coffee. There was never any harm in that.

"Then one day she came to me and asked me to bring it instead. She didn't have to tell me why—I could see. And then when I brought out the coffee, your uncle could tell that I knew. I think that was when he realized that he was in love too."

He made it all sound so reasonable—like a Fellini story—but Patrick's world was still spinning.

"They never did anything they had to feel shame for. Your uncle stopped coming until my sister left, and then he asked if he was still welcome. He was a gentleman as well as a good priest. Don't ever think anything else about him." But Patrick couldn't help it.

He had found a photo of her on the top of a pile of hand-written letters that had never been posted. She was standing before the rotunda. She was very pretty but even Patrick could see she was shy. His uncle had written something on the back too. It read 'Benedetta, summer of 1937.'

The letters were all dated, too. Mostly from 1938 to 1965—a few years before Patrick was ordained. There were a few after that and the last one was written while he was ill. Patrick hadn't read them yet. He was still in shock.

"Patrick. Your uncle was a man, too, and every man has to fall in love at least once—even a priest."

Patrick said nothing lest he betray his own transgression, but he did nod his head.

"Patrick, your uncle was a priest—a good one, too, and he did what was right and proper for everybody. There was no shame then and there should be no shame now."

He beckoned again for whiskey even though Patrick was still sipping his.

"About ten years ago," Giovanni continued, leaning closer to Patrick so no one else could hear, "he was here, on business in the Vatican, and he came by one afternoon. We got to talking and do you know what he told me? He told me all about you and said that you would be by someday. He said I was to look after you like family. Even though he stayed a priest he will always be a part of my family. And so are you."

He drained his glass and rose to leave. He stopped to put his hand on Patrick's round shoulder. "There was no shame, Patrick. Always remember that."

Patrick nodded again and sipped the rest of his whiskey—the first one.

"Can I ask you something?" He looked up into the old man's kind face.

"Anything."

"What happened to your sister?"

"Benedetta? She went away to school for a few years after the war, but she never married."

"Is she still . . .?"

"Yes, yes. She's still alive. She comes to visit sometimes. Perhaps you would like to meet her?"

"I'm not sure. Wouldn't it be strange?"

Giovanni just laughed and walked back inside. "Everything in life is strange," he called back.

*

There was a single tall candle on the kitchen counter when Danny got home. Their bedroom door was slightly open and another candle flickered inside. He had put down his gear and was headed toward the fridge when she called out. "Danny?"

He pushed the bedroom door a little wider but didn't walk in. She didn't like him to see her naked since the baby.

"Oh, Danny?"

She was lying back against the pillows. She was wearing black stockings and a garter belt. She was also wearing one of those bustiers, like Madonna wore—a leopard one. And she had all kinds of makeup on, far more than when she went out with her friends.

She raised her leg so he could see the long black seam that went all the way back down.

"Do you like what you see, Danny boy?"

He was about to say 'fucking-right,' but thought better of it. He stripped to his waist and lay beside her, softly stroking her leg, right up to the garter belt. She looked like one of the women in Penthouse. He kept a copy in the bathroom, wedged between the wall and the toilet. He leaned forward and kissed her. "I love you."

He kept repeating it as she rolled him over and straddled him—just like the way he'd imagined the girls of *Penthouse* did. She even let her hair run along his chest as she pulled his pants down. She started running her mouth down the sides of his belly, but his erection kept getting in the way.

She didn't seem to mind so he lay back and hoped that she was going to do it.

She did, a little, before she sat up and placed him up inside her. She let out a long gasp as he slid all the way in.

"Oh, Danny! Yes, yes. Give it to me." She even ran her hand through her hair and arched her back. Only when she turned toward him again—she looked more like Billie.

"Oh, Danny. More, more, oh, E . . . Danny."

He might have commented but he was gritting his teeth and trying to hold on. She was going mad on him and he never wanted it to end.

But it did. Loudly, too, and woke little Martin. Deirdre got up to get him, wrapping herself in her bathrobe as she went. The same bathrobe she had worn all the time when the baby was born.

*

She felt weird, cradling the baby while she still reeked of sex.

Little Martin didn't seem to mind and turned his head toward her breast. She moved him away and tightened her robe. She had a tough time weaning him. It was mostly her fault; she didn't want to give up that bond.

When she finally got back to her bed, Danny was fast asleep, but she didn't really mind. She kissed the side of his sleeping face.

She was a little ashamed of herself too. It just happened. One minute she was making her husband happy for the first time since . . . and then he popped into her mind.

Only in her mind he sat forward and took her breasts between his big soft lips.

She wondered what Danny would say if he knew. Not that she was going to tell him.

And she couldn't talk to Eduardo about it, though she did imagine that he would just smile if she did. He never actually tried to do anything when he was with her, except with his eyes. She could see the two of them in his reflections, in Portugal, standing on the edge of a cliff as the sun settled into the ocean.

She certainly wouldn't be telling Jean either. At the university, all of her friends had had sex with more than one person. It was one of the things they talked about when they went for drinks—and stayed too long. A lot of times they went wherever Danny was playing and she always found it weird to be having conversations like that while he was in the same room even though he couldn't hear.

And, as the evening went on, some of the women would fall 'in love' with him and some of them were bad at hiding it. It was his accent; they told her they all found it so erotic. And that Danny was really cute, in an artsy way.

That always made her smile. It reminded her of the day in the Dandelion—when she had gone to say she was sorry. She didn't fall in love with him then, but she did get to see him as he might be.

Sometimes, she wondered if she wasn't taking some of that from him. He was doing his best to keep the promises he made when little Martin was born, but she could tell—it was getting harder and harder.

She didn't help, sometimes, when she made suggestions about what he should do. Danny Boyle was never really cut out to be a family man. Her father used to say that he had 'too much alley cat in him,' but she was going to change all of that. After she graduated, she'd get a good job and he could just work on his music all the time. She could even let him build a recording studio in the basement after they got a nice house somewhere. He could even have Frank and Jimmy over as long as they didn't toke up. At least not inside—it wouldn't be right with little Martin.

They would get there. They just had to make a point of making time for themselves as a couple. She didn't need anybody else. She had someone to love—someone who would give up so much for her.

She would make it all up to him. She'd be the best wife he could hope for, even if she noticed other people. There was no real harm in that. He probably did it too.

She kissed him again and turned over to fall asleep, almost face to face with an image of Eduardo.

*

"Ah, son, it's great to hear your voice. Tell me, what time is it over there?"

"It's five hours earlier than it is there."

"Well that doesn't help. I was just having a lie-down on the couch when you phoned. I can't find my glasses and I can't read the clock. It's one of those with the numbers on them. At least with the old ones, you could always tell where the hands were."

"It's almost midday."

"There or here?"

"Are you pissed or what?"

"Pissed? Me? No. Who can afford to be getting pissed these days? Did you see the thing that y'er man Geldof did over in Hyde Park. It was brilliant, though some of the music was shite. They're saying that Ireland gave more per capita than anybody else. It makes you proud, eh son?"

"As a feckin' peacock."

"And did you hear about the Virgin Mary? They're saying you can see her in a grotto down in Ballinspittle. I bet you don't have that yet in Canada?"

"Listen. How's Ma? Has she gotten over us not coming?"

"You know your mother, but I told her it was for the better. After what happened that Indian jet—you can't be too safe. They're still finding bits of it.

"Did you see, too, that they found the Titanic? You're better off staying at home until the baby is born."

Danny waited for him to finish but he was glad he answered; his mother was still pissed about them cancelling their plans. They had to. It was a shock to them too. Deirdre said she was sure it couldn't happen but she didn't seem that upset by it.

"Why don't you and Ma come over here next year—when we have a house."

"I'm game for it, but I'm not sure about your mother. She's not great on airplanes."

"How was your trip to the Costa Del Sol?"

"It was brilliant, son. Just brilliant. Sitting in the sun, drinking good cheap brandies and eating like kings."

"You liked the food there?"

"Of course we did. We found a nice little English pub and they did the best fish and chips. Only everybody was still talking about what happened in Heysel. It was a sad day for Liverpool."

"I thought it was the Italians who were killed."

"It was, but it was still a sad day for Liverpool."

Chapter 10 -1986

IF WE GET TEN THOUSAND FROM YOUR PARENTS, five thousand from mine, plus the two we have in savings, we can do it." They were sitting by the kitchen counter as little Martin sat in front of the Saturday morning cartoons. It was the only way they could have a chance to talk in peace.

"I don't know. My parents don't have that kind of money."

"They do now. Your mother told me that your father just sold the houses they had in Rathgar."

"I know, but that money is tied up in the business. I wouldn't feel right asking for it."

"Danny. You signed over the house when they needed it. Now we are just asking them to return the favor. They won't mind."

"I don't know. Couldn't we just ask your parents for more?"

"My parents don't have any more." Deirdre looked exasperated but it might have been the baby. She was much bigger than she was with Martin and her face was almost round.

"But even if we get it, we still can't afford a mortgage. I just don't make enough."

Deirdre rechecked the figures she had scribbled on the pad. "Of course we can. It will be tight for a year or so but we'll manage. I'll finished studying by the end of the summer if this one," she patted her huge belly, "lets me; then I'll get a job too."

Danny sipped his coffee but he couldn't see it. "But what about daycare? Having both of them in will kill us."

"Martin will be starting school soon so we'll save on that. You'll see."

"I don't know, Deirdre. Frank was just telling me that it's getting harder and harder to get gigs. No one is going to bars anymore."

"Danny, it's almost March; it's the annual dress-in-green-and-get-foolish-and-tell-everybody-you're-Irish time. You guys always make lots of money around St. Patrick's Day."

"Yeah, but what will we do when it's gone? We'll have nothing left over for going out or anything."

"Danny. We have a toddler and another on the way—how often did you think we would be able to go out? And, if you were to go to night school you could learn about computers. Everybody says there will be a shortage of computer people. You could even start applying for promotions."

"What do I know about computers? I need to take my socks off to count to twenty."

"Danny, don't run yourself down. You're a lot smarter than you give yourself credit for. Besides, you'd be doing it for the kids."

"I don't know."

"And that's why you need to go back to school—so you can learn."

He didn't like it when she did that even though it was the only way things were getting done. He had kind of let her take over their finances after he had hidden a bit for himself—to do his own stuff. He felt bad about it but he still had to be a guy—for a while yet.

*

"Are you gonna buy it or not?"

"I don't know."

"Fuck's sake, Danny." Frank looked exasperated. "I've already told him you'd let him know today. He won't hold it forever."

Danny wanted it. It was a great car and the price was right. It was a '76 Chevy Bel Air station wagon with the 400 four-barrel V8. Danny wasn't really sure what that meant but it would be perfect. It was big, just what he wanted for when his parents came over. "It's important to show them how well you're doing over here. Otherwise there was no point to any of it," Frank had advised him as soon as he heard. And it would be perfect for driving the family around. He'd pull Deirdre close to him on the front bench as they wheeled along with the kids in the back seats going to the zoo and places like that.

It would be great for the band's gear too. They had been using Frank's van but it only had two seats and that always caused problems.

"Fuck it. Tell him I'll take it." Danny had stashed almost a grand, and Frank was loaning him the rest without Deirdre knowing. He needed that car. Only how was he going to explain it?

"But if Deirdre asks, tell her that I'm getting it cheaper."

"I will in my bollocks. I'm not getting into the middle of your domestic problems."

"I don't have domestic problems."

"Course you do. Everybody who gets married and has kids gets them."

*

"It's very big. Are you sure we can afford it?"

"But I got it for next to nothing."

"I hope you didn't dip into the house money."

"Of course I didn't. Besides, he's going to take it in payments."

"Danny? Don't you think we should have talked about it first?"

"I would have but I had to snap it up. There were a bunch of people who wanted it." Danny lied, but 'talking about things' just meant Deirdre telling him what they were going to do.

They never got to do the stuff he wanted. "Besides," he continued, "it will be great when my parents come over."

"But it isn't in the budget."

"I know, but you're always talking about elasticity. We can make it work. You always know how. C'mon, let's take Martin for a spin."

"Not until you get a child-seat."

"Oh, yeah. Where do you get those?"

"Canadian Tire."

So Danny spent the first of many Saturdays in Canadian Tire, with all the other married men, walking down every isle. Some of them even pushed carts while they browsed the tools and things that turned ordinary guys into fathers.

*

"Are you sure you know how to drive this thing?" Jerry lit a smoke and looked doubtful. "It's as big as a boat."

Jacinta lowered her sun glasses. "It's very shiny." She fanned herself as Danny climbed in, unlocked the doors and opened the windows.

"It's a bit hot but I'll turn on the A/C as soon as we're in." Danny beamed as he got back out and loaded their luggage in the rear. He settled his mother in the backseat as his father got into the passenger seat and fumbled with his seat belt. He had been drinking the whole flight over and his breath was whiskey sour. And tobacco-y.

"All right?" Danny sat in beside him and smiled broadly as he cranked and cranked once more.

"Does it not work properly?" Jerry asked with just a whisper of a sneer.

"Of course it does; it's just a bit hot." Danny cranked a few more times until the engine caught and began rumbling all the way through the car. "That's the problem with the 400, four-barrel V8, it's a bit sluggish but she's great after that." He wiped his sweat on his sleeve as he turned and backed out carefully. It was the one thing he still hadn't gotten the hang of.

He could handle it out on the road but getting in and out of parking spaces was a bitch. He'd already had a few dings and Deirdre was getting pissed. "We could have gotten something smaller but you just had to get something ridiculous." But it was all very well for her to complain—she had no intention of getting her license. She didn't have the time.

When he was as close as he dared to the cars behind, he began to roll forward, almost straight to the cars in front.

"I think you need to pull on the wheel a bit," his father offered when they had gone directly back and forth a few times.

"Maybe your Daddy could get out and give you some help. It must be so hard with a car like this." She watched him as his face fell and added: "Go on, Jerry. Help him."

Even with Jerry acting like he was on the deck of an aircraft carrier, twirling his arms to urge Danny to turn the wheel more, it took a few more goes.

"That's the problem with owning one of these babies." Danny patted the dashboard as they finally drove away. "But wait 'til you see her out on the highway. She was built for that."

He went into the ramp too fast and had to swerve to make the turn, almost pinning Jerry against the far door, still fumbling with his seatbelt buckle.

"Christ, son. Slow down or you'll have us all dead."

"It's all right," Danny assured him in the most offhanded way he could. "It's power steering, you know? It's power everything." He flicked the locks and raised all the windows together as he accelerated away, out of the airport. "Feel this," he floored it and the car sprung forward. "That's the 400, four-barrel V8."

"Jazus, son. Would you ever slow down a bit? You'll give your mother a heart attack."

"Don't be worrying about me," Jacinta corrected her husband. "Danny's just proud of how well he is doing. You should be proud of him, too."

"I am. I'm just hoping that I can go on being proud of him and not end up splattered across the motorway."

"Well, I feel like the queen back here. This is almost as nice as the cars at your granny's funeral."

Jerry slouched a bit and nodded. "She's very powerful—I'll say that for her. What's she get to the gallon?"

"Don't ask." Danny gritted his teeth a little. He knew what his mother had done. He was glad she was on his side but sometimes, when she started in on his father—she could get very dark. He squealed into another ramp before he applied the brakes.

"Jazus, son. You don't want to brake in the corners. You want to brake before and then power your way into them."

"I told you, it has power steering." He twirled the wheel a little, causing the car to wobble in its lane coming far too close to the wheels of the truck beside them.

"It's lovely and sunny, isn't it Jerry?" Jacinta mused like she was oblivious.

The sun baked down as the 427 straightened out and headed directly south. Danny wanted to take them along the Gardiner, the elevated highway that ran right along the lakeshore, gleaming banks on one side and the sparkling lake on the other.

"Tell me, son. Did it take you long to get the hang of all this?" Jerry was holding on for dear life as traffic merged and parted all around—an almost synchronized ballet at over a mile a minute. "'Cos I don't think I would be able to handle it."

"Ah, you get used to it." Danny smiled over at him with just one hand on the wheel. "So? What's the news from home?"

"You heard that Thin Lizzy died?"

"I heard about Phil Lynott, but I didn't know about the rest of them."

Jerry ignored that and continued. "Jackie Charlton is managing Ireland now. Did you ever think you'd live to see the day?"

"It's all going to the dogs back there," Jacinta sniffed. "They'll all be getting divorced by the time we get home."

"Do you think it will pass?"

"In Ireland? No chance." Jerry was sure of it.

"What would you know about divorce? Maybe I'll give you a divorce and that will learn you."

"Are you kidding me? Now that we have an airport in Knock, the pope will be flying in for weekends. And," Jerry was enjoying himself, "we got pandas now—up in the zoo. I bet you don't have those over here yet?"

"Did you go to see them or did you just walk around outside?"

"Jazus son," Jerry looked away at the lake. "Are you never going to let it go?"

"Is that the lake you were telling us about?" Jacinta piped up from the back to ease the tension.

"Yes, that's Lake Ontario," Jerry cut in before Danny could answer. "It's one of the Great Lakes and that," he pointed ahead, "is the CN Tower. Amn't I right?"

"Of course you are, Jerry. He's," she added to Danny's eyes in the rear view mirror, "been studying up on Canada."

"I just like to know something about the places I'm going— that's all."

"Is it far to your house?" Jacinta tried again. "I can't wait to see my grandchildren. Is the little man getting used to his sister yet?"

Danny checked her in the rear view mirror as he headed down to the DVP, down into the ravine where they would climb back up toward the Bloor Viaduct. "He's great. He's always helping Deirdre out and he keeps asking when he can play with Grainne."

"Ah, God love him. I'm sure he's going to be the best big brother of all time."

"Are we out of the city already?" Jerry asked when they drove along Bayview and turned and climbed up Pottery Road.

"Not at all. This is just a ravine. It runs right through the city. Our house is up on the other side."

"And here," he added a few minutes later, "is Chester Hill. This is where we live."

It was a semi, with a front porch, on a nice tree-lined avenue. Deirdre had hung some potted plants but Danny hadn't gotten around to getting after Frank to move the lumber and other materials. He had been helping them renovate.

Deirdre came out as they pulled into the driveway, with the baby in her arms and little Martin by her side. He got a bit shy in the fuss but Grainne just slept through it all. Jacinta said that it could be a sign of something as she followed Deirdre into the mostly finished kitchen, but wasn't sure what.

"It's a bit of a mess," Deirdre apologized. "As you can see we are having work done. Work that was supposed to be finished by now." She glared back at Danny, who had little Martin on his shoulder, shyly peeping back at the funny faces his grandfather was making.

"The hens are clucking already." Jerry winked and little Martin began to laugh.

*

They all went to Niagara Falls where Danny dangled little Martin over the rail for a picture. He wanted to do the same thing at the CN Tower until his father told him to cop-on. Deirdre could see that stung but she didn't want to step between them. Danny and his father hadn't been right since they got out of the car. She was sad about that. Danny had been looking forward to showing his father around. So when they went to the zoo, Deirdre stayed at home with the baby. She felt it was too hot and too much walking, and she'd have to feed Grainne anyway. It was better if they went without her.

She was hoping that Jacinta would agree and stay with her—just to give Danny another chance with his father. She had told him he should try to resolve it—for little Martin's sake.

"Nonsense." Jacinta had surprised her. "Martin has been telling me all about the gorilla they have there. He was trying to convince me that he could talk with him so I told him I had to see that and I couldn't let him down now?"

"No," Deirdre agreed, and hid her disappointment. She'd been hoping that Jacinta wouldn't mind looking after Grainne for a little while. She really had to find some time to spend on her thesis.

So instead, she stayed at home and hoped they weren't smoking in the car. She had made it clear to all of them—she couldn't have smoke around her children.

Jerry and Jacinta were a little put out at first, but they got used to it. Danny had cleared the part of the back deck that was finished and set up lawn chairs and a little table to put their drinks on. They spent most of the evenings outside. Frank came over a few times and charmed Jacinta right out of her seat. He and Danny would take out the guitars and sing softly as the evening darkened. He knew all of her favorites and in time she began to treat him like her own son. They went out to hear the band a few times, too, and Jacinta came home like she'd been back stage at a concert.

Jerry didn't seem to notice, or if he did he didn't care. He was locked into some type of head game with Danny. It really came out when they were drinking. Danny would make snide remarks about the way Jerry had been when he was a child, so Jerry was striking back through Martin, getting his attention and dividing his loyalties. They made it all sound like they were just slagging each other, but Deirdre knew better. She'd tried cornering Danny about it but he made out like she was misreading it. They were just having a bit of crack and that there was no problem.

"If either you or your brother," she teased Grainne as she wiped her off and changed her diaper, "ever behave toward your father like that . . ."

She looked into her daughter's eyes. They were so different from Martin's. When she first held him, after he was born, he looked up at her and seemed to smile. Grainne was so different. She came out kicking and screaming, tearing as she came. Sometimes, Deirdre resented her for that.

She kept telling herself it was just the baby blues, but she could never shake the feeling that she would never be as close to her daughter as she was with her son. Still, she picked her up and held her to her breast and carried her to her bed. She placed her down, exactly as she had done with Martin, only Grainne squirmed a lot more.

And, when she realized she was being put down, cried and cried until Deirdre went against all that she read about and just gave in. She picked Grainne up and carried her to her own bed. She propped Danny's pillows on one side and lay on the other. She stroked her daughter's flustered head and soothed until they both fell asleep in the cool shade of a hot, humid afternoon.

A few hours later, the phone startled her. It was Danny saying that they were going to stop at McDonald's and not to worry about making supper.

Deirdre reminded him that they had talked about McDonald's—that it wasn't what they wanted Martin to get used to. Danny agreed but said that his father had mentioned it so often that Martin had his heart set on it now.

"So? Did you all have a nice day?" She decided to let it go. The visit was not going the way Danny had hoped. His mother kept complaining she was too hot or too cold when they turned on the A/C. They just had a few window units that Danny had gotten for a great price at Canadian Tire. He said they had to have them in before his parents came over.

And it was worse with his father. They were at each other all the time, while little Martin looked on. But there was nothing she could do. She had her hands full with Jacinta, who seemed to disagree with the way she did everything. She was never direct about it, though, preferring instead to offer sympathies and advice. She said that she didn't want to interfere, only she was concerned for them all. She said she knew how hard it could be to be starting a family—especially so far from home.

She also said that she thought it was time for them to start thinking about coming back to Ireland, now that all the fuss had died down. Canada was all very nice and clean and all that, but were she and Danny serious about raising her grand-children here? She was worried about Danny too. She said he looked so worn out, "but then again he was the one that was having to work night and day."

Deirdre couldn't help it and reacted. She told her mother-in-law that she was going to get a job in the autumn but that just made things worse. Jacinta was horrified that her grand-children would have to spend their days with strangers while their parents worked.

She was on at Danny about it too: that they should forget about it all and come back to Ireland. She'd be more than happy to mind the babies if Deirdre had to go out to work.

*

"So, sweetie? Did you have a wonderful time at the zoo with Granny and Granddad?"

Little Martin ran through the litanies of all that they had seen and done as she knelt down and held him tight. But when he finished, he wanted to sit outside with his grandfather, who had already lit up and was drinking a beer.

"And how's the little one?" Jacinta asked before she followed. "Did my two favorite girls have a nice day together?"

"Just one more week," Danny whispered, and brushed her hand with his before going out to make his mother comfortable.

Deirdre stood in the middle of her almost-remodeled kitchen, staring at her reflection in the darkening patio door and the flicker and flare of candles and cigarettes outside. She couldn't join them. She was still breast-feeding and didn't want to drink—and she couldn't tolerate the smell of smoke.

So she busied herself tiding up the kitchen, forgetting once more that the hot and cold taps were reversed. A friend of Frank's had done the plumbing—when he wasn't rummaging through the fridge for cold beers. He was to come back and fix 'a few little things' but he hadn't.

It was starting to get to her. Some of the doors were sticking and the shower still hadn't been tiled. Danny had taped plastic to the walls but it had become mottled with water and soap stains.

And the basement was leaking—something they only discovered during a recent thunderstorm.

They needed far more money than she had allowed. Frank had tried to warn them, but Deirdre was adamant. She regretted it now. They should have taken it a bit slower.

She would have to get a job after the summer. It was the only way forward but as it drew closer, she had to be honest— she wasn't ready to leave her babies.

Sure, she would find the best daycare, but it was a lot more than that. It was the end of that special time she had with them. It was hard enough leaving Martin for the few hours a day she had taken to finish her degree, but this was different. Everything would be different. They would have to rush out in the mornings, scrambling to drop the kids off while hoping they could still make it to work on time. That was how their neighbors, Cathy and Dave, had been living for the last few years. Cathy only got to see her kids for a few hours each night. And Dave saw them on the weekends while Cathy did the shopping and the housework. What had she gotten herself and Danny into?

She looked at the patio door again when little Martin laughed at something, but she hardly noticed as she only saw her own bloated shape, hulking in her half-finished kitchen.

*

"And one day," Jerry continued with little Martin on his knee, enthralled by every word, "King Conchobar was invited to the house of Culann, the most famous blacksmith in all the land. And on the way over, Conchobar went by the field where Sétanta was playing hurling with his mates.

"'I want you to come with me,' the King told him, but Sétanta wanted to finish the game first.

"'Very well,' said the King, who was very fond of the little boy like he was his very own grandson." He gave little Martin a squeeze.

"Anyway, after he got to Culann's house, he began to have a few drinks and when Culann told him he was going to let his ferocious dog out—to protect them, because in those days, you never knew who'd be hanging around—the King forgot all about little Sétanta. 'Let loose the hound and let's have another song,' he called and they all started singing and playing the finest music that ever was heard."

"Was it like the music my daddy and Uncle Frank play?"

"The very same. Anyway, when Sétanta had finished the game he came up to Culann's house and do you know what he met there?"

"The big dog?"

"The very same. You know, you are a very smart boy. Anyway, as soon as the dog saw Sétanta he came roaring forward with his teeth gnashing and snarling."

"He didn't bite Sétanta, did he Granddad?"

"Not a bit of it. As he came running forward, do you know what Sétanta did? He had his Hurley stick with him—and his *sliotar*. So he throws the *sliotar* up and whacks it straight at the dog. It went right into his big gaping mouth and got stuck in his throat and he fell down dead."

Little Martin's eyes grew moist but Jerry was ready for him. "'What am I going to do now?' Culann asked the King. 'That was the best dog I ever had. How will I ever find another to replace it?'

"And before the King and the Druid, and all the warriors, could say anything, Sétanta stepped before them all. 'I'll get you a new dog,' says he and him only up to their waists. 'And I'll train him myself.'

"But Culann was still very sad. 'Who's going to guard my house and lands until the dog is big enough?' he asked and everyone nodded and looked around at each other.

"'I'll do it,' says Sétanta, 'until the new dog is ready.'

"And he did too, as good as any dog. And from that day to this, he has gone by the name Cú Chulainn. And do you know what that means?"

Little Martin shook his head.

"It means the Hound of Culann."

*

"Did you have to tell him all that?" Danny asked after Deirdre had taken little Martin off to bed. "He'll be having nightmares now."

"Ah, Danny. What harm can there be?" Jacinta sipped her drink and eyed her son and her husband. They were going to get into it again.

"I just don't want anybody filling his head with nonsense."

"What's the matter? Are you afraid that he might want to grow up to be really Irish?"

Danny eyed his father coldly. "That's not what I'm afraid of."

"Well what is it then?" Jerry asked, ignoring Jacinta's efforts to shake him off.

Danny mulled it over in his mind. He resented the way his father was insinuating himself into little Martin's life.

"Figure it out for yourself—just like the way I had to."

"Oh, you're not still going on about that?"

"No. I just don't think that you should be acting the way you are."

"Look, son. I know I wasn't a good father, but can I not try to be a good grandfather?"

"Is that what you trying to be?"

"You know," Jacinta spoke up before Jerry could answer, "there is no need for all of this carry-on. What's done is done and now we should be happy that we all got this far. Besides, your father didn't mean any harm."

"Oh really?"

"Yes, Danny. Your father has some great news for you. He wants you to move back and join him and Donal in the company. Isn't that right, Jerry?"

"Well, I was going to, but . . ."

"But nothing. You know it's the right and proper thing to do. We can't have Danny and Deirdre struggling over here while we're doing so well back at home."

"Who's doing well? Everybody I talk to tells me that people are pouring out of the country."

"Well," Jerry responded, lit another cigarette, and got ready to talk like he was giving a speech. "Things are bad for a lot of people but there's money to be made if you know how. The European Act will happen sooner or later and we'll all be better off. You can see it already. The rich are getting richer but me and your Uncle Donal know how to get rich off them. Dublin is getting full of yuppies and we know how to fix up houses the way they like."

"And what would I be doing?"

"Well, you'd have to learn from Donal and me at first, but then you could be a partner."

"I'd have to learn from Donal and you?"

"It would be grand for you and Deirdre and I could help mind the children," Jacinta added, as if to seal the deal.

"I don't know. I'd need to think about it—and I'd have to talk it over with Deirdre."

Jacinta looked at him and shook her head. "And here was me thinking you'd be delighted."

"Ah, leave him alone. If he doesn't want to, it's no skin off my nose. Maybe he's happier over here now. Living like this."

"But you will think about it?" Jacinta urged Danny again.

"And I'll keep the position open until you get a proper chance to think about it."

Danny stared his father in the eye. He looked like he wanted Danny to take the offer, but Danny couldn't be sure. Jerry had let him down so many times before.

*

"What do you think?" Danny asked after he had relayed it all to Deirdre. She had fallen asleep with Martin and now sat on their bed looking confused. "I don't know, Danny. How do you feel?"

"It sounds grand, but you know my father. He fucks up everything sooner or later. Besides, I don't want to go back there. You know what it's like there—everybody looking at you and whispering about you behind your back. Remember what it was like after the night in the church?"

"Oh don't remind me—only we wouldn't have to struggle so much. It could be better for the kids."

"Are you joking me? Bringing them up with priests and nuns telling them all the things that they shouldn't be doing, and heaven and hell and all that shite. You don't want that for our kids, do you?"

"Of course not, Danny."

"Then we'll stick it out here and make our own lives. Right?"

Deirdre hesitated.

"You do have faith in me, don't you, Dee?"

*

"Well, son. We had a great time, thanks very much. And remember, if you ever change your mind . . ."

"Don't forget the other thing," Jacinta reminded him as she kissed Deirdre and the babies one last time.

"Right," Jerry hugged Danny once more and slipped him an envelope. "There's a few bob in there to help you finish the house."

*

"Thank Christ that's over." Danny almost laughed as they drove away. He reached for his cigarettes and found the envelope his father had given him. "Here," he handed it to Deirdre, "see what's inside."

Deirdre opened it and almost gasped.

"How much is it for?" Danny asked as they drove away.

"Five thousand pounds."

"Holy shit! We should have them over more often."

"Danny. That's very mercantile of you."

"What? I've been putting up with their shite all my life. It's about time I got something good from them."

Chapter 11 -1987

AFTER A FEW MONTHS IT HADN'T GOTTEN ANY BETTER. Rushing out of the house every morning was a strain on them all. Except little Martin. He got up by himself and joined Danny in the bathroom while Deirdre negotiated with Grainne. She was almost a year old and had begun to verbalize—a steady stream of 'no, no, no,' no matter what Deirdre coaxed her with. She refused to have her hair brushed and cried when her pajamas were removed. So many mornings, Deirdre was tempted to just slip something over them but she couldn't. The staff at the daycare had already politely pointed out that Grainne was always fussy in the morning and was taking a long time to settle in.

The daycare was in the university and all the other children were models of good behavior. Some were beginning to make full sentences, even those who were only weeks or a month older than Grainne. And most of the other little girls looked as serene as their mothers, who could drop off their kids without a shred of guilt. Grainne would cling to Deirdre's leg and cry 'no' until one of the staff had to pry her away.

"Don't worry, Mummy," Martin would assure her as she kissed him good-bye. "She really has a good time here—only she doesn't know how to say it yet. Besides, she just has to get used to other kids."

"Thank you, Martin. That's so nice of you to say."

He always kissed her before he wandered off to hang his coat, smiling and talking with all the other kids. It was the only part of their morning routine that was bearable.

When she did speak to Danny about it, he just looked like she was making things unnecessarily complicated. "If it's too soon, you can always quit and stay at home for another year or so. We'll find a way to manage." And that was what she was afraid of. Jacinta hadn't let it go and when Danny called, she'd spend far too long telling him about how well things were going for them back home. "I wish she would just let it drop," was her exasperated response when Danny would relay all that was said. Deirdre always made herself look too busy whenever Danny motioned to her with the phone. He'd look pleading at her but she wouldn't. She never made him talk to her parents— not that her father was ready for it. But at least, now, when he asked after the kids, he'd ask after their father too.

"She doesn't mean any harm. She's just trying to be kind."

"You don't think we should, do you?"

He smiled when she asked him that, when they got to be alone for the first time all day in their almost-finished kitchen. They hadn't got around to painting yet. They should have done it when the drywall was finished but they had waited for so long that Deirdre had gone ahead and started using it. Danny thought that was a bit impulsive of her.

"Sometimes," he said as he ducked into the fridge and emerged with a beer, "I think about our kids growing up all Canadian and that makes me a bit conflicted." He opened the beer and reached for her and pulled her close to him. They hadn't in so long. "But then I remember what it was like grow-ing up Irish."

He shivered dramatically until she laughed along with him, and then took a swig. "She's just being a mother. You know what that's like."

"Danny?" She let him pull her tighter until they were rub-bing together. He had been bugging her for sex and she might tonight, if he'd do her a favor. "What would you think about dropping the kids off—instead of me?"

"Sure. No problem."

"Are you sure?"

"Of course I'm sure. It's almost on my way."

"Grainne can get a bit fussy."

"She'll be fine." He was nuzzling her ears and the cold beer was pressed between them, tingling against her skin.

*

A few weeks later, she got a call from the Center. Martin had hit another kid and she had to go in to talk about it. He'd been acting out for a while. At first he was just a bit sullen but he was beginning to show signs of aggression and the staff had concerns about that. They gave Deirdre some pamphlets to look over and, as it was a Friday, they could all spend the weekend helping Martin to come to terms with whatever it was that was upsetting him.

Deirdre expected him to be a little more taciturn. She had noticed a change in him, too, and had been meaning to talk with him about it but she hadn't been able to find the time.

"Well, Martin. Do you have anything to say before we pick up your sister and go home?"

"I don't like when Daddy drops us off. I want you to do it again."

"Oh, pet." She hunkered down so she could look into his big wet eyes. "Mammy is so busy right now." He didn't say anything and was about to lower his head. "But maybe, Mammy and Daddy will take turns?"

*

"I don't see why it's a big deal, Deirdre. I think he's just being a mammy's-boy. He'll get over it—we all have to."

"I don't want it to be like that for him. I don't want anyone to rush him through his childhood."

"He'll be fine. You're getting worried about nothing."

He took her in his arms again but she was far too tired. And she was still feeling guilty toward Martin. She wanted to go in and read to him before he fell asleep. "How can you be so sure?"

"Because he has you for a mother."

He leaned in but she pushed him away. "I'm going to say good night to him. Would you tuck 'Carrie' in?"

"Don't be calling her that. She'll get a complex."

"She'll be fine. She has you for a father."

She let him kiss her before he went into their bedroom and sat by Grainne's cot. Danny was anxious to move her into her own room but it wasn't finished yet. Deirdre never pestered him about it though. She wasn't ready to have her baby so far away from her. Grainne was still feeding through the night.

She read *The Cat in the Hat* to Martin while listening to Danny singing softly in the other room.

O, Father dear, I oft times heard you talk of Erin's Isle
Her valleys green, her lofty scene, her mountains rude and wild
You said it was a pleasant place wherein a prince might dwell
Why have you then forsaken her, the reason to me tell?

She even stopped reading so they could all listen, drifting off as the verses continued.

My son, I loved our native land with energy and pride
Until a blight fell on the land and sheep and cattle died
The rents and taxes were to pay, I could not them redeem
And that's the cruel reason why I left Old Skibbereen

It's well I do remember on a bleak November's
day
The landlord and his agent came to drive us all
away
He set my house on fire with his demon yellow
spleen
And that's another reason why I left Old
Skibbereen

Your mother, too, God rest her soul, lay on the
snowy ground
She fainted in her anguish of the desolation
round
She never rose, but went her way from life to
death's long dream
And found a quiet grave, my boy, in lovely
Skibbereen

It's well I do remember the year of forty-eight
When we arose with Erin's boys to fight against
our fate
I was hunted through the mountains as a traitor
to the Queen
And that's another reason that I left Old
Skibbereen

Oh father dear, the day will come when vengeance loud will call
And we'll arise with Erin's boys and rally one
and all
I'll be the man to lead the van, beneath our flag
of green
And loud and high we'll raise the cry, 'Revenge
for Skibbereen!'

She woke up a few hours later with the book still in hand.
Martin was sleeping soundly with the hint of a smile on face.
She checked on Grainne, too, sleeping silently. For the first
time since she could remember, the house was peaceful. She
almost made a wish that it might last as she rose and got ready
for bed.

She peeled off her makeup and brushed out her hair. It was far too long but she couldn't cut it until her face didn't look so fat anymore. Maybe after she lost a few more pounds, and maybe change the color a bit—anything so she didn't look so tired all the time.

"Danny?" She called as she turned off the hallway lights. "Are you coming to bed?"

He didn't answer so she went to rouse him. He had fallen asleep, listening to *The Joshua Tree*, sprawled in his chair with five empty beer bottles on the table in front of him.

*

"Okay then, Grainne and I will go with my parents, and you and Daddy will go with Granddad Jerry."

"Yippee." Martin ran off into Jerry's arms and was twirled up in the air. They had gone back to Dublin for his fiftieth birthday.

"Don't be doing that to the child. He's just flown half-way around the world," Jacinta chided as she handed Grainne back to Deirdre. "She's gorgeous. She's the image of you. Don't you think so, Mrs. Fallon?" But she didn't wait for the other woman to answer. "Jerry, put that child down and go get the car.

"He's been like a kid since he heard little Martin was coming over," she complained. "It's been nothing but 'wait 'til I show him this' or 'wait 'til I bring him to the zoo.' I told him not to say that in front of Danny as we don't want to have a repeat of the last time." She waited until Deirdre nodded in agreement before asking, "And how are you managing?"

"I'm fine. Getting back to work was a bit of a strain."

"Sure don't I know? Danny's been telling me all about it."

She smiled knowingly and headed off to get in the car before Deirdre could answer.

"Here. Let me hold the little angel while you get in the car," her mother said and stepped in front of her. "Isn't she lovely, Dermot? She's the image of Deirdre—at that age."

Her father did stop and look for a moment and nearly smiled. "C'mon." he held the car doors open. "Let's be getting home so the Boyles are not sitting outside waiting for us."

"There's no fear of that," Deirdre heard her mother whisper as she climbed inside.

Even though it was Jerry's birthday, she thought Danny and Deirdre should stay with her for the first few days and then, if Deirdre didn't want to change, she could say the baby was settled and it might be better to let her be. She balanced it by hosting a dinner for them all—with wine and all. Deirdre stressed that part to Danny and even Jacinta seemed to think it was fair.

*

"But little Martin is going to stay with us?" she asked Danny as they drove away with Deirdre's father's car following. "And you, too. You know Fallon still blames you for everything."

"He doesn't. Not anymore. Deirdre says he's changed."

"I hope you're right, son. That's all that I can say."

"Is Granddad Fallon mean, Granddad Jerry?"

"No. I wouldn't say that about him."

"I think he is. When Mammy phones, she makes me talk to him."

"Does she have to make you talk to me too?"

"No! Granddad Jerry, you're silly. You're my friend."

Jerry made a face and waggled his thumbs in his ears—the way they had practiced after watching the elephants the summer he was over in Canada.

"Jazus, Jerry, keep your hands on the wheel. Fallon is just behind us and he'll report you for dangerous driving."

"Ma," Danny nodded toward the front seat where Martin sat with the seat belt draped loosely around him. Danny wanted him to sit in the back but his father and his son were conspiring against him.

His mother tried to soothe it over. "It's probably better if he knows what he's really like before we get there—so it's not such a shock."

"He'll hear you, Ma."

"He will not. They don't listen when they are that small."

He took a long look at her but she turned away.

*

"I don't like the way that eejit is driving. And with my grandson in the car too."

"Oh, he's your grandson now."

"Mam?" Deirdre tried to deflect her but her mother was changed. She was never going to let him push his way around the house again. "For years I've put up with it. I'm tired of tippy-toeing around in my own house," she had complained over the phone a few weeks back. She had grown impatient waiting to know if he'd be civil when they visited. "I told him too. I sat him down one night and poured him a shot of whiskey—so he wouldn't be so prickly—and I told him straight."

**

"What did he say?"

"He said nothing. He just sat there looking gob-smacked."

"Oh, Mam. And you were always the one going on about always doing the right thing."

"It was the right thing, dear. He's much easier to get along with now—only he likes to feel a bit sorry for himself."

***

"Don't worry, Dee," her father turned and smiled like she hadn't seen him do before. She never remembered him ever calling her 'Dee' either. She liked it. "Your mother has become a real women's libber, but you know me. I'm nothing if I'm not tolerant and open minded."

"Since when, Daddy?" He seemed almost . . . vulnerable.

"We all change, Dee. We all get older and wiser."

"Help," Deirdre pretended to shout. "My father has been abducted by aliens."

But she said it too loud and woke Grainne, who hadn't slept on the plane. It was such a bad time to fly; she was still teething and was more flustery than usual.

"Ah, now. The poor little one is crying again. Here, give her over to me so you can relax a bit."

As soon as her mother took her, Grainne stopped crying and began to gurgle. Deirdre should have been happy with that, but she couldn't help it and began to cry.

"What's the matter?" her father checked briefly in the mirror. "Are you all right there, Dee?"

"Of course she's all right. She just got off the plane and she's worn out. She'll be fine as soon as we get home. Maybe you should overtake them and we can get on home before them."

"You're right there, missus." He accelerated and swung around the Boyle's car, waving at his grandson as he passed.

"So have you set your scheme in motion?" Deirdre's mother seemed a little indignant.

"Don't be calling it that. We're family now and I'm just going to ask him for a favor. He can say 'no' if he likes."

"Oh, I'm sure you'll find a way of making that very hard for him."

"You don't think very highly of me, anymore?"

And in the silence that followed, Deirdre began to feel a little sorry for him, despite everything.

*

"Will you look at Sterling Moss—it would kill him to have to follow us."

"They're probably just going ahead to get things ready, Ma."

"And you know," Jerry winked over his shoulder. "We could have a quick stop along the way and give them a bit more time."

Danny was about to disagree. Deirdre had warned him—there were to be no stops along the way. Her mother had timed the dinner and she wouldn't want it spoiled. But before he could, Jacinta agreed. "I need a drink before I have to spend the evening with that man. He has a face like a bad-tempered horse."

"Ma." Danny nodded furiously towards Martin, who was busy making long faces with Jerry.

"Well, it's settled then." He patted his grandson on the shoulder. "And you're going to have the greatest crisps in the world."

"What are crisps?"

"Don't you have those over there?"

"We call them potato chips." Danny tried to lean forward between them.

"Well here, we call them Tatyos." Jerry rested his arm on the back of his grandson's seat. "God's only effort to recompense the Irish. That and the best pints of porter."

"Da?" Danny groaned.

"What?"

"Deirdre doesn't want him hearing stuff like that."

"What? The Tatyos or the pints of porter?"

"Pints of porter," Martin repeated into the silence that followed.

"He takes after his grandfather, all right," Jacinta sniffed. "A great man for the pints and not much else."

"Ah, Jass. Don't be talking like that. You're beginning to sound like Old Horseface."

"Horse face. Horse face."

"Jazus. Deirdre's going to kill me."

"Well you may as well have a pint before she does."

"Pints of porter," little Martin laughed as his grandfather carried him inside.

*

"I hope they are not going to be much longer. The dinner will be ruined." Anne Fallon was agitated but didn't want to let it show.

"Well it serves them right." Deirdre had no such reservations. "If they have gone drinking..."

"Sure they wouldn't? Not with the child?"

"And why wouldn't they," Dermot Fallon asked as he stood in the doorway. "Didn't Danny get raised in a pub?"

"Stop that now, you. You know that's not true."

"I was only joking."

"Well it didn't sound like it."

Deirdre checked her watch again. It was three quarters past—five hours later than it said. She had forgotten to reset it on the plane. They had told the Boyles the dinner would be ready at half-past and Danny had promised to make sure they would be there on time. But she wasn't surprised. Nor did she really care that much anymore. She was just far too tired. She'd deal with it all after she just got to sleep for a while. Even if only for a few hours.

*

"They're coming now," Dermot Fallon called from his position by the curtains.

He had slipped Jerry a few quid for the carry-out. They had wine in for the dinner, but he wanted to have some whiskey for later—when he and Jerry might want to have their little chat. He wanted to intercept it, too, in case his wife got to it first and put it away. "I'm sure they only stopped to pick up some flowers or something."

"You're being very understanding."

"Ah sure, we may as well all try getting along—for the children's sake if nothing else."

*

"Ah, now Mrs. Fallon. You shouldn't have gone to all this bother."

"It's no bother at all, Mrs. Boyle. It's the least I could do for our Canadians."

"Here," Dermot nudged Jerry. "Try this wine. I hear it's very good." He poured a couple of full glasses and waited for Jerry to sample his.

"Jazus, that's not bad at all." Jerry sipped and sipped some more before Jacinta poked at him with her elbow.

"And yourself, Mrs. Boyle. Would you like a glass?"

"Well, I'm not a great one for drinking but . . . go on then. It's not every day we have our children home with us."

Deirdre and Danny exchanged glances but said nothing. They had packed the kids off to bed and were anxious to follow them, but it was too early. They both wanted to make it as late as they could—to get over the jet lag.

"Here's," Dermot raised his glass, "to Deirdre and Danny. You're very welcome home."

"And to little Martin," Jerry added, and drank some more.

"And little Grainne, too," Dermot agreed, and topped them up again.

"Jesus," Jacinta whispered to Danny. "Your father would drink with Judas."

"Is everything all right, Mrs. Boyle?" Mrs. Fallon asked from across the table.

"Grand, thanks for asking. I was just saying to Danny that this is the nicest meal I've had in ages."

"Oh, that's so nice of you. I was just saying to Deirdre how nice it was to have the two families together again. We should make plans to spend time together while Deirdre and little Grainne are here. Just us girls."

"Well in that case, Jerry and me will have to plan something for the boys. When we've finished the dinner, we'll go out and have a smoke and talk about it."

"Right enough," Jerry agreed as Dermot drained his glass and poured some more. And when they were done eating and had tidied things away, Jerry and Dermot exchanged glances. "C'mon. Let's have an old smoke for ourselves."

They sidled out in their conspiracy, but Danny stayed. "I'm getting very tired," he nodded at Deirdre. "Maybe we should go to bed."

He timed it perfectly. Dermot was heading out with Jerry and couldn't object about his daughter sleeping with him without being married—even if he was the father of her children. And Jacinta couldn't complain about him staying with the Fallons now that Jerry and Dermot were about to make a night of it.

"Yes," Deirdre agreed, and stretched out a yawn. "Please excuse us but we are worn out."

"Of course you are, dears," Anne Fallon said to smooth any ruffled feathers. "Go on and get some sleep and don't worry. If the children wake up early, I'll be happy to mind them for you."

"Good night, Mam, and thanks for everything. Good night, Mrs. Boyle."

"Good night," Danny added and followed Deirdre upstairs. They checked in on the kids before tumbling into bed.

"What do you think our fathers are talking about?"

"Fucked if I know. Maybe they're trying to figure out the dowry."

"Danny. You have become very coarse since we got here. I hope you are not going to be like that in front of Martin."

"He wouldn't even notice with my father around, buying him everything."

"You're not jealous, are you?"

"Fuck, no. I'm just tired."

*

By the end of the second week, they had done it all. They had been to the zoo twice and to the beach three times—Dollymount, Donabate and Sandycove. It rained a little each time but they had fun and little Martin got to bury his grandfathers in sand. They went up into the mountains, too, to Glendalough, where they all posed for pictures in among the ruins.

They stopped at the Hell Fire Club on the way back and Jerry told Martin about how the devil himself used to show up.

"Don't be filling his little head with all that nonsense," Jacinta chided but Dermot went along with Jerry. "He should know a bit about his own people, and who better to tell him than his two grandfathers."

"Those two have become very chummy," Anne offered in commiseration when she and Jacinta were left alone. "Should we be worried?"

"Ah, no. If your Jerry is anything like my Dermot, it's nothing but blather." The two women linked arms and headed back down toward the car while Danny stood on the hill overlooking the city and tried to avoid looking over at Cruagh Wood.

*

"Do you ever think we'll get like that?" Deirdre asked as she gently stroked his arm. Despite everything, she had begun to enjoy herself, particularly when her mother and Jacinta took Grainne for hours at a time. Between them all, they had managed to wean her and get her to sleep through the night. Deirdre hadn't felt better in years.

"Like what?" Danny asked like he hadn't heard.

"Are you all right?"

"Me? I'm fine. I was just thinking, that's all."

"Did you ever find out what the old men were plotting the other night?"

"No. I haven't really given it another thought, to be honest with you."

"Well, my mother says that my father is thinking of running for the council, but he wants your father to back him."

"That makes sense; they always say that politics makes strange bedfellows."

"But why would your father go along with it? It's not like they really like each other."

"I don't know. Maybe having a councilor around could come in very handy for my father's business."

"You don't think . . .?"

"Sure why not. Everybody in this country is on the fiddle. They may as well get in on the act."

"Danny," she looked up into his eyes. "You are a lot more cynical over here. Did you know that?"

"It must be the air up here," he sighed and shook his head. "It never agreed with me."

*

"Will it be hard for you when they go back?" Anne asked Jacinta as they strolled arm in arm.

"Ah, sure you know yourself, but it's a mother's job to grieve."

Anne Fallon didn't look at her. Jacinta was always a bit dark—having been away in the hospital all those years. "But it will be nice for them to get on with their lives too. Dermot and I were thinking of going over for a visit one of these years."

"Do you think they'll still be there—in a few years? Maybe coming home and seeing how good things are here might change their minds."

Anne Fallon didn't correct her. Things might be going well for her and Jerry, but the rest of the country was suffering. Deirdre and Danny were well out of it. "I think they are settled now. It would be a shame to uproot the children. Not that I wouldn't like to have them closer, but it's a much smaller world than it used to be."

"Well that's fine for you, but not a day goes by but I don't miss my Danny."

*

On the night before they left, they all gathered in the Yellow House, except Anne, who was more than happy to stay home with the children. They promised they wouldn't make it a late night and she was going to serve some sandwiches and pastries when they got home, to make their last night special.

Danny and Deirdre were holidayed-out and ready to go back. They had done all of their shopping, too, buying Guinness golf shirts for Danny and Martin, Irish linen tea towels for around the house, a few kilted outfits for Grainne and a gold Claddagh ring for Deirdre. Danny had surprised her with it—to make up for reverting back into the coarse bollocks he used to be.

Deirdre was happy. Spending time with her mother had brought everything into focus again and Grainne was so much easier to get along with. "She just gets upset when she feels you get tense," her mother had patiently explained. "It's one of the things you have to learn."

She didn't mind when her mother spoke to her like that. She knew she only meant well.

She was looking forward to spending more time with Martin too. She had hardly gotten to hold him since they came over—his two grandfathers were always tugging him one way or the other. Her own father seemed to have warmed to him and even took him on his knee to tell him stories and didn't even get upset when little Martin told him that Granddad Jerry had already told him that one.

"So Deirdre," Jacinta asked as they sat alone while the men drank at the bar. Deirdre didn't mind, her father and Danny were getting along so well. "What would you think about moving back?"

Deirdre didn't even mind her asking but was careful to step around it. "Well, we'd have to wait a bit. Grainne is still a bit young for flying. Maybe Danny and I will talk about it and consider it in a few years."

She had no intention of ever considering it but she wasn't going to say that.

"Don't leave it too long. You don't want them to grow up Canadian, do you?"

Deirdre did but she just smiled. "We'll talk about it once we get settled again, and we'll let you know."

"That'll be grand. That gives me something to look forward to."

*

By the end of the night, the men were singing and insisted on getting a carry-out to keep the night going. Dermot insisted on paying for it too. Jerry didn't argue, as he was getting drunk and was a bit maudlin. "I got to tell you, son," he said, putting his arm around Danny's neck, "I'm so proud of you."

"And why wouldn't you be." Dermot draped himself on the other side. "Hasn't he turned out to be a better man than either of us?"

Danny was about to laugh along with them when he noticed Mrs. Flanagan sitting in the corner. She nodded to him and raised her glass. Danny nodded back and turned away, coming face to face with his own reflection in the mirror behind the bar.

Chapter 12 – 1988

PATRICK REILLY HAD BEEN MORE THAN HAPPY to get back to Rome. He hadn't realized how much it had changed him until he went back to Ireland for his father's funeral. He had missed the sun and the warmth as he led the funeral to the cold windy place where his father would once again lie with his mother.

The old man had died without warning, so Patrick never got to say goodbye to him. But he wasn't too troubled by that; he and his father had long been at peace with each other.

After the funeral, Patrick went through the last of the old man's belongings. His father had never been the nostalgic type and had rid himself of most of his worldly possessions long before death came for him. He had, however, kept two photographs: his wedding picture, in which he stood with Patrick's mother, who looked like a young girl, and one of Patrick the day he had been ordained. Patrick had taken them and packed them carefully between his travelling clothes along with his father's pipe—an old polished briarwood that smelled of fond memories. And, as he turned around one last time in his mother's kitchen, he saw his father's cap hanging on the back of the door. He folded it and pushed it into the pocket of his raincoat and stepped outside. The meadows, that had long been his family's, were fresh and green as the rain billowed down from the hills. Other men's cattle grazed in total indifference as the last Reilly left the valley forever.

When he got back to Trastevere, Patrick placed the photographs on his dresser and put the cap and pipe on the little side table where he kept whichever book he was reading. It suited his room, giving it a more studious feel, and he had to smile at that. His father's death was not really a sad thing. His father had always been a good man and could be assured his place in the better world, but it did mean that Patrick's last real connection with home was gone. He didn't feel sad about that either. A good priest was used to standing alone and apart from life. And it made him feel more like one of the fishermen who had left the trappings of the world behind to walk in the footsteps of the Lord.

In Rome he was free to be alone and apart, unencumbered by human ties, answerable only to himself. He taught at the college with academic dispassion and was becoming celebrated for the clarity he offered his students. Colleagues, too, had begun to seek him out for advice and reassurance.

Patrick gave freely from the growing depth of his own wisdom. He was becoming the priest he had always wanted to be, and when he looked back at what he had once been, the fumbling curate, it was as if he was looking at the life of another man.

He still kept in touch with Joe, writing once a month or so, but that too had changed. He was now advising Joe, whose life seemed to have become impossibly confused. Only Joe didn't seem to notice and still addressed Patrick like a younger brother. Patrick didn't mind. He understood. The more Joe's life grew hectic, the more he needed to think he was in control.

The morning after he got back from Ireland, Patrick made his pilgrimage to the Pantheon. He liked to pray there, imagining his prayers went through the hole in the roof and straight to God's ear. He didn't pray for himself—he prayed for everyone else that they too might find peaceful purpose in times that were growing more and more conflicted.

He also liked to take some time to think about his uncle when he was there. He still hadn't opened the un-posted letters to Benedetta that Mrs. Mawhinney had given him, but the package also contained the musings and diaries of a far-more complicated man than Patrick had ever known. A man who had loved the Pantheon, too, and his writings made so many references to the place, and that he had often spent time there contemplating the absurdity of just one God.

Patrick had found it all very disquieting at first until he realized that the bishop had been privately pondering and not as a layman. The bishop was well schooled in all the layers of theology, schooled enough to see the deeper mysteries that others passed over. He had written eloquently about Pantheism and called Monotheism 'the poor influence of cults of self-justification.'

After he had gotten over the shock, Patrick was able to absorb them for what they were—the secret thoughts of a man who was far more than the functionary he had become. A man who had once seen the result of the evil that came when his Church compromised with the ways of the wider world.

Before, when he served without question, Patrick would have misunderstood, but now he was becoming wiser. Wise enough to understand that his uncle loved his God as he loved Benedetta, with the saddest, purest love of all—hopeless love. And Patrick was becoming wise enough to understand why his uncle had shared them with him. His uncle had known about Miriam all along but hadn't wanted to embarrass Patrick by confronting it directly.

"It is," he had written in the days before he died, "*the type of thing that makes an ordinary man a true priest. The best priests are not those without temptation. Instead, they are those who are tempered in its fire.*" The scrawled letter was carefully folded and placed in an envelope along with all the others. Mrs. Mawhinney must have put it there but maintained her discretion until the end.

Patrick understood. The bishop, who was always so direct and authoritative when it came to diocesan matters, was far more circumspect on personal matters. When Patrick had gone to tell him he had chosen the priesthood, his uncle seemed more concerned than happy. "Are you sure it is what you want?" he had asked from behind his desk. "Are you sure it is not what you think I, or your mother, want? It is a difficult life, Patrick, with nothing to guide you but your own faith in a God who will never speak to you directly."

"It is the life for me," Patrick had tried to reassure him.

"But that's the point I'm trying to make. You won't know that until afterwards and then what'll you do if you find out . . ." He never finished his sentence and it hung over Patrick for years. He had always assumed that his uncle doubted his vocation—or his quality, but now he knew better. His uncle had been trying to offer him a bit of hard-learned wisdom.

He prayed for him every time he went to the old temple. Not for the repose of his soul. If the bishop didn't have it, what hope was there for the rest of them? No, Patrick prayed to thank the bishop for the great wisdom he had left behind.

"Patricio," Giovanni hailed as he crossed the piazza. He seemed more excited than usual and could hardly wait. "Come, come, there is something I want to ask."

*

"I got a letter from Miriam," Deirdre mentioned as they bundled the kids into their car seats. "She got married."

"That's nice," Danny answered after they had all gotten in. He hardly looked at her as he twisted around and backed out slowly. The neighborhood kids were always flying by on their bikes and he had almost hit a few already.

"They got married in Thailand."

"Why there?"

"His parents are dead and she didn't want to do it in Ireland. Besides, she says that he has an affinity with the Orient."

"I thought he'd be sick of it, after the war and all."

"Who's sick?" Little Martin called from the back. He was four years of age and strained against his car seat. Danny would have let him out of it but Deirdre wasn't ready for that.

"A friend of Mammy's."

"Did getting married make him sick?"

"Why would you say something like that?" Deirdre asked without taking her eyes off Danny.

"Daddy said . . ."

"Oh did he now? Well I'm sure he meant something else and he can explain it when he picks you up from school."

"Dee! I can't today."

"You have to. I have a seminar and I won't get out until after five."

"You could still make it."

"I can't. The whole point of going to these things is to net-work afterwards. I told you all of this last week."

"But that means I have to leave early."

"Danny. You work for the government. Leaving fifteen minutes early won't bring democracy crashing down."

"What's democracy?"

"It's when people are fooled into thinking they have a say in how their lives are run."

"Danny. Don't be cynical in front of the children."

"They may as well learn the truth somewhere. They're certainly not going to learn it at school."

"Our teacher says we live in the best democracy in the world."

"Has she ever been anywhere else?"

"Danny!"

He wanted to smoke but he had to wait. He wasn't allowed to smoke in the car or the house or when he was anywhere near the kids, but he'd have one after he dropped them off. If they ever got there. It took two lights to make the left turn.

"I don't know why you come this way."

"I like the view."

He took Pottery Road to Bayview every morning. Going down the hill let him feel like he was going somewhere else—like on holidays and not going to spend most of his day in an office. He'd have to spend the whole day trying to look busy and he hated that but there was a hold on all new projects. He was going to meet up with Frank later. There was a new bar opening in Ajax and they were going to check it out. McVeigh had barred them again; he'd caught Frank smoking a joint in the 'gents.'

They crawled along through traffic, down Bayview and up the Rosedale valley. They dropped the kids off at Orde Street and Deirdre walked from there. It gave Danny a few minutes of peace as he dawdled along with the rest of rush hour, all the way down to Queen's Quay. It wasn't bad down there. He could see the lake, and the islands, and the rusty hulls of the lakers. Except in the winter. Then it was just cold and bleak.

"Supper's in the fridge. You just have to warm it up. And make sure Grainne eats her vegetables."

"You're going to be late?"

"I told you, but I'll be back by nine. Have the kids in bed and then you can go out."

"Bollocks!" Danny muttered as they unclasped the kids and hauled them out.

"Bollocks," Grainne smiled up at him. "Bollocks."

"Are you happy now? She'll be saying it all day."

"What's bollocks, Daddy?"

"It's Irish for great."

"Great, now you'll have the two of them saying it."

"Don't you mean bollocks, Mommy?"

Danny drove away but waited until he was around the corner before he lit up and rolled down the window.

Bollocks, Anto laughed from the rearview mirror but was gone when Danny turned around.

"That's just what I need—on top of everything."

*

"The example of Jesus," was all Fr. Melchor chose to say. He wanted to say so much more but he had been warned. He could teach but he was not to inspire or incite. Everyone had been very clear about that. "Jesus is the role model of self-sacrifice for the greater good."

Philippe Ignatius Madrigal nodded but they both knew he shouldn't have asked that type of question. Fr. Melchor had been very clear: Philippe would have to find his own way.

Over the last two years, he had come to his teacher with many questions that all led up to this. His father was a wealthy landowner and his mother was a devout Catholic. They had managed to bridge their dichotomy but for their son—it was a chasm. He was a good boy and a good student.

John Melchor couldn't help but feel that he was cheating him. He could have said so much more about loyalty to the principle of the poor. He could have made it clear that he opposed those who used the shield of righteousness against what was right, but he couldn't be explicit. None of them could. The university was granted by the rich so that their children could achieve the status of being 'educated' but no one, especially those of tainted reputation, could twist that into anything that might evoke real change.

It was why John was there. He could not walk through the world espousing change as a man but he could as a Jesuit, as long as he was cautious—and considerate. Philippe was almost apologetic. "My father insists. He says that it is the duty of the privileged."

**

"And you don't agree?"

"I want to honor my father but I also want to honor all that I believe in."

Philippe was an earnest young man. He knew what was right, even if it would cost him everything his father, and his grandfather, had built. El Salvador had to change and it would fall to Philippe's generation to pick the path the country would take.

It had been so much easier for John. The Japanese had made his decision for him. His parents did not approve but understood. "Be careful of righteous rage," his mother had warned him. His father had driven him to the recruitment office in the grand old Buick with the spotless white-walls. They sat for a moment as they watched the lines of indignant men shuffle forward, impatient but jovial—as if they were all going on a grand adventure. "I will give you my blessing, for what it's worth, but I cannot claim to be happy about this."

His father, too, was always cautious about anger. He believed it was a sin against the love of God. He had wanted John to finish his education and join the family business. "You are going to join a war that might cost you your life—or worse, your soul."

***

"No one can tell you what to do, Philippe. One can only say what they think is right or wrong."

"Then I will do what is right by my father and maybe then I can then do what is right by me. We must change what we are from within. They say that many of the young officers feel as I do. Maybe we can bring about the change without suffering and death."

John smiled at his own thoughts. He, too, had gone to war to bring a swift end to evil.

"Will you give me your blessing, Father?"

*

John Melchor gave his blessing, for what it was worth, but was troubled as he walked toward his lecture. He wanted to get there before his students. He had a message for them all. He carefully transcribed it on to the grease board and left so they could read it for themselves.

1. The Dignity of the Human Person

Human beings are created in the image of God and, therefore, are endowed with dignity. This inherent dignity carries with it certain basic rights and responsibilities which are exercised within a social framework.

2. The Common Good

While the dignity of the human person is affirmed, individuals live in common with others and the rights of individuals must be balanced with the wider common good of all. The rights and needs of others must be always respected.

3. Solidarity

Human beings are social by nature and do not exist merely as individuals. When considering the human community it must be remembered that it consists of individual and social elements.

4. Subsidiarity

This principle recognizes that society is based on organizations or communities of people ranging from small groups or families right through to national and international institutions. As a rule of social organization, subsidiarity affirms the right of individuals and social groups to make their own decisions and accomplish what they can by their own initiative and industry. A higher-level community should not interfere in the life of a community at a lower level of social organization unless it is to support and enable.

5. The Purpose of the Social Order

The social order must uphold the dignity of the human person.

6. The Purpose of Government

The purpose of government is the promotion of the common good. Governments are required to actively participate in society to promote and ensure social justice and equity.

7. Participation

Individuals and groups must be enabled to participate in society.

8. The Universal Purpose of Goods

The world's goods are meant for all. Although the Church upholds the right to private property this is subordinate to the right to common use and the overall common good. There is a social mortgage on private property.

9. The Option for the Poor

This refers to seeing the world through the eyes of the poor and standing with the poor in solidarity. This should lead to action for justice with and on behalf of those who are poor and marginalized.

10. The Care of Creation

The Earth is God's gift and all species have a rightful place in it. Humans share this habitat with other kind and have a special duty to be stewards and trustees of the Earth.

Pope John Paul II, Sollicitudo Rei Socialis

*

"Dee-dree? Dee-dree Fallon, is that you?"

Eduardo had changed. He looked more like a man. He had grown into his moustache and his hair was combed back, almost blue-black in the evening light. His eyes were dark and his teeth were white, gleaming against his tanned, scented skin. He leaned forward and brushed each of her cheeks before standing back and looking at her. He had always looked at her that way—like he could instantly fall in love with her if she would just give him a reason.

She'd heard the Portuguese were like that. And that they could fall in love even while they were already in it. But he was always polite and well behaved and she liked that. He made her feel like a lady.

"Are you well, Eduardo?"

"I am. And you? Are you well? It is so nice to see you again. Do you have time for a coffee?"

She didn't and she shouldn't, but it was one of those days, in one of those weeks. Grainne was almost three and was becoming more and more demanding. She hardly got to spend any time with Martin anymore. She barely got to read a few pages to him before he fell asleep.

Each night he waited with his books as she scurried and cleared away after dinner. It would go much faster if Danny helped but they decided it was better for him to deal with Grainne. He did that and very little else. The band wasn't too busy anymore but he was playing a few folk clubs. Quieter, pottier places where he could sing his own songs, but he usually came home brooding like he had woken some ghost inside of himself. When he did come home, he'd sit up late drinking and wrestling with it.

"I can't. I really should get home. My husband has to go to work and I have to be there with the kids."

"Twenty minutes? You can spare twenty minutes."

"I can't, Eduardo."

"Ten minutes, then. We can have espressos."

"Eduardo, I'm not sure I should be doing this. I am married and you are . . . ?"

"I am married, too, with two kids also, and I need a little break before I go back to face them."

"I know what you mean."

"Then it is settled. Ten minutes?"

"Okay. But then I am gone."

*

The weekend after Thanksgiving, Danny stood outside McDonald's and smoked, even though it was a cold day. Bright and sunny, but cold. Most of the leaves were gone, shriveled up and piled for bagging—it wasn't proper to burn them anymore. He had spent the morning in the garden, following orders and wrapping shrubs in burlap so the frost wouldn't get to them. He told Martin they were putting on the winter underwear and they had a bit of a laugh about that for a while.

It was one of the few things that made it all worthwhile. His son was growing up not knowing the shadows that had haunted his own childhood. He and Deirdre had made a conscious decision to spare them the burden of religious indoctrination even though it meant sending them to the public school system. The Catholic system was more select, and had a better reputation for discipline, but they had talked about it and, in the end, the good was outweighed by the bad.

He watched his children through the window as he smoked, playing in the ball pit while Deirdre sat on the other side, looking over every once in a while. Martin played with the other kids but Grainne stayed on her own, insisting that her brother leave his new friends and play with her. Danny couldn't hear them but he could read all that passed between them.

It's hard to believe that a fuck like you could even have children.

Anto never missed his chance to catch Danny alone and to spoil his few moments of peace. He didn't just haunt him when he was drunk or high anymore. Now he came to him regularly and always found a way to take the joy out of life.

Danny knew what he was up to. Anto was always a vengeful bastard. Danny wished that he could talk with somebody about it, but who? Who could he tell that he was being haunted by a guy that was whacked for trying to whack him? He didn't want to get into all of that again. And he couldn't mention it to Deirdre. She'd just say that it was because of his drinking—or toking. She was always on him about it. She seemed to think that now that they were parents, they shouldn't do things like that. Danny disagreed: being a parent made him do it. It was the only way he could keep his shit together.

Besides, he wasn't doing any harm to anyone.

He didn't really resent her for being the way she was; she was only trying to get him to improve himself. She said he was too smart not to. Danny was shy about hearing stuff like that but she kept at him. She said she was only chiseling away some of the scales that he had grown against the world.

When she wanted him to change something big about himself, she'd wait until they were in bed. She'd stroke him and get him going and then she'd bring it up. Danny knew what was going on. He was like a dog and he didn't mind admitting it. It was like he was some type of stray that she had taken in off the street. He had often thought far worse of himself.

But he was getting a little bit tired of it all—it never ended. Nothing they had done was ever good enough. They could always do better—it was like her mantra. She said she went to yoga to relax but she seemed like she was more controlling than before. "You should come with me. It would help you quit smoking. And you might not need to drink so much."

He didn't answer. There was nothing to say. If he wanted to keep having sex, he'd keep his mouth shut and go along with her. And afterwards, it was like they had shaken hands on the deal. It took him a few times to grasp that, but he got it now and told himself that it was all about making compromises to keep each other happy.

She wanted to move as soon as the work on the house was finished. Some of the people she worked with had moved to Leaside and she was determined to follow. She had agreed to wait until the spring but she already had the real estate agent lined up. She was reading the 'Homes' section as she watched the kids. He finished his cigarette and headed back inside.

"Excuse me; are you Martin Carroll's nephew?"

She was black and shivered even though she was wearing a coat already. She had the sing-song of the islands in her voice and her eyes were soft and warm, like David's. She told him she was his sister and that he had died a few months back. They had tried to let Danny know but they didn't have his address or his number. She wanted him to know that they had spread David's ashes near the cabana with Martin's.

"Who was that?" Deirdre asked when he came back inside.

*

"Daddy! Martin won't play with me."

Deirdre glanced at him but he couldn't help it; it was out of his mouth before he could stop it: "Martin, play with Grainne."

"Ah, do I have to?"

"Yes you do, and try being a bit nicer, she's your little sister."

Deirdre didn't comment when he sat opposite her. She pretended to be absorbed but he could tell that she had taken the whole thing in and she disapproved.

"Mommy! Grainne needs to go the washroom."

"Do not."

"C'mon, Grainne, Mommy needs to go too. We can go together."

"Don't want to."

"Are you sure?" Danny walked over and joined them, standing closer to his daughter as Deirdre stood closer to her son.

"Are you sure, Grainne? Mommy doesn't want you to have an accident."

"Don't want to."

Deirdre glanced at Danny and back to Martin. "You go on and play, sweetie. Maybe that might be helpful."

He shot away from them like a dolphin released.

"C'mon now, honey. You and Mammy will go to the ladies' room."

"Don't want to." Grainne swam off after her brother, slower, struggling, and leaving a wet trail behind her.

*

"I tried to warn you," Martin ventured from the back seat after they had driven in silence for a while. Danny and Deirdre were both recoiling. They had snapped at each other in front of the kids. Danny thought she should have taken Grainne and saved her the embarrassment. Deirdre thought he shouldn't have snapped at Martin when he complained that no one would play with him now because he had a 'pissy' little sister.

"I know you did, sweetie, and Mommy should have listened."

She looked over at Danny like she wanted him to add something but he just ignored her. She knew he thought she was always mollycoddling the boy and that he'd never learn to stand on his own two feet.

*

"Does it shock you when I speak of him like this?"

Benedetta spoke in cultured English with just enough of an accent to sound truly distinguished. She had a cold steely intellect and often seemed to look all the way inside of Patrick. He didn't mind anymore.

At first it was so disquieting, but over time she had peeled away all the formality and spoke to him like a confidante. She said he reminded her so much of his uncle when he was young. She had gracefully escorted Patrick past any sense of inappropriateness, assuring him that it was nothing more than unrequited love; "the bitter pill that was to be hers in life." She said it as she said everything, without rancor. Benedetta was a grand dame of a person and, over time, Patrick realized that nothing was beyond her gaze. He had fumbled around her for a while, in the midst of the bustling that was Giovanni's family. She often seemed dismissive of them and always wanted to sit near 'Patricio.'

"Not anymore, Signora." She insisted that he call her by name but he wasn't ready for that. "It used to."

She reached out and patted the back of his hand, a soft gentle touch that came straight from her heart. "You will grow to be very wise."

She had told him so much about his uncle, and in doing so, much about himself. Things that he had always felt but could never say. And certainly not to his uncle—one didn't go around bothering bishops.

She was very open about her feelings. She said that she never stopped loving him. She just moved herself out of his life, but no one ever took his place.

"He knew things that others didn't. He could sense things that others couldn't. He understood, too, but was wise enough to keep that to himself. They," she smiled and nodded the side of her head in the general direction of the Vatican, "didn't like free-thinkers."

Patrick was tempted to add that nothing had changed, but he didn't have to. It was implied.

The sun was setting but the night stayed warm. Tourists still crossed the piazza below, their voices drifting up like the burble of a river. Giovanni's roof had a fine view of the city and almost across the river. Patrick came by most Sundays for dinner. He was part of the family now. He liked that. He was introduced as '*Cugino Patricio*' and no one ever questioned it—they all knew and treated him like he was Benedetta's son.

"I often wondered about that," Patrick confided as he sipped his limoncello, an indulgence the old woman had helped him cultivate. He even kept a bottle in his room and poured himself a glass those nights he sat by the window reading. "By the time I really got to know him, he had changed. They made him a monsignor after he got back and then he had to be on show all that time."

"He saw honor in duty."

"Yes, he certainly did."

"One day, you will go back to Ireland as a bishop, and young priests will fear you too. None of them will ever suspect that once you spent your evenings like this."

She waved her hand along the burnished skyline, like she owned the place. And in some ways, he often decided when he was home alone again, she did. Sometimes, when he let fancy run away with him, he thought she was like the spirit of the place, like one of the ancient goddesses whose physical form was being devoured by wind and time, but whose spirit still shone into the eyes of those that could see.

Sometimes, after they had dinner, and they had sat for a few hours on the roof, drinking limoncello until Benedetta grew tired, he would walk all the way back across the river, to Trastevere, where the winds of old ghosts whispered in the trees. And in the shadows of dark little lanes, and the fenced off ruins, statues watched the days come and go.

"I will never leave Rome," Patrick answered with a touch of boyish defiance.

"Perhaps, but first you must do what you were brought here to do."

"Teach?"

"Oh, Patricio. Have you learned nothing from your time among us?"

He didn't feel like she was making fun of him. He felt more like she was encouraging him to see what was right there in front of him.

*

"It's the oddest feeling," he wrote to Joe a few days later. He had told him all about Benedetta, knowing he could be trusted, "but after I talk with her, I feel like I have always belonged here and that everything before was just a separation."

Chapter 13 – 1989

I T'S BECAUSE YOU'RE A WANKER."

Danny was shocked. He would have expected Frank to say something like that, not Jimmy. They were doing a St. Patrick's gig in Ajax, Friday, Saturday and Sunday. It was the first time they had been together since New Year's. The Friday had been wild but Saturday was more forced—like the crowd was only drinking out of a sense of obligation. "Well you can go and fuck yourself."

"What's he done now?" Frank asked as he returned from the bar. He had gone for three pints and someone at the bar insisted on buying the band a round of Jameson too. Large ones.

"Deirdre wants Danny to go to Marriage Encounter."

"What's that?"

"It's where they cut off your balls so your wife can wear them as earrings." Danny carefully placed his pint on the table and reached for the whiskey. "Who bought these?"

"Y'er man at the bar. I wanted to thank him but I couldn't remember his name."

"She's only trying to help your relationship." Jimmy took his pint but declined the whiskey—he was driving.

"What the fuck do you know about my relationship or any relationship for that matter?"

Jimmy didn't answer. He just shrugged and walked off to talk with a few women by the bar. He had just broken up with his girlfriend.

"What the fuck are you picking on him for? He's not the one trying to castrate you."

"I didn't like the way he was talking about me and Deirdre. I think he fancies her."

"We all fuckin' fancy Deirdre. Only, she just wants you, but you are too fuckin' stupid to see that."

"Would you do it?"

"Do what?"

"Go to Marriage Encounter?"

"No, but I don't need to."

"How come?"

"'Cos I don't fuck up my relationships."

"Go an' fuck yourself."

"I'm only tryin' to do you a favor, Boyle. You don't know how good you have it."

"What the fuck do you know?"

"I know that most of the guys in here would cut off their own balls for a chance of being with Deirdre. And I know that you are a morose bollocks that has no idea how good he has it."

"You know nothing."

"Maybe not, but I know that if I had a wife and kids I wouldn't be getting drunk and stoned all the time."

"You know fuck-all about it."

"Boyle! You're an arsehole. I've known you for over ten years and you're still the same little self-obsessed gob-shite. You'd be fuck-all without Deirdre. She's the one who got you into your first house and now she's managed to move you up to Leaside. Do you think that happens to every fuckin' eejit that gets off a plane? Your fuckin' problem is that you have no idea how good you have it. See this," he held up one of the whiskey glasses. "This is half full to me."

"See this," Danny raised his and drained it. "This is empty."

"See this," Frank raised Jimmy's glass.

"What about it?"

"This is your problem, right here."

"Not you, too? Why is everyone so fuckin' concerned with how much I drink?"

"Not everyone, just those who care about you." Frank raised the glass and drained it. "And I'm not one of those anymore. You wanna be a bollocks and destroy your life? Go ahead. Just don't come moaning to me afterwards."

He got up and nodded toward Jimmy and walked back on stage. "We'd like to dedicate the next song to the gentleman at the bar who was kind enough to provide the band with strong drink. And if any of you are offering hash or coke, we'll sing a song for you too." He began to strum like he was thinking about something else. Jimmy doodled on the bass while Danny sulked behind his mandolin. Then Frank began to smile and sing:

> In the sweet county Lim'rick, one cold winter's night
> All the turf fires were burning when I first saw the light;
> And a drunken old midwife went tipsy with joy,
> As she danced round the floor with her slip of a boy,
>
> Singing *bainne na mbó do na gamhna*
> And the juice of the barley for me.
>
> Then when I was a young lad of six years or so,
> With me book and my pencil to school I did go,
> To a dirty old school house without any door,
> Where lay the school master blind drunk on the floor,
>
> Singing *bainne na mbó do na gamhna*
> And the juice of the barley for me.

At the learning I wasn't such a genius I'm
thinking,
But I soon beat the master entirely at drinking,
Not a wake or a wedding for five miles around,
But meself in the corner was sure to be found.

Singing *bainne na mbó do na gamhna*
And the juice of the barley for me.

Then one Sunday the priest read me out from
the altar,
Saying you'll end your days with your neck in
a halter;
And you'll dance a fine jig betwixt heaven and hell,
And his words they did haunt me the truth for
to tell,

Singing *bainne na mbó do na gamhna*
And the juice of the barley for me.

So the very next morn as the dawn it did break,
I went down to the priest house the pledge for
to take,
And in there in the room sat the priests in a
bunch,
Round a big roaring fire drinking tumblers of
punch,

Singing *bainne na mbó do na gamhna*
And the juice of the barley for me.

Well from that day to this I have wandered alone,
I'm a jack of all trades and a master of none,
With the sky for me roof and the earth for me
floor,
And I'll dance out my days drinking whiskey
galore,

Singing *bainne na mbó do na gamhna*
And the juice of the barley for me."

*

They stopped for pizza on their way home from Marriage Encounter while a neighborhood girl babysat. Deirdre wanted them to have some time, just for themselves. To practice acting like a couple again while the example was still fresh in their minds and before it was lost among the trials and tribulations of parenthood. She wanted them to have some time alone to talk about those parts of themselves that didn't revolve around the children. She wanted them to be able to hold hands and honestly tell each other what they were thinking.

She could tell that Danny was cautious, and a little taciturn, but she didn't mind. He had agreed to go and she believed in beginnings. But they struggled to find things to talk about, other than the children.

"Well. I think the move went relatively smoothly." She had hired a moving company even though Danny insisted that he, and Frank and Jimmy, could have managed it.

He nodded along with her, reminding her of a dog wagging its tail. He probably couldn't wait to get home and have a few beers. Then he'd probably start pawing at her, but at least she had his attention for now. "It is a bigger house though. We'll need to start adding new furniture."

"What's wrong with the stuff we have?"

"It's old and it's worn. I want something more in keeping with the house—for when we have people over."

"Are you thinkin' of entertaining a lot then?"

"We will have neighbors over and we want to make a good impression."

"Couldn't we just say we're Irish and that's how we do things? After all, we're supposed to be in a multicultural paradise."

She didn't respond. What could she say? Danny always played the 'Wild Irishman' when he was feeling insecure. He had missed out on a promotion again. He said they told him that they had to pick a more ethnic candidate. It took a few

months to get him to stop making racially insensitive com-
ments around the kids. He wasn't really racist; he was just mad
at himself.

Someone else told him it was because of his drinking and
that only added to his umbrage, half-jokingly complaining
that he was being racially profiled as an Irish drunk. That it
was enough to drive a man to drink.

She had reacted to that. She told him that was propagating
stereotypes, but what she really wanted to tell him was that he
had to grow up and take his job more seriously. She had seen
him at his work parties, acting like a caricature, only falling
just short of saying 'faith and begorrah' at the end of every
sentence.

But she said nothing about that. It would only seem like
she was rubbing his face in it. She had been promoted again,
twice in the last year, and was now making far more than him.
He said it didn't bother him but she knew it did. She tried
joking and said it was the payoff for the first few years—when
they were in purgatory. He had seemed to stiffen at that. Since
the night she overheard his rant against god—the night he
heard that Martin was ill, she had been careful to avoid saying
anything that might evoke that ghost. She had been worried
about him for a while until she put it all in place. They had
both rejected their Irish-Catholic upbringings but while she
dealt with it intellectually, Danny was much more emotive
about things like that. He had reason to be, given all that had
happened with his grandmother, but he was also very self-in-
dulgent when it suited him.

Regardless, their time in purgatory had taken its toll, especially on the way they were together. She had tried telling him
that things would only get better. He wouldn't have to play the
bars anymore—he could just play the folk clubs, but he misunderstood and thought she was taking a dig at him about the
amount of time he was spending over at Frank's. And, after
they had finished arguing in hissed voices so as not to wake the

kids, she cried alone on her bed while he smoked on the back deck.

By the morning she had decided that, if she was going to make things better, she would have to do it for him, too, and the only way that was going to happen was if he freed himself from all the negativity he wallowed in. She understood, but she also said that he had to step out of it now and the best way to do that was through Encounter. The kids were growing up and it would take both of them to see them through until university. Both of them working together as active, engaged parents.

***

"Danny, we're a good team together and we will get all of this sorted too." She raised her wine glass to clink against his. They were sharing a half carafe of red, to help set the mood.

"Yeah, I suppose so."

He was reluctant and that was partially her fault. She was always so busy trying to improve things that she sometimes forgot to give him credit for all the changes he had already made.

"Like with Grainne. I never seem to be able to get things right with her but you always seem to know exactly how to deal with her. I would be lost without you. I mean it." She reached with her other hand and stroked the back of his, the way she did to encourage him.

"Really? Because I always get the feeling that you think that I'm too easy on her, and that I'm too hard on Martin."

"See. This is the stuff we need to talk about. Being a parent has changed and neither of us had good role models when we were growing up." She didn't really think that about her mother but she didn't want to sound like she was just being critical of his parents. "Sometimes I get scared. Do you?"

"Me? No."

"Really?"

"No, I got you to rely on."

"That's so sweet of you." She tried to squeeze his hand in hers. "Danny, do you ever feel like I'm pushing you into things?" She knew he did but she wanted them to talk about it.

"Sometimes, only I'm sure that if you didn't, nothing would ever get done."

"Thanks for saying that. You know I love you and I only want what is best for us?"

"I do, yeah."

"And you don't resent me for doing that?" She knew he did but she wanted that out in the open too.

"Not at all," he assured her but avoided her eyes.

"You would tell me if you did?" She knew he hated talking about his feelings.

"I would, ya, only I don't see the point in going on about stuff like that."

"And that is where Marriage Encounter will help. We can learn how to open up about our real feelings and that way, in time, we'll be able to talk about anything. This is what we all deserve, Danny, the freedom to finally share what's going on inside."

He looked a little dubious so she sipped from her glass, carefully making sure some wine glistened on her lips. "So how do you feel about what we heard tonight?"

*

"I'm fine with it." He pulled his hand away to take another slice of pizza. It really bothered him when they did that in public, holding hands and looking into each other's eyes. It always looked like she was talking to him like he was an idiot.

"Danny, what are you really feeling?"

He really felt like having a few beers and a few tokes and having a quickie in the car on the way home, but that wasn't the kind of stuff they were supposed to talk about. "I don't know, Deirdre. I'm just tired."

"What did you think of what Shirley and Mike shared?"

Danny thought Shirley and Mike were a pair of total assholes, the type that had to be better than everybody else. She had guilt issues and he made a point of assuring her in front of everybody. He was probably gay but couldn't admit it, and she would benefit from a good fuck every now and again—to loosen her up a bit.

"I don't really relate to those kinds of people." He knew he'd get brownie points for saying it that way, maybe enough to get her to drop the subject.

"I think he is a bit controlling and she is not able to find herself in their relationship. I think she has lost her way but is afraid to say it."

Danny couldn't help but feel that she was really talking about them, in some type of code, but didn't let on. He was thinking about what it would be like with Shirley. She was a bit plump but she had great tits, bigger than Deirdre's, and still firm.

"A couple of times," Deirdre continued when it was obvious that he wasn't going to say anything, "I heard things that reminded me of you and me. Did you?"

"Not when Shirley and Mike were talking. I mean, who gives a fuck if he bought her the wrong color car? I think they only came along to try to make the rest of us feel bad?"

"Do you feel bad about us?"

He'd walked right into that trap. Every time he opened his mouth to bitch, she was waiting. "No, I don't. I just feel bad that the little free time we have to spend alone might be getting wasted, that's all."

"That's good, Danny. Tell me more. What do you think we should do, instead?"

He wanted to say sex—on the way home—but he couldn't. Sure it would be great and all, but afterwards she'd make out that it was another 'benefit of Encounter' and another reason for them to keep going.

You know what, Boyle? You don't make any fucking sense, anymore.

He hated when Anto did that. It was bad enough when he came to him when he was alone.

"I don't know, Deirdre." Danny tried to focus on her so he wouldn't become distracted. "I just don't think we need to be listening to other people. They know even less than we do."

"Maybe, but I find it helpful to know how other people manage their relationships."

"But that's the thing, Deirdre. Our parents didn't go around 'managing' their relationships . . ."

He didn't even finish the sentence. He had just proven her point. Again.

You're your own worst enemy—you know that. Right?

"Danny, are you happy?"

"Course I am. Why wouldn't I be?"

"I don't know. You just seem to be getting . . . distracted, again."

"What do you mean by that? Are you saying . . . ?"

She pressed her finger against his lips. "I'm not saying anything. I just want you to know that we can talk about things."

"I do talk to you. We talk every day."

"Yes we do. I just want you to know that you can say anything to me." For a moment, she looked the way she did that day in the Dandelion.

"Well," she decided after looking at her watch. "We should be getting home."

She paused like she was waiting for him to say something.

Tell her. For fuck's sake tell her that you want to fuck her.

I don't like you talking about my wife that way.

Suit yourself, but if it was me . . .

"By the way, I called about soccer and got Martin on a team. They start playing in a few weeks."

"That's great. I'm sure he'll love it."

"The man who runs the league mentioned that the parents do the coaching. Would you be interested?"

"Me? No. I wouldn't have the time to do it properly."

"But you will go to the games?" She rose and for a moment her dress clung to her thighs and against her breasts.

Go on, for fucks-sake. She probably wants it as much as you do.

Don't talk about her that way.

"I'm so glad we started doing this. It gives us time together." She leaned forward as he held the car door for her and kissed him.

Jesus Christ, Boyle. What does she have to do?"

"Me, too," Danny lied. He knew better. If he told her how he really felt, she would be horrified.

When they got home, she did let him nibble for a while before she took his head in her hands. She said she loved what he was doing but she was too tired. "But, I promise I won't be tired on Saturday. We could get the kids to bed early and we could . . ." She kissed him again and went to bed.

*

He sat outside and lit a joint. It was some new stuff that smelt like skunk. The guy who sold it to him said it would blow the top of his head off. Danny hoped so; it was getting very congested in there. *It would be fuckin' great,* he laughed to himself as the stuff began to have an effect, *to just open the top and let all the bullshit blow away.*

He looked up to check that the bedroom windows were closed and the light was off before he reached for the bottle beneath the deck. It was Tequila. He first tried it one night when Deirdre was making 'Mexican,' and liked it. *Enough to keep a private stock—like a gentleman!*

It seemed fair enough. He had worked all day. And then he had gone to 'Encounter.' And Deirdre had gone to bed. He deserved a little 'me' time.

He felt pretty good about himself after a few more hits and another few swigs. But then it started to grow dark inside of him. And hot. It had happened before. He'd slip from being fine one minute to feeling like something was poking at him. Not physically. Something would start poking around inside of him, tapping louder and louder until it threatened to shatter the glass walls he had tried to make between him and the realization of what he was becoming.

He wanted to dismiss it as a bad trip but it was a lot more than that. It was all the shite they had taught him when he was a kid. Right and wrong, and sin, and unworthiness. It all came bubbling up like a broken sewer. It was always there, sludging around in the pit of his stomach, only now it was bilging up into his mouth, overwhelming all of his other senses. Before, he could make excuses for himself—he was just a dopey young fucker acting the tool, but now, married with kids and all, he was becoming a prize fuck-up. Even he had to admit—he was never going to grow out of it.

He had tried. He had tried harder than anybody ever gave him credit for but there was always something, somewhere, that would trip him up. It got worse when he was drunk and that was the real fuck-up. Drinking was the only way he could manage it all.

Mind you, just when he had a few. That was when he was at his best—when he could relax and deal with the kids and Deirdre. He knew she only wanted what was best for them all, but most of the things she wanted to change were things he liked.

When they moved, she was after him to get rid of the car. It was getting old and roared a bit when the exhaust came loose. He said he'd get it fixed but he hadn't. He liked the noise. It made the car feel more powerful. But things were starting to go and she wanted to look at the new minivans.

"There's a green one and a pink one
And a blue one and a yellow one
And they're all made out of ticky tacky
And they all look just the same," he sang softly to himself and that almost made him feel better.

It wasn't just him. Everybody he talked to said the same thing. Women had taken over all the stuff that men used to do. They picked the houses and the cars, and they picked the type of lives they shared. And the men had to do more. Now that the women were working, the men were supposed to do half of everything.

He didn't mind some of it but he hated cooking. Deirdre always made real food but when it was Danny's turn, he'd order pizza or take the kids to McDonald's. It was another running skirmish between them. He couldn't see what all the fuss was about—as long as no one went hungry.

None of it was turning out the way he had been led to believe, and he blamed the way he was brought up. Spending all that time learning about stuff that nobody believed in anymore, but it stayed with him. Like it was stuck to him.

You can never really leave Catholicism, he explained to the Tequila bottle. *They even have a name for people who try. The call them 'Lapsed.'*

But as his insides began to tumble, he calmed himself. It was like Deirdre had said: it was just growing pains. She said that they had to break out of the shells they had been in. She was always saying shite like that. She'd read it in one of her magazines or heard it from one of her friends. She made it seem like you could just go out and get your own set of beliefs and things. He wanted to believe that but it didn't seem to work for him. He could never outgrow the feeling of worthlessness that he had carried since he was little. He used to say that it was beaten into him. Frank and Jimmy used to laugh at that but Deirdre also reacted like it was something she was ashamed of—something that he really should leave behind him.

That was the thing with Deirdre. She always made things sound so easy but she didn't really know him. And he couldn't really tell her because he knew she felt guilty about when they were kids and all.

It wasn't her fault, though; he was fucked from the start. He could work his ass off and try to change everything about himself but he'd still be the same person inside. It was okay for her to go around thinking that she could change her life and all, but he couldn't. The past was still out to get Danny Boyle. He had done bad shit and no matter what you believed in, God,

Karma, the luck-of-the-draw, bad shit always came back to you. That was one of the things they had beaten into him at school.

It really doesn't have to be that way anymore.

He held up the bottle for a moment, as if it might explain why it wasn't Anto's voice, but the bottle was almost empty and had nothing to say. It had sounded like his Uncle Martin. For a moment he thought that was a good thing until he realized that he was just going crazier.

"Enough," he called out, louder than he had intended, and set a few dogs barking in the dark green gardens around. He hid the rest of the bottle, buried the roach in the flowerbed, and snuck off to bed before the whole neighborhood came out. Deirdre would never forgive him if that happened, and she'd be tired again on Saturday.

*

"You know you are supposed to be helping him?"

Anto had a healthy respect for Martin Carroll. When they had been alive, they got in a fight one day. Anto and a few of his mates were slagging Martin as he walked by.

"Are any of you brave enough to stand out?" he had asked over his shoulder. None of them really wanted to; Martin was known as a hard man but Anto had to. Even losing was better than not standing up.

Martin had decked him with a flurry of punches and Anto's mates ran off, leaving him bleeding in the streets.

When he was obviously done, Martin helped him to his feet and gave him a clean white hanky to wipe his bloody nose. That was what Anto remembered most about the whole thing—the clean white hanky. That, and to never mess with Martin Carroll again.

"I'm tryin'."

"Well you're not doin' very well. They sent me down to have a chat with you."

"I'm doing my best, Martin, but you know what he can be like."

"Have you tried frightening him?"

"What? Like acting ghostly or something?"

Martin looked at him like he was stupid. "Didn't they tell you how they wanted this dealt with?"

"No one told me anything. They just sent me back and told me I had to keep an eye on him."

"And they didn't tell you anything else?"

"No."

"This life is as fucked-up as the last one."

"You're right there."

"Well, I'm going back up to find out what is going on. In the meantime, try not to make things any worse, will you?"

"I'll do my best, Martin."

Martin didn't look too impressed as he faded away.

Fuck's sake, Anto muttered to himself. *No one told me it was a test.*

*

John Melchor liked to walk around the campus when he was troubled. He did not venture beyond it where the light of truth was dimmed by the darkness of the souls of the rich. He often tried to be more Christ-like in the way he thought about them, but he couldn't. What value was a man who denied another the basics so he could amass yet more? They paid their soldiers as brigands and lords had done since time began. Hard-hearted men who beat the poor into submission with the assurance of their master's law as a shield.

Philippe had joined the army, despite all that John had not said between his carefully chosen words. He understood. What choice did the sons of wealth have? Philippe would serve his class or be cast out. John had no right to judge.

That was what was bothering him. It was all very well to be teaching what Jesus said about disparity, but even Jesus was circumspect when it suited him. "Render unto Caesar the things that are Caesar's, and unto God the things that are God's." Hardly the words to start a revolution with and hardly the words of a man that had come to die for humanity. John was disappointed by Philippe, but deep in his heart, he was angry at Jesus. He had left the trail of breadcrumbs for honest men to see, but those who followed ended in forests of doubt with nothing but blind faith to lead them out.

John had spoken kindly to Philippe before he left, but in the time that had passed, his heart hardened. Philippe had written breezy, newsy dissertations on the absurdity of military indoctrination. John understood; it was the same when he joined the Air Force and, he reminded himself to boost his flagging spirits, when he joined the Society of Jesus.

He was, in so many ways, a mercenary too. He had fought the Japanese because of his own outrage. It was such a simple matter back then. They went to war to protect themselves against Imperial aggressions. But in the night sky, over Tokyo, when he was dropping napalm on the bedrooms of women and children, it felt a lot more like revenge. Through his sights, he could see each little fire spread into one, leaping around on its own gales, sucking oxygen, and leaving those below to suffocate until the heat melted them into ash. Most of Tokyo caught fire and nearly two hundred thousand people died.

Many of those people were women and children and old people. Some of them were burned alive, while others suffocated before they were burnt.

Afterwards, everyone said the Japanese had it coming after Pearl Harbor, but John Melchor could no longer believe that. Instead, he could picture his handiwork on the streets below. He could see it in his dreams—mothers covering their children that they might shrivel into ashes together. Ashes that were tossed around on the raging winds until they all became a cloud that blocked out the sun that had once shone directly into his heart. He was just twenty years of age.

A much older man came to the Universidad Centroamerica to fight the good fight with nothing but the words of Jesus; it was the Jesuit way. They would right wrong with empirical examination. No one could argue that. No one could deny what was true, except those who dealt in lies and deceit.

He had close friends in that; Jon Sobrino, Ignacio Ellacuría, Ignacio Martín-Baró, and Segundo Montes. When he was with them, it felt like God was gathering them to fight the self-serving logic of those who sold greed as a virtue. Those who violently oppressed the poor to save them from the clutches of godlessness. Those who broke every tenet of humanity for the good of the select few. It was so obvious.

Philippe knew all of that, too, but he had gone and, after basic training, had been placed among the ranks of the Atlacatl Battalion, among the sons of the elite and the ruthless—the Jesuits of Oppression. All John could hope was that some of what Philippe had been taught might survive.

The night was hot and hazy, the beginning of Verano, John's favorite time of the year. Back home they would be getting ready for Thanksgiving, but here, life was reemerging from the rains. His rambling took him toward the house. His friends would have had dinner but would sit awhile to talk into the night, to talk about what might yet come to pass.

He hesitated. Some sense that he could not identify, cautioned. He stood for a moment but it was quiet. He could see the house and he could hear voices speaking softly, but yet he lingered. Something else was prowling in the night. Shadowy figures converged on the house, but John could not make sense of it. They revealed their weapons and began to shoot, gunshots echoing and almost drowning out the stifled cries of terror.

He could see his friends crumple as they died. He could see the shadowy figures of death walk among them, ensuring that none survived, not even the housekeeper and her daughter, who was only sixteen years old. John wanted to step forward and place all that he was between them and death, but as he stepped from the cover of the night, someone turned and shot him.

He lay between life and death as someone stood over him. Someone else joined him and he heard whispers. And, as he faded from life, their words followed him into the dark.

"Porquería" and "Sacerdote Americano."

Chapter 14 – 1990

Jacinta was glad to be on her own in the cold dark church with flickering candles while the wind tested the trees outside. It was where she could always find a few moments of peace when life got choppy. She hadn't wanted to make a big fuss; it was just another birthday, but Gina had disagreed. She had sipped her coffee and smiled. She always seemed to think that Jacinta liked to be coaxed. "But it's your fiftieth. You have to have a big celebration."

"For God's sake, don't be reminding me. I just want to stay forty-nine for a while yet."

After she had excused herself and done the shopping for Jerry's tea, she had a few moments to sit in the church. She didn't believe in all the stuff that went on there, especially now with Fr. Dolan. He had a new way of telling the people what was right and what was wrong. He seemed more like a bank manager advising them about spiritual investments and how to enjoy their rewards. "If Jesus gives us good things," was his favorite mantra, "then we should enjoy them in good conscience."

Jacinta didn't like that at all. She preferred the old days when the bishop would drop by to berate them all for their unworthiness. Fr. Brennan could, too, if he was riled enough, but most of the time he just chided them like he was resigned to the fact that they would do whatever they liked and there was little he could do except set the bishop on them.

And poor, piddling Fr. Reilly. He always wore his heart on his sleeve, God love him. Burning like a candle, hoping that you would go over to him to get warm. She hoped he was doing well in Rome. She'd heard his father had died but he went straight back afterwards. She had wanted to see him, to thank him again. She wanted to tell him that Danny and Deirdre were doing very well for themselves, no small thanks to all the help they got from their loving curate.

Lately, whenever she thought about the Sacred Heart of Jesus, she saw Fr. Reilly's face instead. It first happened in the church. She'd been praying by the side altar. It was just before Christmas and she'd come in when all the worrying about the holidays got the better of her.

It was silent but for the trickle of beads in Mrs. Flanagan's hands, praying away another afternoon, praying for the soul of her son. Jacinta said a prayer for him too. She always did. She liked praying. She didn't think that God was on the other end but that wasn't the point. It was the getting down on her knees and asking for a bit of help. She believed in humility being good for the soul. Jerry told her that was what all the Yogis in the Himalayas said and they spent their whole lives just thinking about it. It was such a 'Jerry thing' to say. He always had his head in the clouds.

Anyway, when she had finished her prayers, she looked up at the stained glass window to see what the weather was like outside. The moment she looked, the sun came out and she forgot herself and stared at it, right through the face of Jesus as He was taken to the house of Caiaphas to listen to all the lies of those who believed in hatred.

She knew she should look away but she couldn't; Jesus was becoming Patrick Reilly.

When she did manage to turn away, the face followed her, even into the gloom around the main altar and in the corner where Mrs. Flanagan prayed. Even inside of her eyelids when Jacinta shut them as tightly as she could.

She tried telling Jerry about it, but he just laughed at her. She didn't care. She had finally figured out what Patrick Reilly had been trying to tell them all along. Patrick's God was not stern and remote, stalking the streets for retribution. Patrick's God was more concerned with people being nice to each other and always being there for the people who needed help, coming through strangers and friends whenever He was needed.

The more she thought about it, the more it made her look at her own life differently too. After Danny was born, when she went running out to drown the baby and was put in the hospital, she thought that Nora Boyle was just being cruel. She begged her parents for help, but they told her that she had to go along with things until she was better. Later, after a few years of staring at the walls, she realized that they were just cowing down to the Boyles.

She tried to tell the doctors, but they told her that she was unsound—what mother would want to drown her baby? She told them she didn't really mean to; it's just she was so angry at Jerry. The doctors turned that back on her and for months talked about her 'anger issues.'

She was only eighteen, far too young to know who she was yet, let alone how to raise a child. And far too young to understand what was going on around her. Everyone had always said she was a bit touched, but never to her face. Except the other children. They never gave her a moment's peace, pulling at her and pushing her and saying awful things about her. She hated them then, but now she understood—they just didn't know any better.

She used to blame the nuns for bringing so much attention to her when she was a child, shy and awkward and not as bright as the other children. But they were only trying to force her to do better. It was all they had from the limited understanding they had about life.

She didn't mind any of that anymore. Everything that had happened had led her to the point where she could sit in a quiet church and grasp the deepest mystery of all. The God that everyone prattled on about and fought about was a quiet strength that fluttered inside all of them. A quiet strength that grew stronger every time they were nice to each other. That was what Patrick Reilly had tried to teach them before they shuffled him out of the way.

"Are you well, Mrs. Flanagan?" she whispered as the two women rose to leave together. It was a regular thing; they would stop in at the Yellow House for a few nips before they both went home to prepare the dinner. And, as always, Jacinta treated.

*

"Listen. It's sound. They'll put in the money now and when the job is done, we pay them off." Donal seemed very assured but Jerry couldn't help but feel that there was more going on.

"How much?"

"Principle and ten percent of the profit."

"Ten percent? Jazus. Wouldn't they have settled for a pound of flesh instead?"

"That's nothing, Jerry. If we tried to raise it on the open market, they'd want our balls as collateral. That's if we could find anybody to take them. Times are tough out there."

"Times are always tough. What I want to know is where the money is coming from?"

"Does it matter?"

"It does to me. I don't want to end up with Shergar's head in my bed."

Donal laughed at that and slapped Jerry on the back—a little too hard. "It's like everyone says: Never look a gift horse . . . Am I right? Listen. They could be selling their daughters as whores for all we care. We just need their money for a while. Afterwards, we'll pay them off and be done with them."

He ordered two more drinks, large whiskies as was befitting their status even though Jerry would have preferred a pint, but Donal was big on keeping up appearances.

"You have to shake hands with a few devils if you're ever going to get anywhere, Jerry. But after this we won't have to anymore."

"That's what you said the last time."

"C'mon, Jerry. It wasn't my fault the deal in Rathmines fell through. How was I to know your man was going to do a runner?"

"I tried to warn you."

Jerry had. He knew the runner from way back—a dubious bollocks if ever there was.

"And I told you," Donal continued like he was explaining something to a moron, "that we'd take a hit now and then. I thought you understood the business by now. I need you as a partner, Jerry, and not someone who waits around to say I-told-you-so every time we hit a bump in the road."

"Bump, my arse, he got us for forty grand."

"Small change, Jerry. Toll money on the highway to riches."

"I hope you fucking know what you're getting us into."

Donal drained his drink and picked up his car keys, the ones for the new Jag. He had to have it to impress clients while Jerry had to make do with the old Rover. "I've told you before—if it starts getting too rich for you, you can quit. I know lots of people who would be happy to buy you out."

He slapped Jerry's shoulder again and left.

*

"Only you can decide, Jerry," Jacinta agreed after he had explained it all to her.

Since he had jacked in the government job and gone full-time in the business, he was always having doubts. Sometimes, she missed the old days when all he had to complain about was 'all the blundering bollocks' that he had to put up with. He wasn't cut out for this. Not that he wasn't smart enough; Jerry had too much goodness in him.

Stuff like that mattered to her. She could see what was going on all around her. Everyone was getting caught up in wanting more and more and none of them were getting any happier.

Though she did like when they took trips to Spain and all, but she was just as happy spending her afternoons down in the shops and in the church. Everyone still whispered about her, behind her back, but now they were just jealous. She and Gina were the envy of them all. Only she never let on that she noticed.

"All that really matters is that you can live with the decisions you make."

Jerry looked at her in amazement ,and that made her happy.

"I know what you mean. The only thing I want now is to be able to look after my grandkids."

Jacinta had to smile at that. Jerry may not have been the best father in the world, but he was making up for it with Danny's children.

"Well instead of throwing me a party I don't want, why don't we go over to Canada, again?"

"How did you know about the party? That feckin' Gina; I told her not to say a word."

"But I'd much rather see my grandchildren again. And my Danny and Deirdre."

"Do you think they'll have the World Cup on over there?"

"It's the World Cup, Jerry. They'll have it everywhere."

"Do you think Danny will be watching it? He was never big into football."

"Oh, stop fretting. Everything will be fine."

"You're right. And do you know what I'm going to do? I'm going to bring over whatever money I make on this deal and give it to him. He'll need it with that mortgage they've got."

*

The days were getting warmer but the crowds of tourists were still thin. By summer they would fill out and take over every street and alley.

Patrick had the day off. It was almost the end of term and he was feeling a bit lazy. Spring in Rome did that. It had rained during the night and the air was fresh with a hint of the ocean. It was a good day to be alive and content, standing by his window looking down on the little streets where life had dawdled by for centuries. When the phone rang, he answered without turning. He was watching an old man and his dog. The old man waited patiently as his dog stopped to sniff every pillar and post, sprinkling those that piqued his interest.

"Patricio, I'm afraid I have to tell you some bad news. Benedetta is dying and wants to see you before she . . ."

Patrick hadn't seen her in a few weeks, not since he had given her his uncle's letters.

He still wasn't sure why he did it. It was like some inner voice called out to him and wouldn't be hushed until he did. He regretted it as soon as it was done. She had taken the letters in her trembling hands and her eyes clouded over. He should have left well enough alone. He had no business evoking old ghosts, no matter what crazy voice popped into his mind. The shock of it all had probably been too much for the old lady.

He pedaled furiously toward the Ponte Garibaldi, across the river and along the Via Arenula. He often thought about getting a moped but there was something invigorating about being a priest in a hurry on a bicycle. He didn't get to feel like that very often anymore. He hadn't worn his collar in years. He was more of an academic now. He said his masses at Santa Maria at a side altar privately, except for a few nuns and the occasional elderly neighbor with time on his hands. And as he wheeled into the piazza, he wondered if he would be called on for the Last Rites. He hadn't done one since Dublin.

Giovanni met him and led him upstairs to the family apartments. Benedetta's room was on the third floor, looking west. She liked to watch the setting of the sun from her bed.

"She has been failing for a while but she's content," Giovanni explained as they climbed the stairs.

She lay like an aged bride under white covers that barely moved as she drew shallow breaths. Patrick had been with so many when death came for them, but she was different. She lay serenely, almost expectant, and smiled when Patrick stood over her and motioned to Giovanni to leave them. When he had gone, she beckoned Patrick closer until he was leaning over her.

"I wanted to thank you," she whispered while staring past his bowed head. "We can be together now."

Patrick wasn't sure so he just nodded. Benedetta had outgrown her religion, so he doubted she was referring to God.

"All these years I wasn't sure."

Patrick knew better than to interrupt and just held her hand and nodded.

"But when I read his letters, I knew. He never stopped loving me, either." She shifted her gaze to Patrick's face so he remained as impassive as he could, only he didn't do so well.

"Do not be shocked, Patrick. We are free now, free to love each other for all time."

She closed her eyes and sighed. He let go of her hand and, out of habit, joined it with the other on top of the covers. But Benedetta wasn't praying—he knew what that sounded like, a hoarse and desperate rattle. She just sighed again and drifted off to sleep.

She died later that night as Patrick sat vigil along with the family. Some cried and some prayed but, after they had covered her, Giovanni took Patrick downstairs and out to the patio. He poured some whiskies and they drank to her memory—and the bishop's.

*

"At this stage, I think we have to assume that no news is good news."

Miriam didn't agree but there was no point in arguing with Joe. He would have done all that he could, phoning friends and the friends of friends, but there was still no word on John Melchor.

Officially, he was not even reported missing, but friends in the Society of Jesus feared the worst. They didn't say that, of course. They said there was still hope. Someone even suggested that there was no reason to believe that he was caught up in the atrocity.

"But that makes no sense, Joe. Why would he just disappear?"

"I don't know, Miriam. All I can tell you is what I am hearing."

He had nothing more to offer into the silence, though she could hear him breathing across the phone line. She knew what he was thinking. John was probably dead and his body lost, but he was too good a brother to say that.

"Thank you for everything you've done, Joe."

"I wish it could be more, sis."

"Well thanks anyway. I should be going, but call me if you hear anything."

"You know I will."

"I do, Joe."

Karl waited until she hung up and was ready to talk. He walked toward her and took her in his arms. She trembled with sorrow and rage but he held her tightly. "Perhaps," he drawled the way he did when his mind was already sorting out what needed to be done, "I can call in a few favors."

She knew he didn't really want to have anything more to do with all of that and appreciated what he was offering.

"I couldn't ask you to do that."

"You don't have to. I'm offering."

He still had friends in the army, friends who owed him, and some of them were privy to what was really going on. Some had just been sent to Panama as advisors.

"I'll just make a few calls," was all he said but it was enough. She knew what he was really saying. He would pull every string he could reach until someone, somewhere, got him what he wanted.

"We still might have to face the fact that the news might be bad." He looked at her like she was a child, but she didn't mind. He was getting all soldierly, sticking out his chin like he was about to lead his platoon back into the jungle.

"I know, but I need to know, one way or the other."

"Are you sure?"

She just nodded. She couldn't tell him that she still had hope. Something inside was telling her that John was still alive—that she would know if he was dead.

"Should we go down there?"

"Not right now. They have started an inquest and they will want to wrap it up neatly. They'll find a few scapegoats. They'll have to; the Jesuits are kicking up a storm."

"For the others but not for John."

"Miriam. John was not among the bodies."

"Then there is a chance that he is still alive."

She knew he was keeping his face tight and she loved him for that. It was a fool's hope but it was all she had.

"There is. And when they find him, we'll catch the first flight and you can give him shit for scaring the hell out of us."

"Us?"

"What's yours is mine."

She kissed him and turned away before he could see how frightened she was.

"You know, we often lost guys in the bush, only they turned up later. And John was in the service."

She knew what he was trying to do and went along with it. "You're right."

"Besides," he continued like he was just sorting it out in his mind, "he's an old fly-boy. Those guys always knew how to hole up well. We had to go looking for one once. He'd been shot down a few days before. We searched for miles and, just when we were about to give up, we found him in a . . ."

"A what?"

It was his turn to look like a child. "A knocking-shop."

It did make her laugh. "Well, maybe you can get them to widen the search but I doubt John would end up in a place like that."

"Unless he was trying to evangelize them."

"Organize a union more likely."

*

"Who put the ball in the English net?" Jerry sang while Danny tried to ignore him. He'd been doing it all the way over to Martin's soccer game in the minivan, singing until Martin sang back: "Sheedy."

In fact, they'd been doing it all afternoon since the goal. They'd stayed in to watch the game. Martin even wore his new 'Irish' shirt. Jacinta thought her nerves wouldn't be up for it, so she took the girls for lunch and a bit of shopping, too.

"Da! Don't." Danny nodded toward the parents all around them. They were mostly women, of British stock but with a spattering of Greeks, Ukrainians, a few Poles, a deranged Dutchman and a few Italians, presiding like royalty. Danny knew them all to 'nod to' but they hadn't really accepted him yet.

They liked Martin though. He was becoming a star player, and to become a 'real Leasider,' you had to have gifted children. Martin fit the bill and would be their 'in.' Deirdre said she couldn't be bothered with all that but she wasn't keen on having Frank and Jimmy over anymore.

"Don't what. Act like a real football fan?" his father asked, innocently enough.

"Just cool it, Da. These people take their soccer very serious."

Jerry looked around at all the parents sitting in lawn chairs along the sideline. Some of them weren't even watching the game properly. "Yeah, they're the Kop, transported," he laughed and began to sing:

For he's football crazy,
He's football mad,
The football it has taken away
The little bit o' sense he had.

He clapped along, trying to get those around him to join in but they didn't. Most of them had suddenly become engrossed with the game, but a few nodded over at them. "Is that your father?" one of them asked Danny.

"Over from Ireland?" another added, like that would explain things.

"Guilty as charged," Jerry beamed at them all. He'd had a few beers during the game and they hadn't worn off yet. Danny's had. He was always careful about that. Deirdre was always after him about it. She didn't want her children's father to ever embarrass them anymore. He'd had a few incidents since they moved. That's why some of the parents were still a bit leery of him.

"And that," Jerry continued and bowed to them all, "is my grandson—number ten."

And even as he said it, the ball sailed across the goalmouth. All the others kids closed their eyes and hopped, hoping the ball would miss them, but not Martin. He jumped straight at the ball and hit it with his forehead, past the flailing hands of the keeper, just as he had practiced with his granddad.

He kept running, past the distraught defenders who were looking at their parents for consolation, back to his side of the field, high-fiving with his team like they did in the World Cup. Some of the parents cheered their approval and began to discuss which of their kids had gotten the assists. And, while the coach of the other team argued with the referee, Martin winked over at his granddad.

"You're welcome, sonny boy. Anytime."

"What's that about?" Danny muttered.

Jerry stopped smiling and turned away to watch the game restart. "It's nothing, son. It's just I was showing him a few tricks."

"That's more than you ever did with me."

"Y'er not still going on with that, are ya? Let it go, son."

"Easy for you to say."

"You don't mean that, son, and some day you'll realize that."

Danny might have said more but Martin had the ball again. He had it close to his feet and had his head up, the way Jerry had taught him. He was faster than the others and kept the ball under some control—as much as the lumps and bumps would allow. He got by everyone else and rounded the keeper, who had come out dispassionately, and banged it into the net.

"Who put the ball in the Rangers net?" Jerry jumped up and began to clap his hands.

"Jesus, Da. Don't be doing that. The parents on the other side will get mad."

"They look harmless enough to me."

"Don't be fooled—they're really hockey parents."

Martin's team won six to nothing, and Martin scored five. He could have had the other but he passed it off. Afterwards, after the coach had given out the frozen treats, Martin came over to where his grandfather sat and put his arm around him.

"You're good enough to play for Ireland," Jerry said laughing. "When we get home I'll phone Jackie and get you on a plane to Italy."

Martin laughed at that but Danny didn't. He was miffed and gathered up the lawn chairs and headed back to the car park while Martin and his grandfather exchanged high-fives again. It was going to be a long four weeks.

*

Martin's team won the next three games, while the Irish didn't fare so well. They drew against Egypt and the Dutch before the shoot-out win over the Romanians. Even Jacinta watched that one, with Grainne on her knee. But it all ended against the Italians.

Martin was in tears but cheered up when his grandfather offered to take him outside to practice some more. "We got to the quarter-finals." Jerry tried to get him to see the bright side as he tied his grandson's boots. "Nobody was expecting us to do that well."

"He's crazy about him," Jacinta remarked as she watched them through the window.

"Which one?" Deirdre laughed. The visit was going so much better than she had hoped. Jacinta had stopped pressuring them about coming home and was still able to work her magic on Grainne. She got her out of bed and dressed without Deirdre having to get involved. She even managed to brush her hair without too much fuss. It made Deirdre happy to see the smile on her daughter's face.

Danny wasn't so happy though. He was brooding a lot but she didn't have time to find out why. It was probably something to do with his father. He still resented him about something.

"You know," Jacinta turned away from the window and sat by the kitchen table. "Jerry has a surprise for you all." She had been hinting about it since she arrived. "I'll let him tell Danny himself, but I want you to know first. He made a lot of money recently and he wants to give you some."

"That's very kind, but we couldn't." Deirdre was tempted but they were doing much better and she didn't want Jacinta and Jerry feeling they had to help.

"Nonsense, Deirdre. Take it while he's offering. It's about thirty thousand."

Deirdre couldn't help it; even as she turned to face her mother-in-law, her mind was calculating all they could do with that. Martin would be playing hockey again this winter, and she wanted Grainne to take up skating too. And ballet. And she really wanted them to be able to take a holiday down south in the winter. "I don't know what to say, Jacinta."

"Just say thanks and don't give it another thought. He'd only spend it all on drink if he didn't have his grandchildren to be helping out with."

Not only did Deirdre thank her, she hugged her too. Even Grainne joined in.

Danny was less pleased when he found out. He said they didn't need his parents' charity anymore so Deirdre had to work on him until he had the good grace to accept it and give thanks. That made Jerry happier than Deirdre had ever seen him, and when they saw them off at the airport, he hugged them all like he might never see them again. Jacinta chided him for being so maudlin and then they were gone.

*

Martin's team won the playoffs, mostly because of his goals, and they were all invited to the coach's house for a barbeque. It was the first time the neighbors had included them, so Deirdre warned Danny to be on his best behavior. He could have two beers but no more. And none beforehand, either.

Danny agreed, for the most part, except for a few swigs of tequila while he was pretending to be tiding up the backyard. But he was going to be on his best behavior.

It was in one of the bigger houses on Bessborough, and Danny and Deirdre had to take the tour on their way through to the back garden. Danny wasn't comfortable; it was far too ostentatious for him but Deirdre smiled and admired it all, like she was in an art gallery or something. She even offered to help in the kitchen while Danny was ushered out to join the other men.

They were gathered around the cooler and somebody handed him a beer, introducing him as 'Martin's father.' They all smiled and congratulated him until Danny almost felt at ease.

They talked for a while about the playoffs and how well Martin had played, and Danny basked in the middle of it all. But not for long—soon they were talking hockey, about Ballard and 'the Great One,' and Danny moved to the edge. He didn't feel qualified to join in.

"Is Martin going to play this year?" one of them finally asked, a swarthy, puffy-faced man who seemed to have sway over the others.

"I dunno," Danny answered as casually as he could. He was happy to have their attention again and happily accepted a second beer. "We're not really a hockey family. We're more into football. Soccer."

"Let me explain something," the swarthy-faced man spoke slowly as if he wasn't sure that Danny understood. "You're in Canada now. Hockey is it here. Soccer is fine for the summer and girls," he added as an aside to the others who stood around and laughed on cue. "But if you want your son to get anywhere, he has to play. I'm holding tryouts next week. Make sure you have him there."

Danny still wasn't sure but the other fathers went to work on him, handing him his third beer and telling he couldn't let his son miss out. The swarthy-faced man was going to form the 'select team' at the end of the season and it wouldn't be wise to turn him down.

*

Danny was still trying to decide a week later as he stood in Canadian Tire, in the aisle with the hockey equipment. The stuff was expensive and he had no idea what some of it was for. The helmet, skates and sticks were obvious but the pads and garters were beyond him.

"You know," one of the fathers from the barbeque sidled up to him, "you can get most of this stuff second-hand."

"Really?" Danny answered and began filling his cart with the most expensive stuff he could find. He had no idea what he was buying but he could get Deirdre to exchange it later. "I don't know if I'd feel right having my son playing in used shit."

When he got home he phoned the swarthy-faced man and told him they were in.

*

So, Danny Boyle became a hockey dad and, though he knew little about the game, he joined in with the other parents, berating referees while sipping his 'Tim Horton's.' He could always be counted on for something acerbic.

He carried a flask, too, and could usually be found among the other fathers, tippling when their wives weren't looking. However, after an out of town Christmas tournament, Martin asked Deirdre to start taking him to games instead. The other parents were always talking about how much his father could drink—and how often.

When Danny heard about it, he was furious and even threatened to pull Martin from the team.

Martin tried to plead with him but Danny just grew more irate until Deirdre had to intervene.

"Go on up to bed, Martin, while I have a little chat with your father."

It was the same way she spoke when Grainne had been acting up, so Martin retired knowing that his mother would sort it out.

"Danny. You're not going to take this from Martin."

"And have him listen to all that gossip."

"Danny. You brought all of this on yourself and Martin, and I think it is only fair that it stops, now. Hockey is the most important thing in his life right now—and being a part of the team, regardless of what you might think."

Danny knew better and stayed silent. He had been drinking too much; even he could see that.

"And," Deirdre continued like she was holding all the cards, "you are going to have to do something about your drinking. I think you may be developing a problem."

"I don't have a problem; I can stop any time I want."

"Good. Then it's settled."

She rose and went upstairs leaving Danny to smolder alone in the dark.

Chapter 15 – 1991

H E HAD BEEN IN DARKNESS FOR SO LONG that he was almost afraid of the light. It was diffused through blinds, but it was still brighter than any light he remembered. A soft hand touched his brow and brushed his hair back from his face. He knew the hand by touch. It was a woman's hand, soft and warm. It was a mother's hand.

He knew her voice too. She had called his name for days, calling him back from the shadows he had fled to. "John," she had called, "John Melchor." She spoke in English but her accent was obvious and her voice reminded him of Philippe's.

He tried to sit up but the woman's hand pushed him back. "Lie still," was all she said. He did not have the strength to try again but he did open his eyes.

Dolores Maria D'Cruz Madrigal had once been a very beautiful woman. Her hair had been dark and her white skin had been smooth. She had once been the most beautiful woman in San Alejo. Her eyes were still dark but soft and now they searched John's for any sign of fever.

"Where am I?" was all he could think to ask. Since that night, he could not be sure what was real and what was dreaming.

She smiled and little creases formed around the sides of her lips. "You are safe now. But you must not try to rise. The doctor will be back soon."

"So I am not dead yet?"

She stopped smiling and wiped his face with a cool damp cloth. "No, not yet."

He could see the question troubled her and regretted it. He lay back and tried to remember.

He remembered the bullets hitting him and he remembered falling to his knees as he watched his friends die. Someone stepped behind him and something cold touched the back of his head. He could feel the gun trembling and tried to prepare for the end. But someone else called from the darkness. They whispered for a few moments and one of them approached and tried to lift him.

That was when he passed out. He came to in the back of a car as it squealed through the night streets. He was carried into a house and placed on a table.

A doctor approached him, a nervous man who wore his spectacles at the end of his nose. He examined the gunshot wounds and shook his head slowly. "He should not have been moved," he chided others in the room. "But they would have found him and . . ." a familiar voice justified.

"They still might," the doctor interrupted and leaned forward with a syringe. "Hold him."

Hands reached from the shadows and held John steady until they all faded back into the gloom.

***

"I am the mother of Philippe Ignatius Madrigal. He brought you here."

Before John could respond, someone else entered and began whispering to the woman. It was a man's voice. It was a deep and commanding voice but it was whispering urgently. John could barely hear but he made out enough. An American helicopter had been shot down nearby and all three crew members had been killed. The man was insistent that they had been killed after they landed.

He blamed the rebels and seemed to think that it somehow involved their 'guest.'

"He is not well enough to be moved," the woman spoke so John could hear her. "He will not leave my house until then."

The man with the deep and commanding voice muttered something but the woman was adamant. "If they find out about him they will know what Philippe did. Do you really want your son exposed?"

The man with the deep and commanding voice muttered again and left.

John tried to rise again. He could not be a burden to them. He could not have them at risk for his sake, but the woman was ready and gently pushed him back. "No, Father. You must rest until your strength comes back."

*

Miriam watched in disbelief. The world was going to war again and there was nothing anybody could do to stop it. The media had whipped them all into a righteous rage with images of premature babies thrown on the floor and gloating soldiers praising their God. CNN was outraged.

Karl had been on the phone all morning but there was still no news. John Melchor had vanished from the face of the earth.

She knew he wanted to say something, something that might offer a little reassurance. She loved and hated him for that. She loved that he cared so much but despised what she must look like to him—frightened and alone in a world that paid lip service to all that she held dear. She did not want pity. She wanted outrage. She wanted everyone to stand up and scream, all at the same time, so the masters of lies would have to pay attention.

But everyone around her was mesmerized by robotic generals showing video clips of pure, clean death, the vengeance of the righteous that only fell on the heads of the despicable. It was all too good to be true.

Miriam knew better. War did not differentiate between innocence and guilt. War was a hungry beast that, when loosed, devoured all that lay before it. There was nothing right about it and all who involved themselves were complicit in murder. In a way, she hoped John had left this world so he would not have to see this again.

"We mustn't give up hope," Karl reminded her, looking at her like he thought she might break.

"No, we mustn't," she agreed, but her soul was empty. Before, when they were actively opposing war, it had seemed so easy. They had 'right' on their side and nothing could threaten them. Sure, they could be arrested and incarcerated, but when the people found out, they demanded their release.

Now, things had changed. The people were bored with what was right. It was too hard—too demanding, so they turned away for reassurance. They believed it when they were told that they lived in the greatest democracy the world had ever seen. Appointed by God and secure in that righteousness, there was no reason for them to question, even those they knew to be dishonest.

"You know," he said the way he said those things that he carefully chose to lift her when she was down, "I was thinking of visiting Canada one of these days."

"Will they let you in?"

"I'm not sure; that's why I want you to come along."

"I see. And where were you thinking of going?"

"Toronto. I hear it's very nice this time of the year."

"It's winter."

"Okay. We can wait 'til the spring."

Miriam smiled and melted into his warm embrace. She knew what he was doing and she loved him all the more for it.

*

Deirdre was really looking forward to their visit. She needed reinforcing. Danny had gotten drunk again, in February, after nearly seven weeks of abstaining. She saw it coming.

At first, he was enthusiastic and had even joined a gym. But as the winter wore him down, he stopped going and sat in front of the TV, night after night. She tried to go along as if nothing was wrong. She took Martin to hockey and Grainne to ballet, leaving Danny alone. She could tell they were all getting on his nerves, but for the most part he kept it bottled up inside of him.

Except when the kids fought. Then all that simmered inside of him would bubble to the surface. Deep down, he was angry at so many things—things that were not directly related to them.

She was getting very tired of him. Life, that was so grey and forlorn to Danny, had actually treated them quite well but he just seemed incapable of seeing it that way. They had used most of the money from Jerry and Jacinta to pay down the mortgage. They had postponed the trip down south so they could send Martin to hockey camp. His coach was sure that, with the proper preparation, Martin could have a future in the game.

Deirdre wasn't so sure, but Martin, being the true Canadian he was, had his heart set on it. In return, to appease her, he kept his grades up and was a model child—except in his father's eyes. Sometimes Deirdre wondered if Danny wasn't jealous of him.

Grainne was a different story. She was only five but was showing signs of becoming very precocious. Deirdre hated admitting it but she was. And even at her age, Grainne seemed to be able to see the fault lines that ran through the family. She could make any squabble with her brother into a family issue. She had Danny wrapped around her little fingers and he could not see it.

Instead, when they did talk about it, he accused her of always siding with Martin. She tried to explain but he wouldn't hear it. In fact, they agreed on less and less.

She was tempted to let it slide. She was busy enough at work and, when she finally got home, drained and worn down, she had little energy for family politics. But she had to deal with his drinking.

**

"What can I say?" he had muttered the morning after as he waited for the coffee to brew. He looked terrible.

"An explanation maybe?"

"Ah, Dee. Cut me some slack. I just had a few beers, that's all. Where's the harm in that?"

It might have sounded reasonable from somebody else. "Danny. We have discussed this and we both agreed that drinking has become a problem for you. You promised that you would deal with it—for all our sakes."

"I know and I was. I just had a few beers. It's not the end of the world."

"Well, I'm not willing to wait until the end begins. I want you to get help."

"I don't need help."

"That's what people with problems always say." Deirdre had done her homework. One of the women in the office had been married to an alcoholic. She made a point of letting Deirdre know that after the last office party, when Danny had gotten so drunk that they had to leave early. She told Deirdre what she had been through and even invited her to an Al-Anon meeting. Deirdre went, for Danny's sake, and heard all that she needed to hear.

"You can't be serious?"

"I have never been more serious."

The people at the meeting had said that the best time to tackle the problem was during the hangover. That was when guilt and remorse bubbled just under the surface. He sat opposite her and sipped his coffee. She almost felt sorry for him but she had been warned against that. Alcoholics thrived on pity.

"Danny. I want you to go to AA meetings."

"Jesus, Deirdre. I'm not that bad."

"Then you'll have nothing to worry about. You can go and find out what it's all about." She had been told that too. 'Just get him to meetings,' they had advised over coffee after the meeting. "It will do no harm to be better informed. Then, if you really don't have a problem, we'll know."

"It was just a few beers, Dee."

A part of her wanted to reach out to him but she had been warned against that too. They had called it enabling. "I will go with you if that helps?"

He seemed to realize that there was no other way out. She had done it. She had forced him into the realization. The people at the meeting had said that was vital.

"Okay. If that's what you want—I'll do it. But you'll see. They'll probably tell me there is nothing wrong and not let me join."

"Then we'll all be happier." It was like shooting fish in a barrel. "There's a meeting tonight, at St. Monica's on Broadway."

"It's not a Catholic thing, is it?"

"No."

"But what if somebody sees me going in?"

"They'll think you got religion."

"Ah, Jazus, Dee. Do I have to?"

*

Danny knew there was no point in arguing. He knew, after the last time, that it was his last chance. Still, it wasn't the end of the world. He would go to the meeting and go along with it all until the heat was off. Growing up Catholic had its advantages.

Still, he sat in his car in the church car park to see what kind of idiots he was going to have to put up with. He thought about sitting there until the meeting was over but he knew better. Deirdre would have been in contact with them and they'd report back if he didn't show. There was nothing for it but to head down to the basement, past the easel with the sign that read: You are no longer alone.

He tried to seem nonchalant but everywhere he looked somebody smiled back at him until he looked away. They must have all been tipped off that he was coming. What the fuck had he gotten himself into now?

I think you should hang around and see what it's all about.

You would. How the fuck did you know I was here?

Kismet, Boyle. Kismet. Anto sounded very pleased with himself.

You don't think I'm one of them. Do ya?

Not yet, but given time . . .

Look at them, Anto. For fuck's sake!

They seem happy enough.

That's because you're dead. Look at them, for fuck's sake. What a bunch of fuckin' losers.

Yeah, and you're a real winner.

But before Danny could respond, the meeting opened with a moment of silence and a prayer. Danny fought the urge to snicker but he was afraid. He was the only sane person in the room and decided to go along with them for the hour or two that it took. That way, if they did report back to Deirdre, she'd know he sat through the whole thing. He could turn this to his advantage yet.

The room was decorated with green ribbons and balloons, and the man who chaired the meeting was a droll Irish policeman. They must have gone to great efforts to snare him. After some rituals that Danny could not understand, and some uninspired interpretation of the clearly legible slogans that stood on little easels around the stage, a man got up to speak. He was from Dublin and Danny was sure that he'd been set up.

The man began to talk about himself and, though his story was very different from Danny's, there were enough similarities. Deirdre must have prepped him too. He talked about his feelings toward God and stuff like that, and how he always felt that he was on God's hit list and how he had a deep feeling of shame that he could never get rid of.

Danny wanted to scoff but it was too close to home. The man talked about growing up surrounded by a veil of lies and Danny couldn't help but pay attention. The man talked about feeling separate and apart from everything going on around him, about feeling like an outsider and how others noticed and picked on him for that. And not just the other kids, but school teachers, priests and nuns and in time, the cops.

He said that he used to question everything—that nothing made sense. He questioned why people lived one way but talked about living another. He said it drove him mad until he found drugs and alcohol. He said when he drank, that it blunted all the jagged edges and he could function with the rest of the world.

Those around Danny began to nod in agreement.

The man said that it was only when he was drinking that he felt comfortable in his own skin—that he didn't feel like he was less than everybody else. In fact, he told them sarcastically, it made him feel a lot better than the rest of them. So he used drugs and alcohol to help him get by and he had done very well for himself—for a while. He had come to Canada a few years before Danny and had worked in advertising. He'd become an art director with an expense account and all. He'd married, too, a model, but he lost it all—and her. She left him as he careened all the way down to the bottom, ending up in Seaton House and panhandling around Jarvis and Queen. But he was sober now for nearly five years and, even though he had a long hard climb back, he was grateful.

He told them he had a special message for newcomers too. He said that they didn't have to wait until they lost everything. They could cash in their misery early and save themselves a lot of grief, and Danny couldn't help but feel that the comment was directed solely at him.

He was unsure of himself as they passed the plate around and he dropped a dollar so they could all see that he was impressed. He almost was. A lot of what the man had said reverberated inside. Danny was nowhere near as bad as him but he could see himself getting there. It almost made him stop and think but everyone around him began to pray. "Our Father who art in Heaven . . ."

And that was enough for Danny. He had spent most of his life trying to get away from stuff like that.

Afterwards, he stood around so that no one could report that he was anxious to leave. He stood near the wall but a few guys came over to talk with him. One of them was the man who spoke.

"You new?"

"Ya. First meeting."

"I'm Sean M," he said as he held out his hand.

"I'm Danny B," Danny answered, showing that he was hip to their ways.

"Do you think you have a problem with alcohol?"

"I might. My wife seems to think so."

The man laughed at that. "Denial, Danny, it's the greatest sickness in the world."

"So," Danny said, trying to brush past that, "do you get many Irish here?"

The man looked at all the green decorations and laughed again. "They're for the church's Saint Patrick's Day dance, but ya, we do. Are we going to see you again?"

"Sure," Danny answered as he measured the number of steps it would take to get to the door. "I mean if everybody thinks I have a problem, I'd be dumb not to find out."

"Ya, you would," the man smiled again before someone interrupted them. Danny seized the moment and fled. He tried not to walk too quickly, but even still, his heart was beating by the time he got to his car. He looked around again. It didn't seem like anybody noticed but he knew they were watching him—for their report.

So, Boyle? What did you think?

Between you, me, and the wall, Anto, I'm not that fuckin' bad. Not by a long shot.

He didn't really believe himself but he had to put on a brave face. He didn't want Anto to know it had gotten to him.

Maybe, Boyle. But, knowing you, you'll get there.

*

"Are you sure it's going to be okay?"

"Of course," Deirdre assured her. Danny and Karl had gone to pick up wine while Miriam and Deirdre prepared dinner. "Danny was insistent. He says he has learned that he cannot hide from alcohol."

"But it will be terrible for him, sitting watching the rest of us."

"He says he'd feel more awkward if we weren't."

"Is he going to make it, Dee?"

Deirdre didn't answer immediately. She had changed. The old Deirdre would have blurted out the first thing on her mind, but this one was different. She looked like a woman now—a woman who had children and a career. A woman who had it all. Miriam would have been jealous if she were someone else.

"One day at a time," Deirdre finally answered, cautiously.

"And you? Are you going to make it?"

Deirdre flashed a doleful smile. "I have to."

Miriam stood closer and gently rubbed her back as Deirdre chopped a little more frenetically. "I'm sure it will be fine."

"I hope so," Deirdre answered without looking up. "It's his last chance."

Miriam wanted to say something but what could she say? She knew nothing about this and there was no point in dragging out all the usual platitudes. "I'm sure it will be fine."

*

"Are you sure it's not going to be a problem?"

Danny looked over at Karl, leaning languidly against the other side of the car. With his elbow out the window and his hat low, he reminded Danny of the Marlboro man. "I told you. I'll be fine. It's one of the things they teach us—at the meetings."

Karl said nothing but smiled as Danny pulled into the car park and got out. He followed, towering over Danny as he walked along beside him. He knew his wines, too, and insisted on paying for them.

"Do you miss it?"

"Every day. But I've also learned to think about what will happen if I have one. Deirdre and the kids would be gone— she's made that very clear. And I don't blame her. I see what I used to be now and I don't want my kids having to put up with any more of it."

"Well good for you, Danny." Karl smiled with his mouth but his eyes hardly flickered. Danny would have to be extra careful around him. He'd probably seen all kinds of things in 'Nam.

"It's not me. I just go to meetings and do what I'm told."

"So you found your 'Higher Power?'" Karl smiled again, but just with his mouth.

"I wouldn't go that far. I just go along with what they say is right—and the steps, of course."

He started the car and pulled out of the car park, checking his mirrors and signaling like a model citizen.

"Well good for you, Danny." Karl repeated, and turned to watch the neighborhood glide past, like he was checking for something.

*

The kids got to eat in front of the television so the adults could sit outside and dine. Deirdre had gone all out with help from Miriam: delicately grilled trout with side salads—green and potato. Karl had chosen light sweetish whites to complement it all. He even helped to tidy things away and helped Danny load the dishwasher. And while Deirdre served coffee, excused himself to check with his message service.

"He's not working, is he?"

"Always, but what can you do?"

"What is it that he does?"

Miriam explained as well as she could until Karl returned and sat down with a big smile on his face: "He's alive."

"Oh, thank God." Miriam hugged Deirdre while Danny sat dumbfounded.

"He's somewhere safe and will be brought out when he is well enough to travel."

"Are you sure?"

"Yes."

"Wait a minute. What did you mean by 'when he's well enough to travel?'"

"He was shot but he is recovering."

"Where? Is he in hospital?"

"I doubt it. All I know is that he's with friends—and he is safe."

"Well, everybody," she raised her glass, "let's drink to John Melchor."

They all joined in but Danny. He'd heard of John Melchor; he'd just never paid any attention to the stories. He heard what had been happening, too, but he assumed it had ended badly. And while Miriam and Deirdre giggled like school children, making so much of a fuss that the kids came out, Karl sat quietly beside Danny and looked at the setting of the sun.

"Thank you," Miriam finally mouthed over at him as things settled down again and Deirdre had gone to put the kids to bed.

"So what is it that you do again?" Danny asked to fill the empty space.

"Investigations." Karl smiled like Danny would understand.

"Like a P.I.?"

"Not really. I'm a contractor. I just sit at a desk digging up information about people."

"Remind me never to get on the wrong side of him." Danny winked over at Miriam.

"Oh, don't worry about him. He's just a big pussy cat. Besides, I'm sure your days on the wrong side are behind you."

Danny looked away. Miriam had never really liked him and Deirdre was probably keeping her up to date on all the stupid things he'd done. "Ah sure, you know yourself, Miriam. One day at a time and all that."

"Well good for you, Danny." Karl smiled again.

They spent the rest of the evening talking about John Melchor and sipping wine until Danny got tired and went to bed. Deirdre didn't kiss him goodnight—because she had wine on her lips—and said she would stay up for a while yet. Karl had just opened another bottle.

*

Danny was beginning to figure it all out. As long as he went to meetings, Deirdre stayed off his case. He had even memorized all the slogans for when she lapsed. 'Live and let live,' was his favorite and that always deflected her. 'One day at a time' and 'Easy does it' became passwords to procrastination. Nobody could ride his ass anymore. He even told his boss.

Deirdre thought that he shouldn't but Danny knew what he was doing. His boss had always indulged him on account of Martin and became even more supportive. Danny could flit out any time to go to a meeting. He'd even invented a young man he was helping as a sponsor. It got him out of the office any time he liked.

He had to change groups, though. One of the guys at the 'Broadway' could see right through him. "Still bullshitting to beat the band, eh Danny?" he'd ask while searching Danny's eyes.

"Ah sure, you know what they say: Fake it 'til you make it."

"How are the steps coming along?"

Danny began to avoid him after that and, in time, changed groups.

Sometimes, it got to him but he was able to rationalize it. Everyone wanted him to stop and he had—almost seven months and counting. He had done his part. Now it was up to everybody else to get their shit together.

"Danny? Could you take Grainne tonight? I have to work late."

He pretended to look concerned. "I'd love to, Dee, but I told this guy I'd take him to his first meeting." It was perfect. It got him out of anything. He'd been to the ballet rehearsal before and it really bothered him. He didn't like sitting around looking at young girls, at least not until they were older. "I suppose I could tell him to find someone else to take him—only he's a bit shaky."

Deirdre wouldn't hear of it. She'd find someone else. She never wanted anything to come between Danny and all he had to do to recover.

"Are you sure?" Danny asked, to rub it in. He was enjoying his immunity from responsibility. If he was going to suffer, then so was everybody else.

Are you sure you're doing this right?

What? I'm staying sober. That's what she wanted and that's what I'm doing.

You're such a fuckin' asshole, Boyle. I think I preferred you when you were drinking.

So did I, Anto, but she didn't. She wants me sober and that's what she's going to get.

You still have no idea what it's about, do you?

Sure I do. Don't drink and go to meetings, and fuck the begrudgers.

I haven't heard that slogan before.

That's because you don't go to enough meetings.

Pride, Boyle.

What about it?

It comes before the fall.

*

By the fall, everything was going great. Deirdre was even having sex with him again. Sometimes, he felt a bit bad about all the bullshit but what could he do? He went to meetings four nights a week and on Sunday mornings over in the hockey arena. He even gave out his number so that guys in the program would call the house. Deirdre was impressed.

"Gimme a roast-beef on rye and a bottle of Carlsberg."

He wasn't planning on getting ripped or anything. He just figured that he had learned enough about it now and that he could control it. Everybody at the meetings said they couldn't but Danny had come to realize that he wasn't like them. He just had some issues that he had to sort out—they were real alcoholics.

The beer went down well and he went back to work after he had stopped to pick up some gum. He'd finally been promoted to Senior Supply Coordinator. He was doing the same shit but for better money. His boss said he'd deserved it—for all the changes he'd made. His boss even said that when he was ready to retire, he'd recommend Danny.

Life was good and would only get better. He just had to keep it up for a while longer and show that he had really changed. He'd sneak a few beers now and then but, at home, he'd be the model of reformation. He wasn't really alcoholic; he just needed to sort out a few things. He had a bottle of tequila in the back shed. It had been there for months and he hadn't touched it. That meant something. Danny Boyle could take it or leave, just like any other man.

*

"John just arrived in Panama City. He's being checked out in a military hospital and you can talk to him later."

Miriam dropped her coat and hat in the hallway and rushed inside. "Where was he? How is he? When is he coming home?"

Karl laughed and kissed her cheek. "Slow down. I'm just getting the details as they come through. He won't tell anybody where he was, only that he was safe. You might want to talk with him about that. It could raise complications."

"How?"

"They'll want to know, and they'll want to know how much he knows. Talk to him, okay? It's for his own good."

"That has never been John's biggest concern."

"Miriam. This is serious. He has to tell them what he knows."

Chapter 16 – 1992

"What, I don't hear from you for almost a year and now you show up looking for a place to stay?"

"C'mon, Frank. Deirdre's kicked me out and I've got nowhere else."

"For how long?"

"Just until I get my act together."

"That long? Well, you better come in then."

Frank showed him to the spare room. It had a bed, covered in laundry, and a chest of drawers that was spilling over with socks and underwear. Half the floor had been sanded and the tools were still in the corner.

"You can move all that stuff into the basement." Frank looked a little embarrassed.

Danny knew he could count on him. For all his gruffness, Frank was a decent human being and a good friend. They tidied up enough space for Danny to unpack his bag and went downstairs to have a few beers.

"So what happened?"

Danny had gotten caught and all of his charades exposed. "I don't know, Frank. Since we moved to Leaside, she's changed. Nothing is good enough for her anymore."

"You never were—that's the real problem."

Danny laughed along as Frank passed the joint. It was like old times, only they were older.

"I heard you were going to meetings."

"I know. Can you believe it?"

"I can. Why did you stop?"

Danny handed back the joint and opened the bottle of tequila. He had brought another, and two two-fours as well. He didn't want to be showing up empty-handed. They'd put some in the fridge and the rest in the basement. They were well stocked for the weekend at least. He hadn't stopped going to meetings—he just hadn't stopped drinking either.

"Because I'm just a drunk."

Frank shook his head and had another hit. "Do you know what the difference is between a drunk and an alcoholic? Alcoholics go to meetings."

"Do you think I have a problem?"

"I think you've got lots of problems."

"I'm serious, Frank."

"What do you think?"

Danny took the joint and had another few hits and thought about it while Frank got another few beers. It was going to be one of those rare times when Danny could sit and talk honestly with someone else. Frank had always been a good friend. All the slagging and snide remarks were just his way of being friendly—the Dublin way.

"I think it's all a big load of bollocks, that's what I think."

Frank finished the joint, took another swig of tequila and popped his beer. "Of course it is, but that doesn't mean that you can fuck-up everything."

"You don't know what it's like, Frank. You've never been married."

Frank glanced at him to see if he was 'having-a-dig' and sat back like he was going to have to explain it all. "I never got married because I knew I would only fuck it up. Every time I get together with a woman, I end it before I do something stupid."

Danny was about to wise-crack but Frank held up his hand. "Don't fuckin' try to make a joke out of it, Boyle. I'm tryin' to tell ya something."

He waited while Danny sat back and picked another joint from the soapstone box on the coffee table. He kept them there, neatly lined up and each one perfectly rolled. He had made the coffee table himself, from burnished scrap metal with a sheet of smoked, tempered glass on top. He sat back in his red leather armchair. He had found it in a house he was renovating and had recovered it himself. The couch was black leather, covered with a palomino hide, and the walls were covered with paintings. Other people's junk, but in Frank's house they came together like an enigma. Desolate and distorted faces hung side-by-side with sunflowers and Bateman-like prints of animals in the north. Frank had put in pot-lights and tracks. It was the perfect room for men to share their souls.

"Every time things are going good with a woman, she wants to go to the next stage—the living together and having children and all that. I'm not up for that, Boyle. Some of them tell me that I would be a great father, but I know. You can't be the way fathers used to be. You know, down in the pub with their mates and only coming home when they had to. My auld fella was like that. My ma used to send me down, on payday, to get the money from him before he spent it all. He'd hand it over, no problem, and he'd give me money for sweets too."

He took another swig and passed the bottle. "I'd be like that, Boyle, and no woman today is ever going to settle for that. That's why I'm still on my own."

"You know what, Frank?" Danny slurred a little; they were really getting through the tequila. "You're the only one who makes sense anymore. And you're right. Only I had to fuck everything up before I could understand that." He lowered his head into the stinking cesspool of his reality. The tequila had turned inside of him. "Did I ever tell you about my old man? Now there's an interesting character. Beaten down and broken, even before he got started. He didn't even have the balls to stand up for my mother when my granny had her locked up."

Frank didn't say anything so Danny continued, talking about all the shite that had been his life. About all the lies about what was good and what was bad, about all the little runts that picked on him and about Martin, the only shining light.

"I still miss him, you know?" He tried to look defiant but there were little tears in the corners of his eyes. "He was the only one who was ever really straight with me. Deirdre was for a while. But once she came over, she changed. Now all she wants is to make everything better.

"I suppose she was right but there was no room for me in her brave new world. I was supposed to change too. I was supposed to stop being me and become one of those 'involved' fathers. I didn't mind that, Frank. I mean I love my kids. Who wouldn't? But I'm not one of those guys who can live in the little pockets, ya know? Storing it all up for 'boys-night-out' or fishing trips.

"I went on a few of those. Just a bunch of sad bastards sitting around drinking and longing for when they had real lives of their own. They were all lawyers and managers and fuckers like that, but every one of them was miserable. They all knew they were dying inside.

"But, do you know what. This is all getting very fuckin' heavy, man. Let's just take out the guitars again. Let's put the fuckin' band back on the road. Eh?"

*

"Is Daddy never coming home again?"

Deirdre clutched Grainne to her breast. Her little body was warm and tucked in like they had never been pulled apart. "I don't know, sweetie. Daddy is very sick right now and he has to try to get better."

"If he gets better, will he be able to come home then?"

Deirdre was going to reassure her but Martin was standing in the doorway. She knew he was hurting, too, but he smiled and came toward them.

"Or course he will, silly. After he gets better."

He sat on the bed and tried to wrap his arms around the two of them.

"You know that I will never leave you," he added as they laid his sister under the covers.

"She knows that, sweetie. She knows she has the best big brother in the world."

"I meant you, Mummy. I'll never leave you."

Deirdre tried to pick him up but he was far too heavy and slid back down until his long legs reached the floor. He was almost up to her breasts.

"You say that now, Martin, but one of these days one of those pretty little girls at school is going to catch your eye."

"I know all that, but when I grow up and get married, you and Grainne can come and live with us."

"I'm not sure what your wife will think."

"It'll be okay. I'll tell her before we are married."

It was funny but Deirdre began to cry. She had been so brave for so long. She had been exactly what they told her she had to be. She had been consistent and firm. She had quietly noted and catalogued each one of Danny's transgressions. Not for her sake—for his—so she could lay them out as evidence before him, to convince him to see himself for what he really was.

They told her it would be hard. They told her that she had to learn detachment. But they never told her how gut wrenching it was to sit with her children and explain why she wouldn't let their father come home. What choice did she have? She could never be one of those women who kept it together for appearance's sake. She was doing the right thing. She had to keep reminding herself of that, especially when she felt guilty and re-questioned her motives.

*

Sometimes things just happened.

She had taken Martin to a game in Brampton. He'd been pumped for days. The coach had talked it up — 'urban against the sub-urban.' "This is it, guys," he had briefed them after the last practice. "This is when we start finding out who has it and who doesn't. Brampton has won the last four years. They're going to think they just have to show up. But they don't know what I know about you—you're not quitters or losers. You're winners. You are going to Brampton to kick butt."

The parents gathered round and nodded to their kids. Coach's words were 'gospel.' Except Deirdre. She just studied Martin's face but she couldn't tell what he was thinking.

"Do you like your coach?" she had asked as they drove home.

"He's all right."

"What do you think of all the stuff he says?"

"I don't really listen. He's only a select-team coach."

When they got to the rink, all the other fathers were seated behind the team's bench in tiers, reading *The Globe and Mail* while sipping on their 'Second Cups.' They greeted each other politely but they were on edge, each hoping their kid wouldn't fuck up. The coach had warned them all that there were going to be changes—if they were to move up to double 'A.' Stuff like that really mattered to them; their kids were currency.

Deirdre never sat with them, preferring somewhere off on her own. She didn't like hockey but she paid very close attention to everything Martin did. She had to be able to discuss it with him on the way home.

*

"Dee-dree? Dee-dree Fallon? You're the last person I expected to see here."

Eduardo looked the same. Dark and suave with just the tiniest twinkle in his eye.

"What can I tell you, Eduardo? They've made a hockey-mum out of me. What are you doing here?"

"My son is here with his team. They're tykes. None of them can even skate yet but you know hockey, it's worse than religion."

They both laughed and he reached forward to kiss her cheeks, but she leaned back. The Leaside fathers were all watching them over their rims or fluttering business sections.

"May I sit with you?"

As she moved her bag from the seat beside her, she stole a peek at the Brampton parents. Husbands and wives with blankets and cushions and cups of 'Tim Horton's.' She might have felt like Juliet but she was far too cynical for that.

She had known that Danny was drinking all along, but what really hurt was the way he was using the AA program. It almost felt like he had taken their last hope and wiped his feet on it. She had done everything to support him and it was all lies.

"So, how have you been?"

"Oh, you know. Parenthood, eh?"

"Ya," he agreed. "Tell me about it."

And for some reason she did. She told him everything and it felt good even if it was an indulgence. She knew he still carried a torch for her and felt vindicated when his eyes began to blaze with outrage, even as the game went on.

It was getting tense. Leaside was proving to be far more than Brampton expected, especially Martin. "Hit him," the Brampton parents yelled every time he touched the puck. "Hit him into the boards."

It was a bad idea. Martin thrived on that and stick-handled around like a Gretzky. He scored twice and assisted on another despite all the hacking and slashing, even pushing back when they squared up to each other just like they did in the NHL. "That's it, Boyle. Show 'em what you're made of. Now let's finish them off," the swarthy-faced coach spoke loud enough for the whole rink to hear.

"Hit him harder," the Brampton parents replied, but Eduardo just sat and listened until Deirdre was done.

She couldn't help it and when she had finished recounting all the terrible things, she began to cry like a little girl. She let him put his arm around her. None of the parents were watching anymore. There were just two minutes to go.

"I am so sorry to hear that."

"Thanks," Deirdre mumbled through her teary, snotty tissue. But she wanted more from him than that. She wanted him to hold her and make her feel like she wasn't so God-awful alone in the world, that she wouldn't have to spend the rest of her life sleeping in her empty bed. She wanted him to kiss her, right there in front of everyone.

The Leaside parents rose in their seats and Deirdre was grateful for the distraction. Martin had the puck in his own end. She knew he wouldn't rush forward with his head down the way the other kids did. He slowed and looked, like he was evaluating what was in front of him. The other center was tired; he'd been sent on to shackle Martin. But he was big and slow and couldn't turn and Deirdre knew that Martin would go straight at him.

The other center braced himself to make a hit but Martin slid the puck between his skates and picked it up on the other side. Someone was dragging at him with their stick as he burst forward, through the neutral zone, toward the blue line. Brampton were all lined up like skittles with Martin's wingers on the edges. He faked the pass to the right and cut left. The defender tried to push him wide but Martin drifted toward the corner until he had space to turn. He cut inside and glided in behind the net, just like number '99.'

The defenders were afraid to follow and the goalie had to look over his shoulder to see. Martin pushed to the left and the goalie followed, still looking back. Martin pushed to the right and as soon as the goalie's skates moved, pushed left again and reached forward and tucked the puck into the corner of the net. It all came so easily to him.

"Could I meet with you again? Maybe for lunch sometime? I work downtown."

"Why?" Deirdre smiled but decided to let fate take its course.

*

"You played so well. Mommy is so proud of you."

Martin seemed pleased but she could tell; he was thinking about something else. He was like that. Other kids would need even more affirmation, but not Martin. 'Quietly confident,' always came to mind.

"Who was that man?" he asked without looking over at her.

"He is a friend of Mommy's from university."

"Is he a nice man?"

"Yes. He is."

"Are you going to see him again?"

"I'm not sure."

"I think you should."

"Martin," Deirdre mentioned casually as they pulled into the driveway, "I don't think we should tell Grainne."

*

"Danny Boyle, you bollocks." Jimmy laughed and hugged him tight. He was looking very well with a very buxom blonde on his arm. "This is Anna. Anna, this is Danny from the band."

The party was getting loud and Danny had to strain to hear what she was saying, leaning over her as he did. He was a bit tipsy already. He'd been drinking since midday. Frank told him he'd be wasted, but Danny didn't care. He was going to have a good night—the first in years.

"So what do you think?"

"Of what?" Jimmy asked.

'Of putting the band back together.'

"Danny, you've got to be fucking kidding."

"I'm deadly fucking serious. Me and Frank are gonna go for it."

"I dunno. I'm kind of involved in a studio project right now. I'm not sure I'd have the time."

"Well, in that case," Danny said as he swayed around in a slow circle, "you can go and fuck yourself. Me and Frank don't need you."

Anna looked concerned but Jimmy just laughed. "Just like old times, eh? Okay, I'm in."

"And this time," Danny announced to the whole room, "we're going to do it right."

He wandered off in search of beer, laughing with the old crowd and stealing kisses from their wives and girlfriends.

Billie arrived after eleven. She looked like she had come from the opera or something. She had her hair up and wore a pearl necklace. She wore a short black dress that showed her shape. She was still a fine looking woman.

"Danny boy." She smiled and let him kiss her cheek. She wore an expensive fragrance that filled his mind with wicked thoughts. "You haven't changed a bit."

"Are you kidding? You're the one who's looking great. Jazus. Come here and give me another hug."

He held her as close as she let him, smelling her hair and feeling her warmth against him. She'd been drinking, too, and she was high. Her eyes were huge and deep, but he could see that she still had feelings for him, even after all that happened.

*

"It was a mistake," she told him as she scurried around collecting her expensive lingerie from the floor. "We shouldn't have done this."

Danny couldn't disagree more. They had fucked half the night away. Their bodies remembered each other, despite the booze and the coke. She had a few lines and let Danny snort some off her body for old time's sake.

"What?" he asked impishly as he watched her dress.

"This, Danny. We shouldn't have done this."

"Then why did you?"

She turned away and looked at herself in the mirror. She laughed for a moment before turning back to him. She had been doing so well. She'd left the museum and now worked for a private art dealer in Yorkville. She arranged parties and created buzz.

"I don't know," she answered and her own honesty seemed to trip her up. "I guess . . . well, I guess I should be going."

She stepped into her heels, rising higher while flicking out her hair, tumbling freely now down her shoulders. She almost made it to the door before she turned. "I did it because I just broke up with someone."

"Me too."

"Don't kid yourself, Danny boy. You're still married."

Danny rose and wrapped the sheet around his waist. He stepped forward and took her in his arms. "Not anymore."

He knew that got to her. It was always different with her. Deirdre was always looking at him like she was trying to find something to change, but Billie just accepted him for what he was—and she still loved him, despite everything.

*

"It's not like I think marriage is final, but because of the kids . . ."

Deirdre wanted to say the right things. She didn't want to give Eduardo the wrong idea, but neither did she want to say anything that might drive him away. She liked getting together for lunch. It was so intimate, almost like dating. She wouldn't be what drove him and his wife apart, but if it were to happen . . .

"I understand."

"Do you?" She smiled and resisted the urge to reach forward and stroke the back of his hand. He was having problems too. His wife had become everything he hadn't wanted. A stay-at-home, full-time mother who suspected every moment he spent out of the house.

Deirdre knew how lonely he had become—almost as lonely as her, but it shouldn't become more. It was bad enough that they met and shared what they did. They both had children and they didn't want to make things any more complicated than that.

"So, are we to go on denying ourselves the chance to be happy—together?"

He motioned for the bill and wiped his lips one last time. He tugged at his cuffs and stole a glance at his watch. He had to hurry back to the office. His wife called every few hours.

"And what makes you so sure that we could be happy together?" She shouldn't have asked but she liked to tease him a little. He always tried to seem so assured.

He tapped his heart and winked at her. "Because I have never stopped loving you."

*

"I am sorry, Ms. Fallon, but something must be done."

Deirdre knew she was right. It was the second time Grainne had hit somebody and it was still the first term of grade one. She was belligerent at home, too, only there they could deflect her. But it wasn't fair. Martin had to tiptoe around her, even when she turned on their mother. He tried. He talked with her and let her watch all her shows. He even played dress-up with her but, in the long run, something had to be done.

"Am I correct in understanding that there have been some changes in your family life?"

Deirdre nearly laughed aloud. People couldn't say 'shit' any more, even when they had a mouthful. "Yes, Grainne's father and I are separated."

"I see." The teacher nodded like she was hearing it for the first time. "And have you been to any type of family support?"

"Yes," Deirdre lied. She'd had enough of all the ways people used to deflect reality.

"Grainne doesn't seem to know this."

"I can't understand that," Deirdre bluffed.

It was how she dealt with issues at work, and teachers were so easy to handle as long as you remained superior. "We have made a point of getting as much help as we can."

"I see. In that case I'm not sure how to proceed. Normally, we would insist on a suspension but, if you are in counseling, we should give it some time and see how things are in a few weeks."

Deirdre had pulled it off. She couldn't afford to take time from work right now and she had no one to turn to. "I think that's best. Our family therapist thinks Grainne is resisting. That's probably why she didn't want to mention it, but we are all confident that we can expect a breakthrough any day now."

She'd get to work on it as soon as she got home. She would make whatever deal she had to, to make everything right again. She stole a glance at her watch and waited until the teacher smiled. They had nothing more to discuss for now.

"Well thank you for coming in so quickly, Ms. Fallon, and I am sure we will have everything back to normal in no time. Grainne is such a bright little girl. I think she could be one of the smartest children I have seen in a while." She led Deirdre outside where Grainne sat on a bench. She didn't seem the slightest bit concerned.

Deirdre almost laughed about that as she started the van. Grainne was smart. Too bloody smart and she would have her work cut out getting her to come around.

"Sweetie. What are we going to do?"

"I want to see my Daddy."

"Daddy is at work right now. Maybe we can call him instead."

Grainne flew into a rage and pounded her feet against the back of Deirdre's seat. Deirdre waited for it to blow over but Grainne kept going, kicking and screaming until her mother broke.

"If you stop," Deirdre said in her most controlled voice, "I will take you to Daddy's office."

"I want to see my Daddy, now."

"I can't drive while you are kicking my seat."

"I want to see my Daddy. Now!" She repeated it a few more times until she had blown herself out and settled into a sulk.

Danny wasn't in the office, so Deirdre took a chance and drove to Frank's. Danny wasn't there but Frank agreed to watch Grainne until he arrived.

"Are you sure?" Frank always had a thing for her and Deirdre felt bad about imposing on him, but she had to get back to the office.

"No problem. I'll let her play with the power tools. Kids love that."

Deirdre felt like a whore when she kissed his cheek, but she knew Frank would get after Danny.

*

Frank even agreed to have Grainne and Martin over for the weekend so Danny and Deirdre could have some time to try to sort things out. He'd even take Martin to hockey. He and Grainne could start fights with the other parents. "Just kidding," he added when Martin looked concerned.

"They will be okay?" Deirdre asked as she and Danny sat down to dinner. They had decided on a nice little place on St. Clair where they made great pizza.

Danny looked different. He didn't look so 'pinched' anymore. He even wore a 'Blue Jays' hat—everyone was wearing them since the World Series.

"It's Frank that I'm worried about." He tried to sound relaxed but he was hesitant, forcing himself to seem natural. He'd been different on the phone. They had talked and agreed; they had to do something for the kids' sake.

When the waiter took their order, Danny ordered a beer. Deirdre ordered a glass of wine and tried not to react.

"You're not going to say anything?"

"Would it make any difference if I did?"

"It's not like that, Dee. It's just that I have found out something about myself. I'm not an alcoholic."

She fidgeted with her placemat and waited for him to continue.

"I know you think I am but, after months and months of going to meetings, I figured it out. I'm just a heavy drinker who has other issues."

The waiter returned and placed their drinks in front of them but neither of them reached for theirs.

"I'm learning to drink normally, now. I know you don't believe me, but you've always been on my case and that's part of the problem too. I know you mean well but it's not working for me."

He paused and waited for her to comment, but she didn't. She knew she had to be different with him. Her time alone with the kids had changed her.

"Well?"

"I'm not sure what to say, Danny."

"Well then, what would you say to a clean slate? You don't bug me about my drinking and I won't get so drunk all the time?"

She really wanted to cry. He was never going to be what she wanted him to become. She had been fooling herself all along. Miriam had warned her, back when they used to get together for coffee in Bewley's. Danny Boyle would never change his spots—just like most men.

It was all an illusion. Women of today were no different than their mothers. Not really. Sure, they could have their careers and speak openly about orgasms but, at the end of the day, they were still the ones it all fell to. They still had to be the heart of the family. Only now they had to do it while juggling all that liberation had brought.

She could end it all and start fresh with Eduardo. Except she wasn't prepared for all that entailed. Grainne would never accept it. His wife would never accept it. She sipped her wine and smiled at Danny. He knew he had her over a barrel. He knew what Grainne had been up to. He wouldn't have encouraged her, but he wouldn't have discouraged her either. If Deirdre was going to put her family back together, she was going to have to settle for the same old Danny Boyle.

He'd make some effort. He wasn't a bad person—just a very flawed one. But he was the father of her kids and they came first. Women could have it all until it broke them.

Deirdre raised her glass. "To a new beginning."

*

So, as the year drew to a close and Mary Robinson settled in at Áras an Uachtaráin and Ireland agreed to the Maastricht, Danny Boyle moved back home.

The war in El Salvador was over, too late for the seventy-five thousand, and the Charlottetown Accord died, but Mulroney signed the NAFTA deal. Better times were just around the corner.

A colonel in the Atlacati Battalion was sentenced to thirty years for killing John Melchor's friends and Philippe's kindness had gone unpunished. Apartheid was ending but so was Tito's peace in Yugoslavia.

Los Angeles burned with rage for a few nights and, in Russia, they found the bodies of Nicholas and Alexandra.

The British finally outlawed the UDA and Sinead O'Connor ripped the pope apart, even though he finally lifted the Inquisition on Galileo. Bill Clinton would be taking over in the White House and Danny Boyle sat in the midst of his family, drinking moderately and overseeing a new peace.

And on Christmas Eve, he even took out his guitar and they sang carols like any normal, happy family.

Chapter 17 – 1993

"I CAME OVER AS QUICKLY AS I COULD."

Jacinta looked at her and felt better. She was the only one she would dream of calling in the middle of the night. She tried to smile but cried, so Gina hugged her tight.

"How is he?"

"They said that we got him here in the nick of time—but you never know with heart attacks."

Gina made the sign of the cross from her head to her breast and across her shoulders before looking up at the ceiling. It almost made Jacinta smile. Gina was just like the rest of them, religious-less until death showed up. She didn't mind; Gina just didn't know any better.

"Ah, poor Jerry. And you, it must have been an awful shock for you."

It was awful, but it wasn't a shock. Jerry had been complaining for a few days but neither of them took much notice of it. If he was really sick, he should have gone to the doctor.

But he didn't, and after dinner he sat beside the fire and smoked like a chimney. He had a few whiskies, too, but she didn't begrudge him. Things were very tense at work. Donal was flying higher with every new deal and Jerry just wasn't cut out for that type of thing. Jacinta had told him. "You'll end up in an early grave," she had warned.

"But at least I will be able to pay for a grand funeral," he had laughed, "and I'll leave lots of money for you too. You'll be able to go off and get yourself some young fella to love you for your money."

"Me?" she laughed along with him. They did that a lot. They had spent far too much time crying. "What would I want a man for? I've had enough of men for one life."

"Admit it. Being with me has spoiled you for all the others."

She had looked away and sipped from her glass of sherry like she was dismissing him, but it was all in play. They had great fun together and, given how they had started out, that was far more than she could have hoped for.

He'd even gotten a bit frisky when they went to bed. They hadn't in years and she was about to make fun of him again when he clutched his chest. She thought he was kidding around until his breathing got strange.

She didn't panic though; she was very proud of that. She phoned for help and followed the instructions they gave her until they came. It was only when she was in the back of the ambulance that she began to shake. They gave her a blanket and, in the hospital, one of the nurses got her a nice cup of tea. Jacinta didn't want to be a bother but the nurse was so nice, saying how brave she was and all.

*

"Do you think that work caused it?" Gina looked concerned and a little guilty. "I've been telling Donal to ease up a bit. I told him that Jerry wasn't as young as him and to take it easy. But would he listen? He's gone plain mad for money and nothing else matters anymore."

Jacinta thought about consoling her, but she was too tired. Now that she had gotten through all the excitement, she was worn out.

"But this is going to cost him. Mark my words." Gina looked very determined and a little mean. Things were not great between her and Donal.

"It wasn't his fault," Jacinta said but her mind was wandering. They were well enough off that Jerry could quit working. But it would be better if he could get a retirement package—if Donal had any heart left. "Jerry's just getting a bit too old for all of this. I think he should retire. Do you think Donal would let him?"

"He better not try to stop him. Not after this."

"What I meant was," Jacinta continued as calmly as she could. She didn't want Gina to fly into a rage and get Donal's back up. "Do you think he would see his way to giving Jerry something to retire on—buy him out like?"

"It's not up to him."

"What do you mean?"

"It's all in my name. He signed it over last year so he could fiddle the taxman. I decide things for him now and he'd do well to go along with it."

Jacinta said nothing. She was thinking about the day she took Gina to buy her wedding dress. She worried for her back then—about what she was getting herself into. Life with Donal was never going to be easy, but Gina was a great one for looking after herself. Linda and Brenda always said that she got too hard, but Jacinta understood. She had to. Things had changed between men and women. Women could stand up for themselves now and Gina had become more than a match for anybody. Jacinta could never see herself being like that but she didn't have to. She and Jerry had become partners for life. That was how things were supposed to be.

"Mrs. Boyle," The nurse called from the hallway, "would you like to come and see your husband now?"

Jacinta rose in a fluster with Gina attending. "Is he . . ."

"He's out of danger. The doctor will explain more to you later but for now you can go in and see him." She might have meant just Jacinta but Gina took her sister's arm and they both marched in to Jerry's room.

"Ah, Jaze, Jass. I'm sorry you have to see me like this." He was pale and looked very worn out and had tubes and wires all over him. Jacinta didn't mind. She leaned over and kissed his damp brow.

"Sure amn't I always happy to see you."

"And here was me thinking you'd be happy to see the back of me." He tried to laugh but he wasn't well enough.

"Don't be making a joke, Jerry Boyle. When I get you home it'll be no laughing matter. Isn't that right, Gina?"

"You better listen to her, Jerry, if you know what's good for you."

*

Deirdre sat back as Eduardo read:

Ms. Fallon epitomizes the type of candidate the Advancement Committee is seeking to promote. As a woman, and an immigrant, she has consistently achieved the highest ratings in her employee evaluations. She continues to demonstrate the leadership skills we are looking to promote and has a proven track record.

Ms. Fallon is also a mother of two and is a role model for all young female employees. I have no hesitation in forwarding her name for consideration for the newly created position of Manager, Internal Career Development.

"Wow! They really love you." He handed back the memo and smiled.

Deirdre smiled back. Eduardo could always find ways to insert words like 'love' and 'passion' into every conversation. They were having lunch in *Ramboia*, on College. He wasn't concerned about being seen there. He told anyone who asked that she was his contact with the bank, and it was strictly business. Besides, he wasn't the only businessman dining with someone who obviously wasn't his wife.

"I'm sure it's no more than you deserve. You have such passion and commitment for everything you do."

It was so nice to hear someone say that. She had shown it to Danny, too, but he was not so enthusiastic. He congratulated her, of course, but with just a hint of condescension. She knew what he was thinking: that she was being promoted because she was a woman. It had happened again—he had been over-looked for another promotion. "You have to be a handicapped, black, or lesbian to get anywhere these days. It's discrimination. Reverse discrimination and nobody can say shit about it. Misandry," he smirked as he handed it back. "I'm a victim of rampant misandry."

*

"You don't think it's just because I'm a woman?"

"That sounds like your husband speaking."

Deirdre felt a twinge of guilt, laughing about Danny with another man. She was always careful not to take sides when Eduardo complained about his wife.

"Yes, he did have something to say about it."

"His problem is that he doesn't appreciate you."

So many things dangled between them. Things that she could almost reach out and touch so easily. Delicious little intimations to be savored, even as they ate. He was always so attentive, holding her chair for her as she sat and holding her coat when she rose. He ordered the wine—just a half carafe, carefully selected to complement the food and the conversation. Danny always ordered by price. If it cost more, it had to be better. Eduardo was a lot more discerning about everything.

"I am sorry," he corrected himself. "It's not my place to comment."

She smiled at that too. He liked to trespass a little, like he was testing her defenses. Some nights, as she lay alone in her bed, while Danny sat in front of the television drinking beer, she wished he would not hold back. She wished he would reach out for her and push himself on her, gently but persistently.

But they had a pact and she shouldn't encourage him. "Do men ever appreciate what they have or are they always fixated on what they don't?"

It was his turn to smile. She liked to test him too. To call him out for being the bold little boy that she could see inside his expensive suits. He poured their wine and raised his to his nose before he answered. "Women are not the only ones who mourn the death of love."

That always got to her, the Portuguese lugubriousness that he wore around his heart. He had told her of his race's poets and had tried to explain *Fado*. He said sorrow was essential in the Portuguese spirit. He called it the "suppressed memory of all that had been lost in the *Reconquista*." His skin was coffee-colored and his eyes were brown. His forefathers were Al-Andalusians.

"Married people do not concern themselves with love; they are too busy compromising."

Even as she said it, she realized how sad it sounded. They had a form of peace at home. Not harmony—more of a working truce. Danny complied with all she asked of him and in return, she let him be. It was workable for now, but she couldn't help but feel she had lost control. Everything she had hoped for was put to one side. Danny said it was the same for him. He said that being married and having kids was a job in itself. They just had to get through the next few years until the kids were a bit older and then they could be a couple again.

She didn't argue with that; there was no point. It would only set the cat among the pigeons.

They had patched things up enough to become a functional family again. Grainne had stopped hitting people and Martin and Danny had an entente. Martin's stature had grown and his coach had recommended him to St. Mike's. Danny was basking in the reflected glory.

It should have been enough. Many women she knew would have been happy with what they had, but Deirdre wanted . . . not so much more, she wanted what they had to be real.

"Yes. We have all become so busy."

Eduardo had been promoted too. His company was keen to lose its Anglo image and seem more diverse. He was a poster boy for the up and coming ethnic. He knew that, and he knew how to turn it to his advantage.

"I will be traveling more," he announced with just a hint of suggestion. "Across Canada mostly, but I am hoping to go further."

"I may have to travel, too. I might have to go to Montreal in a few months."

He just nodded as he drained the rest of the carafe into their glasses. "Maybe we might have the chance to have lunch there sometime."

*

When she got back to her office, she closed the door and took a few moments for herself. They had crossed the line they had said they wouldn't. It was only going to be a mutual support thing. Voices in her head warned her but they were the voices of her mother and Miriam. She loved them but she could never model her life on either of them. The world had changed far too much for that.

Still, she and Eduardo were lying to themselves. Little white lies to rationalize what they were really doing—putting themselves into situations where things could 'just happen.'

She had heard so many people say it: they had left their husbands for someone else because 'it just happened.' Fate, kismet, love, anything but confronting the truth. She and Eduardo were flirting with the possibility of having an affair. She knew they shouldn't tempt fate but, without those moments she shared with him, life would be far too bleak.

As she sat back into her desk, she picked up the postcard he had once sent to the office. From Alfama, where he had been thinking of her. He said he wanted to bring her there and to Sintra, but when she thought about it, she couldn't see herself there without her kids.

*

"Please excuse my entourage." John Melchor laughed as he joined them. The two suits that had followed him since he came back found a table close by. Karl, who had risen to shake

John's hand, nodded toward them but they pretended they weren't there.

"FBI?"

"Most likely."

"Why?" Miriam asked with a tone of displeasure that almost sounded maternal.

"I presume it is for my own good," John laughed aloud. "Why else?"

"Why else, indeed. I'm just surprised that you don't have a few cassocked Jesuits in tow too."

"We managed to give them the slip down in El Paso."

They decided to meet in San Antonio, in a restaurant by the Riverwalk. Karl had been working there for a few months. John had been closeted away with an old friend, his old pilot, out near Uvalde. The FBI stayed in a motel nearby.

"So," Karl drawled, "what have you been up to?"

"Yes," Miriam joined in, "please give a detailed account of yourself."

"You would have made a great Mother Superior."

She didn't respond to that and an awkward silence settled.

"I'm sorry," John Melchor finally said in Karl's direction. "I forget that things have changed."

"Don't worry about me, padre."

"Ah. Another military man?"

"He was a Marine," Miriam answered for him. Karl was often taciturn about his past and his present.

"A *Teufel Hunden*? I was a flyboy, but I'm sure you know that."

"Well?" Miriam tapped her finger in mock impatience. "How long is it going to take for you boys to go through your rituals?"

"Military formalities—you wouldn't understand."

"Careful, there, Jar-head. Nuns are always trumps."

"Anyway," John continued after sipping his beer. He hadn't had one in so long. "After what happened, I was a guest of some friends who risked everything for me. I won't reveal any more detail, other than to say that without them, I would now be answering to the Boss, himself. They kept me until I was well enough to travel, and by travel I mean being smuggled out.

"Anyway, I got to Panama City, where a reception committee waited. Old friends of yours, I presume?"

Karl nodded but said nothing. He was watching the two suits trying to seem nonchalant as they strained to hear what was being said.

"They were very welcoming and all that, but they were far too interested in my hosts. Sadly, I couldn't tell them anything."

"Well, that explains your entourage," Karl muttered without moving his lips.

"Yes," John Melchor sighed like it saddened him. "That and my priors, but I couldn't risk it. Friends put their lives on the line and not all of our people down there can be trusted. Nothing sinister, I just think we get far too cozy with the wrong people."

Their food arrived and changed the topic. John Melchor hadn't had a good burger in years and even stopped to say grace. Miriam had a salad and Karl had chicken wraps but John ordered the works: a cheeseburger with fries and onion rings, and a large Coke. He had finished his beer and slurped a few mouthfuls before he slathered his food with ketchup, relish and mustard.

"Death wish?" Miriam smiled at him.

"Not really. I am being sent back to Rome in a few weeks and I have every reason to believe they will lock me in a cellar somewhere, with only bread and water. I'm just indulging myself—a last supper, if you wish."

By the time they had finished eating, they were all caught up but were not ready to part. John decided to finish things off with a scotch and Miriam joined him. Karl decided to stick with coffee and excused himself.

*

"He seems like a good man," John ventured when he was gone.

"One of the best. I have been so . . ." She was going to say blessed but it didn't seem appropriate. Sitting with John brought all the old habits back. "Fortunate."

"Karma."

"It hasn't been so kind to you."

"It is not the end yet. I will reserve comment until then so as not to tempt fate."

Miriam couldn't help herself and reached forward to touch his hand. "It must have been so horrible."

*

John tried to shrug. It had been. It haunted every night he slept in the Madrigal house, waking at every noise and never sure where the world ended and his frightened mind began. "I will deny ever saying this, but I can tell you: it terrified me. Not just for my own sake. Watching them die like that—it was like seeing the devil face-to-face."

"You never believed in the devil before."

"I do now and he is man. We were not born in God's image. No God could be so vile."

*

Karl stopped at the other table on his way back and returned with the two FBI men in tow.

"I decided that if we are going to sit around for a while that we should all get to know each other."

The FBI men seemed unsure but John was very gracious. "Yes, come and sit. We are all friends here."

They introduced themselves and sat, close together like they were joined at the hip. One was older and more care-bitten. The other took his lead from him.

"May I ask why you are following me?" John asked in a kindly manner.

The older one weighed his answer for a moment. "Protection."

"That is so considerate. I suppose you are aware of my criminal past?"

The older one looked at his hands while the younger one seemed to blush.

"Padre," Karl implored, "don't give them a hard time. They are only following orders." He almost made it sound Germanic.

"Forgive me," John bowed to them. "Perhaps you would join us in a drink. We are celebrating old friendships and I have begun to consider you my friends."

The older one looked a little pissed but was considering it. "And then you would report us?"

"No. I have nothing against you. I was just trying to be civil."

The older one looked at Karl for a moment and then the younger one. "A beer. Thank you."

Karl ordered the beers and had another coffee. He winked at Miriam to let her know he was enjoying himself. When the beers arrived, the younger waited until the older one drank. "Go on," Miriam encouraged. "No one is going to find out—unless we are all under surveillance."

John and Karl both laughed but the FBI men just looked pained.

"She's just kidding, man. Take it easy." Karl sat back and lit a cigarette. He didn't smoke too often but it suited him.

In time they got to disagreeing even though the FBI men were affable enough. They saw the world through the limited view that such men had—a world of terror that would reach out to take away all they held dear. They pointed to the bombing in the basement of the World Trade Center as proof that there were those who would attack the American way of life.

John Melchor argued that terrorists were not born, but made. Made by the actions of those that supported tyranny—like those who had gunned down Archbishop Romero at the altar. Those that American governments had befriended and armed.

And when things seemed to be getting heated, Karl insisted they walk across to the Alamo, to remember those who had died in the cause of American Imperialism. Miriam could see he was enjoying himself but she was getting tired. For men, the problems of the world were matters for the mind, like Gordian knots. For her, it was much more a matter of the heart, albeit a bleeding one. She worried for John Melchor. The cruel lashings of the world would only spur him on and he was getting far too old for all of this. But they all stood reverently in the old mission. Each one had answered their country's call; John over Japan, Karl and the older FBI man in Vietnam, and the younger one in Kuwait. They all had that in common.

*

It was one of those nights when the breezes woke old ghosts. Rome was full of them, doleful souls of the slaves and saints who had died to make the place great.

It was too warm and Patrick couldn't sleep. He sat up and read for a while as the murmurs of life dwindled. The city was noisy most of the time but there were a few quiet hours, after the last of the night-lifers had drifted off and before the early morning rustling began. Giovanni often said that in those few hours, if you listened intently, you could hear the talking statues of Rome.

After he tossed and turned a few more times, Patrick gave up and got dressed. When he was a young curate, he was often called from his bed. It was an imposition he bore with all the grace he could muster. Some weeks he was lucky if he got one decent night's sleep, especially when Fr. Brennan was failing. He didn't miss those days but he didn't regret them either. All of that had led to this—a tranquil place to sit and watch the world.

Sometimes when the news of the world was troubling, he wondered if he shouldn't be doing more with himself. He still got letters from Miriam and she was still fighting the good fight. She still railed away against all that was unjust and Patrick admired her for that.

She had written to him about John Melchor, about his recent troubles and that he was on his way over. Of course Patrick agreed to meet with him but he was unsure. His life was an idyllic island. He spent his days with his nose in a book, only taking it out to share what he had found there. His students loved him and the college was proud of that. They thought his kind of priest was what was needed in a world that grew more secular by the day. All of Europe was becoming one in that, except in Yugoslavia, where the old fault lines were tearing the people apart.

He had been able to ignore most of that by focusing on all that had gone on before, accounts of the days when kings and popes wrestled for the reins of power. He found great comfort in that, that the more things changed . . .

He crossed the Tiber at the Ponte Mazzini. He had no direction in mind; he would just wander until the sun came up and the cafés opened.

He was unsure about meeting John Melchor because Jesuits always made him nervous. They were the best and brightest and had a bad habit of looking through people. And this one was tainted by notoriety. Patrick had made discreet inquiries. John Melchor was a black sheep—the type that once ended their days in ashes.

By the time the sun was about to rise, he was standing in the Campo De' Fiori. The cafés were beginning to flicker to life but it was still calm. A delivery van scuttled across and then it was quiet. He had been there many times during the hot afternoons. He came by but had never said 'hi' to Bruno as his uncle had once suggested.

Bruno had been waiting. His likeness had stood there since 1899, a few years after Pope Leo had issued the *Humanun Genus.*

The Masons had put him there, forever staring off toward those who had consigned him to the flames back in 1600. Patrick had never understood what his uncle had meant but it was that kind of night.

"Hi."

So! You've finally gotten here.

Patrick was startled and looked around to see who might be playing a prank.

Over here. It was his uncle's voice. *Up here.*

Patrick approached the base of the statue. It had to be a prank, something Giovanni might have thought up.

Do not be afraid, Patricio. It was Benedetta's voice. There was no mistaking it.

Patrick looked around but he was alone in the piazza. Except for a few cats and a man washing down a patio.

"Uncle?" He whispered loud enough. "Is that you?"

Were you expecting Giordano?

Don't tease your nephew. That's not nice.

But Patrick had heard enough and scuttled away. Not so fast as to draw any attention to himself, but fast enough. He bustled along narrow streets and lanes until he got to Giovanni's. He was sweeping and setting out his tables and chairs.

*

"Patricio. What has you out so early?"

When he returned with a coffee he sat down and searched Patrick's face for a moment. "Would you like to tell me what the matter is?"

"There is nothing the matter." Patrick raised his cup and gulped his coffee down in case he was sleepwalking.

"I see."

He waited until Patrick was a little more settled and tried again. "Patricio?"

Patrick checked to see that no one else was listening before he asked: "Tell me about the talking statues."

*

"I can't fall asleep."

Grainne stood in the doorway. Her hair was tussled and she dragged her raggedy doll along behind her. They had been to see *Jurassic Park* and she was far too young but their father was sure it'd be fine. Martin was a little scared, too, only he didn't let it show. He knew it was just a movie and stuff like that was supposed to make you jump and laugh about it later. He pulled his blankets back. "You can lie down here if you like."

Grainne didn't hesitate and bounded in beside him. "Whatcha reading?"

"My hockey magazine."

"Does it have pictures?"

"Yeah. See." He flicked through a few pages but she didn't seem interested.

"Does it have pictures of anything else?"

"No, silly. It's for people who only like hockey."

"Do you only like hockey?"

"I love hockey. When I grow up I'm going to be the best."

"Better than Gretzky?"

"No one can be better than Gretzky." He put his arm around her and let her rest her head against him. He knew what was bothering her. Their mother was away and things were different when it was just their father looking after them. He let them eat in front of the television but he never cooked. Their mother had left stuff in the freezer but their father never bothered with that. Instead they ate pizzas and burgers and fries. It was all right but it didn't really feel good.

"I miss Mommy."

He squeezed her a little tighter. "She'll be home tomorrow evening."

"But what if there are dinosaurs were she is?"

"She's in Montreal, silly. There are no dinosaurs there."

"How do you know?"

"'Cause they have a hockey team there and dinosaurs are afraid of hockey players."

"But what if they are hiding and jump up at her plane?"

She was getting sleepy but he knew she would persist. He didn't mind; she just wanted to feel safe.

"Dinosaurs can't jump that high. Besides, Mommy is not afraid of anything."

"She gets afraid of Daddy when he's drinking."

"That's because Daddy is Irish. Back in the Stone Age, the Irish killed all their dinosaurs. Granddad Jerry told me all about it."

"Did he kill any?"

"I don't think so—he's too nice. Besides, he would have just been a little kid back then."

She was nodding off and just smiled back. "Mammy says we are going to go to Ireland to visit him and Granddad Fallon. He's not as much fun."

"He's all right. He's just different. Granddad Jerry told me that they are friends."

"Granny Fallon is nice. She doesn't smell like cigarettes."

She was almost there so Martin put away his magazine and turned down the light. He brushed her hair away from her face and began to whisper:

> Up the airy mountain,
> Down the rushy glen,
> We daren't go a-hunting
> For fear of little men;
> Wee folk, good folk,
> Trooping all together;
> Green jacket, red cap,
> And white owl's feather!

Just like his mother used to do with him when he couldn't sleep.

Chapter 18 – 1994

S O HE'S BACK ON THE DRINK?"

"He is, ya."

"And there was nothing you could have done?"

"C'mon, Martin. You know what he can be like. Besides, how was I to know that Deirdre was going to take him back?"

"Yeah, that was unforeseen."

Martin could tell that Anto had tried, in his own limited way. He didn't understand what was going on yet. He wasn't open to it. "But you have to start allowing for stuff like that. You used to be good at figuring out the angles."

"Ya, and look what it got me."

"Get over it, will you. You're getting a chance, now, to put everything right."

"But why does it have to be with Danny. Isn't there another way?"

"You and Danny are bound to each other; that's how it works. You got killed while you were trying to kill him. You guys owe each other."

"Ya but, he still gets to live."

"Yeah, Danny Boyle has a great life."

"He would if he wasn't a total fuck-up."

"Anto, listen to me. You have been given a chance to clear your slate, you know? To address your karma imbalance."

"Karma imbalance?"

"Penance, if you prefer."

"It still sucks. Why can't I just be dead and get on with it?"

"Because of your mother."

Anto didn't say anything for a while.

"What's she got to do with it?"

"She's the one who keeps praying for you. And as long as one person prays for you, you get another chance."

"They get you coming and going."

"Don't be cynical."

"I'm not." Anto was trying to seem defiant but Martin could tell—the mention of his mother had unsettled him.

"Martin, can I ask you something? Why are you still here?"

"Because I volunteered."

"Why?"

"Do you remember Danny's grandmother?"

"Ya. She used to tell me that she would have me off in the Borstal all the time."

"Yeah, that's her. Anyway, I'm doing this for her. She asked me, a long time ago." He paused to reflect. Promises were promises and had to be kept no matter what. "So what's Danny up to these days?"

"The same, drinking and lying, but they are all going back to Dublin soon—his father is almost done."

"Are you going with him?"

"Do I have any choice?"

"You always have choices, only sometimes they are for the worse."

*

Danny had taken the kids and his mother to the zoo. They were going to stop at the Garden of Remembrance, too, so that Jerry could have the house to himself and could have his nap. He'd been overdoing it again and his color was bad. Jacinta insisted: "You've done enough river-dancing around. Stay home and rest up for yourself. We'll all be back in few hours."

Even little Martin agreed: "Don't worry, Granddad Jerry. I'll tell you all about it when I get home, after your nap."

It almost made Jerry's heart burst with joy and sorrow.

Deirdre had gone out to have lunch with her sister. She and Johnny were back for a few weeks, too. Deirdre had brought them over one evening. Jerry really liked them, especially their kids, and managed to sneak them some sweeties when their parents weren't looking.

He had the house to himself and settled into his armchair and listened to the Wilburys. He didn't care too much for Dylan or Petty; they reminded him of the shite Danny used to play, but the rest of them were all right.

Danny had gotten a lot better though. He played Christy Moore stuff, now, and the Pogues. It was a pity that he ever got mixed up in all the shit. He could have been good. But he'd done all right for himself and Jerry was proud of him. He'd never say it though. They weren't really the type of father and son that did stuff like that. But at least they were a lot better than him and his father. Not that he had any issues about that anymore. The heart attack had shaken all of that out of him.

It had taken over too. Everywhere he went, it came with him, and no one he met could see past it. "Are you minding the old ticker?" they'd ask, and they wouldn't let him smoke any more. Dermot let him have a drag on his, once in a while, but he never let him have a full one. And when he went to the pub, he could only have just one pint a night. He told Jacinta that he was losing the joy for living but she told him that he was just thinking of himself.

He tried to agree with her and looked forward to seeing his grandchildren again. He had been counting down the days. Only now that they were here, he realized he wasn't able for it anymore.

*

He woke as Deirdre came in.

"Were you sleeping? I hope I didn't wake you."

"No, girl, I had to wake up anyway to take my pills."

"Would you like me to get them?"

"No at all." He tried to get up but he struggled.

"Sit down right now or I'll tell Jacinta and Martin. I'll get them for you. And I'll make us a nice cup of tea too."

He sat back and, without thinking, reached toward the little table where he used to leave his cigarettes. He hadn't had one in weeks.

"Ah, that's grand," he said as he sipped when Deirdre brought the tea. He sipped again and swallowed his pill. "I'm sorry that you have to be spending your holidays looking after me."

"It's just a cup of tea, Jerry. It's no big deal."

"It is for me. I can't do anything for myself without looking like your . . ."

"My father?" Deirdre laughed. Her father was putting on weight and looking a bit purple from time to time.

"Well, I wouldn't like to be saying."

"Oh, it's okay. It's all my mother goes on about."

"She's a good woman for doing that. Jacinta is always on at me, too, about getting me out for walks and all. Us men would be lost without our wives."

Deirdre looked at her cup, like she was deciding something. "Jerry? Why don't men ever listen?"

He knew what she was asking. "We're always listening, girl. Only we don't always understand for a while. We have to try all the other ways before we start doing things the right way."

"Pride?"

"Ah no, not entirely. I think a lot of it comes down to just being plain stupid. It takes us forever to grow up and admit it."

Her eyes were a bit moist so he decided he'd said enough. He knew she was looking for a bit of direction. Deirdre was a good girl and she would do the right thing. And if he only knew what that was, he'd tell her and try to save her some heartache. In a way, he was glad of the heart attack. It gave them all something else to be talking about. He and Jacinta were being so careful not to say the wrong thing.

Jerry had wanted them to leave the kids and to go off and have a few nights on their own, but they all thought it was a bad idea. They thought the kids would be too much for him and Jacinta, even after Martin and Grainne promised to be good. He and Jacinta didn't take sides and let them sort it out for themselves.

"Will he ever grow up?"

Jerry reached out and put his hand on hers. "Sure of course he will, but, if he's anything like me, he'll need a bit of help yet for a while."

*

"And when I was young, I used to come here with your daddy's granny."

Grainne's eyes grew wider and wider as she took in all the hustle and bustle that was Bewley's. "Was she nice?"

"Yes," Jacinta decided very quickly. "She was the nicest, kindest person. And she loved your daddy. She used to say that he was an angel." She stole a quick glance at Deirdre but she had her head down, smiling as she watched her own daughter's face.

"Daddy said she used to lie to him."

"When did he say that, sweetie?" Deirdre glanced up but Jacinta didn't flinch.

"When he'd been drinking."

"Grainne!"

"No, that's all right," Jacinta assured the two of them. "Grainne, darling. It was different back then. Back then people used to say things to children to try to keep them away from harm. They didn't mean them as lies."

"Did you ever lie to my daddy?"

"Grainne!"

"No, Deirdre, let her have her say. We're all family and we've been through worse."

She turned back to her granddaughter and smiled as the waitress returned with their tea and coffee and the big dish of ice cream, with a chocolate swirl in it.

"Grainne, pet. Sometimes you say things to people to try to help them. They're not really lies. They're just little white lies. There's no real harm in them."

Grainne looked toward her mother, who just smiled like she agreed, and turned back to licking her spoon. But Jacinta knew she was still listening. Grainne was like that; she was always taking everything in. It didn't bother Jacinta, but she could see it bothered Deirdre. She was always so tense around her daughter. Jacinta understood; it was a lot easier just having a boy and Deirdre was always very good with Martin, and Grainne could get a bit like Danny sometimes.

"Well," Jacinta looked for safer topics to talk about. "I hope you're all having a nice visit."

"We are." Deirdre started smiling again. "It so nice to be back—for the kids especially. And I got to see my sister. We have been missing each other for years."

Deirdre looked so beautiful when she smiled. Hopefully Danny could still see that. Jacinta had warned him. She had told him that he would never find anyone as good as Deirdre ever again, but she wasn't sure he'd heard.

"Well I'm glad. I know things haven't been great recently."

"No. They haven't. But it's okay now. Danny and I, and Grainne and Martin, have all talked and we are all going to try to make things better. Haven't we, sweetie?"

Grainne nodded but never looked up from her spoon.

"Well, I know that you'll all do fine." Jacinta raised an eyebrow to see if Deirdre had anything else to say about it.

She didn't and a silence settled for a while.

"Will you and Jerry be okay?"

"Oh we'll be just fine, Deirdre. Don't you or Danny be worrying about us. I'll take good care of him until you all come back the next time. Things weren't always rosy between us but, at this stage of our lives, we're happy to be the ones looking out for each other."

"Is Granddad Jerry going to die?"

Jacinta had almost forgotten Grainne was there. "Not at all, pet. He's going to live to see you all grown up. Who knows, he might even dance at your wedding."

"Ew. I'm never getting married."

"Ah now, little girls have been saying that since time began."

"I mean it. Getting married just makes people unhappy."

"It does, but it also makes people very happy too."

"Are you happy, Granny?"

"I am, pet. Only I had to grow up before I came to realize that."

Deirdre waited until Grainne was finished and took her to the toilets. Jacinta had seen the little tears in the corners of her eyes. Jacinta hadn't meant to upset her; she just didn't want her giving up too soon. Not that she'd ever blame her. And she would never shun her. Deirdre and the children would always be a part of her and Jerry, no matter what happened.

She had done all that she could but there was no getting through to Danny. She had tried, in whispers so as not to disturb Jerry. She told him he had to stop his drinking but he just smiled and nodded his head, like he had heard it all far too often. It wasn't all his fault, though, not after the way things were when he was little. Only he hadn't learned how to move past them. In a way he was the same little boy that came to see her the day he was confirmed. Only then, it was the nuns closing like a veil between them. Now he was doing it himself. He was closing himself off from everyone who loved him. As his mother, she was going to have to do something about it.

"Are we all set then?" She forced herself to smile when Deirdre and Grainne came back.

*

"I don't mean to upset you; it's just that I can't stand seeing you like this."

Her sister meant well but she didn't understand; her life with Johnny was so much different. They got to go around the world and never had to settle down.

"I know you mean well, and you're probably right, but I just can't do it right now. The kids are too young."

"I don't think there's ever a good time to be breaking up a family," her mother added as she stirred her cup, over and over, in slow circular motions.

Deirdre sat between them, at the kitchen table where they once shared everything. Her father and Johnny had taken Danny and the kids for a drive. Johnny wanted to visit the Powerscourt waterfall.

"But there's no point in you being miserable, Dee." Her sister was always on Deirdre's side, even when Deirdre wasn't. "The kids won't be thankful, you'll see."

"I'd give him one more chance, if I were you." Her mother always wanted to see a bit of good in every one.

"Mam! How many chances does she have to give him? Danny has a problem and he won't deal with it until he has lost everything."

Deirdre knew she was right; she'd heard the same thing at Al-Anon meetings, and from Eduardo, only his opinion might be a little bit biased.

"Well, I think she should give him one more. Have you told him this is his last chance?"

"Of course she has. She's been telling him that for the last few years, only he doesn't seem to be able to get it."

Deirdre had. When they got back together, they had talked but she knew he was just going along with her. He was smirking a lot, even as he was agreeing to everything she said.

"Grainne," her mother pleaded, "we don't all get it right from the start. You and Johnny were very lucky."

They were. Johnny was a good husband and a great father, when he wasn't working. Her sister used to tell her that, before their kids came along, she used to get lonely when he became absorbed in a painting.

"God knows. There were lots of times when I nearly gave up on your father, but marriage is about the good and the bad."

That's what Deirdre often told herself, when she was alone in her bed, crying herself to sleep.

"Ah but, Mam, we all know you're a saint for having to put up with him."

They all laughed at that.

"Poor Daddy, he hasn't been the same since women got the vote."

"Now, now. Leave your poor father alone. He's doing his best."

"He is?"

"He is. It wasn't easy for him having the two of you as daughters."

"Us? He should be proud of us."

"He is. Now."

"Well I still think that Deirdre and the kids would be better off doing what has to happen before any more harm is done."

Her sister was right, but Deirdre couldn't bring herself to do it. Not yet. Not until she was satisfied that she had given him every chance. After that; she would do whatever had to be done.

*

Deirdre had been putting off meeting up with him; it wasn't the right time.

She'd missed him and the reaffirmation she felt just being near him. He had called a few times but she had always said she was too busy. It wasn't a total lie; she was, and she needed time to let everything settle again.

She was, when she was honest with herself, becoming paralyzed. She could function from one day to the next, but she couldn't bring herself to think about the future. Eduardo seemed to sense that and didn't push her. He just wanted her to know that he was always there at the other end of the phone if she needed to talk or anything.

She often thought about phoning him, especially at night while Danny sat downstairs until she was asleep. Their marriage had become little more than a functional agreement. They did what they had to do together as parents. For the most part, they were civil to each other for the kids' sake, but they weren't really a couple anymore.

Danny had been acting out a little too. Drinking more, almost challenging her to say something.

She didn't. She overlooked it and asked if there was any news on his father. All they had were functional conversations, nothing more.

She missed caring about him but she had learned something else at Al-Anon. They told her that she had to learn to detach. It was confusing. Where was the line between detachment and indifference? She couldn't find it any more.

Danny had probably erased that, too, with all of his encroachments. They might have been cries for help but she had nothing left to give him. But it still wasn't the right time to do anything. The kids were still too young and the news of Jerry wasn't good. It just wasn't the right time.

Eduardo called again, at the end of October, to say that he noticed Leaside was playing in Markham the same weekend his son was playing. Perhaps they could meet for hotdogs?

She would have made some excuse but, the previous Sunday morning, Danny had crossed the wrong line. Martin and Grainne had been having a tiff and were getting a bit loud. Deirdre was determined to stay out of it and just read the newspaper, absentmindedly chiding them every once in a while.

**

"You'll wake your father!" she reminded them again, but it was just a token effort. He had woken her when he came to bed.

So Martin and Grainne argued some more and she went on reading the paper, trying not to smile as she enjoyed a moment of restitution. Until Grainne took it too far. "Daddy. Daddy. Daddy. Martin won't let me watch my shows." She even ran to the foot of the stairs, too, to make sure he heard.

Deirdre sprang up but it was too late; Danny was already pounding down the stairs.

"Would it be too much to ask that one morning—just one fucking morning—I get a bit of peace and quiet?"

"I'm sorry, Daddy, but Martin made me cry."

"Did not."

"Did too and he tried to pull my hair."

Deirdre reacted instinctively. "Martin, is that what really happened?"

"No, Mum. She just won't let me watch my show—and hers is stupid."

"It's not stupid. It's for girls."

"Girls are stupid."

As Deirdre watched, she knew what was going to happen next. Grainne started slowly, deliberately, so that everyone but her father could tell: she was going to throw her brother in front of the bus, again. She pouted her lips and scrunched up her face and began to tremble, voluntary at first until it all bubbled up from inside and poured out through her eyes.

Deirdre never expected what happened next. Danny grabbed his son and hauled him up level to his face. "Can't you see that you made your little sister cry? What kind of a cruel-hearted bastard are you going to grow into?"

"Danny!"

"Danny nothing. I'm sick and tired of you not keeping this little gurrier on a leash."

It was Martin's turn to cry, though he tried to hold it in.

"Not so fucking tough, now, eh, Gretzky? If I ever catch you making your sister cry again—I'll fuckin' ..."

Deirdre reached forward toward Martin, glaring at Danny as she came. She wanted him to know that, in that moment, she despised him.

He seemed to recoil and lowered Martin. "I'm sorry."

He might have said more but Deirdre stood face to face with him. She didn't say anything. She just wanted him to know.

He withered a little and turned to go.

"Don't you ever speak like that again in this house. Do I make myself quite clear?"

Even the kids stopped and looked at her. She had never, ever, spoken to anyone like that before, not even the night Anto followed her home. But then she was only afraid for herself.

"I'm sorry," he mumbled and slunk off toward the basement.

"Right, you two." The kids were still standing in shock. "Get upstairs and get dressed. We are going out for brunch."

It worked. They both shot off, almost leaving what just happened behind.

She took them to the Sunnybrook, right across the road from McDonald's. She wanted them all to have bacon and eggs and sausages, with warm toast and jam, but Grainne wanted waffles and Martin wanted a burger, so Deirdre just had coffee and watched them.

She had been very stupid—and careless. She could have headed it off. It could all have been avoided if she had just stopped to think. She had put her son in danger so she could make her point. Yes, Danny was supposed to get up and spend some time with the kids, but she knew better. She had made a huge mistake and would never let it happen again.

***

"Can all girls cry whenever they want to?"

Deirdre should have said no but she didn't feel like it. When she was alone with Martin, she almost felt free. She was taking him to the tournament while Grainne stayed with a neighbor. She hadn't asked what Danny was doing. It didn't matter; she had said yes to Eduardo.

"Yes, Martin. I do believe they can."

"Can you?"

"Probably, only I don't like crying."

"I wasn't crying, you know? When Dad was being all . . ."

"I know, sweetie."

"Do girls cry because that's the only way they get their way?"

"Not all girls, sweetie."

"It's still not fair. Boys always get blamed whenever stupid girls cry."

*

She had dropped him off at the door along with his hockey bag and had gone to park when Eduardo arrived. He was so happy to see her and parked right beside her even though he still had his son's bag and they were a long way from the door.

"Dee-dree." He leaned forward and kissed her cheeks, right between her hat and scarf. "And you are perfectly dressed for spending the day in a rink."

He wore a leather bomber jacket and blue jeans. It was a good thing she had brought something to sit on. He hauled the heavy bag from the back of his van, so like Deirdre's only newer. "I swear to you," he laughed as he slung it over one shoulder, "next year—swimming."

"Oh, Eduardo. That's so un-Canadian of you."

"Well, I admit it then." They were walking briskly but he wasn't getting short of breath. "Besides, I was very good at swimming."

She couldn't help it and briefly imagined him in a Speedo, rising up from the warm surf as the sun set on the Costa De Caprica. She was still thinking about it as she held the door for him and watched him walk in. He had been back to Portugal during the summer. His skin was a little darker and he smelled like a shower—a long hot shower.

She watched him check in with his team and hand the bag over to his son. The coaches took it from there and would keep the kids 'focused' for the next few hours.

"So how was your trip to Dublin?"

"Nice. The weather wasn't great but I got to see my family again. That's always nice."

"And your parents came to visit too. Yes?"

"Yes." It had been a bad idea, seeing them so soon, but her mother told her that her father was insistent. He wanted to be there for Danny while Jerry was going through what he was going through.

"And did they enjoy themselves?"

"They became total Canadians for a few weeks. My mother insisted on barbequing every evening and my father wore shorts and a t-shirt the whole time. Such Euro-trash, eh?"

"Oh, you don't mean that. I'm sure it wasn't as bad as all that. Besides, my family always barbequed *sardinhas*. The Fire Brigade is always calling around. It was very embarrassing at first but now my mother makes them stay and eat with us."

His smile always made her tingle deep inside.

**

But it was worse than she let on. Danny and her father went drinking every evening and when she complained, her father sided with Danny. "You're getting a bit shrill there, Dee. Relax and let a man enjoy his holidays."

Her mother rolled her eyes but didn't comment, though Deirdre overheard them at night, arguing softly as they went to bed. "The last thing that boy needs right now is a boozing buddy."

"Let it go, Anne. I'm only trying to help him keep his mind off things."

"Well I think he should be minding things."

"You don't really mean that. You know as well as I do that his father will be dead before the year is out."

But the night before they left, her mother whispered to her in the kitchen. "Don't worry, pet. If you ever divorce Danny—I'll understand, because the minute I get off the plane, I'm divorcing your father!"

***

And for some reason, she shared all of that with Eduardo, over hotdogs and rink-cold hot chocolate. She was testing him. She wanted to see if he was ready. Would they take that great leap together and land in each other's arms? Or would they fall into a jumble of tangled and broken emotions?

She had to risk it, but she needed some sign from him that she wasn't stepping out into an abyss.

It almost seemed like he knew. He sat and listened with his chin in his hand, his long slender finger resting against his lips. She couldn't tell if he was smiling but his eyes were sparkling.

"And will she leave him?"

*

The question hung in the car, all the way home. Leaside had lost in the finals and Martin was quiet but not despondent. Martin didn't get like that. Instead, he replayed every play while thinking of how much better he would do it the next time.

Both of them were.

The house was dark, the only one in the lit-up street. And, as Deirdre struggled to find the lock, the telephone rang.

"It's Gina. Danny's aunt. I'm afraid I have some very bad news."

Chapter 19 – 1995

JEREMIAH BOYLE WAS LAID TO REST BESIDE HIS PARENTS on a bitter afternoon in November. The wind whipped down through the gap in Glenasmole and tore at the mourners. The rain pelted them, too, so Fr. Dolan had hurried everything along. Only Danny had made the trip and stood, swaying slightly, as his mother greeted everyone who came. "You'll come back to the house to send Jerry off in style?" Those that accepted nodded in quiet deference, dripping rain from their hats and umbrellas as they did.

When they got home, Jacinta sat beside the fireplace sipping whiskey to ward off the chill. Gina and Anne Fallon organized the kitchen and served sandwiches and tea for those that wanted it. Danny was no help. He was even worse than his father—at his father's funeral.

Jacinta had liked Bart. He had danced with her at her wedding. He was nice to her and told her not to pay Nora too much mind. "She's not used to having other women around her, but don't worry, she always does the right thing in the end."

"I'm very sorry for your troubles," the mourners offered, but Jacinta hardly heard; she was deep in her own thoughts, swirling like fog inside her. And she was getting mad at Jerry. He could have tried to look after himself but it seemed like he just gave up in the end. Deep down inside, she understood.

Jerry was never going to be content unless he could be Jerry and she couldn't help but feel a little admiration for that.

"She's still in shock, God love her," the mourners agreed when she didn't respond.

But that was all well and good for him; she was the one left alone again. Just like when she was sent to the hospital and he ran off to England. Except then, she was still able to believe that one day she would get out.

"I brought you a cup of tea," Anne Fallon insisted, and held it before her until she took it in her trembling fingers. Jacinta didn't want it, but she knew Anne was just trying to be nice. "Drink it now. It'll do you a bit of good."

Jacinta sipped it. Sure, there was still Danny, but he was no good to anybody anymore. She was angry at him too. No matter what he had had to put up with, he had no right to show up in the state he did. God only knows what he must be inflicting on Deirdre and the children.

And they'd be gone one day, too, and she'd probably never get to see them again. Deirdre and her mother would try to hold it all together for a while, but once a family was broken, it shattered everything.

"I'm very sorry for your troubles."

Mrs. Flanagan stood over her. She had her coat on and was ready to leave. She'd had her cup of tea and didn't want to be a bother. She'd only come over to share her condolences. She looked down at Jacinta with that same look and Jacinta was mad at her for that. She was always looking like she expected Jacinta to have some kind of answer that would make everything okay.

"Thanks, Mrs. Flanagan. That means so much more—coming from you."

Mrs. Flanagan seemed content with that and left, pathetically shuffling away. Jacinta would never allow herself to become like that. Jerry was gone wherever he was gone and no amount of kneeling and praying the afternoons away would ever change that.

She was angry at Nora too. Not for all that had happened. Jacinta was mad at her because here, at the end of it all, she was going to have to deal with everything alone.

"Mrs. Boyle," Fr. Dolan addressed her as he sat in the chair opposite her. He was like that—very pompous. Jerry used to say that he behaved like he had invented the whole business of God all by himself. "May I offer my sincerest condolences?"

Jacinta was angry at him too. He was the one who had driven poor Fr. Reilly out. Jacinta had heard it from Mrs. Dunne a few weeks before she died.

"And though I didn't get to know the deceased as well as I would have liked to, I can say with certainty that he will be sorely missed by the community."

Over the years he had managed to finagle donations out of Jerry for the youth club and things like that. Jerry, the soft-headed old fool, had been more than happy to hand it over too. "So they're not out getting into drugs and things like that." But she knew better than to say anything. "Thank you, Father," she managed before lowering her head and staring into the coals.

"It's at times like these, Mrs. Boyle, that even I struggle to accept the Lord's plan."

Jacinta might have snorted. There was no plan. People just got born, lived their lives and died. All that mattered was whether or not they had been good to each other along the way. Fr. Reilly had told her that, only not in so many words. Fr. Dolan was a different kind of creature—more of a salesman.

"But we that are left behind must struggle on. Perhaps, after your mourning, we could talk about an idea I had to make sure that your husband's good name is remembered, along with the good names of his parents. May they all rest in peace."

Jacinta didn't look up. Instead, she stared into hottest part of the fire. It made her face flush and her eyes began to sting but she wouldn't look away until he left. She knew that he had been on at Jerry for money for something or other a few months back.

"Well, I leave you to your mourning. You will want a mass?"

She had to look up at that. Jerry always said that he was like an insurance salesman. And that the price of the mass kept going up. 'Money for old rope,' he used to call it. She just nodded to get rid of him. She knew that he knew she had very little time for him.

And in time, they all left. Neighbors first, until it was just Anne and Gina, cleaning and putting away. Danny had passed out and gone to bed.

"Will you be all right?" Gina asked from the doorway. Anne stood behind, putting on her coat, but ready to stay if she was needed.

Jacinta just nodded as Gina came over, kissed her head, and then left her alone with her grief.

*

After Danny came back, more dark and brooding than ever before, and his mother came to visit for almost three months, Deirdre begged Miriam to visit. At first, Miriam felt that she and Karl were too busy, but she finally got it: Deirdre really needed to see her and spend some time with her. Miriam had to check with Karl first, but she was sure that they would be able to visit over Thanksgiving—Canadian Thanksgiving.

They offered to stay in a hotel but Deirdre wouldn't hear of it. She wanted to be able to sit and chat, over coffees, in her own recently remodeled kitchen, with pot lights and stainless-steel fixtures. It mightn't be the type of thing to impress Miriam but it made Deirdre feel better about herself. She had most of the house re-done after Danny 'moved' into the basement.

He had built a bar down there. It was some tacky 70s stuff that Frank had torn out of a job. Danny was delighted with it and, as it was on the opposite end from the laundry room and the kids' TV room, Deirdre couldn't care less. He had an old couch down there, too, and spent his nights there.

It was strange for them all at first, but Martin just acted like his father wasn't around anymore. Deirdre knew what he was doing. Martin was embarrassed, only he'd never let it show. She was doing the same thing, herself, and for a while it seemed like a very good arrangement—for everyone except Grainne. Deirdre didn't like her going down there but it was the only way she could spend time with her father.

Sometimes, when they had all gone to bed, Danny would take out his guitar and sing and play softly to himself. It drifted up through the vents, along with the traces of his cigarette smoke. He had put filters in all the vents but it just made his music muffled. She could just hear his voice, softly cracking and wavering, as she lay staring at her ceiling. But it wasn't really Danny anymore, just the ghost of what he might have been. Things could have been so much different, but they weren't and now all that was left was to clear up the mess and get on with the business of living.

The next time would be the last; she had promised herself, even after she had debated it from all sides. It was what was best for all of them, even Danny. Only, she'd have to wait for the inevitable to come around again. Danny was in a vortex and every time, like now, when he clung to the edge, clinging on for dear life, she was tempted to reach out with her toe and crush his fingers and get it over with, once and for all.

She would never do it. Instead, she would just stand there, beyond caring, and let life take its course. It would be better for them all in the long run.

And she couldn't do anything while Jacinta was over. After Jerry died, Gina put Jacinta on the payroll, as a director, and Donal knew better than to object. And she gave her money to come to Canada, too, to spend time with Danny. Deirdre wasn't consulted until it was all arranged. Danny mentioned it while she was sitting at the table with the kids and retreated to his lair before they could discuss it. That's what upset her—that she had no say in the matter.

Still, she was determined to see it through with as much grace as she could muster. She liked Jacinta but she also knew what she could be like sometimes. And the last thing Danny needed was someone to drink with. Deirdre had tried getting him to talk—at least about his father, but Danny had closed down completely. He lived inside a pall of gloom and made everything around him seem less and less worthwhile. He still talked with Frank, who had tried everything to get him to snap out of it. He was on the verge of giving up too.

It was going to be hardest on Grainne. She had started to look to her mother for reassurance but Deirdre had nothing to give her. She tried reaching out and holding her but they had never been that close. Perhaps after her father was gone things might change, but for now there was nothing else to do but wait.

**

"The point is, Ma," Danny had said, looking over the rim of his glass for emphasis, "nothing is like they say it is. We all get tricked into believing that there is good in the world but there isn't. It's just a whole bunch of people running around distracting themselves until their time is done. That's all, and the sooner we all accept that, the better."

They had been drinking all day since Danny got back from the liquor store with a fresh supply.

"Ah, now, Danny. That's an awful dark way of looking at things. I prefer to try to see things a bit more positive."

"Right! And look where that got you."

Jacinta's eyes welled up again. She had done a lot of crying since she came over, for herself, for Jerry, and for Danny. She hadn't meant to. She had wanted to come over and just spend some time with him—time that would be spent remembering Jerry for all the good he had done. She just wanted to be able to talk about him until she was satisfied that there was nothing more she could have done. She wasn't angry at him anymore. Now she felt like if only she had looked after him a bit better . . .

"Life is a load of shite, Ma, and anyone who tries to tell you different is just trying to sell you something."

He wasn't her son anymore. He was a man full of bitterness and badness. He had a meanness about him, a dark bitter meanness that burned like a fire inside him. She wanted to tell him to snap out of it for the children's sake if nothing else, but it wasn't all his fault. It was like a hereditary disease and she could see the same look in little Grainne's eyes that Danny used to have when he was a child. She hadn't been able to chase it away then, and it wasn't for her to do now.

At the back of it all, Jacinta still blamed herself. She shouldn't have gone running off that night with the baby in her arms. What did she think was going to happen after that? And she could have gotten out of the hospital sooner. Instead of sitting around feeling sorry for herself, she could have just gone along with all they told her and she would have been out years earlier. She could have done it for Danny's sake. It was no wonder he was turning out the way he was.

"What are you crying about now?" he asked.

"I was just thinking back, pet, that's all."

"There's nothing back there that's worth crying about anymore."

"Ah don't say things like that, Danny. It was where we were all born and bred, and it's where your father was laid to rest. It wasn't all bad between him and me, you know? He and I had a lot of good times, too. It just took us some time to get to know each other."

"Jazus, Ma. Don't be trying to make a saint out of him, for Christ's sake. He was a miserable, gutless bollocks. He was the one who let them put you in the fuckin' loony bin."

It hung in the air between them for a while, then slowly wafted away, out toward the hall.

"Don't be saying things like that, Danny. That's all done now."

"Well, maybe you can forgive him but I never will."

Jacinta choked back a few tears but she was determined to try to set him straight. "We all make mistakes, Danny boy, and we shouldn't be so quick to judge. I made my fair share too."

"Tell me about it. And I'm the one still paying for them."

**

"Mum?"

"Yes, Martin?"

"Why did Granddad Jerry let them put Grandma in the loony bin?"

**

"He must have overheard something and got the wrong idea. You know I'd never say anything like that to him."

Deirdre tried to remain calm. She didn't think Jacinta had, but she wouldn't put it past Danny. He was so desperate to rationalize the state of his own existence that he was only too happy to tear at everybody else's, especially his son's. She got that; it was part of his disease but it didn't change things.

"And I doubt Danny would have said that." Jacinta was wringing her hands but they both knew better. "Would it do any good if I had a word with him? The poor little chap. It's not right that he should be going around believing something like that."

Deirdre thought about it. Her first reaction was to say that Jacinta and Danny had done enough damage, but she couldn't. Besides, she knew that Danny was spoiling for a fight and it was better to lie low until he got past that. She knew his pattern so well. Jacinta's visit, and all they had talked about, had stirred it all up inside of him. Anything she did or said would just light the fuse.

She wasn't worried for her own sake, but she was for her children's. If she could just get them to all keep their heads down for a little while longer his anger would turn to cold brooding and, in time, that would have to come bubbling out. He would go on one more wild spree and that would be it. That would be the reason she needed.

"No, Jacinta. I have already talked with him. I told him that he must have misunderstood."

She hadn't. She had told him that his father was very sick and he shouldn't pay any attention to anything he said right now. Martin, being as perceptive as he was, asked why Grandma Jacinta hadn't said it wasn't true.

**

"Grandma Jacinta is . . . well she's so upset about Granddad that she is not being herself right now."

"Is she going crazy again?"

He said it in such a matter of fact way that she had to be honest. "I think we all are." She wanted to see him smile again and he did, but like he was forcing it for her sake. So much damage had been done already. 'The wreckage of the past.' She had heard the phrase so often and was finally coming to realize exactly what it meant. "Martin. It's a really bad time for everyone right now. It's just like in hockey. Sometimes you just have to force your way to the . . . goal."

"It's called the crease, Mum, and I hate when you try to talk hockey."

"But you do understand what I'm trying to tell you."

"Yeah, I get it."

"Sweetie, I need you to know that Mammy will deal with it."

"Are you going to make Dad leave again?"

She thought about reassuring him but she wanted to know what he thought Grainne would do.

"I think I might have to."

"I think so too."

"What do you think Grainne will do?"

They fell silent for the rest of the drive home, but when they were hauling his bag from the van, he hugged her for a moment. "It's going to be all right, Mum. I'll look after her."

**

"He didn't misunderstand anything."

And even as she said it, Jacinta lowered her head and began to cry. At first, Deirdre just sat there, with the table between them. She had never had to deal with Jacinta like this before, not personally. But she had to now. She rose and cradled her mother-in-law's sobbing head against her. It was the same thing she had done with the kids, so many, many times, but it felt weird. So she squatted until she could look up into Jacinta's teary face.

She looked so much older from there and so frail and frightened. She cried openly and honestly; Martin had over-heard them and she hadn't stood up for Jerry because she was afraid that Danny would erupt and spoil things for everybody. "But I see now, I'm not doing anybody any good being here."

"Oh, don't say that, Jacinta." Deirdre handed her a box of tissues. She kept one in every room.

"Deirdre," Jacinta wiped her face and tried to look deter-mined. "We both know what's really going on and the last thing you needed right now is a visit from your mother-in-law."

"No, Jacinta. Don't think like that."

"Now, Deirdre. Don't be trying to tell me what to say or think. Wasn't I doing both before you were born." She had raised her head and smiled through the last of her tears, like she was letting Deirdre know she was going to be on her side now. "Not that I was ever great at it."

She seemed to mull over that for a bit as Deirdre squatted and waited. Her thighs were killing her but she distracted her-self by thinking of all the tightening she was doing. Besides, Jacinta seemed a lot happier.

"Do you mind if I ask you something, Deirdre?"

"Yes?"

"From before?"

Deirdre knew what was coming but got ready to smile anyway.

"Did you get back with Danny because you felt guilty?"

Deirdre had to smile at that. Jacinta wasn't crazy—she was just far too perceptive. Maybe that's where Martin got it. "Which time?"

Now it was Deirdre's turn to cry a little, but she fought against it.

"Oh, now I've gone and upset you even more. It's Danny that should be out here crying instead of you. You are a good, kind woman, Deirdre, and the best mother to my grandchildren. You deserve a better life than this and I'm going to start seeing you get it." She nodded to her own thoughts as Deirdre rose to take it all in. Jacinta was giving her blessing and Deirdre loved her for that.

"And I'll begin by getting out of your hair and letting you get on with what has to be done. Do you need any money? I wanted to give you some, only I don't want himself to know about it."

It was done; they were joined in conspiracy. "Thank you, Jacinta, but I don't think I'll need it."

"You will. Besides, if you dangle it in front of himself like a carrot, he'll follow it, right out the door."

*

Jacinta went home a week later and by then she could tell, Deirdre was sorry to see her go.

She had spent the last few days taking her grandchildren shopping. The three of them went off on the subway every day to the Eaton Center. It was a bit noisy and busy, but it was the least she could do. Besides, Martin and Grainne loved it. Jacinta bought them whatever they wanted and felt better about things. Doing them a bit of good did her the world of good. And Deirdre needed some time to herself. And as far as Danny was concerned—it was better that they start getting used to being without him.

She thought she saw him flinch when she told him she was leaving, but then he just smirked and shrugged. As long as he had his drink in front of him, he didn't care.

She thought about him on the plane home too. It was time for Deirdre and the kids to leave him for their own sake's, but she was worried about what would happen to him after that. If he took the money she had left, he could get a flat somewhere and not end up in the gutter. And, after a few months alone, he might come to his senses. It was probably too late for Deirdre but he could still make things better between him and his kids. It would be work, but it could be done.

Only he'd need help.

The first person she thought about was Fr. Reilly, but he was no good to her now.

And then she remembered that day he became the face of Jesus. People still laughed when she told them, but she had seen it. Right in front of her.

That was it. She'd do whatever had to be done so that some good would happen to Danny. When she got home, she'd go down to the church and have a chat with the Virgin Mary. Then she'd tell Mrs. Flanagan that she was going to take her to Rome so she could pray near the pope.

Jacinta didn't believe in all that but Mrs. Flanagan still did.

It could only bring good; goodness always did.

*

"I know. I know. It's just guilt but it just keeps creeping back in. What do you expect from someone who was schooled by nuns?"

"Deirdre, I'm the ex-nun and even I think that's nonsense. Catholic wives have suffered enough."

"You're right, and I know what I have to do. And I will; only I'll most likely have a few breakdowns along the way."

"Does his mother know?"

"She does and even she agrees."

"Well, there you go then."

"It's not his mother I worry about."

"Grainne will be fine. It will be hard on her for a while but you'll see: in a few months things will look so much better—for everyone."

"You have no idea what that little girl can get up to in a few months."

"Deirdre. Get hold of yourself. She's the child and you're the adult."

"Are you trying to tell me that my daughter is spoiled?"

"Yes, but don't worry; they're all spoiled these days. I blame 'girl power.'"

"Miriam? Have you sold out on feminism?"

Miriam hugged her and laughed. "This was not what all those poor bras were burned for."

They needed to lighten up before the kids got home from school.

*

"I am trying, you know?"

Karl was always difficult to read but Danny knew that whatever he said to him would get back to Deirdre. He didn't like Karl and he couldn't stand the ex-nun, but now that they were here, he'd be on his best behavior. He knew he was on thin ice since his mother left.

"How?"

"I'm just sticking to beer."

"And does that cut it?"

"Look, I'm Irish. For us, cutting back is like other people quitting."

Karl didn't smile; he just looked bemused.

"No, I'm serious. I'm going to get it together again. It's just with my Da dying and all—a lot of unresolved issues, ya know?"

Karl nodded as if he did.

"It's got me thinking about the way I am with my own kids too."

Karl just looked at him and Danny couldn't tell, but decided to pour on a bit more. "I'm going to start making changes. Big changes."

"Can you do it on your own?"

"I have to. I can't go back to those meetings. They're always saying that it's not about religion but then they're always going on about God and all. I've had enough of all that. This time, I'm going to beat it on my own."

"Well, I wish you the best."

It almost sounded like he meant it, but Danny knew better. He and the ex-nun where just waiting for him to fuck-up again so they could persuade Deirdre to throw him out. Sometimes, he wished they would so he could just get it over with. But then he'd think of Grainne. Martin would be delighted to see the back of him but Grainne was still 'his little girl.' She'd end up just like the way he was.

He was hanging on for her sake. He was going to tone it down. He'd even talked to the doctor about anti-booze pills, only the doctor wouldn't give them to him until he stopped. He was going to, in the new year. There was no point now; it would be Christmas in a few months.

He'd have to take it easy, though, and not fuck up like he did every other year. He'd do it for Grainne's sake.

*

He had just one glass of wine with dinner—turkey with all the fixings.

Deirdre and the kids really got into Thanksgiving. They'd all spent Saturday morning down at the St. Lawrence buying sprouts and cheeses and cranberries and little gourds to decorate with. He used to go with them before, but he hadn't the last few years. He didn't think they would have wanted him there anymore.

When they'd finished eating, he helped Deirdre tidy up. They had managed to get back on civil terms but it was just for show. He knew that she despised him—she couldn't hide it anymore—so they put everything away in a silent ballet. He wished there was something he could do but there wasn't; she just didn't believe in him anymore.

He resented her for that and the little flutters of rage fanned old embers smoldering beside the combustible pool of shame that sloshed around inside of him. She was making him pay for his sins, with Miriam and Karl just sitting there, watching them like they were watching a play or something.

He was sick and tired of people looking at him like that. They'd been doing it his whole life.

Only when Karl did it, it was like he was looking at something that was dying. The ex-nun just looked right through him like he wasn't even there anymore.

When they'd finished, he went to check on the kids. Karl had brought them the *Lion King* video and they were happy, curled across each other on the basement couch, out of earshot. He had a few bottles behind the bar—just in case—but he couldn't go near them. Even though they were watching the movie, their eyes followed him around.

So he headed back to the kitchen where the ex-nun was going on about Fr. Melchor again. The old coot was being shipped back to the catacombs and she was worried about him. She was saying that he hadn't been the same since he'd been shot.

There's a lot of that going around, he whispered to Anto, but he didn't answer.

He'd been very moody lately, like he was getting exasperated, and that just pissed Danny off a little more. Even the poor fucking ghost who had been sent to haunt him couldn't stand him anymore.

Fuck the begrudgers. He smiled to himself and hung around the door to the basement.

*

"Are Mammy and Daddy getting a divorce?"

"I don't know."

"Why do people get divorced?"

"It's like the circle of life thing."

"How?"

"Well first people get married. Then they have kids and then they stop liking each other. Not everyone, just those who get divorced."

"What happens after a divorce?"

"It's great. You get to live in two houses and you get two presents, too, for Christmas and your birthday. And daddies have to take their kids to the zoo and stuff, more often."

"How do you know?"

"Some of the guys on the team have parents that got divorced."

"Do the kids have to be split up?"

"No, silly. Besides, I told you before. I'll always look after you."

"Even when I get divorced?"

*

"I couldn't, Mrs. Boyle. That's just far too generous."

They were sipping their sherries in the Yellow House. It was a cold wet day and the church was cold and damp. Fr. Dolan had the heat down so low that when they rose, their knees were aching. Jacinta thought she was going to be in there all day as Mrs. Flanagan checked off her rosary beads, one after the other.

"It's nothing of the sort. It's just Jerry's company is sending me over and I can bring one guest."

It wasn't a total lie. She had told Gina all about her plan and even though her sister didn't seem convinced, she was very enthusiastic.

"Well, it's still very generous of you, but it wouldn't feel right."

"But you have to come with me. Knowing me, I'd only get lost or something and besides, they'd have to hear your prayers there."

"Well, only if you're sure."

"I am. I've been reading about it too. All kinds of Irish people have had their hearts buried there."

"Well that's nice, but my heart has already been buried."

Jacinta raised her glass. It wasn't going to be easy, but it was the least she could do. Besides, she'd find out where Fr. Reilly was and they could have a nice visit. He'd understand what she was trying to do.

Chapter 20 – 1996

IT HADN'T SNOWED IN A FEW DAYS but there were still mountains of it piled along the sides of the road, taking up half of the sidewalk and making crossing streets almost impossible. The salters had been busy and pools of brown slush were everywhere.

And it was as cold as fuck. Christmas, New Year's, and all that went with them had come and gone, taking all joy with them and leaving nothing but bills and remorse. January in Toronto was almost the worst time of the year.

February would be worse though. Cold and dark and each time it would snow, it would have to be piled higher and higher. For a few years, Deirdre used to take pictures of him standing in it for scale, but Danny was getting sick of shoveling the cars out. And it never failed; just as he finished, the plow would come around and block the driveway again.

And he was broke. And there was talk of layoffs. But Deirdre was out of town for the night so he could go 'off leash' for a little. He phoned home but had to leave a message. Martin never picked up when he saw it was him.

But at least he'd told them; he was going to stay in the office for an hour to catch up on a few things and they should go ahead and heat something up for themselves and he'd be home soon.

He felt a bit bad about it but it had been a rough day. Since the 'Common Sense Revolution,' everyone was scared. It was bad enough that they had to suffer 'Rae Days,' but now they were to be sacrificed on the altar of fiscal evangelism. He had seniority but you never knew. At best he would have to do more for less while the wealthy took another tax holiday. It just wasn't right. *This country was made by immigrants coming over and spending their wages. Cutting their wages was going to fuck it all up. Maybe from now on they're just going to let in people who already have money.*

He needed to drop into the Windsor, just for a quick one, to chase away the blahs. He'd only have the one and see who else was prowling around.

*

"Ah, it's yourself," Jimmy McVeigh greeted him, cordially but with a hint of suspicion, like he was welcome, but only for a while. "And what will it be?"

"Just gimme a pint there, Jimmy, like a good man." He really wanted a few whiskies, to ward off the chill, but he knew better. Jimmy had made it very clear the last few times he was in. He had a very good idea of what was going on with Danny and didn't want him getting drunk there. "Has Frank been in lately?"

"No. We haven't seen him in a while."

Danny assumed they had another row but when Jimmy placed the pint in front of him, he leaned so only Danny could hear him. "He's been laying off it for a while now. Drying out a bit, don't ya know?"

He looked like he was waiting for some reaction so Danny just raised his pint. "The first since New Year's."

It went down a charm, slithering down to where his nerves were all in knots, loosening them and letting him breathe again. But he drank it slowly like he was savoring it and not to seem like he was needing it or anything, even though nobody along the bar was paying much attention.

Most of them, in groups of three or four, were just getting in a few quick ones before facing home. They were the ones that could still manage to enjoy themselves. They'd spent the whole day smiling in the face of shit-storms and they deserved a bit of time before going home and having to face more. They never said stuff like that but Danny knew; they just hadn't gotten around to getting honest with themselves yet.

He ordered another without thinking, from the barman, but Jimmy looked up from the till at the other end of the bar. Danny pretended he didn't notice. He'd just have this one and get himself the fuck home. It was too fucking depressing trying to have a drink in public.

He checked his watch before beginning the second one—so they'd all know that he was keeping track of the time. And he'd drink the second one faster. And he'd order a taxi too. There was no point in going back for the car, and the cab would make it all seem more respectable.

He felt better when he thought like that—like he wasn't such a bollocks after all. Sure he'd had a spot of bother every now and then but he was going to get it all together this time. He'd just have these few and then get ready to start taking the anti-booze. That would show them.

He'd stay on them, too, at least until Paddy's Day. He'd have to go off them for that, but he could go back on them again and there'd be no harm done.

Mind you, if he didn't go off them—that would really show them. Then, by the summer, he could have a few beers in the evening and not have everybody making a big deal out of it.

That's what always drove him back on it—everybody making such a big deal out of nothing. He just liked to sit in the basement and have a few beers while he listened to some decent music. Deirdre and the kids were always listening to shite.

Besides, they were a lot happier without him. He would have fucked off on them only he wasn't like that. His father had done that to him and there was no way he was ever going to be like that with his own kids. He'd been doing his best for them and, considering the example he'd been given, he wasn't doing too badly.

Only Martin didn't see it like that. He was developing a real attitude and Deirdre was letting him get away with it. If it wasn't for Grainne, Danny would be gone and fuck the pair of them. Nothing he ever did was ever going to be good enough for them.

He thought about having a third but he didn't. He was feeling good inside and it wasn't just the booze. He was really going to get a grip this time.

"Not for me," he announced loudly when the barman stopped in front of him. "I'm going to grab a cab and get myself home to the wife and kids."

"Goodnight," Jimmy acknowledged from the other end of the bar.

As he stood outside waiting, Danny thought about Billie and all the times they had together. He never should have left her. That's why everything went to shit. Not that it was Deirdre's fault; it's just that they weren't really very good together. He and Billie were so much better. They understood each other and accepted each other for what they really were and not what they wanted to become.

That was the thing with Deirdre; everything always had to be improved and then improved again. Life was just one big project after another. She was probably like that because of her work. He'd tried telling her that, but she didn't even listen to him anymore. She never really did and had always treated him like a child—an errant one that always needed scolding. But what could he do now? They had made their bed . . .

Still, he'd get his act together if for no other reason but to show them he wasn't the only problem in their world.

"Bayview and Millwood," he told the cabbie as he hunched into the back seat. "But I need to stop at the liquor store on the way."

"There's one on Church."

"Great." He knew it well; it was just around the corner from where he used to live on Jarvis. He was just going to pick up some rye. He had a bottle of coke that he had to finish.

*

After the flight back, Deirdre felt the way she imagined Danny did. A few days in Calgary always made her feel like that. That and being traipsed around the country like a trophy; the bank's poster-girl. Women, for all the changes, were still a currency.

Toronto had looked nice from the air, but once she landed and retrieved her case, the one with the wonky wheel, and gone outside to wait for a cab in the wind, it felt like desolation.

Danny used to sing that song—the one by Dylan—but she'd never really liked it. She used to say it was because of Dylan's voice but the truth was she just didn't like looking at things that way. She got it; she just didn't see the point. Life was difficult enough. Danny used to say that she was the one in denial and that if she ever really looked at the world, she'd understand what he was going through. "It's all bullshit," was his old tired mantra and sometimes she almost agreed with him. But that was the toxicity of his world spilling over and the only way she could stop it was obvious.

She would. She just had to wait until the right time.

Was there ever a good time to break up a marriage?

She'd called again before she left the airport but no one picked up. She was getting anxious.

She had hoped to catch the earlier flight so she could have missed rush hour, but her V-P needed her to stay for the whole meeting in case anybody asked a question he couldn't handle. No one did but it was just as well. He was old and really only liked to talk about himself and his struggles, growing up in Westmont, in Montreal, and having to adapt to a new life in Forest Hill. Two days of his company and now she had to go back and face her own wonderful life. But then she thought of Martin and, even though the 427 was down to a crawl, she smiled. He'd be twelve this year. Time was flying by and he was in such a hurry; he hadn't waited and was becoming a teenager already.

And Grainne was worse. Boys had begun to dominate her life, along with what her friends thought. Deirdre was so tempted to sit down and have a talk with her but who was she to be offering anybody advice about anything?

Christmas had been painful. They got through it but it hadn't been easy. Danny insisted on trying to involve himself again. To be fair to him, he had stayed relatively sober, but it was too late. She wanted to tell him that but she couldn't be bothered, and by the time they had the nights to themselves, she was far too tired. Besides, he'd slink back down to the basement while she climbed the stairs to her large empty bed where she'd think of Eduardo.

He phoned just before New Year's. She wasn't happy at first—with him calling the house, but he told her that he had to hear her voice. He'd spent the last week going from family to family.

She envied that even though he described it as a miasma of mustached aunts force-feeding him while all his balding, greasy uncles looked at him with suspicion—like they knew he was going to turn his back on all that was proud Portuguese, and especially Azorean—"the proud heritage of the children of a penal colony." His cousins, who worked in construction, always made him out to be gay, or worse, a Canadian.

"It sounds wonderful."

She really meant it. Anything was better than the cold, cautious life she had made for herself and her kids. After she hung up, she let herself think about what it could be like with him. He was warm; even his call had briefly chased the chill from her heart. He wanted to see her but she couldn't. Not during the holidays and not until after her trip. He tried to change her mind but she wouldn't. She would make a clean break before starting a new life with him and she hoped he would do the same. He never talked about his wife anymore. Not that she wanted him to, but sometimes she wondered about the woman whose life she could shatter by just saying yes.

Traffic was lighter along the Gardiner and the city was lit up like a tree. It started to snow softly as the cab turned up the Don Valley where they slowed again.

Everybody would be home by now and hopefully Danny had fed them, even if he had just heated something up. She was tired and later, after she had tucked the kids into bed, she might pour herself a glass of wine and soak in a bath. Danny would stay in the basement and she could have an hour or two to herself. But the house was dark when the cab pulled up outside, and that wasn't a good sign. She hoped the kids had gone to friends but there was something ominous.

"I'm home," she called to check after she had let herself in and turned on a few lights. They might be downstairs watching TV. No one answered, even when she called down again, so she went to the kitchen and found Frank's note.

*

"Martin called me and told me that Danny was drunk and terrifying them. I went straight over and got them. I hope you don't mind. I just didn't think they needed to be around that."

"Are they okay?"

"They're fine. They were a bit shaken up but we had pizza and watched *The Lion King*, twice."

"Frank, thank you so much for doing this."

"It's no problem. I like kids, especially the ones I can give back."

"I'll be straight over. Have they eaten?"

"They're just finishing."

"More pizza?"

"No. I cooked spaghetti."

Deirdre's heart was beating too fast. She was angry and relieved. "Is Grainne eating it?"

"She is. She even helped me make it. Do you always add ketchup in yours?"

"Of course not. That little . . ."

"It's not bad; maybe you should try it. Is he still there?"

"No. There's no sign of him."

"I told him to fuck off out of there and leave you alone, only I'm not sure he got the message. I've never seen him so bad."

"He didn't hurt them, did he?"

"Not really. They said he came home and went into the basement for a while. Then when he came up he just started yelling at them and calling them names and stuff. Martin said that he tried to stop him but Danny just told him to fuck-off. That's when they phoned and I went straight over.

"Danny was back in the basement by the time I got there, but I warned him. I told him that I'd beat the crap out of him if he ever talked to them like that again."

"I'm sorry you had to deal with that, Frank, but I'm so glad it was you."

He had them all ready by the time she got there. Grainne wanted to stay—they were having so much fun. "Uncle Frank let us make a tent with sheets in his living room."

He'd even slept in an armchair so they would know he was nearby.

*

"I know I crossed the line. I don't know what came over me.

"I'm sorry," he added when she didn't answer. She didn't dare open her mouth. Not until she gained control over herself. She was fit to kill him.

"And I know you've heard it all before, but this time I was going to stop. I'm going on the pills, only I just had to have a few to get ready."

She held her hand over the mouthpiece so she couldn't hear the way she was breathing.

"You were right all along. I am an alcoholic. I admit it now."

She couldn't care less. Nothing he could say would ever change how she felt about him again.

"I'm going to go back to meetings, too, as soon as I get straight." He was staying in a hotel downtown, trying to dry out before ... "I don't suppose ... ya know. If I get my act together?"

"No, Danny. It's all over. This time you have," she was surprised how calm her voice was because her heart was still pounding, "pushed me way past my limit and I am going to start divorce proceedings."

"Ah, now, don't say things like that. We haven't even had a chance to talk about it."

"Did you give me a chance to talk about it when you decided to come home drunk and harass my children?"

"Ah, Dee? C'mon. You know me better than that."

"Oh, I do, Danny Boyle. I know you far better than that and that's why I'm going to make this easy for you. You are going to get your things out of my house and you are going to stay away from us, or I will lay criminal charges."

"Dee?"

"You heard me. What's it going to be, Danny? I'll be making the call right after I get your answer."

"Okay, okay. You win, Deirdre. You finally got me exactly where you wanted me. I surrender. I won't fight you on any of this. But is there any way I could still see Grainne?"

She wanted to step on the only piece of his heart that she could still hurt, but she didn't. She wasn't going to be one of those women who used their children as weapons. "Not for a while."

"I understand."

"No, you don't. You have no idea."

She was on the verge of breaking down and crying. This was it. This was the moment she never wanted to have to live through but she remained calm. "It might be better for us to have no contact until everything settles down."

She probably should have screamed at him and gotten angry, but what was the point?

"Maybe after I go to meetings for a while?"

She had to be civil for the kids' sake. They both hated him right now. She didn't want that to be their last impression of him. "Just get sober and then we'll talk about things."

She leaned back against the wall when she finally hung up. She felt gutted and relieved and had to make herself laugh. "I have just expulsed the biggest piece of shit . . ."

"Was that Daddy?"

Deirdre had no idea how long Grainne was standing there. "Yes, pet."

"Is he not coming home?"

"No, sweetie. Daddy needs to go away and get better."

Grainne looked at her for the longest time. It was unnerving. "Will he be okay, all alone?"

"I don't know, sweetie." She was trying so hard to be what a good parent had to be—especially a good single parent.

"Course he will, silly," Martin tousled his sister's hair as he walked into the kitchen and went straight to the fridge. "Daddy's Irish. Mum? Can we make nachos?"

"Yeah," Grainne joined in and left all thoughts of her father swirling behind her. They always made nachos together, extra cheesy on one side with extra peppers and less on the other. That side was covered in ketchup. They even cut some limes to put in their drinks.

She waited until they were totally engrossed before she put on Ricky Martin and danced all the cobwebs away. She danced, utensils in hand, from the counter to the table and back again. Shaking and gyrating everything dark and angry from inside of her. Deirdre and Martin and Grainne were having a little fiesta, to keep their spirits up.

*

After he had taken Jacinta's money and found himself a nice flat, Danny went on the anti-booze. He was really going to do it this time. The thing with the kids had made it very clear—he had become everything he had once hated. Even his own father never got that bad.

It was a lot tougher than he'd thought. He was going to have to avoid everything that had once been any part of his life. He tried sitting in bars drinking soda waters, but it drove him mad. Not only could he not get drunk, but he had to listen to everyone telling him that he was doing the right thing. Some of them even put their arm around his shoulder, smothering him in their booze breath.

So he just shuffled off to work each day, did whatever had to be done, and scurried back to his apartment. There was little else to do in February. He just sat and watched TV until something stupid made him cry.

You're beginning to act like a little girl.

"Fuck you, Anto. Is it not enough that my entire life is shite without you coming by to rub my nose in it?"

Careful, Boyle. I'm the only friend you have left.

"I suppose you're happy now—seeing me like this?"

I'm delighted, Boyle, but not for the reasons you're thinking of.

"What's that supposed to mean?"

Figure it out for yourself, Boyle. I had to.

He tried but he couldn't stop thinking about drinking.

But from the moment he woke and realized it was going to be another dry day, he kept telling himself that he was doing it for the kids. It was getting harder and harder but he didn't give in and had to make-do with binges of self-pity and bursts of self-loathing. He was smoking two packs a day and his whole life stunk.

So it wasn't so surprising that he got drunk on St. Patrick's Day. Only he was still taking his pills, too, and had to be taken out of the Rose and Crown in an ambulance. He had passed out in a washroom stall. He hadn't been feeling too good.

*

"Fuck it. Okay. You can stay with me for a while."

Danny had phoned him from the hospital. They had kept him for a few days and wanted to send him home with Valium, only they didn't want him to be alone. "They think I'm a bit suicidal, Frank. Can you believe it? Me?"

Frank wanted to tell him to go fuck himself but he could hear his desperation. "Yeah, yeah. I'll come and get you."

He wasn't ready for this; he had only been sober for eight months.

And he should have talked to his sponsor first, but, fuck it, it was done now. But there would be rules. Danny the-fuck-up-Boyle wasn't coming over to flop.

Besides, people at the meetings were always saying that helping others was what kept them sober. Even if Danny didn't make it, Frank would be all right.

He was still angry at him, though, and struggled not to become furious. What he should do was lock Boyle in the basement and only let him out to meetings. But he didn't. He took him home and looked after him. Not that it was hard. Danny was out of it most of the time and that made Frank leery. There was no way he got all that Valium from the hospital.

"Okay," he announced when he finally caught Danny awake. "My house, my rules. You're going to meetings or you can't stay with me."

"Ah, Frank. Where am I?"

"Fuck that shit, Boyle, and listen to me. This is your last warning."

"From you or from the higher-fucking-power?"

"We're going to a meeting on Sunday morning. That gives you a day to get your shit together. Now hand over the Valium."

"But they're prescription."

"And from now on, you're only getting them from me."

"I will in my bollocks. I'm not staying here to be treated like this. You've just lost yourself a friend."

Frank didn't try to help him as he swayed when he got up from the couch. He steadied himself and tried to look indignant. "You know, I always thought you were smarter than that, Frank. I never figured you to be one of the sops that soaked up all that religious shit."

"It's spiritual, not religious."

"What's the difference?"

"You're the one crashing on my couch."

*

"When did you realize that you were, ya know, an alky?" They were driving to their seventh meeting in two weeks and Danny was trying so hard to look like he was beginning to believe.

"I'm not an alky, I'm an alcoholic—I go to meetings."

"No, I'm serious, Frank. When did you know?"

"Well, you know when my ma died a few years ago? I went over to see her and the last thing she told me was to stop drinking. Of course, being the bollocks I was, I didn't. Then every time I got drunk, I'd end up seeing my mother's face, crying. Every time until I couldn't ignore it anymore."

He quickly wiped at his eyes and Danny couldn't help it and began to blub too. When he thought of his own mother, she looked the way she did in the hospital, only now it felt like he was the one stuck inside and she was just visiting. "I know what you mean. I'm just worried it's too late for me. I've fucked over too many people."

"It's never too late, Boyle. Not if you really want it."

*

"Hi. My name is Simon and I'm an alcoholic."

"Hi, Simon," Danny and Frank answered back in unison along with the rest of the meeting.

"And tonight," Simon continued, "I have a message for those who have struggled with the program."

"That's right up your alley," Frank snickered toward Danny.

"For ten years I came to meetings and went along with everything, but deep down inside, I just wouldn't accept a higher power. And for most of those years, I managed to stay for a few months here and a few months there. I once made it to almost eleven months but I always went back out."

Half of the meeting nodded along while others just kept their heads down.

"You see," Simon explained, "I was a priest, and a priest who doesn't believe in God is never going to be at peace.

"The God I believed in, the one that I studied and based my life on, became dead to me. I was angry at Him for all the terrible things He allowed to happen. I believed Him to be indifferent to all the suffering and heartache around me."

He paused for a moment to take a drink of water and to settle the emotions that were causing his voice to waver.

"I used to sit in meetings like this and feel sorry for all you poor fools who were getting sober on a lie. I used to think that I knew so much more than all of you, only I didn't know how to stay sober.

"Finally, I was given my marching orders and left the priesthood. They offered me some options, but do you know what? I was so far gone that I even thought I was superior to them. I left and devoted the next few years of my life to getting drunk. I told myself that I was on a mission to find God, and I can tell you," he smiled, "He wasn't to be found in any of the watering holes from here to Montreal. And I know. I drank in every one until they threw me out too."

He went on to talk about how bad things got for him and many nodded along. It was the same old beaten track for all of them, one way or another. He had lost everything and ended up swigging from a paper bag in Moss Park and sleeping in Seaton House when he could afford it. That was where he met Albert; he was running the meetings there.

"He used to be one of the drunken Indians that hung around outside the Canada House. I met him in the park at Queen and Church a few times. He remembered me and, after the meeting, came to talk with me. He had been sober for over a year and asked me how much more suffering I needed before I'd stop.

"I didn't want to talk to him but he was the only person I had talked to in weeks. Seaton House, as some of you may know, is not a great place for conversation."

A ripple of laughter wrinkled through the room as those who had been there agreed.

"We were more into snapping and snarling at each other like a pack of wild dogs. But Albert cornered me and wouldn't let go. So I gave him the sad story about how I was a priest who had lost God. How was I ever going to get sober?

"It worked on most people. Nobody else knew what to say and left me in peace. Not Albert though. He just looked at me, through those huge big glasses he wore, and he had a huge bulbous nose. He calls it his whiskey nose. Anyway, the next thing he said to me was one of those moments when it feels like the higher-power is talking directly to you: 'You can borrow mine, if you like.'

"I was angry and glared at him but he just smiled and walked off. He came back the next morning and took me out for a coffee and I went because I had nowhere else to go. And we started doing that every morning.

"He brought me back to meetings, too, but I just fell into my old habits, acting like everything was just fine because I couldn't stand the idea of anybody feeling sorry for me. But Albert could see right through me. 'Simon,' he said to me one morning, 'when your people came they took away everything we believed in, our lands, our way of life. Everything.' He said it in such a soft understanding way. 'But you could never take away the Great Spirit. It's still here. It's in all the good things in the world. It helped me to get sober and it will help you too.'

"So for a while, when I tried to pray, I kept thinking of God in full head-dress."

*

"What did you think of the speaker?" Frank prodded as they drove home.

"Yeah. I'm still thinking about it."

"Can you imagine being a priest that doesn't believe in God? That's fucked, that's what that is."

"Yeah. I wonder how he handled drinking the wine during the mass, ya know? Transubstantiation goes right out the fucking window."

"Fair play to him, though. He's got his shit together now."

"Yeah."

"What did you think of the stuff Albert said to him?"

"I'm still trying to figure that out."

"Stop trying to think it, Boyle, and just feel it."

"Easy for you to say—you're fucked in the head anyway."

"Then how come I'm sponsoring you?"

"Because you'd only fuck it up without me."

"Fuck you, Boyle, ya ungrateful bollocks."

They laughed for a while but fell silent as they waited for the light to change at Queen and Sherbourne, across from the Canada House, as the former friends of Simon and Albert swayed and tottered back toward the mission before it shut.

"You know I'm kidding?"

"I hope you are."

"C'mon, Frank. I know what you're doing for me, and I know I don't deserve it, but thanks."

They were stopped again at Broadview, across from the strip joint, kitty corner to the Jamaican place.

"I shouldn't really be telling you this, only she's pestering me."

"Who?"

"Billie. I met her the other day."

"Ah, Billie. How's she doing?"

"Not so great. She just got out of rehab. Coke and booze."

"Is she going to come to meetings?"

"Yeah. She said she'd be at the Welcome Group on Sunday night."

"We'll have to go and see her."

"Just don't forget: no sex for a year."

"Since when?"

"Since ever. No emotional involvements for the first year. You heard them."

"A year? How the fuck are you supposed to do that?"

"The three 'M's.'"

"What?"

"Meetings, meetings and masturbation." Frank smiled. He didn't tell him that he had been talking with Deirdre too. Grainne was asking to see her father and Deirdre wasn't sure.

**

"I think he's ready. He's been sober long enough. Not that I'm taking sides here, but it just might do him some good."

"Frank, I would never think that you were taking sides; you've been an angel through all of this."

"That's me, Danny-fuck-up-Boyle's own personal angel."

"Is he going to make it?"

"One day at a time."

"It's too late for me, Frank. I think he should know that."

"He does, Deirdre, but it's not too late to go on being their father."

"Okay, Frank, but on one condition. You go with them."

"I was going anyway. I miss them more than he does."

***

As Danny slept as contented as he could be, separated from his wife and children but struggling to make some things right again, Anto sat on his bedside table.

"You're good," Martin repeated. "You can go. Your clearance came through."

Anto didn't look up. He was thinking about all the stuff Danny told him his granny used to say, about Danny being an angel. He didn't look like one, snoring and slobbering into his pillow, but he looked at peace for the first time in years—almost the way he looked when they were kids. Anto had done his penance but he couldn't help but feel that he still owed Danny a little more. "I can't."

"Of course you can; you've cleaned your slate."

"I dunno, Martin. I've spent so much time with the stupid bollocks, I have to stick around to see how it all ends."

About the Author

Peter Murphy was raised in Dublin, in a house full of books. After a few years studying life in Grogan's, he wandered through the cities of Europe before setting out for Canada, for a while, and has been there ever since, raising a family. He is also the author of the novels *Lagan Love* and *Born & Bred*.